The DEASt File

S. J. Garrett

Other Titles by S.J. Garrett

CHRONICLE Series
Chronicle of Destiny
Chronicle of Summer

ETERNITY Series
Ghost Eyes

DESCENDANTS Series
Shadow on the Sea

3rd DISTRICT Series
The Shaughnessy File
The Carmichael File

PROLOGUE

There was a place known as the 3rd District.

When viewed from a plane, it resembled a small triangle located at the edge of New York City, New York. From space, it could not be seen. It was not a landmark. It was not a place of great historical import. It was, for all intents and purposes, a backwater area in a bustling city of hundreds of thousands of people.

It was also the place where magic lived. If your life crossed the roads of 3rd District, it was said, then you would find true love and live happily ever. You would find a true faerie tale story.

This story is one of them.

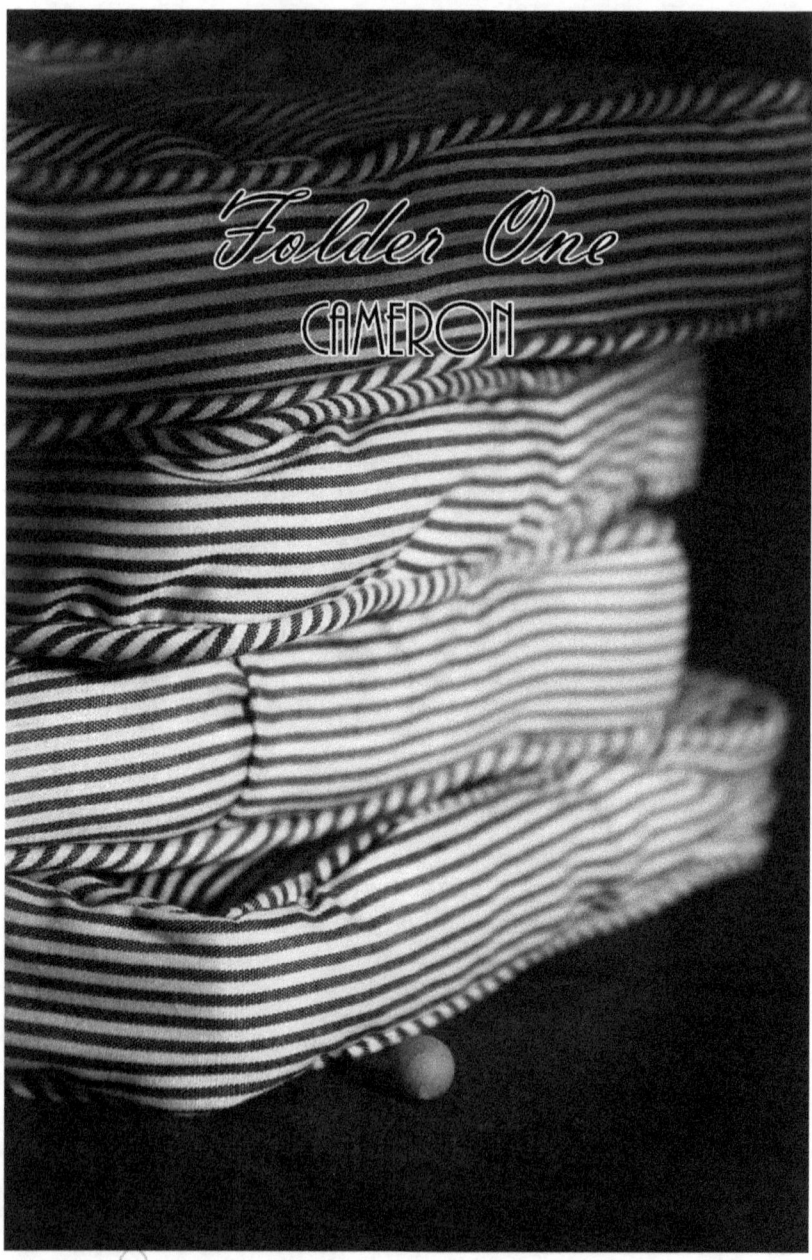

Folder One
CAMERON

CHAPTER ONE

There were two agencies in New York that companies fought over to have as their designer for ads and campaigns. One company, owned by the Lucino family, was known as Just In Time, Inc. The other company, owned by the Dease family, was known as Two More Minutes, Corp.

Two More Minutes had been formed by Viktor Dease and built from the ground up. When he had married, his wife, Lorcana, had become a partial shareholder. When they had been blessed with two sons, one two years older than the other, Viktor had been wise enough to leave the future of the company in their hands.

Though not very old, Viktor knew not to tempt fate. He wrote up a will and a trust for the company. When each of his sons turned twenty-one, they would each inherit fifty percent of the company, thereby making them the sole proprietors. Kenneth and Cameron, though children, loved their father's company and looked forward to being in charge.

Viktor acted not a moment too soon. Five years later, when Kenneth was twelve and Cameron was ten, Viktor was diagnosed with lung cancer. He passed away within another two years. Lorcana stepped in to take over the company, and though she led well enough, the employees found her to be an unpleasant woman to work with, and for, in equal doses. There wasn't a single person who didn't look forward to the day the two boys would grow up and take over . . .

(One year ago . . .)

The boardroom had filled to the brim with executives. It was a power meeting to let one of the larger conglomerates in New York look for a new and unique style to promote their product. They had considered going to Just In Time, but something had swayed them toward Two More Minutes.

Part of the reason might have been because the company was owned half by Lorcana Dease and the other half by her son Kenneth Dease. He had inherited his share of the company on his twenty-first birthday weeks before and had already made sweeping changes that seemed to be nearly revolutionizing the company.

His younger brother, Cameron, was only nineteen. He would not inherit his share until he turned twenty-one as well. The not-yet-partner put in partial time at the company and the rest into college where he swiftly blazed through Business and Advertising degrees. Same as his brother before, he would complete his Bachelor's degrees within the coming year, marking a scant three years to completion; both brothers had graduated high school early as well. Though neither liked hearing 'prodigy' applied to them, they certainly ticked off the right boxes to earn the moniker.

The power meeting had both brothers present and sitting in to observe and participate. The executives of the other company, be they male or female, couldn't have been happier with that arrangement. The brothers looked as alike as two peas in a pod, nearly resembling twins. Both had shimmering platinum hair and oddly piercing gray-green eyes, and a terribly devastating beauty.

Lorcana disdained sharing the spotlight with anyone, even her own sons, and dictated everything they did—up to and including the way they dressed. Or rather, she only now dictated to Cameron. She had lost control over Kenneth weeks before.

The elder brother had taken swift advantage of the newfound freedom. While Cameron still had to wear his hair short and dress in a suit that did not do a bit of justice to his form, Kenneth had already started letting his hair grow and had immediately taken advantage of

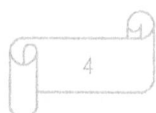

the family tailor to get a properly fitted suit for himself. He finally looked, and felt, like he belonged in the room.

Anger and upset churned in Lorcana. As soon as Cameron turned twenty-one, the company would be completely out of her control. It was *her* company. She had married for it. She had given birth to two sons for it when she had hardly been able to stand her husband's touch. Now she would lose it all.

Still, her smile stayed calm and competent as she explained the campaign that she had displayed on the room's large computer screen. "As you can see, we went with a family theme."

One of the executives drummed his fingers lightly on the top of the table. "It's an old campaign."

Kenneth and Cameron exchanged a quick look. They had tried telling their mother that the company wanted a fresh and modern look, but she was so set in her ways she could be the poster woman for cement retail. Their idea, or rather, Cameron's idea, had been to get away from the family theme and move toward the young couple one. Their generation would start buying now, and continue buying through the future—if they could be hooked.

Cameron cleared his throat. "If I may, we do also have a second idea for you to view."

"Cameron, don't speak until spoken to," Lorcana told him gently, but with an edge to the tone.

He seethed and swallowed his anger. Kenneth just narrowed his eyes fractionally and slid the portfolio holding Cameron's concepts across the table. One of the company's graphic designers had mocked them up on the down low to keep Lorcana from knowing. "Then allow me to speak for him. He and I have both discussed this idea. I find it to be a fresh new look that I believe you'll like." He ignored the warning look his mother shot his direction.

The executives gathered in closer to look at the offer, and they all began to smile. "This is just what we wanted," one female said. "Something new and young. Something to bring in all those 'just legal' youths that want to have a romantic dinner."

Lorcana stopped behind her sons' chairs as the conversation lifted in an excited buzz. "We'll discuss this later," she warned quietly, her tone icy, and she continued down the line.

Cameron and Kenneth exchanged another look. "For the love of god," Kenneth muttered, "hurry and grow up, Cameron, before one or both of us commits murder."

(Present)

The 3rd District. On the surface, it was a place where the sights and sounds of old America could be seen. Only the insides of the buildings had been modernized. All the exteriors stood the same as they had for over two thousand years. The only modern building in the District was the Enforcers' Headquarters, the company owned by Rhianna Taber and Eric Mason.

Enforcers protected the people of the 3rd District and had for centuries. Some people felt fairly sure Rhianna and Eric had run it for centuries too, but there were few who worried over it. The 3rd District was a place where magic gathered. No child born there was born without a special gift.

It did not, however, make the people less 'human'—though some assuredly had less than human blood. They loved and they hated. They cried and they laughed. Eric Mason stood on the doorstep of a small home in the middle of the District and knew that the news he bore would only bring tears. He took a quiet breath and lifted a hand to knock.

The door shortly opened by a slender young woman with surprisingly bright hair. It looked not quite orange and not quite red, and was instead an interesting combination of both that resembled rust. Her eyes glowed dark brown and filled with lively humor as she smiled at Eric. The smile turned a normally cute face into a nearly beautiful one. "Mr. Mason!" Like all residents, she knew Enforcers on sight. "Can I help you?"

He cleared his throat. "May I come in, Sarah?"

Sarah Davidson stepped back easily to let him enter. "Of

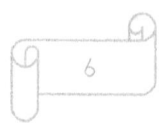

course. I hope it is quick. I need to go to the airport and pick up my mother and father."

He closed his eyes and cursed mentally. "Sarah, please sit down." He opened his eyes and saw the smile on her face fade. She was young, only twenty, but she held a razor sharp intelligence paired to a nearly psychic-level of astuteness. The look on her face implied she may already know what he needed to say, so he got straight to the point. "There was an accident."

She slowly sank down to sit on the side of the couch. Her dark eyes seemed far too large for her face. "I see."

He knelt in front of her and covered her hand gently with his. "Sarah," he said quietly, "I am sorry. The entire plane went down, and there were no survivors. There was a failure in the engines that could not be avoided. Rayna and I checked and double-checked and there is no mistaking the truth. Neither of your parents survived."

She turned her gaze toward the window and then straightened her back. "At least they were together," she murmured. "They were such lovebirds. They'd have suffered without one another." She turned back to him. "The family company will fall to the shareholders, won't it?"

The Davidsons had owned a small but very profitable ad company that had worked exclusively with small businesses. It had been primarily owned by her parents, but shares had been split amongst investors. Among them was the Shaughnessy-Tavoularis Conglomerate, a company Eric knew very well indeed. "Yes," he admitted. "But there is an alternative."

"What is that?"

"Before coming here, I spoke with Mel Shaughnessy and Kalliope Tavoularis. You are the sole heir to the portion of the company owned by your parents. If you are willing to sell all of that to Mel and Kalliope, they will ensure the company is not dissolved entirely. It will continue to operate as it is, but it will be co-owned by Shaughnessy-Tavoularis."

She let out a long breath. "So, in other words, I give up the keys to the castle that is rightfully mine in order to avoid being the princess devoured by the wolves of the wilds?"

He had to smile. "I suspect Mel and his wife would resent that."

"I suspect you're right." She got to her feet and walked over to the window to stare almost blindly across the landscape. The grief would come later. She would deal with it when she could. Right then her only choice was to accept the deal being offered so generously. Enforcers, and Mel and Kalliope, had gone out of their way to try to help her. The money would support her until she got a job, and she would not endure the guilt of seeing a few dozen people lose *their* jobs. "Alright," she finally said. "What do I need to do?"

It was mostly a lot of paperwork, she discovered. Lots, and lots, and lots of paperwork. She met with Mel and Kalliope multiple times and was able to reassure herself that they would do a good job of maintaining the integrity of her parents' company.

Thankfully, the other complications of her age had been handled by Enforcers as well. At twenty, she was not yet a legal adult. The law raising the age of majority had been in place for many years, and it had eliminated the gap between eighteen and twenty-one. Enforcers had very persuasive lawyers on hand, though. Sarah, so close to being legal, was given her independence and would not need a guardian for her last year as a minor. Effective immediately, she was an adult.

But because she would not own the company, she would not receive funds from it. She also wouldn't have a guardian to help support her until she got up and running. She would need a job to help pay for her living expenses as well as any further college courses she might want to take. The sale price of the company had been *beyond* generous, but that money would not last forever, and she had too large a practical streak to waste time.

Eric helped yet again. He sent job offers her direction that he thought she might be interested in. Finally, she decided to apply for one. It was with the Dease ad company known as Two More Minutes. The position would be as receptionist and secretary to the owners.

She would be doing clerical work, but at least she would be surrounded by something she loved.

The night before she was due to start working there, she found herself looking around her new apartment and realizing that she was lonely. She could no longer turn and have her parents there to share her laughter and her odd sense of humor. And, finally, she let herself grieve.

CHAPTER TWO

As Sarah got ready the morning she was due to report in to work for the first time, she stood in front of her closet and fidgeted. She had been told that she needed to be 'casually professional' but that term had such a broad interpretation. She also had the soul of an artist, so she balked at wearing anything resembling a neutral.

Aware the clock was ticking, she grabbed a soft yellow sweater and a pair of black slacks. She paired them with a pair of yellow heels, a black scarf for her hair, and some sassy silver hoop earrings. "Body armor," she decided.

Because it was getting late, she beat a hasty retreat to the kitchen, gulped down coffee, then just as quickly left the apartment and went to get her motorcycle. It was a guilty pleasure, and she knew it, but she couldn't bring herself to sell it. The gas still, barely, cost less than public transit.

She reported in twenty minutes later to the high-rise building that the Deases owned and operated from. The company only took up the highest floors of twenty through thirty; all other floors had been subleased to other companies. No other ad companies, of course.

She studied the directory and felt her amusement well. Executive Services for Two More Minutes sat all the way up on the thirtieth floor. She snorted. "So hot air *does* rise. I always wondered about that."

The other people in the elevator lobby began to laugh. Since that bank of elevators only went to the top ten floors, one man felt

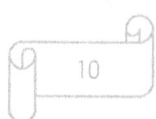

safe saying, "You must be the new girl. Welcome aboard. And good luck with the piranha."

"Piranha." She contemplated that as they got on the elevator. "I assume we are discussing my esteemed new boss Lorcana Dease?"

"Bingo! Give the girl a prize."

She shot him a sassy grin as they got off the elevator. "I'd rather have a cookie." She waited in bemusement for him to open the large glass doors that signaled the entrance to Executive Services. She had never understood the need that men had to leap to open doors for her. Was it the hair? She hoped it wasn't the hair; she had never really seen herself as a ginger so much as a paprika. She had a soul (artistic though it was).

As she walked around the corner, she saw a vast open space heralded by a tiny reception desk. Behind the desk sat a series of short cubicles. None reached over three feet tall. If someone sat up, they would likely resemble a gopher emerging from a golf hole. "Wow," she said. "Groundhog Day must be fabulous. If the pit sees its shadow, there's another month of piranha bites."

That made everyone start laughing. One woman with a riotous mane of curly auburn hair walked over with her hand held out. A genuinely warm and welcoming smile lit her face. "I hope you're Sarah!"

"I am indeed," Sarah agreed sagely. "Have been for twenty years, though my mother used to swear they tried to name me Penelope. Apparently I balked."

The other woman grinned. "I'm Louise Pram. We could use someone with your sense of humor around here."

Sarah took her hand and very expertly hid a subtle flinch. Her skin was so sensitive that even the nearly non-existent rasp of her associate's fingerprints felt painful. She been dealing with it for all of her life, so she had learned to suck it up and ignore the discomfort where needed. "Nice to meet you, Louise. And I promise I packed plenty of piranha food. Hopefully the biting won't be so pronounced."

Louise smiled. "Lorcana, I presume. If we were discussing Kenneth and Cameron . . . well, if they didn't feel like my brothers, they could bite me any time and any way they want."

"And *how*," came a chorus from several voices in the pit.

Muffling a giggle, Sarah followed Louise over to the receptionist desk. It turned out to be bigger than she had initially thought. The small stature was an illusion created by the preponderance of office supplies and surplus items that had been placed everywhere. "Is this the supply office?"

Louise coughed. "No, we have a supply room."

Sarah began to test the quantities of pens on a pad of paper. Half of them didn't work despite having ink inside, and the other half were empty of ink entirely. "Mmhmm. I'd rather have pens that no one else has chewed on. At least I know where my teeth have been." She tossed out or chunked in the recycle bin what was beyond repair or out of date—one pad of paper still listed Viktor Dease as in charge—and then grabbed the nearby cart and loaded it down with the rest.

Louise watched in utter fascination. Sarah had wasted no time in wading in and taking charge. Cameron and Kenneth would absolutely *love* her. This was one person who might just have the backbone to look Lorcana in the eye and tell her 'no.' "The supply room is a closet around the corner," she offered.

"Make sure there's coffee left," someone called. "The Deases ought to be in soon."

"Will do!" Sarah gave a sassy salute and looked at Louise. "I've heard that the two males are very handsome. And your comment of earlier . . ."

"They're *gorgeous*. Almost identical, actually. Most think they're twins on first look."

She grinned. "Resident eye candy is always a welcome thing when working a desk. Do promise me that they come through often."

"Not often enough," Louise said wistfully, and then she and Sarah exchanged a look and began laughing.

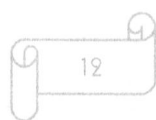

"I hate my life," Cameron muttered at his brother as they walked into the building. "Scratch that. I hate my age."

"Six months," Kenneth sympathized. "In six months you'll be twenty-one. The hell will then be over."

"Hell is right!" Cameron crossed his arms and glared at the elevator panel as the cab rose steadily. "Any ideas I have need to come from you so I don't get chewed on! I can't even pick out my own clothes, talk at meetings . . . Shit, I wouldn't even be wearing a decent suit if you hadn't told Mother to jump off."

His big brother pulled an innocent face. "Well, it looks bad on the company, you see, that we all don't dress for success. She would hate to have someone think our work was as sloppy as the way she forced you to dress."

Cameron muttered something uncomplimentary under his breath toward their mother. He could not argue that he owed Kenneth a *lot*. Kenneth had taken a lot of the brunt of their mother's wrath for most of their lives, and especially over the last two years since he had taken over his rightful share. The only reason he hadn't moved out of the family home was because he *refused* to let Cameron face Lorcana alone, or be lonely.

Truthfully, Cameron and Kenneth alike had had relatively lonely lives because they had never really been able to make and keep friends. The only real friend they had made in their lives had been Louise, who had effectively adopted them as her baby brothers from the moment she had been hired. They just kept it quiet lest Lorcana decide to fire her.

And if friends had been scarce, girlfriends had been far more so. Which would have been fine if Cameron had not felt a need for a romantic or physical relationship, but he did. Thinking it, he demanded of Kenneth, "Can you get her to allow me to have a girlfriend while you're busy convincing her to not be a bitch about my clothes?"

"You've had a girlfriend."

"Sneaking around with a girl and making out in the backseat of a car is not the same as having a girlfriend," he muttered. "Call me a stupid romantic, but I want to be with a girl I can actually *date* and, you know, maybe fall in love with and marry."

Kenneth cocked his head. He, too, had felt a similar lack of companionship as his brother, but he'd had more patience to wait. Once Lorcana had been fully removed from the picture, he would start looking around as well. "So, in that vein, what kind of girl do you want?" He had his own ideas about what his brother needed. Cameron had carried heavy chains for a long time, and Kenneth thought he needed someone with serious spunk who could bring humor into his life. If he found the right girl for his brother, he would encourage it however he could.

"Hmm." Cameron contemplated things and finally grinned. "You know, I don't think I have an actual preference. I think I'll just know a girl I want when I meet her. I think I lean toward cute girls, though. Never really been interested in cover models, y'know?" He pushed open the doors to Executive Services and then came to a quick stop. "Whoa."

Kenneth stepped around him and lifted a brow. The reception desk looked unexpectedly immaculate, and a dish of candy sat at the front. "Ooh. M&Ms." He grabbed a few. "Either we're being bribed or the new girl started today. Or both."

"Okay, she's good. Did you meet her?"

"Nope. Mother did not bother with an interview; just hired her based on her resume." Kenneth glanced around and spotted the brunette in question. Technically, she was one of the graphic designers, but she served as office manager as well. Lorcana wouldn't actually hire a *real* office manager, or an actual Executive Secretary, so Louise pulled double duty without double pay—for now. "Hey, Lou! Where's the new girl? We want to introduce ourselves."

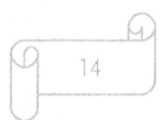

"She went to the supply room. After clearing out the mess, she discovered she had nothing but chewed up pens." Louise grinned. "She said that if the pens were to be chewed on, she'd rather it be her own teeth. She knows where they've been."

The brothers exchanged a grin. That alone promised they would like their new secretary. Cameron opened his mouth to say so when he spotted Lorcana standing in the boardroom doorway and tapping her foot impatiently. She was looking at the clock and her lips were drawn into a thin line. "I hate Mondays," he muttered. "She stores up all that ire over the weekend."

Kenneth patted his shoulder sympathetically without a word. Cameron took a quick breath to brace himself and then heard an unfamiliar female voice softly exclaim, "Wow! That's a good gene cookie dough!"

"Cookie dough? Don't you mean gene pool?" one of the other employees asked curiously.

The first voice giggled. "Cookie dough. You know. Cookie cutter cuties."

Cameron forgot his mother. He instantly turned and headed toward the direction of the voice. He could feel himself grinning, and that alone was a first because he almost never grinned on Mondays. He swung around the corner near the supply room and saw one of the graphic designers standing with a young woman he didn't recognize.

He knew, however, that he would never be able to mistake her for anyone else. Her hair was *amazing*. It was straight as a pin and fell to her waist in a fascinating shade of rusty orange. She looked average in height, probably only five or six inches shorter than his five-ten, and her figure seemed subtle rather than curvy. No one would call her pretty, necessarily, but she was cute as hell. He adored her on sight. "We have munchkins in the office!" he proclaimed.

Sarah turned with a grin. "I do not represent the Lollipop Kids, Mr. Lion. And I traded Toto in for a less frilly bike. That basket was just too 1940s."

The other nearly added in his own wise comment when he looked closer at Cameron. There was something in the younger man's eyes and corner of his smile that served as a red flag. Covering a grin, the man edged back until he could sneak away without notice. Had their new princess caught the eye of one of their favorite princes? It was too fabulous for words.

Cameron didn't notice the exit as he held out a hand. "Cameron Dease."

"Sarah Davidson." She took his hand and braced herself, but to her surprise, he didn't hold her hand too tightly. His fingers were strong and warm, and the little rough edges didn't hurt. If anything, it felt quite enjoyable. Her shoulders relaxed. "I'm your new slave labor. I mean receptionist. Shoot. I always do that."

"You mean we didn't make the fine print small enough?" He lifted her hand to his lips and bowed with all the courtly grace of a prince from hundreds of years before. He simply couldn't resist. Something about her just seemed to demand old-world manners. "Welcome to the company, Sarah." He grinned. "A baking company, so to speak."

She smiled impishly. "Well, I could have called you bad boy bookends." The words came out of their own will, which was just as well because she had mostly forgotten how to speak. Her heart had gone into such overdrive, it seemed a miracle she could string any words together. Louise, damn her hide, had lied. Gorgeous? Cameron Dease was sin incarnate.

"Let's go back to cookies." He eased closer without conscious thought and flattened a hand on the wall behind her head to effectively cut off the rest of the office. "And speaking of cookies, have lunch with me."

"I probably shouldn't. You're my boss."

"Not for six months, I'm not. I'm someone who *might* ask you to do something, but I'm not your boss. And even if I was, you can be friends with your boss around here. It's a family company. Informality is cool." His eyes searched her face. She had the most impossibly

kissable mouth he had ever seen. He would start with friendship and then see if she wanted more as badly as he was beginning to think he did. "Just lunch," he coaxed.

"Might as well give in," Kenneth offered dryly from their side. "He won't give up until you do."

She blinked and then looked back and forth between them. "I thought cloning humans was illegal."

He laughed. "Okay, we're keeping you." He reached over and caught Cameron's collar. "Leave her alone."

"I'll cry," Cameron warned as he was dragged away. "Please?"

She sighed as if she had been asked to climb Mt. Everest with a toothpick, but she grinned to take the sting out of it. "Oh all right." She couldn't help but like him. He looked like someone in need of some serious laughter. She would just have to ignore her hormones. Seriously, where had they been since puberty? She had been sure they would sleep until she was eighty.

When she returned to her desk, several other coworkers pounced on her. "You go girl!" Louise said. She started to clap Sarah on the shoulder but caught her faint wince and arrested the movement. Poor thing probably had a sunburn. "You didn't mention you had a fishing pole with you."

"I didn't catch him," Sarah protested on a laugh. "We're just having lunch. He's just being friendly. He looks in some serious need of a friend."

"We wouldn't argue that," a man admitted. "Lorcana works Cameron like a slave. Until he's twenty-one or married, he's firmly under her control. It's the worst thing ever, especially because Cameron and Kenneth are incredible at what they do and Lorcana is only so-so."

Sarah tilted her head. "We have permission to call them by their names?"

Louise grinned. "Kenneth made the decision. He said that there were too many Deases running around. If we're going to curse at them, he would rather know precisely who we're cursing at."

"I'm going to like it here," Sarah decided mischievously.

Inside the meeting room, Lorcana glared at Cameron as he and Kenneth walked in. "You kept me waiting." She hated to be kept waiting by anyone, even her own child. Perhaps especially by her own child. Her sons looked far too much like her dead husband for her own tastes.

Cameron felt himself bristle slightly. All the relaxation and fun he had gotten out of his meeting with Sarah seemed to fade away. "I was introducing myself to the new secretary," he told Lorcana politely but with a bite to the words. "I thought it was the proper thing to do since she'll be answering the phones and needs to know who to give messages to."

She walked over to the door and looked across the room to where Sarah had begun to get the computer up and running. Her familiarity with the machine was visible. Lorcana gave a quick nod. "She came highly recommended from Enforcers. Eric Mason himself vouched for her work integrity and skill, and Rhianna Taber had nothing but high praise for her personality. Her other professional references came from Mel Shaughnessy and Kalliope Tavoularis-Shaughnessy. It seemed a waste not to hire her."

And thank god for it, Cameron thought, but he felt more curious than ever about Sarah's history. She could claim two of the biggest companies in America as professional references? It was fascinating, especially since he knew that Enforcers usually only worked with people in 3rd District, and if she was from 3rd District then she was probably not human. He couldn't wait to ask.

"So what is this all about?" Kenneth asked his mother as he sat down beside his brother. "You indicated that this was an urgent meeting. You've come to an important decision of some sort?"

Lorcana linked her hands behind her back as she began to walk around the table. She had been thinking, and thinking, and she knew that she faced losing the company in six months. That Cameron would claim his share was inevitable. Her only hope in holding any control over him was to ensure he married a woman of her choice and blackmail him into signing a pre-nuptial agreement giving his shares to his wife. She could then have the wife sign them over to her. "I've been thinking about things," she said, "and I have decided that Cameron needs to get married."

Cameron choked on his coffee and Kenneth did likewise. "What?!" they both demanded, and loudly enough that several people outside the meeting room looked toward the doors in surprise.

"You're out of your mind!" Cameron shot to his feet. "Why should I get married? You won't even let me date!"

"You're my precious baby boy," she cooed. "I only want your happiness. To that end, I will simply have to select your bride myself. You're still under my guardianship for six months, Cameron. I just want you to be happy."

He felt slightly ill as he sat down. There was no doubt in his mind that any woman *she* picked would make him utterly miserable. She only associated with people who were just like her.

"Here's my idea," she said decisively. "I'm going to invite properly eligible women in for an interview. If they pass the first round, they will come back for a second. Once we've narrowed it down, then we'll have the perfect candidate."

Slightly green at the edges, Kenneth shifted in his seat as she continued on outlining her plans. He leaned over to his brother and murmured, "We need to find a way to stall for time. Six months. We can manage that, right?" Louder, he said, "And when will these . . . interviews, as you put it, begin?" Interviewing for a bride. The idea alone was disgusting.

She beamed. "Why, I thought I might start things up this week. There's no reason to wait. I'm sending out the notices this afternoon!"

Cameron groaned and dropped his head onto the table. "I'm so screwed," he said under his breath. "My life is over." His eyes shifted to the clock. Three hours until lunch. He could endure. Seeing Sarah again would make it better. He just felt sure of it.

As lunchtime drew closer, Sarah had become very comfortable with her new job. She always learned very quickly, and she had been a receptionist for her parents' company whenever their regular had called in sick or gone on vacation.

She was also vividly aware that the meeting that morning had not gone well. For one thing, she and everyone else had heard the shouting. For a second thing, Cameron had left the room looking as if the world was falling down around his head. He had disappeared down the hall to his office, and even from the front she had heard the door shut hard.

She'd had enough. She got to her feet and went over to the coffeepot to pour two cups. With both in hand, she headed for the hall. "Last on the left," Louise said helpfully as Sarah went past. She hid a smile to herself. The entire office would encourage this budding romance if they could. They adored the Dease brothers, and Sarah seemed *perfect* for Cameron.

Sarah moved down the hall and her brows drew together as she realized that Cameron's office was actually a glorified closet next to the supply room. She peeked around the now open door, saw him sitting with his head on his desk, and resolved to remove his clear anxiety. Injecting surprise in her voice, she stepped into the doorway and said, "Hey! They told me that this was the strip club, darn it."

He lifted his head and smiled. He couldn't help it. She came like a breath of fresh air into his windowless little closet. "I could always take my shirt off."

"Let's not, Harry Potter. It might make the others jealous." She walked over and sat on the edge of his desk to offer one of the cups of coffee. "Is this your broom closet under the stairs, Mr. Wizard?"

"Less broom and more dustpan." He looked around with a sigh. "I'd settle for a single window."

She also glanced around. "You need some paintings. Maybe a painting that *looks* like a window. You could hook a little fan to it and make a fake breeze." She propped her chin on her hand. "And add a plant or two."

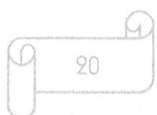

He tilted his head as he considered her ideas. "I always thought it was a waste of time since I would be leaving."

She laughed. "And you want to be miserable in the time you remain here? Just take the stuff with you." She swung one foot lightly, and he was tickled when he realized that she had an anklet with small ladybugs on it around her ankle. "What happened this morning?" she asked. "I see tooth marks. You got nommed pretty hard methinks."

He leaned back in his chair on a sigh. "My mother wants me to get married."

A pause, then, "Are we talking Cinderella or . . .?"

"I wish! No, she's going to be interviewing potential brides as if hiring someone for a job." He put his head on the desk again. "I can't guess at her reasoning, but it sure as hell can't be good."

"Well, why not look for your own bride?" she offered.

"I'm not legal. She'd have to approve."

"There are *always* loopholes," she pointed out. "Maybe you could find a bride you like and ask her to pretend to be someone your mom might like." She shook her head slightly. "I can't fathom it. A parent doing something like this to their child."

He smiled at her. She really was just what he had needed to feel better. "Your parents must be good ones."

She lowered her gaze and again felt the pain well up without stop. It still hurt to even think of them. "They were," she whispered. "You know the plane crash three months ago? They were in it." She clenched her hands into fists at her sides. "I'm sorry. I need a moment. It hurts so much."

He got to his feet and pulled her into his arms without thinking, wanting only to bring back her smile. "It's okay," he said softly. "I know how you feel. When my father died . . . it was horrible. It was years ago and the pain still sneaks out and slaps me." His heart tightened fiercely as he felt her burrow against him and tuck her head on his shoulder. She felt so . . . right in his arms.

She gave a soft sigh and closed her eyes. She had never been held by anyone other than her parents because it always hurt too much to feel physical contact. For some odd reason, Cameron seemed incapable of hurting her. Even the feel of his shirt wasn't abrasive to her skin. She could still feel each individual thread, but it seemed as oddly soothing as the alluring scent of his skin and cologne.

The mood had shifted to something oddly intimate, and it alarmed her more than a little. To regroup, she sought refuge in humor and sniffed at his collar. "Lavender."

He coughed and released her. "So what?" he asked. "I like it."

"But it's a *girl* scent," she said, putting a whine on the word 'girl.' She was rewarded by a swift grin. "But that's okay," she told him. "I have a preference for fruit, so we shouldn't clash and create The War of the Smells."

He leaned over and sniffed at her hair. It smelled like blueberries. He figured it was just his own bad luck that he adored blueberries. "You're right. Do bakers chase you down on the streets?"

"Only the random ones who sell cookie cutters to parents-to-be," was the teasing retort.

Laughing, he held up his hands. "Okay, I know when I'm defeated." He leaned down and softly touched her cheek with his lips. "Sarah, thank you. You showed up right when I needed you most. I guess it was a lucky coincidence."

Listening outside the door, Kenneth had to smile to himself. He had taken a peek at Sarah's personnel file and recognized her home address. She did indeed live in the 3rd District, and there was a fairly common belief that, when it came to 3rd District, there was no such thing as coincidence. If anything happened, it happened at the whim of destiny.

He lightly rubbed his hands together. There was no law against helping destiny, and he fully intended to help his brother and Sarah. They just . . . belonged together somehow.

CHAPTER THREE

By the time lunch arrived, Sarah was at home with her new job and her new coworkers. By that time as well, her coworkers were absolutely in love with her. Her sense of humor could only be called contagious, and she was quick to respond if someone needed help. She won their eternal devotion by walking around and refilling coffee cups; they were working on a rush order and hadn't had time for a break.

Sarah also resolved to do more office work than strictly assigned to her, to allow Louise to do her *real* job. So, after negotiations and outright emotional blackmail, she got Louise to hand over the tedious task of typing up letters to some of the company's clients to give them status updates. She was so involved in her work that she didn't realize she was no longer alone at her desk until she heard giggling. Without looking up, she asked, "Is that Jason or Freddie behind me?"

Louise tucked her tongue in her cheek. "Well, certainly not Freddie. And if Jason looks that good without his hockey mask, his victims died happy."

Cameron snorted. "Gee, thanks, Lou!" He leaned down to look over Sarah's shoulder. "You type like a demon." He grinned. "And you misspelled 'gratitude.'"

"You distracted me," she accused. "And if you're going to type, type fast." She fixed the typo and tried to ignore the tempting scent of lavender and male skin that teased her nose. She saved the file, locked her computer, and swiveled on her chair. With a smile, she asked, "Ready for lunch?"

"I was ready before I started work." He tugged her gently to her feet and kept a firm grip on her hand as he hauled her behind him out of the office.

"I need my purse!" she protested on a laugh.

"My treat. Stop fighting. Don't make me carry you out."

"Be still my heart, you charmer you." She gave a sigh as she was hauled toward the elevator. "Why don't you just throw me over your shoulder? Good grief, Cam, you couldn't get more caveman-ish if you were swinging a club and wearing a loincloth." Her mind promptly diverted by the mental image and she dragged it back. She was *not* going there.

"I'm desperate," he admitted. "Mondays always suck, but after you left me, my mother started sending me emails of pictures of 'possible candidates.'" He ushered her into the elevator as the doors opened. He didn't admit out loud that he had mentally compared the pictures to Sarah and found them lacking. He was well aware that he was already getting in over his head. He just didn't care.

She leaned against the wall and watched curiously as he used his keycard to access an unlisted floor. "Wow," she said solemnly. "And here I thought the company would have policies against sending dirty pictures."

"Ha. I wish they were dirty pictures. At least then I'd have a *reason* to feel so offended. The photos were of very nice businesswomen. Some posed, like for portraits, and others were more candid, as if caught at work. Mother wanted me to see what my 'choices' were. Choices, my ass! I won't have any say in it."

She linked her hands behind her back. "What about going along with things?" When he lifted a brow, she explained, "A marriage of convenience. Don't sleep with her unless you and she mutually want to. When you're twenty-one, divorce her."

"It crossed my mind," he admitted as the elevator stopped and the doors opened. "But the damage would be done. I have this sinking feeling that Mother is doing this to get her hands on my share

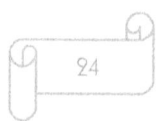

of the company."

"Yeah, that wouldn't be a surprise. Company rumor mill works better than the Starbucks coffee grinder." She stepped out of the elevator and followed him up a single flight of stairs. When she pushed open the door at the top and stepped outside, she was surprised to find herself standing on the roof of the building. Further surprising was the realization that the roof was, in fact, a giant greenhouse and atrium. "Wow," she breathed.

"Follow me." He took her hand and drew her into the open doors of the atrium where trees and plants of all shapes and types instantly surrounded them. If it hadn't been for the glass ceiling, someone would forget they stood on a roof in New York City. He studied her face and knew bringing her there had been the right idea. "Like it?" he asked softly.

"It's amazing!" She turned in a slow circle. Impulsively, she took off her shoes to feel the grass under her feet. "This is my idea of a break room!"

"Dad built it way back when he had the building built." He led her through the pathways until the sound of running water grew loud. "But he never gave Mother access to it. The only two keycards are in Kenneth's and my possession. She knows that, but she doesn't really care. She hates most forms of nature, though, I guess to be fair, it's probably as much because she has a lot of allergies as much as anything else."

"So nature hates her as much as she hates it?"

"I plead the Fifth on that one."

She grinned as they rounded a large bush and found a large pool with a waterfall tumbling into the center from some artfully stacked rocks. A picnic lunch sat only a few feet away. She walked over and sat on the edge of the stones lining the pool. "So if the roof leaks, I know who to blame, right? Can you swim in this? It looks pretty big."

"Yup. Twenty feet diameter, seven foot deep at the lowest point." He moved closer and sat down beside her, far closer than was strictly polite. He also leaned in so that she couldn't mistake that he was close. It came as more of an instinct than a conscious decision. He *had* to ensure that he had her attention. He knew he would lose her if he didn't. "Ken and I come here to escape. We know when the other is here, so there won't be interruptions." His breath swept across her nape. "If you look straight ahead, you can see the skyline."

Her heart began to beat harder than a snare drum in a school band. He felt hot and secure, tempting and sinful. If she leaned back, she would be leaning against him. Would he hold her? The depth of her longing to know was a little frightening, so she again sought refuge in humor. She squinted out the windows. "I can see my house from here."

He laughed and eased back. He moved over to the picnic blanket and began to unpack the basket. When she had joined him, he offered her a soda. "I saw that you live in 3rd District."

Her lashes lowered slightly, her eyes watchful and waiting for judgment. "Yes, I do. I was born there."

He visibly brightened. "Then you're not human?"

She blinked at him. "Wow, executives are getting more tactless these days." Her gaze turned wary. "Where's the other shoe, and why do I feel like it will hit my head?"

He scooted closer. "Not from me," he assured her. "I think it's fascinating and amazing. I've met Mel Shaughnessy and his wife. They *totally* can't be human. They hit a chord between terrifying and protective. It was wild."

"Hee." She muffled a full giggle. "Audra and Mel do that." She hesitated and then went with her instincts. "They're werewolves. I've known Audra my whole life, so I knew Mel even before he, uhm, became a professional reference for me. So, yeah, they aren't human. And I'm . . ." She searched for the words. "I wouldn't say I'm not human. But I'm . . . different. Here." She held out a hand.

He curiously took her hand. Goosebumps rose on his skin as he felt a tingle of *something* going through his fingers. Power. It was the only word he could bring to mind. If asked to describe it, he would

have never been able to. It simply was. And watching her eyes slowly darken to black from brown seemed oddly erotic. He wanted to make her eyes darken with desire instead of power.

Her fingertips moved over his hand as light as a feather, as if reading him. Then she blinked, her eyes cleared, and she smiled. "You fell off your bike when you were six, and you scraped up this hand." As his eyes widened, she grinned. "There are tiny scars on your hand. I read them." She released his hand. "My skin is so sensitive that I can feel the individual threads in cloth. My clothes are specially made because of it."

"How can you handle touching people then?" he wondered.

She looked at him, startled. "I didn't think you'd pick up on that." She looked away. "It *is* painful, to be honest. Especially because I can read things people have done if I am touching them. Mostly it is in relation to injuries and such." Inner honesty made her admit, "But you don't hurt me. I'm not sure why."

He eased even closer to her and framed her face with his hands. He leaned down and softly brushed his lips over hers, careful to make sure it was just friendly. He had the feeling his Sarah might be a little skittish when it came to romance—and just as inexperienced as himself. "Good," he said softly. "Because I'm a very touchy-feely sort of person and you seem like someone in need of serious hugging."

"I could handle that." She smiled. "Friends who can't hug aren't worth having." She gave him a quick one. She released him with hidden reluctance and reached for something to eat. She would be double damned if she admitted that she wanted more than friendship. She was going to throw toilet paper on Eric Mason's prized sports car if she found out he had known she would click with Cameron. "How goes the shark work?"

He munched on a carrot stick. "It sucks, for me at least." He considered her. "As a consumer, would you pay any attention to the same ad you'd seen a million times before?"

She snorted. "No. I completely tune out." She nibbled on a

sandwich. "I take it your mother is stuck in a rut."

"Stuck? Hell, she put a door over the top so she can't get out." He fell over onto his back and linked his hands behind his head. "There's a company that wants to promote shoes. My mother wants to go the old-fashioned route of using models. I keep trying to say we need to jazz it up. Maybe use dancers. Appeal to the younger generation like you and me." He opened one eye. "How old are you?"

"Twenty."

"When's your birthday?"

"Next month." She grinned. "I'm older than you are."

"I like older girls." He went on without missing a beat, "But my point is that we're the new generation of shopper. You need to appeal to us too. We'll be here a lot longer than the older generation. Catch us now with flashy or entertaining ads and keep us with the quality of your product. We'll keep going back."

His style wasn't that vastly different from her parents' so it felt comfortable to her. "Why not go ahead and have Kenneth force your mother to take the idea?"

"Because she said she won't go along with it without support from some big name dancer to be in the ads." He sighed. "And without her support, how can we hope to get any dancers involved? I don't even *know* any dancers!"

"Have you ever been to the Faerie Club in 3rd District?" she asked curiously.

"Sure. Who hasn't? That place is awesome! I'm a decent dancer, but I danced with Aenya Michaels once. Friggin' world champion dancer. She left me in her dust." He sat up with a grin. "Maybe we could go together some time. Relax after work."

"Sure." She wasn't entirely listening, though, as her mind worked very quickly. She had gotten to know all of the Shaughnessy family members during the dealings with Mel and Kalliope. She had met Aenya Michaels, formerly Shaughnessy, as well. She had a strong feeling that if she asked the older woman, she would be glad to assist. Aenya's dancing skills were well known; they had single-handedly turned the Faerie Club into the hottest spot for young adults. She had also won a world dance competition with her husband two years prior.

She startled out of her thoughts as Cameron eased closer to her yet again. He was sitting right beside her now, but slightly behind her. The difference had her suddenly feeling enveloped in his presence. Her pulse kicked into overdrive and she strangled an urge to turn her head and kiss him. She really wished he would stop looming over her like that. It had to be bad for her blood pressure.

The soft hitch in her breath couldn't be disguised by the sound of running water. He slowly ran a finger down her arm and watched as goosebumps followed his touch. A giddy sense of delight and triumph seemed to meld with the steadily growing hunger he had for her smile and her outrageously lovely body. She wanted him as badly as he wanted her. And he felt no guilt whatsoever for being willing to take advantage of her apparent sensitivity to him. "Know something?" he murmured into her ear.

She fought a shiver as his breath teased her. She knew her skin was sensitive everywhere, but her *ear* was an erogenous zone? Whatever genetic gods had put her together had to have been smoking something. "What?" She tried to ease away before she did something stupid.

He just slid even closer. "I think I'm falling in love with you." Her head jerked around and he fought the urge to lean in and take the kiss he craved. They were nose-to-nose, and their lips almost touched. "It's just a warning," he said, his voice slightly huskier than normal. "Because if I do fall in love with you, I will be having you come hell, high water, or my mother."

"Whoa." It was the best she could manage. She had never before heard such a blatant declaration of intent. In fact, she had never known any man with the confidence or courage to consider making one. It terrified her on more than one level, and she sought for balance. "Well, fine then. Since I might be falling for you too, we'll have to see who gets there first, if at all. Kind of like trying to get to a sale at Sak's on Black Friday."

He grinned and eased back. He was beginning to understand her, and in his understanding, he was beginning to form a plan. "Well, we need to go back to work before you're late. Much as neither of us probably wants to go back."

It was to her credit that her knees weren't still weak and she looked perfectly calm as she got back to her desk a few minutes later. The calm gave way to laughter as she saw the post-its that had been stuck all over her monitor. They all said different things, but the general theme was the same: if she wanted Cameron, she had the full support of her coworkers. "I'm not replacing those from supply," she scolded, but with a smile.

The others just grinned and went about their business. After cleaning up the mess, she did likewise. She was, however, still thinking swiftly. As she observed Kenneth and Cameron going into another meeting with Lorcana, she made up her mind. "Someone have a home phone book?" she called. Sometimes, things called for old-fashioned methods. The number she needed could not be found online.

Louise brought one over to her. "What are you up to?"

She flipped pages swiftly. "I'm doing my good deed for the month." She dialed the phone and waited for a few moments. When it was answered, she smiled. "Hey there, Ruthie. Is your mommy there? It's Sarah." Louise opened her mouth and Sarah shook her head. "Aenya? Good afternoon! How are you? Listen," she continued, "I have an idea to run past you."

Ten minutes later, Louise's eyes looked huge as she watched Sarah hang up. "You did not just call Aenya Michaels and ask her to support Cameron's idea."

"Actually, yes I did." Sarah smiled. "It's too complicated to explain, but I know the Shaughnessy family and all its extended branches. Aenya is only four years older than I am. She's one of the nicest people I know. She also knows the complications of bad business owners. She was glad to help."

Twenty minutes later, in the meeting, Cameron felt as if he was hitting his head against a brick wall. His mother wouldn't give way for anything. "Can't you see?" he exploded as he leapt to his feet. "You're going to destroy the company like this! You want it so badly and yet you keep choking it!"

"Don't you dare take that tone with me!" Lorcana snapped back.

"Cameron's right." Kenneth's voice was clipped. "Our business has dropped twenty percent over the last few years. It was only when I took control of my rightful share," he used the phrase deliberately, "that the business started growing again!"

Lorcana opened her mouth to retort sharply when the door opened behind her. She whirled around and shouted, "You are to *never* interrupt a meeting! Get out, now!"

Sarah didn't bat a lash and looked past Lorcana to Cameron. "Your guest is here." Her eyes twinkled and asked him to play along.

He blinked. "Well, uhm, show them in."

She stepped to the side and gestured gracefully. The slender young woman who had been standing behind her walked into the room and swept her honey colored gaze over it swiftly. She had grown up under boardroom tables playing cards with her youngest older brother, and yet she had never heard anything as ridiculous then as what she had heard now. "My name is Aenya Michaels. Which of you two handsome males is Cameron?"

Kenneth's jaw fell open. Lorcana could only stare in shock. Cameron felt a bit off kilter himself, but he recovered and got to his feet. "That would be me." He took her offered hand and wondered when he had entered the looking glass without noticing. "Thank you for joining us."

Her eyes sparkled. "I was glad to hear from you." With a casual sort of confidence, she sat down beside Cameron. She knew it would piss Lorcana off and didn't care one way or another. "When you contacted me with the request that I dance in an ad, I was quite honored. I know what it's like to fight for a dream."

Lorcana whirled on Sarah. "You are not to take any more requests from Cameron!" she ordered sharply. The *nerve* of the girl!

Sarah met her gaze head-on. "Does Cameron draw a paycheck?"

"Well, yes, but . . ."

"And is he a Dease family member?"

"I don't see what . . ."

"Then I will continue to do as he asks me." She lifted her brows. "My job description was that I would be secretary and support to *all* members of the Dease family who work for the company." She gave a graceful and yet subtly mocking curtsy. "Now excuse me please. Kenneth is horrible at filing his papers."

Kenneth grinned swiftly. "Job security." He wanted to laugh out loud. He also wanted to hug Sarah. She had not only done the impossible, but she had stood up to Lorcana at the same time. If it was the last thing he ever did, he would see her get together with Cameron. His baby brother would finally have someone to fight at his side.

Boxed in by her own words, Lorcana had no choice but to go along with Cameron's idea. She would die before admitting that it was a good one, and she sure as hell wouldn't admit to being impressed by Aenya. Aenya was a Shaughnessy by birth and it showed; she was a shark to her core and held her own during the negotiations as well as her elder brother might have.

It was the end of the day by the time the meeting ended. Kenneth had a dinner date and had to hurry out. Lorcana was still in a snit so she took off for home. Cameron got out into the office area and looked around swiftly but Sarah had already left for the day. Disappointed, he wondered how it was possible to know someone for just one day and know they were vital to your existence.

Aenya stepped up beside him. "Walk with me, Cam. I'd like to talk to you, if you don't mind."

"Not at all." He fell into step beside her and glanced at her curiously. "Did Sarah call you?"

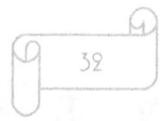

"She did." She smiled. "Sarah . . . well, it's her choice to tell how and why, but she got to be very dear to the Shaughnessy family. We've taken her under our wing, so to speak. We told her that if she ever needed help, she could call on any of us. When she told me what was going on here, it annoyed me."

He lifted a brow. "Why?"

"Two reasons. One, because it was stupid." She grinned impishly. "I'm Sullivan Shaughnessy's daughter, and I own my own club. I know stupid business when I see it. And the other reason is because of you." She sighed. "You probably wouldn't remember since I doubt you read the paper when you were fourteen, but, I was forced into a contract with my father. Any man who found out where I danced at night could marry me."

"Yikes." He winced in sympathy.

"My father did it because he loved me and worried, but it still made me mad. It worked out though." She smiled. "I met Hiro. Sneaky bastard found out where I danced *and* stole my heart." She grinned when he laughed. "But the thing is . . . it wasn't coincidence." She turned to face him as they waited for the elevator. "3rd District was involved. And it was involved with my brothers as well."

"Magic."

"It's more than that." She shook her head. "It's a joke, but it's true. There is no such thing as a coincidence around 3rd District. The fact that Sarah is here, that you've met, that you're falling for her . . . it's not a coincidence."

He tilted his head slightly. "Destiny?"

"You know, I'm not sure." She smiled as she got onto the elevator. "But I can say that I'm sure that someday you'll have everything you want. Dreams come true in our District, Cameron." She waved her hand. "See you in a few days to get the rest of the details taken care of."

He smiled but he was thinking hard as the doors closed. He had always believed in magic and in destiny. He had always thought that perhaps there was some being out there, some deity that watched over lovers. The idea that the entire 3rd District might be protected by such a person was an incredible one.

He thought about things critically as he returned home and went to his favorite place in the garden. He had known Sarah for only a single day but he already craved her presence. He wanted to see her again, to talk with her. He wanted to hold her and remove the lingering traces of grief. He wanted to make love to her, to sleep with her all tangled in his arms.

He was so deep in his thoughts that he didn't know Kenneth had joined him until his brother spoke up, "I know they say 'ask and ye shall receive' but I've never known a guy who asked for a girlfriend and found love."

He glanced up at Kenneth with a wry smile as his brother sat beside him. There were two years difference in their ages, yet they had always been as close as the twins they resembled. "Short date?"

"Eh, she canceled. No worries. Tell me about Sarah."

"I want her so badly it hurts," he admitted. "I'm looking forward to work, Ken. I *want* to go to work so I can see her." Awe and pride entered his voice. "Did you see her stand up to Mother?"

"I don't think a princess could have done better. Her parents named her well." Kenneth linked his hands behind his head. "So what do we do? Mother won't change her plans, especially not over someone like Sarah. But *I'm* on your side, you know that."

"Yeah." He let out a long breath. "The first thing is to convince Sarah that we can be more than friends."

"Is she at least attracted to you?"

His grin turned dangerous for a moment with masculine satisfaction. "Most definitely. I plan to take full and complete advantage of that. In the meantime, if you can think of a way to get her on Mother's radar as a potential bride without getting all of us in trouble, please let me know."

"Gladly."

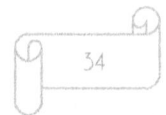

Cameron was the first one at work the following morning, an inner instinct telling him that Sarah was the type to arrive early and leave late. Much to his delight, he found that he was right, and she was already at her desk a full thirty minutes before she was due to start. The entire office wouldn't be arriving for a while yet either, and the area remained nice and quiet.

She didn't know he had joined her. She had her email open but didn't see it. She was still thinking about the same things that had kept her up all night. She had never expected to meet a man that she couldn't bear to be away from for more than a few hours at a time.

She was a virgin by choice (and practicality because of her abilities) but every time she looked at Cameron, all she could think of was throwing on sexy lingerie, climbing onto his lap, and settling in like a dieter on an illegal binge. Why she'd had to fall in love with a person she could never have, she didn't know.

Her skin tingled suddenly and she knew he stood behind her. Ignoring her fluttering heart, she said, "And here I thought the office wasn't haunted. Are you the ghost of hot men past?"

He laughed and leaned down to wrap his arms around her shoulders. "I'm more like the ghost of piranha food past."

She snickered and turned as he released her. More than happy, she returned the hug he had given her. "You're here early, Cam. You trying to be prepared for the auction?"

"Auction?"

She quirked a brow. "Your mother had me contact five of the first brides. They'll be here today bidding on a certain cookie dough cutie."

He groaned. "I wish you were talking about Ken, I really do." He rested his chin on her head and held her closer. She definitely wasn't very curvy, but that just meant she fit perfectly in his arms. "Promise to have lunch with me. I'm going to need you."

Her eyes softened as her heart swelled. There was nothing like being needed by the man you loved. She wanted to take away the sadness in his eyes. "Cam . . ."

"Whoops!" Louise covered her eyes as she entered. "I see nothing. I hear nothing. Just let me get my coffee."

Cameron laughed and released Sarah. "I was just stealing a hug. I need her to keep me sane."

Louise grinned at Sarah. "Not fishing, huh?"

She stuck her tongue out. "I'm just lucky that way." Good luck, she mouthed to Cameron as he headed down the hall. After a moment of thought, she turned and began to type up a document. When Louise joined her, she said, "If Lorcana wants this to be an interview, the candidates ought to have a duty statement."

Her supervisor's brows slowly lifted as she saw what Sarah was typing. "You're an evil woman. Damn, we should have found you sooner."

The five candidates had arrived by ten o'clock. Sarah checked them in but intensely disliked all of them. They were beautiful, cultured, intelligent . . . and radiated an aura of pure ruthless manipulation not dissimilar from Lorcana. Talk about like recognizing like.

Still, she remained friendly and polite and had all of them smiling once they were seated. She simply didn't have the heart to be rude or mean. Casually, she handed out the duty statement. "These are some of the duties you will be undertaking once you marry Cameron Dease. You'll also find a fact sheet about your potential groom."

One female said, "He's only twenty?! I'm not going to marry a man seven years younger than me, I'm sorry." She got to her feet and held out the statement to Sarah. "My apologies, but I didn't know he was that young."

Sarah just smiled. "That's understandable." She snorted mentally in derision. Cameron was more mature than half the males

she knew who were older. He had been forced to grow up early just to survive. "Are there any more questions?"

"There aren't any executive parties?" another asked warily.

"No. Lorcana prefers to keep thing strictly professional. She does not encourage fraternizing with other employees in any fashion."

The woman made a disgusted sound and got to her feet. "Sorry. I have a high profile name. I have to be seen. Please give my apologies." She swept out with all the drama of a Hollywood star, and Sarah almost rolled her eyes.

The other three were clearly ambivalent but they remained for the interview. Sarah played her role and showed them into the meeting room and then escorted them out when they were done. Her anger grew with every passing minute. Every time she caught sight of Cameron's face, it looked more and more haggard. It seemed as if the strain was aging him rapidly.

Kenneth left the meeting first and he looked no less stressed. He stopped on his way out to give Sarah his key card. "Cam wants you to meet him for lunch. He worries that Mother might sense something between you and get rid of you."

"But we're just friends," she protested.

He just smiled and walked away. She really was cute as hell. If he hadn't felt so much like a big brother to her, he would have fought Cameron over her. Maybe she had a sister, or a best friend like a sister. It was doubtful though. Perfection was rarely recreated, much to his regret.

With a sigh, she locked her computer and grabbed the lunchbox she had packed. She pointedly ignored the cheers and waves she got but inside she smiled. She worked with smartasses. It made her feel good.

By the time Cameron got to the roof, he was in desperate need of her presence. Her sense of humor and her calming manner. Her soft and fragrant skin and hair, so vastly different from the perfume other women wore. Most of all, he needed her touch to remind him that there was someone who needed *him*.

When he saw her standing at the edge of the pool, a soft wind fluttering her hair, emotion welled up inside him. He was in love. This beautiful creature was the only one meant for him. Riding with it, he moved forward and wrapped his arm around her fiercely. He buried his face in her hair. He couldn't imagine his life without her now.

She wasn't sure what to do for a moment. There was something inside him, some wild and driving emotion that seemed to echo what was inside her own heart. Could he really, possibly, love her as much as she loved him? She shied away from examining it. Things were complicated enough. Instead, she turned in his arms and hugged him tight. "It's okay, Cam. You're safe now."

After a few moments, he reluctantly released her. "I'm sorry. I just . . . needed to be near you."

Warmth unfurled inside her. "Just call me your lode stone. I steal all the yicky stuff and make you feel warm and squishy."

He laughed and drew her over to the picnic blanket. Much to his surprise, he saw the lunch set out. "Wow, where'd you score this?"

"I made it." She felt pleased with his startled look. "Spoiled little rich boy with a piranha for a mother and servants to do everything, I figured you might like something other than fancy gourmet food."

He couldn't have been happier. "Good call!" He dug eagerly into his share. The first bite made his taste buds happily dance. Her cooking skills rivaled her sense of humor for being her best feature. If he ever managed to get a ring on her finger, he would beg for her to make lunch every day. He would even be willing to share her lunch skills with his brother. "I bet none of those 'potential brides' could cook like this."

"Well, maybe, but I doubt they have time." She worked her way through her own share. "They're your stereotypical high-power executives who believe they don't need time for family." She shook her head. "I can think of three large corporations, three of the largest in New York and/or America, and they're all about family. Shoot, I can think of four if you include Enforcers. Sorry, but it's a lie to say you can't have it all. It's all about delegation and killing stereotypes."

"Didn't one of the leaders of Enforcers get married a while back?" he asked curiously.

"About ten months ago, yes." She smiled. "He's so in love with her. She's another of 3rd District's . . . um, miracles."

"Oh yeah!" He snapped his fingers. "I remember her! She was in a coma for like sixteen years and came out of it okay."

"That's Rayna. She's really nice, but not a pushover." She tucked her hair behind her ear. "How bad was it, Cam? Did you even like any of the women? If you like one, there's always the chance you could fall for her and turn something bad into something good." It took a lot of effort to keep her voice from quivering. She wanted him for her own, but she wanted more for him to be happy.

"Ha. Not hardly." He looked at her directly, his eyes more green than gray. "I'd rather have you for my wife."

She took a small, sharp breath. What was she supposed to say to *that*? Her muscles tensed as she prepared to scoot back away from him. "Well, that's certainly the best proposal I've ever had, better than the one in third grade from Oliver Persnickle. He gave me a toad."

His hand shot out and wrapped around the back of her neck, stopping her before she could get away. His other hand closed over her wrist, and he jerked her onto his lap and up against his chest. Her shocked brown eyes slowly widened even as his narrowed slightly. "Don't, Sarah," he warned softly, intently. "Don't hide from me. I see right through you."

She swallowed hard. His body was hot and hard and she wanted nothing more than to merge everything she was to him so they would never be apart. She couldn't breathe, couldn't feel, couldn't *live* without him. "Cameron," she strove to sound patient, "we're friends. That's all. Friends can't get married."

"We're more than that," he told her, "and I'll prove it." He swiftly turned and tumbled her down onto the blanket. Before she could blink, he had covered her body with his own to keep her pinned. He cuffed her hands over her head. "I'm in love with you," he said quietly, and so intensely that she had to believe him. "And I warned you what would happen if I fell."

His hot mouth cut off any response she might have wanted to give. He didn't just kiss her; he consumed her as if he was devouring her. She could only manage a strangled moan as hunger pounded through her body. Everywhere their skin touched brought a dizzying pleasure that was both physical and mental. Information poured into her mind as fire seemed to pour into her blood. Both fed her craving for more.

She arched toward him wildly, ravenously returning the kiss. Her teeth scraped over his lower lip, where he often bit down when he was thinking hard. A low rumble came from his chest and he returned the rough caress. When she gasped, he slicked his tongue into her mouth. She countered and the kiss grew ever hotter until both were shaking.

He broke free on a curse. "Damn," he muttered, pressing a hot and wet kiss to her throat. He resisted the urge to sink in his teeth and mark her as his. "I've never been that turned on by a kiss before." He slowly pressed against her, his aching erection rubbing against her stomach. Her eyes darkened and lust happily clawed at his body. "If you doubt me," his voice sounded rough, "then feel free to check."

"I didn't bring gloves to handle dynamite." Her breath hitched and her body arched helplessly as he released her hands so he could open her blouse. For the life of her, she couldn't move or escape, and she really had no care to even try. Her entire body felt drugged on him, quivering helplessly for more of the wicked pleasure he could give.

He stopped to lavish kisses over every inch of skin he uncovered. By the time he had the blouse halfway open, she was writhing beneath him desperately. She had never imagined her sensitive skin might react like that. "You're evil!" she managed to say, but the words came out as almost a sob.

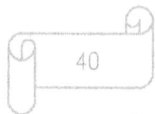

He muttered something wordless and unclipped the front clasp of her bra. Her hands shot down to cover herself but he caught her wrists and pinned them again, baring her to his gaze. "You know," he said huskily. "I've seen women with better figures."

"But . . .?" she asked breathlessly.

"But I can't seem to remember them. The only thing in my mind is you." He nuzzled the gentle curve of her inner breast and nudged her bra cup aside. Hungrily he closed his mouth over the hardened point of her breast and sucked strongly.

Her back arched and a thin cry came from her throat. She began to shake in his arms and tried to fight free. Her body didn't seem to be her own anymore. She was drowning in pleasure and wanted more, but she was terrified of the strength of her desire. She felt wound so tight that she thought she might break in two. Why wouldn't it *stop*? "Cam," she managed to plead. "Stop."

"You'd hate me if I did." Still ravishing her breasts with his lips and teeth, he began to unfasten her slacks. When they were open far enough, he slid his hand inside them and her panties, seeking the heart of her. Savage satisfaction filled him as he felt the evidence of her arousal, slick and burning against his fingers. "If we were just friends," he said fiercely, "then we wouldn't feel like this."

She couldn't respond. She desperately grabbed for his arms, needing him as an anchor as his softly stroking fingers made the wicked delight worse. One long finger slid inside her body, and her senses came apart in a blinding shockwave of ecstasy. The waves washed over her, each stronger than the last, until she arched wildly underneath him.

Her cry muffled by his hungry kiss. He held her there, his other hand keeping her pressed close. When the tension seemed to flood out of her and she went limp, he gentled the kiss. He slowly lowered her back to the blanket and began to softly smooth his hands over her skin. It was self-inflicted torture. He wanted nothing more than to take her where they were, knowing her desire as intimately as he could, but they had no time.

"Okay," she finally managed to say huskily, "you made your point. I concede defeat." Pleasantly satiated, she slid her arms up around his neck. "But how am I supposed to go back to work and not have every single person there know exactly what I was doing? Or rather, *who*."

He had to laugh at that. She wouldn't be his Sarah without her sense of humor. "The same way I'm not sure how to hide what I *wasn't* doing, and wish like I hell I had been." He kissed her again and lingered over her taste. "Invite me over for dinner tonight." His green eyes burned like gems, and there was no doubt in either of their minds what would occur.

She had never believed in fighting the inevitable. "Come over for dinner," she whispered, "and stay for breakfast."

"Deal!" He kissed her again just for the sheer torture of it and then forced himself to let go. Still, he watched her hungrily as she put her clothes back into order. Except for the flush to her skin, her slightly swollen lips, and the glow in her eyes, it was hard to tell that she had been tumbling over a picnic blanket. Her hair seemed miraculously tidy, and he wanted to muss it up. "Do you believe that I love you?"

She looked at him for a solemn moment before leaning over and framing his face as she kissed him tenderly, giving him all the generosity of her love. "Yes," she said softly against his lips. "And I love you too, Cam. I'm sure you know." She curled closer as he hugged her tightly. "I'll think of something," she decided. "If I have to, I'll get Audra to come beat up your mom."

"Audra?" It took a moment for the name to click. "Audra Shaughnessy?" His eyes widened. "You wouldn't."

"I would. She's a protector of kids. And she's known me since I was a kid." She grinned mischievously. "If I tell her I want you, she'll find a way to make sure I get you. By the fastest means possible."

"You're evil. I knew I loved you." He kissed her again, and then released her entirely. His eyes seemed to glow with happiness despite his obvious frustration. "Let's pretend nothing happened.

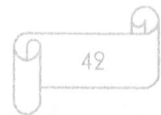

And then tomorrow we can say that nothing happened the day before, but most definitely did the night following."

She just giggled.

CHAPTER FOUR

Sarah was an intelligent young woman. She stopped in the women's restroom to see how bad the damage was to her appearance. Her hair pleased her with its lack of tangles, but there was no mistaking the effects on her face. Some cold water thankfully brought the flush to her cheeks down to normal and brought down the swelling of her lips.

Her eyes, well, she couldn't do a thing for them. Anyone with half a brain would look at the expression in her eyes and know she had just been well loved. Her humor couldn't help but find it fascinating. She wondered if anyone would have the absolute nerve to say a single thing.

She was back at her desk just as lunch ended, and she knew immediately that Cameron had to have already passed through. Everyone immediately looked at her intently as if to confirm a theory. Based on the smug looks, she could only assume they had guessed right. Then again, it wouldn't be hard to miss the contrast between him looking so frustrated and her looking so relaxed.

Louise wandered over and leaned on the counter. Casually, she examined her nails. "Have a good lunch?" she asked blandly, but a hidden note of laughter gave her away.

Sarah considered her words. "It was certainly an interesting lunch. I've never had cookie dough quite like that before."

Louise was hard-pressed to keep from laughing or grinning. Good for Cameron! She had been hoping he would get more ruthless with Sarah. Considering her 'just ravished' expression, it was fairly

obvious what had occurred on the roof. "Going to be having more?"

Sarah smiled wryly. "I think it's my dessert tonight." The entire conversation was absurd but she enjoyed it too much to care.

"You go, girl." Pleased, Louise headed back to her desk.

Down the hall, Cameron was scrolling through Google to find a florist when his brother walked in unannounced. Kenneth studied his younger brother and a smile began to play around the edges of his mouth. "Good lunch?"

Cameron looked over and smiled wryly. "I'm a masochist, but I got my point across to her."

Kenneth shut the door behind him so that no one could walk in. He sat on the edge of Cameron's desk and contemplated the search results on the computer screen. "Then that means we only need to deal with Mother. You know there's no way she'll approve of Sarah, not after she so beautifully stood up to her."

"I'll think of something." Cameron's eyes burned intently as he leaned back. "I'm not willing to even pretend. I'll have Sarah as my wife or no one else." He raked his hands through his hair. "I hate to consider it, but, if it comes down to it, I'll either get a lawyer to have Mother's guardianship revoked, or give up the company entirely. I want to be *happy*, and I guess it's time to decide what that means to me. At the least, I know it includes Sarah."

Kenneth nodded slightly. "I stand by you for either choice. I'll be proud to have Sarah for a little sister." He grinned. "But I might suggest a cold shower in the gym downstairs unless you want Mother to get suspicious. You look a bit, uhm, *distracted*."

Cameron took the advice to heart, but he got the strong feeling that Lorcana already sensed something. Whenever he saw her passing through the office, she would always take a moment to study Sarah intently. It probably wasn't helping, he thought wryly, that he couldn't help but look at Sarah himself. Every time he did, he thought of lunch and the night ahead.

When the bouquet of flowers arrived for Sarah, she found herself all the more amused as she signed for them. There was no card to indicate who they were from, but she (and her coworkers) all knew. Kenneth also knew because he winked one of the times he walked past her desk. Impulsively, she put one of the flowers over her ear, just to enjoy seeing Cameron's eyes light when he looked at her. Lorcana glared at her, but she just looked at her blandly. She had combed the official employee handbook, and Cameron had been right: no rules existed against fraternization. As long as all parties were willing, their private lives were their own.

She rushed home as soon as the day ended. She wanted to get her apartment cleaned up and herself prepared. Damn it, it was going to be her first time, and she wanted to make sure it was special for them both. She was in love and she was going to give herself to the man she loved. That seemed worth some candles and silk.

Once the apartment was clean, she set up electric candles around the living room and bedroom and then contemplated her closet. She didn't want to wear anything that was *too* hard to get back off, and yet she didn't want to be obvious. Finally she settled on a sheath dress in stark black. It was plain and elegant, but it also flattered her hair and skin. She sassily wore nothing underneath it.

Her heart jumped when her doorbell rang. She quickly hurried over and peeked out the spy hole. Her mouth went dry. Men who looked that hot should have been illegal. Or strippers. Cameron still wore his work clothes, but the shirt was partially unbuttoned and his tie hung around his neck. She wanted to muss him up even more, and she opened the door to say, "Alright, the stripper is here. Now for the real fun."

He grinned. "I even brought pizza." He waved the box under her nose temptingly.

"What, no fancy fish or French food we can't even pronounce?" She clucked her tongue as she shut the door behind him. "I feel so cheated."

He ran his eyes over her slowly and felt his hands almost literally itch to touch her. She had never seemed exceptionally beautiful before, more cute than anything, but right then she was the

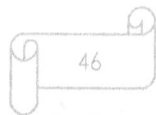

most beautiful woman he had ever seen. He studied the snug form of the dress and how there didn't seem to be any lines marring the flow of the silk. "Are you wearing anything under that?" he asked huskily.

She lowered her lashes with a smile as old and feminine as time. "Perfume."

"Per . . ." He swallowed hard as desire ripped through his body faster than the speed of light. "*Just* perfume?" He put down the pizza on the kitchen counter before he dropped it. If she didn't stop smiling at him, he was going to pounce on her. The candlelit atmosphere just made it more difficult to keep his hands to himself.

"Maybe." She stepped forward and slid her hands up to link around his neck. Her body molded to his perfectly as if they had been meant to go together. "Dinner first, or dessert?" Her lashes fluttered closed as he bent his head and began to trail soft kisses over her ear. Shivers rippled through her body with lazy waves of pleasure. "Cam?" she whispered.

"Hmm?" She even tasted like blueberries, as if she had deliberately worn his favorite flavor and scent just for him. He wanted to taste every inch of her from head to toe, and he ran his hands slowly down her back and over the curve of her bottom. Just as he had thought, there was nothing beneath the dress but her.

"I've never done this before, just so you know." She buried her fingers in his hair, delighted with how it felt.

"I know." He smiled as he lifted his head. "I had guessed that might be the case. Know what?"

"What?"

"I think I've done this before."

She arched a brow, bemused. "You only think?"

"Well, I can't seem to remember anyone else. Just you." He softly took her lips, drawing the kiss out until both their heads were spinning and their pulses beat hard in unison. There was something about her that made him want to take his time, to shower her with all the love they both had missed out on.

Drowning in him, swept away on the drugging pleasure of his touch, she could only catch a startled breath as she found herself lifted into his arms. "Despite my name, I'm not some . . . princess. Put me down."

"I thought girls like romance." He took his best guess and headed down the hall toward where he could see more candlelight.

"Well I'm sure most do, and I do for sure, but . . . it's unnerving." She held on tighter to his shoulders as he lowered her slowly to her feet inside the bedroom. "I didn't imagine this would happen," she whispered. "How can you know someone only two days and know that you had been waiting for them your whole life?"

"Magic." He pulled her closer and kissed her again, shuddering as the taste of her spread through his body and soul. He eagerly ran his hands down over her back and savored the resilience of her skin. It felt ridiculously soft.

She could only manage a faint moan as his touch sent off wild streamers of pleasure through her body. It was as if her skin had become hundreds of times more sensitive to him now, and the barest brush of his skin against hers made her hunger for him grow. "Cameron," she whimpered into his kiss.

He lifted his lips long enough to catch her dress in his hands and slowly peel it upward. He tossed it to the side and for a moment just studied her naked figure with possessive delight. She was still no centerfold, but she was the most incredible thing he had ever seen. "You're beautiful, Sarah," he whispered.

"So are you." Curiously unafraid or shy, she began to unbutton his shirt the rest of the way. When it was finally open, she watched hungrily as he shrugged out of it. He was smooth skin and hard muscle, and put every fireman calendar she could remember to shame. And he was hers. Delight filling her, she skimmed a finger along the line of his chest. "So do you work out, or was this literally God's gift to women like me?"

He grinned, a little flustered but a lot pleased. "Both. I was lucky enough to be born attractive. And I'm not lazy enough to waste

that. Ken and I both work out."

"Wow. Bet that alone gets the pulse rate of the other gym-goers up."

He gave in and laughed outright. On a burst of happy energy, he scooped her up into his arms and tumbled her down across the bed. He kissed her wildly, deepening it until her body arched helplessly toward him and her fingers clutched at his shoulders for an anchor.

Hungry for everything, he began to trail hot kisses down her body, lavishing the inner curves of her breasts with caresses. His hands stroked slowly over her sides again and again until he thought he could feel the sensitivity himself.

She took a breath to tell him to stop teasing her when his mouth closed over the point of one breast. She twisted against him on a strangled cry, her desire sharpening to a razor point until she was at the edge of release in moments. Her body began to shake, her legs moving restlessly, as he switched his attention to her other breast.

Sensing her desperation, he slowly slid one hand down to ruffle the rust colored curls at the apex of her thighs. His touch slid lower and he shuddered as he felt the slick heat waiting for him. He wanted to be inside her so badly it hurt, but he also didn't want to hurt her. He wanted her wild in his arms.

She struggled to breathe as his knowing fingers teased and tormented. Somehow he knew exactly how to touch her to drive her insane but not give her the satisfaction her body craved. As his teeth scraped lightly over her stomach, she gave a thin cry. "Sadist!"

He released her on a low curse and stripped the rest of his clothes off. He swiftly returned to her, and his playful pounce sank them both deeper into the soft feather bed. With a touch of desperation, he kissed her again, his tongue surging into her mouth to tease and torment. She returned the kiss just as ravenously, and her fingers raced over every inch of skin she could reach. Her fingers skidded over a few odd scars on his back and the knowledge ripped through her mind. Tears filled her eyes and she clutched him closer. "I love you!"

He dragged her closer and braced her legs over his arms, opening her completely to him. His erection pressed against her opening, sought entry, and slowly he flexed his hips to push inside. Electricity rippled down his back with raw delight and he fought the urge to drive deep. He wanted to always remember that first moment.

Her breath caught and she dug her nails into his shoulders. Her skin was so sensitive that all she could feel was sheer pleasure. It had to be some sort of biological chemistry that made him so very different, but it seemed such a paltry term for what existed between them.

He kissed her again as his arms shifted to hold her as tightly against him as he could. She wrapped herself around him like a vine, some deep instinct urging her to bind him fast to her so that he could never get away. He began to drive in and out of her swiftly, every thrust sending her excitement higher and higher until she thought she would break apart and her thin cry was muffled by his lips.

Something broke. The snapping tension seemed to ricochet through her entire body and soul all at once, the rapture as all-consuming as it was dimly terrifying. She could only clutch onto him desperately as she felt herself drown in ecstasy. And when he shuddered, caught just as she was, her arms tightened and she held him closer as it took them both.

It was a few breathless minutes before he found the energy to lift himself enough to look at her. She looked content, sleepy, and sated. It was a face he wanted to see more often. There were dozens of faces he wanted see on her. He wanted to wake with her in his arms and fall asleep with her at night. Forget having a girlfriend. He wanted her for his wife. There was no law against skipping certain stages when you knew what you wanted. "Are you happy?" he asked softly.

For an answer, she wound her arms tighter around his

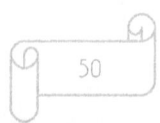

shoulders. "Ask me when I'm not glowing. On the bright side, we won't need a night light."

He laughed and kissed her lightly. Even with just that, he felt the stirring inside of hunger for her again. Still, honesty, and bedrock integrity, made him say, "Sarah . . ."

"It's highly unlikely." She opened her eyes to smile at him. "I'm due to start my period in a few days, but I'll go to the doctor and get some birth control." Her lashes lowered. "That is, if we're going to be doing this again."

"You bet your ass we will. In the meantime, I'll take care of things for us." He smoothed a hand down to rest over her stomach. "If the timing was wrong, and you are pregnant . . ."

"Yes?"

"Whatever you decision you make, I'll stand beside you completely. And if you decide to keep it . . . I'd be more than willing to be a dad." He rolled over onto his back and took her with him so that she was sprawled over the top of his chest. "And even if we're in the clear, I'll do whatever it takes for you, Sarah. My mother has stopped me from having everything else I wanted. She won't stop me from having you."

She curled closer and rested her head over his heart. "I felt them," she whispered. "The scars on your back. She beat you?"

"Only once. My father caught her and threatened to divorce her if she ever laid a hand on me or Ken again." He ran his hands lightly over her back. "But enough about that. Want to know something funny?"

"Sure." She propped her chin on her hands to study his face in the candlelight. "I'm always interested in a laugh."

"This was the first time I ever made love in a bed." He grinned when her brows lifted in disbelief. "I told you. My mother never let me have a girlfriend. My previous experience consists of sneaking around with girls and testing the shocks of cars. Fords have some good ones, by the way."

She giggled softly. "Makes me wish I didn't own a motorcycle."

He should have known! "You own a motorcycle? That seems slightly out of place for my princess."

"Ha. You're just jealous. Men can't stand when a woman has a better vehicle than they do."

"Sad but true." He linked his hands behind his head. "My car is so old that the original owner was named Flintstone."

"Must be bad in heavy rain."

"Tell me about it. The breaking is hell on my shoes." When she laughed, he held her even closer against him for a moment, savoring how it felt to be there. "I wish I could spend the whole night and wake with you, but my mother might notice I was gone all night." He nuzzled her ear softly. "When I turn twenty-one, I'll move in with you long enough to give my mother time to move out of the house. Then you're coming home with me. As my wife."

It wasn't the most romantic proposal she had ever heard, yet it felt utterly perfect. She smiled and closed her eyes as she cuddled closer. "It's a date."

He left close to one in the morning, and only because he had forced himself. She found it exceptionally hard to sleep without him there to snuggle against. She loved the way he felt against her skin. Her cheerful mood was so strong that when she dressed for work, she took the time to put some curls in her hair and some makeup on. She also wore a skirt that was *slightly* shorter than 'professional' but only an adept eye would notice without a ruler in hand.

She was the first one to the office, as was becoming habit, and she got coffee going. While she contemplated some tea for herself, strong arms suddenly went around her waist. Delighted, she snuggled back against her lover. "I thought you were the perpetually late one."

He smiled and hugged her tighter. He had missed her insanely

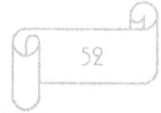

and had never before noticed how cold and lonely his room could be. When he had seen her standing at the coffee machine, he hadn't been able to keep his hands off her. "Yes but if I get here early, I have enough time to steal a kiss or two."

She turned around to wind her arms around him. "Steal away, my prince. But I might steal them back."

"Promise?" He lowered his head to kiss her when he saw down the collar of her shirt a few shadows on her breasts that weren't from the light. Shocked, he unbuttoned the first two fastenings to see better. Sure enough, there were bruises on her fair flesh. "Oh god. Sarah . . . I . . ."

She laughed and covered his mouth with a hand. "No! It's not your fault. Well okay, *technically* it's your fault. But it's not that you hurt me. Remember, I told you my skin is sensitive. Well, that also means that I bruise faster than a grape. I fell down the stairs once and looked like I had gone ten rounds with the champ. I think I won, but I can't promise it."

He let out a breath. "Okay. I just don't want to hurt you." He gently re-buttoned her shirt and then skimmed a finger over her curls. "Did you make yourself prettier for me? And how short *is* that skirt? I'd swear it wasn't proper, but maybe it's just my wishful thinking."

"I just wanted you to have a fair comparison of me against the potential brides." She fluttered her lashes for emphasis.

"You win. Hands down, you win."

Kenneth stood around the corner and listened to the conversation. He had known instantly when he had seen his brother that morning that Cameron had been rolling around a bed with Sarah and enjoying himself immensely. On one hand, he could not have been happier. On the other, he was worried. He did not want to see Sarah get hurt and he had no doubts about his mother's ruthlessness. Bruises would be the least of the problem.

Her unique gift was certainly interesting though. He filed it away for later review. Something told him it might be usable in ensuring his little brother's happiness. Deciding he had eavesdropped long enough, he came around the corner and headed for the coffee. "You sure you don't want to run away with me instead?"

"I'll fight you over her," Cameron warned, but with a smile.

Sarah clasped a hand to heart. "Why, lucky me. I have the two most eligible males in the building vying for my hand. I don't know how I'll ever choose."

Cameron glanced around, and Kenneth grinned. "It's clear."

"Good." That said, he grabbed Sarah and kissed her so hard that her toes curled inside her shoes. When he released her, he asked, "Now who wins?"

She could only dangle in his arms, her head spinning wildly around her shoulders. "I think I do. Whoo boy." Her sharp ears detected footsteps and she quickly stepped away and smoothed her hair and clothes.

Cameron's good mood was visible to everyone, and more than one smiling glance went Sarah's way. She looked completely unruffled, but there was an added sparkle in her eyes. Even Lorcana noticed and her ire steadily grew, as did her suspicions.

She felt fairly sure Cameron was screwing the girl, and under other circumstances she might not have minded. In fact, if Sarah had been the type she could easily control, she would have wholeheartedly approved of the relationship, especially since it seemed clear that Cameron wasn't thinking with his brain in relation to her.

But the girl had had the absolute nerve to stand up to Lorcana and she despised that. Who did she think she was? She was a nobody from the backwater 3rd District, and she had no fortune to call her own. She came recommended by Shaughnessy-Tavoularis but that meant nothing in the grander scheme of things.

Still, she decided to play it by ear. "Well," she said to Cameron as she entered the meeting room. "You look extra cheerful this morning. Finally decided that I'm right about this whole situation?"

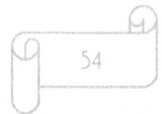

"No, but I've decided to make the best of it." He shrugged and propped his feet on the table. He knew she hated it and therefore did it on purpose as much as he could. "I long ago came to the conclusion that you hate me and want to do everything you can to make us miserable because you are."

Her jaw dropped. Kenneth's did too but then his shock faded to be replaced by sheer delight. Sarah had put some serious steel in Cameron's spine. He couldn't have been happier. And, while Lorcana paced away, he swiftly wrote Sarah's name in on the list of candidates. He knew full well that his mother wouldn't recognize her name; why would she bother herself with such a trivial thing? She barely remembered Louise's name half the time. Something needed to be done, and he could nearly feel a presence urging him to act.

In the front area, Sarah was already beginning to check in the potential brides. A part of her wanted to tell them all to keep their hands off her man, but she covered it with a friendly smile. Really, what could she say that wouldn't get her and Cameron into trouble? She would have to play along until they found a solution.

Two potential brides walked out when they saw the duty statement. The others remained and she did her part to make sure they felt welcome. Observing her, Cameron thought to himself about how she truly seemed to be a real princess in disguise. He fought the urge to rush out there and make it plain that he wanted her only.

Lorcana, going down the list of names, didn't even know who she was calling for as she walked out of the room and said, "Davidson!"

Sarah's eyes widened and she looked around. There were no other brides left, and she was the only one who had the last name of Davidson. She warily got to her feet and walked into the meeting room. "Er, yes?"

Shocked, Lorcana stared at her. "What are you doing in here?"

She blinked. "You called my name."

Lorcana looked down at her list swiftly, and this time looked closer. "Kenneth!" she snapped at her eldest son. "This is your handwriting! Why is she on the list of brides?"

He linked his hands behind his head. "I figured Cam ought to marry the woman he's in love with. Where do you think he was last night?"

With the doors standing open, there was no one who hadn't heard him. Everyone fell silent. Cameron and Sarah mutually stared at him in wide-eyed shock. Lorcana couldn't find her voice at first and then her fury rose wildly. Her face turned red as she whirled on Sarah. "You're fired!" she screamed. "If you think you can sleep your way to the top, you're sadly mistaken, you little bitch!"

"You mean like you did?" Sarah lifted her chin slightly. "You knew Cam had been with me last night when you saw me this morning." Her voice remained perfectly calm. "The only reason you're so mad now is because you *know* that your son stands on the cusp of a happiness you will never have." She turned to the door but briefly stopped and looked back. "You are a pitiful woman, Lorcana Dease."

She held onto her composure until she reached her desk. The pain welled up sharply and she grabbed her purse as she fled out the doors. She knew Kenneth had been trying to help, but it had backfired in the worst way possible. She would never see Cameron again; he would be under twenty-four hour surveillance. How was it fair that she fall in love and have her heart broken all within a twenty-four period?

Cameron's temper blew. He leapt to his feet and slammed his hands on the top of the table. "I've had it!" he shouted. "I've had it! You've done nothing but ruin my life! And for what? A company you don't even know how to fucking run! Well, you know what? I want Sarah more than I want this damn company! Unlike you, I know how to love. I know that it's more precious than any shares, no matter their value! Keep your greed! I hope it keeps you warm. I'll have Sarah as my wife or none other! I'm retaining a lawyer in the morning and having myself relieved of your guardianship! If it means giving up the company, then *so be it*!" He ran out of the office swiftly but Sarah had already left. Cursing, he headed for the stairs.

This time the silence was absolute. Kenneth said nothing. Pride filled him over his brother's actions, and he could not regret what he had done. It had spurred Cameron to do something long overdue. Still, Kenneth could not shake that feeling that he had somehow been manipulated into causing the events. His eyes drifted across the room to a potted plant that, curiously, had begun to bloom with white roses. Where had those come from? They had not been there before the idea had struck him to write down Sarah's name. More magic?

Shaking, Lorcana braced her hands on the table. She had never seen Cameron like that. A part of her was shocked because he had never looked more like his father. She had loathed Viktor, but a part of her had respected him as well.

Someone knocked lightly on the door and the two Deases looked to see Louise standing in the doorway. Politely, she asked Lorcana, "Did we hear you fire Sarah, and Cameron vow to give you the company in order to have her?"

"That about sums it up," Kenneth confirmed.

"I see. Well, in that case we quit. And by we, I mean the entire graphic department." She removed her badge and dropped it on the floor. "We're not going to work for you, Lorcana. We only stayed this long because of Kenneth and Cameron. Bring back Sarah and Cameron, and we'll return. Until then . . . I guess the company is temporarily shut down. Goodbye."

Kenneth and Lorcana both walked over to the door and watched in surprise as every single employee shut down their computers, gathered their bags, and left. Lorcana felt sickened as she watched all of her carefully laid plans fall apart. If only that little bitch had never arrived. "What coincidence is this that I decided to hire *her*?" she asked scathingly.

Kenneth glanced at her as she walked off and decided not to mention the lack of coincidence around 3rd District. She would never understand. Still wondering what in the hell they were supposed to do next, he headed out of the office. He would find where Sarah lived and have a talk with her and Cameron. Maybe the three of them could find a way to win it all.

CHAPTER FIVE

When Sarah got back to 3rd District, she stopped to visit a friend on her way home. They had been friends since kindergarten when they had discovered that they had nearly identical names. It had started as just something to giggle over and then had evolved into their own inside joke. They enjoyed seeing people do double takes.

Things had happened so fast over the last few days that Sarah hadn't had time to tell Sera about the changes in her life. Now she desperately needed her friend's levelheaded, pragmatic, personality, and her quick thinking.

Sera Thomason was watering the flowers in front of her home when she sensed her friend. She looked over at Sarah and snorted. "Well. Someone got laid."

She had to smile. "Is it that obvious?"

Sera tossed short black hair streaked with hot pink out of her gold colored eyes. "Well, to someone who knows you. You have that nicely relaxed look about you. Now you want to tell me why there's so much sadness in your eyes as well, and who I have to kill?"

Sarah took a deep breath. "You know I went to work for the Deases, right?" When Sera lifted a brow, she sat down on a tree stump. "To make a long story short, I fell in love with Cameron Dease."

Sera's gold eyes began to resemble flames as her ire grew. "And he took advantage."

"No." She put her head in her hands. "It would be easier if he had. No, he loves me too. We became lovers. And now his mother has fired me because she's a cold-hearted bitch who wants to make Cameron suffer. She'll have him under lock and key until either she marries him off or he turns twenty-one. Probably the former before the latter."

Sera drummed her fingers on her arm and contemplated the merits of turning into a wild boar and goring Lorcana Dease to death. "All executives are pricks," she noted. "You're better off without any of them."

"You may think that," Sarah said softly, "but you don't know Cameron and his brother. They're different, Sera."

Sera wasn't an empath, but she didn't need to be in order to feel her friend's misery. With a sigh, she relented and sat beside her. "So, what do we do?" Sarah glanced at her, and she smiled and nudged her shoulder. "Hey, we're friends. That's what friends do." Abruptly, a frown marred her brow. "You *were* careful right?"

Sarah coughed. "Well . . ."

She groaned. "Sarah!"

"He made me forget my own name!" she defended herself. "And he was lucky to remember to take his socks off! I was going to go on the pill or something, but I guess it's moot now."

"You know what?" Sera hugged her. "If you do end up pregnant, I'll hire some big thugs to kidnap your Cameron and get him away from his mother. Then you two can 'live in sin' until he's legal."

Sarah hugged her back. "Thanks, Sera." She sighed and got to her feet. "I'm going home. I just can't make my brain work right now."

Sera watched her go and then crossed her arms, a scowl darkening her lovely face. Sarah had been her best friend since they were children. Just as Sarah had stayed by Sera's side through the death of her father and her mother's ailing health, Sera had stayed by Sarah's side during the loss of her parents. Thinking that her friend was suffering and she couldn't do anything pissed her off.

"Excuse me?"

She looked over at the male voice and her brows rose sharply.

The young man on the other side of her fence was downright gorgeous with platinum hair and eyes more gray than green. Her eyes narrowed suddenly as she saw that he wore a suit. She got to her feet slowly and walked over to him. Her delicate nose instantly caught a whiff of Sarah's perfume. "You must be Cameron."

Cameron watched the slender female like one would watch a wild animal. She looked quite furious, and he was fairly sure she knew Sarah because of it. A sixth sense told him that Sarah had been through the area lately. He had tried her house first, but she hadn't been there. "I am," he said. "Do you know where Sarah Davidson is?"

"Yes." She bared her teeth. "Now ask me if I'm going to tell you."

He narrowed his eyes. "Are you her friend or not?"

"Oh I'm her friend." She narrowed her own eyes in return. "And as such I'm not going to watch her be torn to pieces by some little boy who can't cut his mother's apron strings."

Temper flared in his eyes and she wondered if he would let it loose. Then, to her everlasting shock, he suddenly dropped onto his knees. "Please," he said, his voice low. "I'm begging you. Where is Sarah?"

"Get up," she begged. "You're really freaking me out here!" She hated seeing men grovel, and his sincerity was so strong that she felt as if she had been kicked by it. He suffered as much as Sarah did. There was one severely lovesick man in front of her right then. She sighed. "Look, I don't want her hurt again."

"I'm going to do my best." His gaze hardened. "I've disowned my mother. It means disowning my company, but I want Sarah more."

She lowered her gaze slightly. "Sarah should be at home by now. She was in no condition to go anywhere else."

He leapt to his feet and gave her an enthusiastic hug. "Thank you!" He swiftly ran off down the road, leaving one very bemused shapeshifter behind him.

"Yeah," she murmured, "you're definitely the one for Sarah."

Back at the company building, Kenneth paced rapidly in the lobby. He didn't know what to do. All he knew was that he had to do *something*. He couldn't stand to see his brother and Sarah suffering, and he was doubly sure that he didn't want to see the company fall into Lorcana's hands, even in part. Cameron had shed blood for his share—literally.

As he swung around again, he came to sharp stop in surprise. Standing just behind him was a short young woman with snowy white hair. Her purple-gray eyes seemed to laugh at a joke only the universe might understand. And she was *tiny*. At only five-eleven, he still felt like a giant. "Er, can I help you?"

"Actually, I can help you." She walked over and held out a sheaf of papers. "I'm from Enforcers."

"Because of Sarah?" he asked shrewdly.

"Mmm."

It wasn't quite an agreement, but something told him not to ask more. He took the papers and unrolled them. His experienced eye instantly recognized that he held a contract. He read it over quickly and then had to go back and read it again. He began to grin slowly. "This is great." He looked up but the young woman had disappeared, leaving behind the scent of roses. "Thanks," he murmured.

He wasted no time in heading for home. The servants at the manor were quick to clear his path. He rarely got that kind of a look on his face, and when he did, you got out of his way.

He didn't bother to knock on the study door. He just walked right in. "Look," he said curtly, "let's call a spade a spade. You want Sarah gone. I want peace in the house."

Lorcana slowly looked at him, her eyes narrowed. She knew he wasn't helping because he was on her side. "Your brother's *happiness*

doesn't matter?" she sneered.

Icily, he retorted, "I'd rather find a way to bring him back than to deal with you by myself." He slapped the contract down on the desk. "This is a surefire method. You play nice for one night and we get everything taken care of by morning. This contract says that if Sarah can feel a *pea* through a mattress, then she can marry Cameron. If not, she's out."

"Oh please!" she scoffed. Even she recognized the scenario. "A faerie tale!"

"Fitting for someone from 3rd District, no? I'm not telling them what they're signing. They won't even know. But with their signatures on here, they're trapped into the outcome."

She tapped a scarlet fingernail on the top of the desk, but she couldn't find any way that she *wouldn't* win. Even if the little twit was 'different' in some way like rumor stated, there was no way she could possibly feel a pea under a mattress. "Won't it be squashed?" she asked reluctantly. "I always wondered about that."

"Eh. I'll freeze it beforehand." He met her eyes. "One night. You can pretend to be less than a bitch goddess for one night."

Her face tightened. "You're pretty bold, Kenneth Dease. How dare you talk to your mother like this?"

"Please. Let's be honest here. You married Dad because you wanted the company. You gave birth to me and Cameron under duress because he wanted kids and would have divorced you otherwise." Something cold moved in his eyes. "Dad loved us; he told us all along what you were really like. If he had known he would die and leave us in your *tender* care, he probably would have quit smoking."

She muttered something vile under her breath. With vicious strokes, she signed the contract. "Now get out of my sight," she ordered sharply.

"Gladly." He tucked the contract in his pocket and walked out of the study. It took considerable effort not to slam the door behind him. Now all he had to do was find Sarah and Cameron and get their signatures on the contract without telling them what was going on. He could only hope they still trusted him.

Sarah was curled up on her couch crying into a pillow when she heard the doorbell ring. Unwilling to deal with anyone, she didn't move. She felt miserable and alone. If it was Sera, she would apologize later. If it was a salesman, he could get lost. And if it was Eric . . . ooh. He would *so* get it.

A fist pounded on the door and she nearly jumped out of her skin. Her heart froze in her chest as she heard Cameron calling, "I know you're home, Sarah! Open the damned door. Please. Let me in."

She carefully walked over to the door but didn't open it. "Why are you here?" she asked achingly. "You're just going to make it worse."

"Open the door." His voice softened. "Sarah. Please. Let me in." He held his breath as the silence stretched, then his heart began to beat again as the lock turned and she opened the door. His beating heart promptly broke as he saw the puffiness under her eyes and traces of tears on her face. "Sarah."

Before she could blink, he had moved to catch her in his arms and lift her off her feet. It felt so good to be held by him that all she could do was wrap her arms around his shoulders and cling on.

He walked into the apartment and kicked the door shut. Still holding tight to her, he walked over to the couch and sat down with her on his lap.

"Why did you come here?" she whispered again. "It just hurts more."

"Because I love you." He eased her back and gave her a little shake so that she looked at him. "I'm not losing you, Sarah. Do you think I want any life without you around? Who would I go to when I

needed a laugh? Who would I share horror stories of bad coffee with? Who would I make love to just for the sheer joy of sharing my body and heart with?"

Her lips trembled. "You're going to make me cry again!"

He wiped away her tears softly. Quietly, seriously, he said, "I told Mother that I'm getting a lawyer in the morning." He held her when she tried to jerk away. "I'm relieving myself of her guardianship. Yeah, I lose my shares. Big deal. I want you more."

"You can't *do* that!" she cried. "Cam, you *can't*! Men don't give up multi-million dollar companies for women!"

"This man does." He turned sharply and pressed her down onto the couch. His eyes darkened to more green than gray as he pinned her. "Read my lips, Sarah Davidson: I am *not* giving you up!"

When Kenneth suddenly cleared his throat, both lovers looked at him in surprise. "Sorry," he said, "the door was unlocked." He shut the door behind him. "I guess I'm interrupting."

Cameron very reluctantly helped Sarah sit back up. He didn't let her slide off his lap, however. "A little," he conceded. "But I assume you're here for a good reason. And hopefully it's a better idea than what you tried this morning."

"Yeah." He walked over and sat down on one of the chairs facing the couch. "I am *really* sorry, guys. But something needed to happen. We would have been stuck in status quo forever." His smile turned wry. "And, Cam, there isn't much of a company to give up."

"Wha?"

"When Sarah was fired and you vowed to give up the company in order to have her, everyone in Graphics quit." They stared at him, and he raked a hand through his hair. "Seriously. Louise came to the door and told us very politely that she and the others had stayed for me and you, and they would not work for Mother. They then walked out. They won't come back unless you do."

"I would say that's impossible," Sarah said softly, "but I never really believed that word even exists."

Cameron jerked a thumb at the window and the District that

lay beyond it. "Par for the course around here, isn't it?" He raked a hand through his hair in a manner not dissimilar from his brother. "So now what do we do? I mean . . . I hate to see the company go under, but I'm not giving up Sarah."

"I would hope not!" Kenneth said. "Look, here's the thing. I had words with Mother. And I may have gotten to an agreement with her."

"Did you sell your soul?" Sarah muttered.

"No, no. It's okay. I got her to agree to letting you come over for dinner and to spend the night. To give you and Cam a chance. I even got her to sign a contract." He pulled the papers out of his jacket. "I just need you two to sign as well so she can't welsh."

"Can I read that?" Cameron asked warily.

Kenneth met his eyes. "Do you trust me, Cam? If you do, then sign without reading this. I promise that tomorrow morning everything will work out."

Cameron and Sarah exchanged a long look and then both nodded slightly. What did they have to lose anyway? Without reading the contract, without bothering to even skim the surface, they both signed at the bottom next to Lorcana's name. "Man, I hope this works," Cameron sighed. "I'm not looking forward to facing my mother."

Sarah wasn't feeling entirely sure herself, but she couldn't let either Cameron or Kenneth down. Cameron was willing to give up a multi-million dollar company for her. Kenneth had put his neck on the line. That was worth finding some courage. "I'll go pack a bag, I guess." She rose to her feet and headed to her bedroom.

The minute she got out of earshot, Cameron demanded, "Tell me straight, Ken: are you getting yourself in trouble over this?"

Kenneth shook his head. "No. And, besides, what can she do to me? I'm an adult. The sooner she's out of our house, the better. You and Sarah can redo the master for yourselves."

Speculatively, Cameron said, "You know, you sound entirely confident that somehow this is going to work out. What do you know

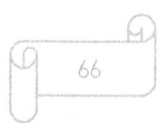

that we don't? Should I have been reading between the lines on that contract after all?"

His brother smiled. "Let's just say that simply by being exactly who and what she is, Sarah is going to ensure you both have a happy ending."

Puzzled and yet amiable, he went to help Sarah. Really, at this point he was playing it all by ear. He had always believed in magic, and Aenya's words seemed to, rather appropriately, dance constantly in his mind. He really wanted everything to work out perfectly.

"How do you guys handle dinner?" Sarah asked as she sensed him in the room. "I mean, when I'd have dinner with the extended Shaughnessy family, they were super casual, but your mother is, uhm, a little straight-laced."

"How tactful." He grinned a little. "Why don't we plan on making it fancy? That way you can prove that you're not some poor secretary and I can happily admire you all night. Can you wear that black dress?"

"Maybe." Her eyes began to sparkle merrily as her humor returned. "But I'm not going to tell you what I'll have on under it." She paused, and then murmured, "Or what I don't."

"I foresee myself sneaking into your bed sometime tonight."

"The man's a prophet! And I thought I was the one with the wooky mojo in her bloodline."

The mutual good mood lasted until they got to the Dease family home. Despite her best efforts to keep her smile, Sarah found herself highly wary as the two brothers escorted her into the large manor. The wariness faded, however, as soon as she met the housekeeper. In fact, she began grinning.

The older woman was as plump as a large bird, had snowy white hair, and sported a cherubic-like face. She seemed to descend out of nowhere and grabbed Cameron by the ear. "Cameron Dease!" she scolded, her voice far more youthful than her appearance lent itself to. "What's this I hear about you falling in love?"

"Ouch! C'mon, Tia! Let go!" He wiggled free and rubbed his ear. With a wry smile, he gestured at Sarah. "Meet the woman of my dreams."

"Hi." Sarah smiled angelically. "I'm the woman of his dreams. I'm usually called Sarah."

Tia studied her intently and began to smile. She had a feeling she was going to like this young lady very much. "I'm quite happy to meet you, Sarah. I am Tia. I run the household. I've also raised both these terrors since they were but toddlers."

"Oh so you're the one I need to bribe to get all Cameron's secrets." She nodded sagely. "We'll have to talk price later. I can offer homemade cookies."

With a rich laugh, Tia clapped a rather alarmed-looking Cameron on the shoulder. "I believe I might just be buyable for that price." She took the suitcase Sarah carried and winked saucily. "Should I put this in Cameron's room to save everyone some trouble?" Cameron's cheeks turned pink, and she just clucked her tongue at him. "As if your Tia didn't know!" She tweaked his nose. "I want grandbabies to spoil."

As she disappeared down the hall, Sarah started giggling. "I'm going to like her!"

"Tia is awesome," Kenneth agreed with a grin.

Cameron sighed fondly. "In case you hadn't guessed, she's Ken's and my *real* mother in all the ways that really count. C'mon. We'll give you a tour of the place. You'll like it here."

She didn't just like it. She *loved* it. Despite the size and grandeur and the occasional servants wandering around, it felt like a home. Since she knew full well that Lorcana didn't even know what a home was supposed to be, she could only guess it was Tia that had made sure her two 'sons' felt comfortable. At least she could understand better now how Kenneth and Cameron had become such amazing men despite their birth mother's influence. Love could make all the difference in the world for any child.

Cameron's bedroom was on the third floor. It was also almost

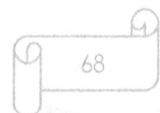

as big as her entire apartment, and her eyes widened in wonder at the giant bed taking up a chunk of the floor space. "Holy cow. Was that designed by NASA or something? I swear it defies all laws of spatial relations. Who divided by zero?"

"Hey, I like lots of room."

They exchanged a look. Then, as one, they both ran forward and jumped on the bed. She would have gone skidding off the other side as her silk skirt found no traction on the equally silky covers, but he hastily grabbed her and yanked her back. Sprawled in the middle of the bed, they both started laughing. "That was fun!" she managed to say.

"I'm just glad I caught you! I took a noser into my dresser once. Dad swore the only reason I didn't have a concussion was because my head was so hard!"

"Like father like son?"

He grinned. "So he claimed." He sat up and felt his heart twist as he looked down at her. Her rusty hair had tangled around her shoulders, and glowed more brilliantly orange than ever against the blue comforter. She looked so perfect there in his bed, as if she had always belonged. Unable to resist, he leaned down to kiss her. She sighed softly into his lips as the kiss deepened, and a shiver rippled through her body as he skimmed his fingers down her sensitive skin.

"Ahem."

Against her lips, he muttered, "Go away, Tia."

Tia gave a ladylike snort. "You can work on my grandbabies later. Mrs. Lorcana has said that she wants dinner to be formal, and that you're to be dressed and downstairs in fifteen minutes."

She disappeared from the doorway and he reluctantly released Sarah. "I need to start locking the door."

"That would be more effective if she didn't probably have keys to every door." She scooped up her suitcase and spotted the door leading into the bathroom. "No peeking!" she scolded him as she went in and shut the door.

"Spoilsport! It's not like I haven't seen you naked."

"Yes, but I'm shy."

"And the sun rises in the west, I'm sure."

"See, I knew that stuff about it rising in the east was just a governmental conspiracy."

Grinning, he went into his closet to find clean clothes. As he changed into black slacks and a blue dress shirt, he couldn't help but think again about how much he owed his big brother. Kenneth had done a lot over the last nearly two years to act as a deflector for him, helping him win battles he might not have been able to fight alone. Even the minor scraps, such as the clothing he wore. Kenneth deserved happiness too.

"Shoes or no shoes?" Sarah suddenly asked from the bedroom.

"Shoes. When Mother says formal," he said wryly as he walked out of the closet, "she means . . ." His words trailed off as he saw her. She had done that strange female thing to her hair and face where it didn't *look* like she had done anything, but suddenly her features were more pronounced and her hair was pinned in a way that begged for his fingers to take it down.

The black dress clung to every curve of her body without being too revealing. Having become intimately acquainted with every inch under the dress, he approved wholeheartedly of anything that showed it off. "You're not cute," he told her.

She arched a brow. "I'm not?"

"No. Right now you're gorgeous. And sexy. I thought I preferred cute girls, but I'm becoming a big fan of sexy ones."

On a sigh, she rose on her toes to kiss him happily. "I love you, Cameron Dease. Never change."

"In general or specifically?" He linked his hands around her waist.

"I meant in personality. I would take it as a favor if you at least changed your socks once a day." Her eyes twinkled. "Some change is good for you."

He lowered his forehead to hers with a smile. "The changes you've brought sure are." He held her for a moment and then let go.

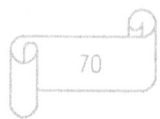

"Let's go eat dinner with the devil. No food fights, though."

"And the long spoon I brought would be such a good weapon, darn it."

CHAPTER SIX

Kenneth and Lorcana were already in the dining room when Cameron and Sarah arrived. Kenneth got to his feet with a smile when he saw them enter. "You sure you won't run away with me instead, Sarah?"

"You don't like the color blue as much," she told him innocently, "and it goes with my hair so well."

Despite herself, Lorcana found herself asking, "Blue and orange?" Looking at them, she could certainly *see* that the colors blended nicely together, but she hadn't the faintest idea why. She knew advertising when it was good, but she couldn't grasp the art behind it.

"Complimentary colors," Sarah offered kindly. "Like red and green, or yellow and purple." She let Cameron hold her chair and sat down gracefully. "Most people don't know why they work, but they know that they do. I only know because I spent a lot of time with the artists who worked for my parents' company."

"Oh, did they own a business?" Lorcana smiled coolly. "I thought most of those in 3rd District were middle or low class."

Cameron's hands curled into fists under the table, and Sarah covered them gently with one hand. Sweetly, she said, "As a matter of fact, there are few people in the 3rd District who don't own whatever business they work at. We can lay claim to the hottest club in NYC, and one of the most affluent bed and breakfasts as well. The president has even stayed at the Gentle Brook Inn; did you know?" Blithely she continued, "Anyway, my parents owned a small ad company that worked with small businesses."

"What was it called?" Kenneth asked curiously.

"Analogous Ad Company." She smiled. "More color puns." Aware that all three Deases were now staring at her in shock, she blinked. "Did I say something odd?"

"Your parents owned AAC?" Cameron sat back in his chair. "Wow. We tried to buy stock in the company but we couldn't bid high enough. I didn't even make the connection that the reason the company had been bought by the largest shareholders was because the owners had died."

"I couldn't run it by myself," she said softly. "I had to let Mel and Kalliope take over. It was better than seeing it be destroyed. I couldn't have endured that."

"Then you're an orphan?" Lorcana asked.

"Yes, but I'm a legal adult. The Enforcers themselves got me the lawyer that gave me my independence. And I turn twenty-one next month." She smiled angelically. "I've been acting like an adult since I was eighteen though; my parents trusted me to think for myself."

Even Cameron couldn't guess at whether or not she had deliberately insulted Lorcana. His mother was fairly certain she had, but she couldn't prove it. Frustration simmered under the surface in Lorcana. It seemed as if everything she did to make the girl realize she wouldn't fit in just seemed to backfire. "You know," she said, a little bite in her words, "there are a lot of rumors about 3rd District. People say that those who were born there aren't even human."

Sarah sighed gustily. "I told my parents that too, but they *insisted* that they hadn't stolen me from aliens. And my childhood tutor often threatened to eat one of us kids for misbehaving, but I think she might have been a vegetarian, so I doubt she meant it." She propped her chin on her hand. Something powerful flickered across her brown eyes. "If I was able to cast spells, you wouldn't even know I'd done it until too late."

A chill went down Lorcana's back and she rubbed her hands

over her arms. She just felt sure she had seen . . . something in Sarah's eyes. It was with much relief that dinner was served at that moment and she didn't have to try to find a retort. She wasn't even sure she had one.

"So you don't have any artistic talent?" Kenneth asked Sarah curiously.

"Define talent." She smiled. "I've always said I had the soul of an artist but lacked the skill to express it. I can draw stick people, but that's only because my best friend *is* an artist and was patient enough to teach me. I've seen her sketch portraits of people on the fly. She's amazing."

Cameron thought about the cocky young woman he had met when he had been looking for Sarah. The slender female had definitely had style and flair, but she had been a lot more . . . forceful than he had come to expect out of freelance artists. She wouldn't take any crap from her clients, that was for sure!

"What made you decide not to go to college?" Lorcana asked politely. "Couldn't you make up your mind on a major?"

Sarah's eyes widened innocently. "What makes you think I didn't go to college? As a matter of fact, I'm currently trying to earn a dual major. I've been studying Advertising and Computer Information Sciences. I've had to take a brief sabbatical since I need to save money for my next semester; my parents were helping to support me. However, I recently entered a scholarship contest and made it to the finals, so I might be set within the next month or so."

"What was the contest?" Cameron kept the grin off his face with effort. The way she seemed to deflect or counter Lorcana's every comment was fabulous.

"Interested students had to write a five-thousand word essay to explain and promote a personal, home grown computer program. In the finals, we actually had to build the program. I decided to take my 'art for dummies' knowledge and built a program that, with only a little input from the user, can accurately and efficiently match colors for everything from interior design to clothing trends."

Kenneth whistled between his teeth. "That's a lot of programming!"

"Tell me about it! I was awake until two a.m. more nights than I can count. Anyway, if I win, I'll be able to have my degrees within the next year. I only have a handful of classes left." She tilted her head and her curls bounced lightly. "Of course, you wouldn't have known that, Lorcana, since I didn't feel the need to put down a 'pending' degree on my application unrelated to secretarial skills. I didn't want you all to think I was using my degree to get my foot in the door."

Lorcana's back teeth clicked together. "Dessert!" she nearly barked at the servants.

While they were all eating, Kenneth took a brief hiatus from the table for a few minutes. When he returned, Lorcana just stared at him. He inclined his head ever so slightly and retook his seat. Mollified, she clenched her hands together and told herself it would all be over soon. She hated Sarah. She hated more the way Cameron looked at her. And she absolutely loathed the fact that there was the smallest seed of respect inside her for the younger woman. She had style, grace, and class.

Clearly thinking the same thing, Kenneth said wryly, "You know, it's so funny. Cam and I are always teasingly called princes because we're set to inherit a modern castle. You're completely the equivalent of a princess whose kingdom was lost."

"Yes, but I'd never do well in exile," Sarah countered woefully. "I'd have no one to talk to. I'm a people person. By the time I returned to civilization, I'd be talking more than the local politicians."

Lorcana threw down her napkin and got to her feet. "I'm going to retire for the evening. Good night."

Everyone was silent while she left the room. Finally, Cameron smiled and said, "That was like a round of tennis! Back and forth, back and forth."

"It's probably the only love your mother will ever know."

"Ouch!" He gave her a smacking kiss. "That was petty, and awful, and I love you all the more for it!"

"You should hear what I've been biting back!" She blew out a breath. "I don't think I've won any points, guys. She still hates me. She still doesn't want me anywhere near Cameron because I make him happy, and if he marries me, she loses all control of the company. It's your guess which she hates more."

"Well, no use thinking about it right now," Kenneth said softly. "Let's just go to bed and deal with things in the morning." He winked. "Try to actually sleep, okay, guys?"

"Tia wants grandkids," Cameron argued, grinning. "We should try to oblige."

"I must be insane to be anywhere near you two!" Sarah got to her feet with a smile. "Your time will come, Kenneth Dease! And I'm going to enjoy watching it."

"It would only be fair," he agreed.

Cameron slipped his arm around Sarah's waist and escorted her out of the dining room. "Damn," he said softly, "that was unreal! She really tried to put you through the wringer." His arm tightened possessively. "You really held your own, though. I was really proud of you."

She rested her head on his shoulder with a sigh. "Thanks, but I'm not overly optimistic about the future. Unless she's swapped with a pod person in the middle of the night, there's no way she'll ever give her blessing tomorrow morning."

He shut the bedroom door behind them and leaned against it. His green eyes were dark and intense as he watched her kick off her shoes. "So what if she doesn't change her mind? I don't care, Sarah. For once in my life, I'm going to make my own decisions. I'm going to fight my own battles. If she still digs in her heels, you and I are going back to your apartment *together*. We can both get new jobs. We can make it work."

"Enforcers has good lawyers." Her smile was slight but real. "I could call Eric Mason or Rhianna Taber and ask for help. They'd give it without hesitation." She took a long breath and then began pulling the pins out of her hair. "What's done is done."

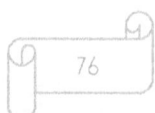

"Stop." He had moved closer without her knowledge and his voice had gone husky with desire. "Let me." He buried his fingers in her hair and sent the remaining pins flying. The few curls in her hair were already stretching out, and he wrapped one around his finger. "Your hair just doesn't like to bend to anything. Just like you."

Her lashes fluttered closed as his hot mouth began to trail kisses over her jaw. That wonderful, now familiar, heat was spreading inside her body. Of their own will, her hands lifted and spread across his chest. He was so hot. Hard and secure, a seductive promise of comfort and pleasure all at the same time. How was it that even his clothes couldn't hurt her skin? They weren't like her clothes; they weren't specially made. It seemed as if everything he was permeated everything he wore. "Cam."

He slowly caught handfuls of her dress and stripped it up over her head. His mouth went dry as he saw what had been hiding underneath. The dark blue silk barely covered her breasts and rode high on her long legs. Sexy garters held up smoky stockings. "I'm glad I didn't know this was under your dress," he managed to say. "I'd have gone crazy."

Her lips curved slowly. "It was an eighteenth birthday gift from my friend. I never thought I'd have a reason to wear it." She wound her arms around his neck and pressed teasingly against his body. "Think you can get it off me without ripping it?"

"Watch me." He bore her down onto the rug, his mouth eagerly rushing across every inch of fragrant skin he could reach. He sensed as much as felt her flinch slightly and immediately rolled over so she was on top. "I didn't even think." His hands stroked slowly up her legs and played with the garters as he went. "No rug burns on your body. No marks at all this time."

By the time they climbed into bed, she wouldn't have cared either way if she had rug burns or not. Seriously, what he could do to her body had to be illegal somewhere. As he pulled the covers over them, she drowsily curled closer against his side. The silk sheets felt deliciously decadent against her skin, which was even more sensitive than usual thanks to him. Thank goodness for his rich-boy preference for the really high thread count sheets. She could sleep on these safely.

"Comfy?" he asked sleepily. He tugged her even closer possessively.

"Mmph." She tucked her nose against his shoulder.

"Good."

Her comfort didn't last long. He shifted position and she naturally adjusted herself to follow. Problem was, as she settled down again, something pressed painfully into her back. It felt as if she had laid down on a rock! Agitated, she tried to find a place to lay that didn't dig into her tender flesh, but the more she moved, the worse it got.

Her restless movements finally got to her lover. "Jesus, what's wrong with you?" He rose onto one elbow to eye her intently.

"There's a lump in the bed!"

He sighed as he understood. "It's probably just a spring. I don't feel anything." He laid down again and dragged her on top of his chest. "Here. Now go to sleep!"

That was easier said than done since feeling him pressed along every inch of her body was highly distracting. But, finally, she was able to drift off to sleep. Once she let herself relax, she realized how comfortable she really felt. He made a nice bed.

She awoke in the early morning to the feel of his hands moving over her body slowly. She surrendered to his touch with a sigh into his kiss. If this was how she was destined to wake every morning, then she was going to be a very happy woman.

As real sunlight began to come in the window some time later, she reluctantly rolled off his chest. The lump in the bed instantly stabbed into her back again. "Ouch!"

"Alright, that's it!" He rolled out of bed and dragged her up as well. "I'm finding this mysterious lump of yours." He began to strip off the covers.

She walked over to the mirror and turned to see her back. She

winced. The black and blue bruises were spreading with a vengeance. "May I recommend that we keep my bed?" She rolled her shoulders carefully. "I'm going to be stiff all day. And it hurts. Do you have aspirin around?"

"Yeah, in the medicine cabinet." He sighed. "I can't find anything wrong with the bed, sweetheart. The springs seem to be fine. I guess it's a good thing we'll be using your bed; at least we know it won't make you look like you went three rounds."

"Tell me about it! Now help me get my bra on. It hurts to move my back muscles right now."

"I'd rather help you take it off." He fastened the clasp in the back and then tenderly skimmed his fingers over the bruises. "I'm sorry, Sarah." He gently pressed a kiss to the worst of the marks.

"How were you supposed to know?" She smiled over her shoulder. "Next time I feel something wrong, I'll say something rather than just toss around. I don't think either of us got the sleep we wanted. But let's let Kenneth think we were working on Tia's grandbabies and make him jealous."

He laughed and helped her pull on a sweater. He then got dressed while she packed up her things once more. After a moment of thought, he pulled out a suitcase of his own and began to throw items into it. "I'm an optimistic guy, but I'm not an idiot," he told her. "I'm sure we'll be leaving together."

"I know." She let her fingers entwine with his as they left the room and headed downstairs toward the dining room to get some breakfast and have the final showdown. When they walked in, she was surprised to see both Kenneth and Lorcana staring at her intently. "What?" She automatically looked down. "Is my sweater on backwards?"

"No, not at all." A smug smile began to curse Lorcana's lips. "How did you sleep last night, my dear?"

Instantly wary, she said, "Well enough, thank you, despite the fact that my tossing and turning kept us both awake."

"Tossing and turning?" Kenneth asked.

"Yeah." Cameron sighed. "There was a lump in the bed that she could feel and it bruised her something fierce. I didn't feel anything myself, so I finally made her sleep on top of me."

"Which was vastly more comfortable than a pillow top bed anyway," his lover said impishly. To her shock, Lorcana suddenly walked over to her and grabbed her arm. "Ow! Hey, let go!"

Lorcana tugged Sarah's sweater away from her back and stared in horror at the sight of the bruises covering her fair flesh. "That . . . that's impossible!" She backed up sharply, her face white. "It's impossible!"

"What did you do?" Cameron demanded of Kenneth when his brother started laughing. "Damn it, Ken, I knew you were up to something!"

"Here's that contract you signed." Kenneth pulled it out of his back pocket and handed it over.

It didn't take Cameron long to figure it out. "'Should Party 2 be able to feel to feel a single pea through a high quality mattress, Party 3 will be given full permission and authority by Party 1 to marry said Party 2. This contract will be Enforced to the highest . . .'" He trailed off in shock. "*This* is what we signed?"

"That was a *pea* that I felt?" Sarah yelped.

"I stuck it under the mattress last night." Kenneth grinned. "And there's no denying the evidence that you felt it; you've sure got the bruises to prove it. And that means that you've both fulfilled the terms of the contract, little sister." He glanced at his mother coolly. "And because she signed as well, she can't deny the terms. Cameron has full permission to marry you even though he's not yet legal."

There was nothing Lorcana could say to that. Before her eyes, every one of her plans had crumbled and fallen apart. *The girl had felt a pea through a mattress!* It should have been impossible, but not even she could find a way that this could have been a set up. The bruises on Sarah's back were very real, and they looked very much like what one would expect of someone rolling over a small object.

With a violent oath, she stalked out of the room. Her office

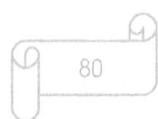

door slammed so hard that it shook the entire manor. Kenneth said nothing. Cameron and Sarah said nothing. Then, suddenly, Cameron grinned. "I'm not knocking my luck!" He grabbed Sarah's wrist. "We're getting married *right now* before she finds a way to renege!"

"Ow, my wrist! Yikes!" She grabbed his shoulders for balance as he instead scooped her up and headed with purpose toward the door. Her head spun around on her shoulders. The emotional rollercoaster of the last three days was beginning to take its toll on her thoughts and emotions. It seemed too good to be true. But that contract . . . she had recognized the language. They *had* been set up all along, and she couldn't even be mad over it. She was getting everything she had ever wanted.

An hour later, they were signing the legal paperwork that would make them husband and wife. They had been expecting a long wait, but as soon as they arrived, they had been shown right in to a judge rather just see the clerk. He even took the time to walk them through all the other paperwork they would have to do to make the federal government happy.

"Are you keeping your maiden name?" he asked Sarah.

"Hmm." She thought about it and then smiled. "No, I want Cameron's name. His last name, anyway. I'd look silly answering to his first name."

"Here's the documents you'll need." He slid them to her with a smile. "Just fill them out and bring them by when you can. I'll take care of the rest."

"Not that we're not grateful," Cameron said, "but you're definitely going above and beyond the call of duty. It's not election year, is it?"

The judge laughed. "Not at all, son. As a matter of fact, Rayna Mason from Enforcers called me and told me that the two of you were on your way. I owe the Enforcers a great deal, and this was the least I could do to repay the debt."

Cameron was still pondering that when they finally left the courthouse. "Rayna Mason?"

"She's a specialist with Enforcers," Sarah offered. "She's Eric's wife. You know, the girl who was in a coma for sixteen years."

"How did she . . .?"

She sighed. "Cam, we were set up. From the beginning, probably. That line in the contract about it being Enforced is standard language in all Enforcer contracts. I'd bet money that Kenneth got it from Rayna or Gwyn, or even Eric."

"So the outcome was never in doubt."

She smiled up at him. "Seems so."

"Wow. I guess I didn't need that suitcase after all." When she laughed, he swung her up into his arms and around in a quick circle. "I'm going to love you forever, Sarah Dease." His grin widened. "I like how that sounds. And it'll look great on a name plate for a desk."

"I was fired, remember?"

"I'm in charge now, so you're rehired. You'll be my personal secretary this time. I'm not sharing you with my brother."

She giggled. "That's not fair to him, Cam. I can be both your secretary."

"Okay, fine. But I'll only share you there."

"That's fair. I mean, he's practically your twin, but he's just not my type."

"We'll have to find his type."

"Right now?"

He headed for his car. "Later. Much later. Maybe tomorrow. There's no law against having a honeymoon before a ceremony."

Content, she held onto him tighter. She had changed her mind. She wasn't going to throw toilet paper on Eric's car. She was going to send him and Rayna a *big* bouquet of flowers to thank them. She owed them both so much.

Kenneth was watching the guesthouse be cleaned out when

his cell phone rang. He walked away to answer it, but no one was there. Puzzled, he went back to the bench he had left the contract on only to discover it had disappeared. In its place sat a single white rose. Oddly unsurprised, he just smiled. Everything had worked out perfectly. Now he wouldn't need to worry about Cameron's happiness anymore.

It was just a shame that Sarah didn't have a sister.

CHAPTER SEVEN

Rhianna Taber was the face on the front of Enforcers. Eric, as her partner, was normally the one in the shadows. He only went to a meeting when someone had screwed up. Rayna was in charge of Enforcers' information technology section and had the ability to hack into any system in existence. Her sister, Gwyn, worked in the legal department as a consultant. Gwyn's husband, Taylor, was a part-time consultant; he owned his own video game company.

Having all five of them together in one place usually meant that there was something big in the works. So when Rhianna walked into the conference room, she said idly, "We're scaring the natives."

Rayna giggled softly. "Well, naturally." In her arms, contentedly sleeping, rested a baby girl with a cap of silvery hair. "You want to hold her?" she asked.

"Gimme." Rhianna happily took baby Glory to cuddle her. "She's the closest thing to a niece that I have." She sat on the edge of the desk and smiled at the white-haired woman next to Rayna. The two sisters were as nearly identical, if not more so, than the Dease brothers. "Well?"

Gwyn Vincent pulled out the contract and put it on the table. As they all watched, the word 'Complete' appeared across the front. "Done and done well, I might add. Trade you." She took her niece while Rhianna picked up the contract.

The older woman wrote down some notes and then slipped it into a folder that also reflected as being complete. "I have a drawer prepared," she noted. "Room for at least three files. I presume, of

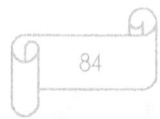

course, that there will be at least three."

"Naturally," Taylor agreed absently without looking up from his sketchpad. It went everywhere with him. "I mean, we can't just leave it there."

"One down and two to go, so to speak," Eric offered.

"And just what have we got in mind for part two?" Rhianna arched a brow.

Taylor put down the sketchpad where the others could see. He had just finished drawing an old-fashioned genie lamp. Even as they all watched, smoke began to lift from the spout on the page. With a flash, the lamp disappeared from the page and appeared in the middle of the table. "Fun," he decided.

Rhianna began to smile. "I always knew you had untapped abilities that would be useful."

"I know." Gwyn shot her husband the impish grin that he had always loved. "Isn't he great?"

Status: File Begun
Analysis: The most important things in life are more than skin deep.
Beauty, love, and humor. A true princess has all three.

Folder Two
KENNETH

CHAPTER EIGHT

As Cameron's twenty-first birthday drew ever closer, things began to get busy. Lorcana had moved into the guesthouse because she adamantly refused to live under the same roof as Sarah. Since her sons, and daughter-in-law, weren't inclined to share space with her either, it worked for them as well.

Everyone who worked for Two More Minutes came back to work happily when they received word of the outcome. Louise was distinctly the most pleased since Sarah's new position as Executive Secretary meant that *she* was the office manager. That gave Louise plenty of time to focus on her graphics work. Now if they could only find a lead graphic designer! She hated being in charge.

It was two weeks before Cameron's birthday and Lorcana was facing the end of her career. The only reason she even remained in the company at all was because Kenneth and Cameron were transitioning her out. Transitioning her! As if she was an old retiree of no use anymore. She had *earned* this company and now it wouldn't even be hers anymore.

If she wanted to keep a hold of her business, then she needed to find a way to control Kenneth. She didn't fool herself into thinking it would be easy. He was an adult, and he was one of the more intelligent men she had ever met. He was also ridiculously stubborn and unfailingly honest. No, getting him under her control would be damned near impossible.

But not completely.

It stung her that she was even thinking of going this particular route, but she was desperate. She had nothing to lose by grasping at straws. She had already learned that there were indeed some things beyond mortal comprehension. A lowly secretary who could feel a pea through a mattress was one of them. An ancient lamp that might grant wishes was another.

The rumor of the lamp had come to her from one of her cronies as another of those silly 3rd District legends. Supposedly this lamp had a genie inside that could grant wishes. The difficulty lay in that it had been lost into a well somewhere, and there wasn't anyone who could get it out.

She wasn't ready to give up yet, though. There had to be a way!

Kenneth had spent most of the previous six months working elbow-to-elbow with his brother to make sure that Lorcana's departure would be as seamless as possible. While Cameron took on more and more of the internal work, Kenneth found himself working externally to find clients, work with the ones they already had, and oversee their publicity department.

It didn't help any that they didn't have a lead graphic designer anymore. The last one had finally retired the year before; he had been around since the company had been formed by Viktor Dease. With that spot empty, Kenneth had to start reviewing applications with Cameron and prepare to conduct interviews. And worse still, they were in the middle of a big job for an auto company.

When Sarah walked into his office with a cup of coffee, she smiled wryly as she saw him leaning back in his chair with a cloth over his eyes. "I have caffeine, Ken." She brought the cup over and put it down in front of him. "You need a break."

"I need the next two weeks to be over." He straightened and pulled the cloth off his eyes. "Mother is making things as hard as she can for us, and you know it. I can't shake this chill I get whenever I see her." Grimly, he added, "I get the feeling she's up to something."

"You need to get your mind off things," his sister-in-law scolded. "You need to get out of here for a while. Take a day off, Ken, c'mon."

"I have way too much work to do. But," he added as he got to his feet, "I *will* be outside to do it, promise." He smiled suddenly. "You boss Cam around like this too?"

She grinned. "I'd hate for him to be bored."

There were many mysteries in the world, and most of them hid in the 3rd District. Some of them were more of ironic destinies than mysteries, though, Sera Thomason decided to herself as she headed home from her part-time job. Her *former* part-time job since the owner had decided to cut back, and she was the cut he had decided to make. Friggin' stuck-up business owners in Brooklyn. She would have rather dealt with the small businesses in her District any day, but no one needed a budding graphic designer.

"Mom, I'm home," she called as she walked into her house.

"Welcome home, honey." Cecily Thomason looked up with a smile as she saw her daughter walk into the living room. "Did you have a good day?"

"Got canned." Sera plopped down on the tattered chair that her Golden Retriever loved to chew on. "So I guess I'm job hunting. Again. Hey, Milly." She ruffled her dog's fur as she ran up with her favorite rope in her teeth. While they played a light game of tug-of-war, Sera tried to surreptitiously eye her mother. "How do you feel?"

Cecily sighed. "As well as can be expected. Doctor Matthews said he would come by later to check on me. Really, he fusses worse than you do."

"Hey, he has the degree that tells him when fussing is required. I'm just a worrywart." She glanced at the clock and then went into the kitchen with Milly on her heels. "I'll get your medicine."

For the last few years, Cecily's health had been rapidly declining. It seemed as if everything was happening all at the same time. She had been diagnosed with so many things that Sera wasn't even sure she remembered all of them. Every single one required medication to keep it in line. Both mother and daughter had insurance through Enforcers, but that didn't make the payments any easier. Sera worked every odd job she could and sold her art on the corners to make ends meet.

If it hadn't been for the fact that Doctor Lewis Matthews was a childhood friend of Cecily's, Sera doubted that they would even be able to afford to go to a doctor at all. Lewis was more than willing to make house calls and let Sera pay off any bills by mowing his lawn or babysitting his two twin daughters; the widower claimed she kept him sane by entertaining the two five-year-olds. She loved both kids, so couldn't argue the deal worked for everyone.

Her stomach churned as she saw that the medications were running very low. She knew she could ask Sarah for a loan to cover it, but she hated the idea of owing anything to anyone, even her surrogate sister. And she really didn't want Sarah to start worrying again; she was finally happy with her new husband.

There weren't many options left for Sera. She didn't have her degree, and she couldn't get into her chosen field yet. A lot of people were cutting back on part-time workers, and she couldn't go full-time until her mother was strong enough to be home all day by herself. She was going to be stuck in fast food, if she could even find one of *them* hiring. On a sad sigh, she knelt and hugged Milly. "Oh well. We'll make it work, right? Maybe I can train you to do some tricks and we can join the circus."

"Woof!" Milly licked her face enthusiastically.

"Yeah. I can see it now. Sera and her amazing Slobber Dog." She swiped a hand over her face. "Man, your breath smells. Let's go for a walk and you can eat some flowers or something. But not Madelyne's this time! She'd kill us."

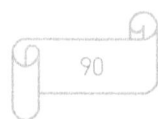

CHAPTER NINE

Kenneth was a big believer in understanding his clients. If they wanted to promote to a certain type of people or a certain area, then he needed to visit them and find out what they needed and what they were like. He had a personal pet peeve about seeing billboards in rural areas, or ads for things that people in the area might never need.

Having briefly seen the 3rd District, and having talked to Sarah about it, he knew that it was an untapped area for advertisers. AAC had been their only company because no bigger places would work with such small businesses. Kenneth and Cameron wanted to change their company's standing on that, so Kenneth knew he needed to find out what the District needed.

It was to his advantage that he wasn't known there in the way he was known other places. He deliberately dressed down, opting for the most casual jeans and shirt he could find. In fact, he found himself enjoying the efforts. He so rarely relaxed anymore.

He opted to take the bus as well. Really, his pretty Volvo would have been totally out of place. In fact, if they had allowed it, he would have completely gotten a real horse. The 3rd District was the perfect place for it.

The closest bus stop to the District still had him walking a few blocks. Not that he minded the exercise. He hadn't been able to get to the gym for weeks either. As he walked across the street that marked the entrance to the District, he took a deep breath. The air was somehow . . . cleaner there. It had to be part of the magic.

When he rounded a corner, he was brought up short by several males not much older or younger than himself. He hated to profile people, but he couldn't stop his shoulders from tensing when he saw that they didn't look at all as if they belonged in the District.

"So what's a guy like you doing out here?" one asked slyly. "This isn't a safe part of town, you know." He slipped his hands into his pockets. "What do you say you hand over your wallet and we'll let you go?" A very low and vicious snarl from behind the males had them going white. "Sera."

"Yeah," came her mocking voice, "but I ain't the one snarling at you. That would be Milly. She thinks she's a Rottweiler right now."

Kenneth glanced over the male's shoulder to see a shockingly beautiful young woman holding the leash of a distinctly unhappy Golden Retriever. The dog had her ears back and every single tooth bared as she growled low. "Rottweiler, huh?"

"You should see her German Sheppard impersonation." Sera bared her own teeth in a mockery of a smile. "Should I demonstrate it?"

The thugs weren't that stupid. They ran off as quickly as was possible. As soon as they were out of sight, Milly stopped growling. She sat down and began to wag her tail happily. With the canine equivalent of a grin, she woofed at Kenneth. He found himself grinning. "Thanks for the save, Milly."

He shifted his gaze to his rescue dog's owner. It was with much male appreciation that he studied her long legs and generous figure. They were more emphasized than disguised by her tattered jeans and peasant shirt, and both articles had been liberally streaked with paint. His eyes met her wryly-amused golden ones, and he grinned. "Hi."

She decided she had to like him. She grinned. "Hi. A bit out of your way, aren't you? You're not from the District."

"I felt like visiting." He offered a hand. "Kenneth."

"Sera."

"S-A?"

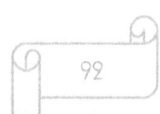

"S-E. And thanks for asking." She snorted. "Most people never guess right." She laughed when Milly barked. "And this is Milly. She's supposed to be a Golden Retriever."

"She makes a great Rottweiler." He knelt to pet Milly and she wagged her tail harder. "All bark and no bite, aren't you? Hey there, beautiful." He laughed when she licked his face. "Best action I've had in months. Thanks."

He was gorgeous and he loved dogs. Sera automatically gave him points for both. He also looked eerily familiar but she couldn't quite put her finger on it. She hadn't seen *him*, precisely, but she felt sure she had seen someone *like* him.

He got to his feet and his grin widened as he realized how tall she was. She stood only one or two inches shorter than his five-eleven height, and that suited him *just* fine. He liked tall girls. In fact, she was the best of his favorite two female worlds: tall and curvy. The twain didn't usually meet, but here they were rolled into a black haired, sardonic package.

"I'd like it to be stated," he said, "that I am very much attracted to you, and therefore I will be doing my best to get you to go out with me. Tell me you're legal," he begged.

She *really* liked him. "I'm legal," she assured him. "But you're going to have to work hard to get a date. I'm not really a date-type girl. I've never seen the point. I'd as soon stay home and get my sketch on."

"You're an artist?"

"Budding." She tied Milly's leash to her belt loop and tucked her hands in her pockets. "You want to see the District? I can show you around. I live here. Born and bred, in fact."

He fell into step beside her. "So you're gifted?"

"Ooh, how tactful you are! Most ask if I'm not human."

"Are you?" He smiled. "I don't mind either way. Well, as long as, you know, you're not going to have an alien come out of your chest."

"Nah, that's not our shtick around here. We lean toward the

more traditional types. Faeries, werewolves, and so on. I'm human, but I'm gifted." She had never been embarrassed by her gift, and she could feel genuine interest and acceptance from him. "Actually, we're not really that secretive about it. We don't flaunt it, but we don't lie about it either."

"Well, what do you do?"

"Shift."

He considered that. "Are we talking about morphing objects?"

"No, myself. I'm a shapeshifter."

"Hmm. I have two reactions to that. The first is 'holy cow!' The second is 'that's so cool!' You can pick your favorite." He smiled when she laughed at him. Her laughter seemed to make her eyes glow like coins. He was even fond of her bright pink hairstreaks, and he had never really been into that before.

"I like them both. Wah!" She threw out her arms for balance as Milly darted to the right and nearly pulled her off her feet. She landed safely in Kenneth's arms when he shot forward, and Milly, deciding this was a new game, ran around them happily, tying them both up in the leash.

"Idiot dog," Sera muttered. She held onto Kenneth's arms for balance as she glared at her pet. Her legs were firmly tied to his and moving might knock them both rather painfully over. "Sorry about that."

She turned her head to meet his eyes and realized that they had come almost nose-to-nose. Because they stood so close in height, they were effectively on eye level. His ridiculously sexy mouth was so close that she could have kissed him without moving at all. Her breath lodged in her chest and her pulse began to hammer as she saw his darkened gray-green eyes watching her with hunger. "Uhm."

His hands tightened on her hips as he pulled her closer. "I'm going to kiss you," he murmured huskily.

"No, you're not!" She flattened her hands on his chest and leaned back as much as she dared. "I just met you!"

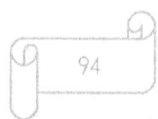

"Then you had better find a way to get us untangled. And I'll kiss you later when we've known each other a few more hours."

"Grab the leash," she muttered. Her eyes flew wide as his hand slid hotly over her hip and pointedly grabbed the leash where it pressed against her bottom. With more haste than grace, she grabbed her power and let it take her.

His brows shot up as she suddenly disappeared and a bluebird appeared in midair in her place. "Wow." He held tighter to the leash as Milly realized it was loose and tried to run off. Firmly, he yanked back. "Sit."

Milly sat. Sera flew back a step and turned back to normal. Very warily, she reached out to take the leash from him. "Okay, Kenneth. I have ground rules for you. Hands and lips to yourself unless I say otherwise, got it?

"It wouldn't bother you if you weren't attracted to me just as badly."

"I won't deny that." She wrapped the leash around her wrist. "And you definitely get points for not freaking out that I turned into a bird."

"It was fascinating." He fell into step beside her once more as she headed down the sidewalk. "What can you turn into?"

"Most anything, but there are caveats to it. I have to have a rudimentary understanding of the physiology of whatever I'm becoming else I retain some human features. When I was a kid, I accidentally turned into a bird-human hybrid. I was molting for weeks after."

"Did you get your power from your parents?"

"Yeah. My mom is a shifter. My dad was a conjuror type."

"Was?"

She lowered her gaze. "He died six years ago."

"I lost my dad ten years ago," he said softly. He curled his hands around hers and laced their fingers together. "I know how much it never stops hurting." He brought her hand to his lips briefly. He had a feeling he was in danger of losing his heart to his lovely shapeshifter. It wasn't just desire. It couldn't be, not when he ached to hold her and take away her sadness. "So what do you do, Sera? Do you sell your art?" He knew 3rd District had a strong handcrafted market.

"Sometimes. Mostly I have a bunch of part-time jobs. Well, I did." She scowled. "I just got fired. I *hate* executives and big business. It's all about the bottom line. What pricks."

He groaned mentally. If that wasn't the worst-case scenario, then he didn't know what was. "You hate all executives, or just those that don't care about the lesser man, or woman?"

"All of 'em. Ain't met one yet that I liked. Well . . . okay, I guess there's one I like. My best friend married one a few months ago. He's cool." She tried to tug her hand free, but his grip stayed firm. Reluctantly, she let it be. It was sort of nice to walk holding hands. It almost felt like having a boyfriend, and she hadn't had one of those in two years. It just hadn't been worth the time.

Kenneth was worth every minute, and she liked him more and more every moment. Maybe she would let him kiss her. Oh, she didn't doubt she would enjoy it. Just his presence alone was enough to give her heatstroke. She could only be glad she didn't have any sort of elemental power. She would be starting fires for sure.

"So." He changed the subject pointedly. He needed time to find a way to tell her who he really was without her killing him, *or* running off. "Tell me about the District. I read about how it doesn't have a lot of flashy advertisements and it intrigued me. Seeing it now, I realize what they meant. There aren't a lot of posters or billboards, are there?"

"We're a historical landmark," she retorted dryly. "You think they had billboards back in the 1800s? Please. We like our advertising to be external. Internally, we pass out flyers and stick notices in mailboxes. People have tried to pay Enforcers to put up big signs and stuff, but Rhianna and Eric adamantly refused. If *we* want to advertise, we mostly go the poster route or word of mouth."

"Television?"

"Who can afford it, Ken? It's so expensive!"

Bingo! He couldn't have been happier. Offering cheaper means of television advertising to businesses like those in 3rd District would probably be the perfect place to start. They didn't need much else, although he was pretty sure some discount poster services might be appreciated as well. "Digital or hand-drawn?"

She blinked in bemusement. "I actually understood what you're asking. Go me. Mostly hand-drawn around here. It's that 'old-school' thing. I help out with a lot of that around here when I can. I'm a pro with both acrylics *and* Photoshop/Illustrator. I'm trying to get my degree in Graphic Design."

"Okay, we have to talk. Seriously." He glanced around and saw a quiet bench sitting under some shady trees. "Come over here."

"As if I had a choice," she said dryly as he dragged her along. "What's the deal?" She sat down and tethered Milly to the bench so she couldn't get away. "Something up?"

He sat beside her and took her hands. "Okay. Here's the deal. I . . ." He trailed off as he watched the sun filter across her face. It caressed her skin and made her eyes shimmer with power and mystery. Her short hair seemed to simply beg to be mussed up more by his fingers.

He cupped her cheek with his hand and leaned forward to kiss her. She tasted like sunshine and magic, her lips soft and perfectly made for his. His free hand curled into the back of the bench as he fought to keep the embrace light. The little purring sound she made did nothing for his control, however. He eased back a breath and asked huskily, "Going to hit me?"

"Not if you kiss me again." She slid her hands into his hair as he pulled her closer again. The shivers were starting from the inside out, spreading in heated waves of delight. Dear god, the man knew how to *kiss*. It was stupid, it was probably tacky, and she didn't give a damn. As the kiss deepened, something low in her body clenched with sharp longing. Every nerve ending came alive all at once.

When he slowly broke the kiss, she had to force herself to

release him. She looked into his darkened eyes and saw the same swirl of volatile emotions inside him as churned inside her. "Uhm." It was the best she could say.

"Still not going to date me?" He nipped at her lower lip teasingly. His hands slid down her body and then up again, savoring every inch. "I'm not feeling very casual, Sera."

She shuddered as his mouth found a sensitive nerve in her neck and teased it with his teeth. She was going to go crazy if she didn't get his hands on her soon. "Neither am I," she managed to say. When he lifted his head and looked at her, she accepted the inevitable. She had been doomed from the moment she met him. "Oh, the hell with it. Kiss me again."

His lips curved and he slowly slid into the kiss, his lips teasing hers into opening for him. She found herself going under for the third time before she had realized she was in deep water. Slowly, reluctantly, she eased back until there was a breath between them. "Where have you been for the last five years of my life?" she asked huskily.

He ran his thumb over her lower lip. "Only five?" His voice sounded just as thick with desire as hers.

"I didn't realize how nice the male of the species was until I was sixteen." Her lips began to curve. "Of course, at sixteen, you don't have real standards yet, so I thought the paperboy was hot." She took a long, steadying breath. "Five years later, I think have figured out what I like. Even saying that, I don't think I ever set the bar so high as for a man like you."

His eyes lit. "Compliments aren't going to help me find self-control, Sera." His hands again skimmed up her sides and then down. "But I must confess I had a similar thought when I saw you. I've always liked tall women. And I like curvy women. I never thought I'd get both in such a spectacular combination."

"You're so bad for my pulse." She eased back entirely and untied Milly. "I need to be heading for home."

"I'll walk you there." He stood and took her free hand with his.

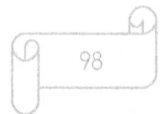

"I want to spend more time with you. And if I know where you live, I can come back tomorrow and pester you mercilessly until you go out with me."

"Gee, I've always wanted a stalker." She smiled as she bumped her shoulder against his to be sure he knew she only joked. "I seriously like you, Kenneth. I'm not normally quick to like people, but I can't seem to help myself with you."

He mentally crossed his fingers and prayed that he could build enough of that like to ensure she didn't hate him when she found out his identity. He just couldn't bear to tell her yet. It was too wonderful to spend time with someone he knew liked him for himself. "So are you on your own or do you live with your mother?"

"I live with my mother." Her gaze lowered. "She can't live alone. She's been so sick lately. It's like everything at once has hit. Among the many other things eating at her, she's diabetic, has Crohn's disease, and just got diagnosed with kidney stones." Her voice broke and then steadied. "Worse, the doctor is now worried about her heart and her liver. She can't eat much; the medications make her sick. She's lost twenty pounds in a *month*." She swiped furiously at her eyes. She *refused* to cry.

"I'm so sorry, baby." He brought her hand to his lips for a long moment, hurting for her. "Is that why you work so hard?"

"Someone has to. I had to put school on hold. I was *so close* to my degree, Ken. I only had general education left. But all my school money had to go to pay for the hospital and the doctors and the meds. I've tried applying for grants and scholarships, but so far no luck." She shook it off. "What about you?"

"I finished my major in three years. Business mostly. I want to run my own company." He shot her a teasing grin. "Will you still like me when I'm high on the food chain?"

"Will you promise to be honest and have goodwill for us lower peons?" Her voice was just as teasing. "Don't worry, Ken. I like you as you are, so unless you completely changed your attitude, I'd still like you. I'm usually a good judge of character." Milly woofed and she laughed. "And so's she."

It was something at the least. "Hey, you want to get lunch?" he asked. "My treat." He grinned when she eyed him. "It's not a date, promise. When I have you on a date, you'll know it." His fingers skimmed down her arm slowly. "Trust me."

"Hoo boy," she said under her breath. Impulsively, she asked, "Do you want to have lunch with me and my mom? I bet she would like the company."

"I'd be honored. And I promise to behave myself. She doesn't have to know I'm trying to seduce her baby girl."

"You're so bad." She just shook her head as she led him toward her home. "Don't be alarmed by the appearance," she warned him. "We keep the area looking ramshackle so that people won't try to bulldoze in."

Even with the warning, he was still slightly nonplussed by the residential area. Anywhere else, he would have called it a slum. But here . . . it seemed oddly inviting. It had to be the people. Residents of all ages wandered around, working in yards, setting out laundry, or simply lounging on porches. Everyone knew everyone else. "Just like you're your own town," he murmured.

"Bingo." Sera unlocked the door and took Milly's leash off so that she could bound inside happily. "Mom!" she called. "I found a stray. I'm going to feed him."

"Sera," Cecily scolded as she stepped into the doorway. When she spotted Kenneth, her exasperated look turned to a smile. "Oh. That sort of stray." She studied him with a mother's speculative eye. "And you are?"

"Kenneth." He smiled. "Sera saved me and I bummed my way into a meal. Please pardon the intrusion, Mrs. . . . ?"

"Thomason. But Cecily is just fine. It's nice to meet you, Kenneth." She sighed as Sera darted forward and helped her sit down. "How do you do that? I don't even know I'm tired before you do."

"You shouldn't be up yet." Sera frowned deeply. "You just got

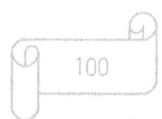

over the flu."

"I have to do something," her mother said gently. "I can't let you take all the weight." She smiled when Sera hugged her tightly. "I love you too, honey."

A little pain clenched Kenneth's heart. He'd had Tia growing up, but it had never been the same as this. He had never known what it was like to have a mother that loved unconditionally. He envied Sera a little, and he certainly understood why she was so determined to help Cecily.

"What's wrong?" Sera asked. "You look sad."

Candidly, he admitted, "I was just envying you a little. My mother hates me and my brother. She always has."

"Her loss." Cecily's lips firmed in a way that indicated Sera might be a chip off her mother's block. "Mothers like that don't deserve the name."

"I can't agree more."

"Sit." Sera shoved him into a chair.

"Woof."

She grinned. "Milly's cuter, sorry." She competently began to assemble the ingredients for two sandwiches and a vat of soup. Over her shoulder, she asked, "What was with the interest in advertisement in the District?"

"Morbid curiosity. I've never seen a street without a billboard. That, and I want to find a niche for myself, and I'm interested in all kinds of things." He watched her unashamedly, not noticing Cecily watching him in turn. "You're a graphic artist, right? Can I see some of your work? Or anything you've done?"

"Over the door," Cecily offered.

He turned his head and was struck silent by the brilliant poster. It was an advertisement for the Faerie Club, both hand-drawn and digital all at the same time. The top left started out sketched and then slowly evolved into full digital color by the bottom right corner. In the middle, in the middle of a dance, was a couple. They looked normal in the drawn portion but wore fantastical costumes in the digital.

Across the bottom, it read '*Where magic happens.*'

"Wow. Damn, you're good." He tried to remember their advertisement for a lead designer. Had they insisted on a degree? He sure as hell hoped not! Sera would be *perfect*. She had the skills and the personality alike to get the job done.

Cheeks pink, Sera said, "Thanks." She put down a sandwich in front of him and gave her mother a bowl of soup. Content, she sat down with her own sandwich. "Don't feed Milly scraps, no matter how pitiful she looks."

He laughed. "I'll do my best."

They played cards after lunch while Cecily kept things legal. Kenneth was having so much fun that he had no idea how late it had gotten until he saw the clock. "Oops." He grimaced. "I need to go." He had two meetings, and he would be running to one of them. He reluctantly got to his feet. "I'm sorry to run out."

"No, it's okay." Sera walked him to the door with a smile. "Come back anytime." When his hand gently framed her face, she leaned in with a soft sigh to meet his kiss. Her fingers curled possessively for a moment into his shirt. "Come back soon," she said softly.

"Will you miss me?" he asked just as softly. It took considerable willpower to not kiss her again.

"Probably." Her lips curved. "Kiss me again to be sure."

He did so with a smile, lingering over her flavor until he knew he was in danger of not leaving at all. He slowly released her and stepped back. "See you tomorrow." As the door shut quietly, he took a deep breath. He needed a cold shower. In fact, he needed five. He was also suddenly beginning to understand what had happened to Cameron when he had met Sarah. This love at first sight thing was volatile and scary all at the same time.

Sera walked back into the living room and found her mother lifting a brow. She winced. "Well."

Blandly, Cecily said, "I admit, I'm old-fashioned enough to think that at least one date should occur before kissing commences, but

I'm also still healthy enough to not blame you in the slightest. I didn't think men were grown that gorgeous in New York."

Sera sat down on the couch with a laugh. "You and me both! He's also witty, personable, and has such a giving heart." She sighed deeply. "I think I'm in love with him. I know we're all wired for true love, but *really*? At first sight?"

"It happens for some." Cecily smiled. "And for others, you need to test the waters before you find the real thing. What's important is to treasure each moment and fight for it. If you're one of the lucky ones to find the real thing from the beginning, then you need to do whatever you can to keep it."

Sera rested her head on her mother's shoulder. "He's a good kisser too."

"The best ones are, honey."

CHAPTER TEN

Kenneth made a point of getting to the office early the next morning so that he could rearrange his schedule. He wanted to spend as much time as possible with Sera. He knew it was absolutely critical to build up her trust before he told her the truth.

As he scowled at his calendar, Louise walked into his office. She studied him for several moments before a smile teased her lips. "Kenneth, how long have I known you?"

"Huh?" He blinked at her. "Five years. You started as an intern when I was starting college." He had always greatly respected her for that simple fact; she was only four years older than he, but she had moved up the ranks quickly.

"Based on that long history, and the lack of formality around here, I'm going to be blunt." She sat on the edge of his desk. "You look like a guy in serious need of getting laid. There's steam coming off your head, boss. Who's the lucky girl?"

"Her name is Sera."

"Well, there's irony."

"Tell me about it." He sighed. "She's also, still ironically, from the 3rd District as well. Unfortunately, she hates executives, and I happened to meet her incognito. So she likes me, but she's temperamental enough to possibly kick my ass when she finds out the truth."

"Okay, are we talking about a mutual case of the hots or . . ."

He raised his hand. "Hi, I'm Kenneth Dease and I'm a victim of love at first sight."

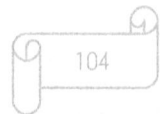

She winced good-naturedly. "And another good man bites the dust. What about her?"

"I *think* it might also be mutual, but I don't think she'd admit it if it was. If anything, there's definitely mutual attraction. I couldn't keep my hands off her."

"Or your lips?"

"Them neither. She wears a rather addicting cinnamon lip-gloss." He raked both hands through his hair this time. "I'm trying to rearrange my schedule so I can free up some time this afternoon to go see her again."

Tongue in cheek, she said, "I hadn't seen those wings before."

"Wings?"

"You know what they say about moths and flames, right?"

"If they looked like Sera, the moths went happily to their doom." He found a smile suddenly. "Why are you still single, Lou? If you weren't so much like our sister, Cam and I would have been fighting over you."

"I'm picky," she retorted dryly. She got to her feet. "Let me know if I can help, okay? Cam's happy. You need to be happy too."

Through some creative finagling, and strategic excuses, he managed to clear his afternoon. The instant his last morning meeting ended, he rushed home to change clothes and then made a beeline for the 3rd District. He felt bemused at himself as he headed for Sera's front door. His heart beat faster than a snare drum, and he was fairly sure he was holding his breath. He had always thought people grew out of those reactions once puberty ended.

Sera was washing dishes when she heard the doorbell. She dried her hands quickly and hurried to answer, her breath held with anticipation. She had been hoping all day to find Kenneth on the other side. Thus far she had been disappointed twice. Once by a kid selling cookies and the other by Dr. Matthews.

This time, when she opened the door, she was rewarded by the sight of Kenneth on her porch. He looked windblown, sexy, and slightly flushed as if he had run the entire way to see her. "Hi." It was the best she could manage, and it came out as breathless as she felt.

"Hi." He curled his hand around the back of her neck and drew her in for a hungry kiss. The taste of her was rich and wild and as potent as the power inside her. "Missed you," he said against her lips as he eased back. He rested his forehead against hers. "Did you miss me?"

"Are you nuts?" Her laugh came out shaky. "I was going out of my mind." She curled against his chest and rested her cheek on his shoulder. His arms closed around her tightly and she felt something inside eagerly soak up the feeling. It wouldn't have been so bad if it had been just her body—though it hadn't helped her sleepless night any. Her heart and her soul seemed starved for him.

"I cleared my afternoon for you." He smiled. "I'm all yours for the rest of the day." When she lifted her head, he leaned in and nibbled at her ear. She had triple pierced ears, and he found it sexy for some reason. "I'm at your command."

The man was temptation incarnate. She knew she could invite him to stay the night and he would be more than willing. She even knew that she wouldn't regret it. He had been right the day before. Whatever there was between them was not casual. It never would be. But it was certainly volatile, and well out of her experience. She needed a little more time. She wasn't nearly as impulsive as most people thought.

"What's going through your mind?" he murmured, his hand cupping her cheek. His eyes searched hers. "I can see so many things flickering across your eyes. Secrets and mysteries." His lips brushed hers. "Tell me everything."

From the living room, Cecily called dryly, "Hi, Kenneth."

He lifted his head with a grin. "Hi, Cecily," he called back. He dropped a kiss on Sera's nose. "I guess the good moms always know everything."

"Boy do they! Get some rest!" she called to her mother. "I'm taking Kenneth with me to pick up the terrible two and drop them at Brian's shop!"

"Have fun!"

"Terrible two?" Kenneth asked curiously. A stab of jealousy made his eyes greener than usual. "Who is Brian?"

"The closest thing to a big brother I have," she assured him with a grin. "Why, Ken, are you jealous?" She got her answer when he dragged her against him and kissed her so hotly that her toes curled in her shoes. "Oh." It was the only thing that came to what remained of her mind.

"Who are the terrible two?" He looped his arm lightly around her waist.

"They're my mother's doctor's daughters." She laughed when he blinked. "Tammy and Tawny. Identical twins. Super cute but super scary smart for their age. They're about five or so. I babysit them in exchange for free doctor's visits for my mother. I also pick them up from school and deliver them to Brian's place. He's Doc Matthew's nephew."

"Biggest little town in New York," he murmured.

"That's one way of putting it."

The elementary school that the two girls attended sat right outside the District. Kenneth carefully kept an eye on the area just in case anyone spotted him. Thankfully, he didn't see anyone who would have reason to recognize him.

It wasn't hard to tell who the girls were. Not only were they most assuredly identical, but they also spotted Sera and gave happy shrieks as they ran down the sidewalk and jumped into her arms. They talked over each other and at the same time, each trying to be the first to tell their favorite person about what they had done that day. He couldn't help but grin as he watched.

"Okay, okay!" Sera put them both down. "Calm down! You can talk my ear off on the way to Cousin Brian. First, meet Kenneth." She turned them around so that they could see him. "Ken, meet Tawny and Tammy. Tam is the one with the short hair."

He knelt down to their height and smiled. "Hi. Nice to meet you." He offered his hand and smiled when they both shook it.

"Are you Sera's boyfriend?" Tawny asked shrewdly.

"No," Sera said.

"Yes," he said at the same time.

The twins giggled as the two adults eyed each other. "Don't encourage him," Sera scolded them with a smile. She took Tammy's hand. "C'mon, troublemakers. And that means all three of you."

As they walked, the girls chattered five miles a minute. It was to Kenneth's credit that he not only managed to keep up, but he was also able to ask questions and listen with obvious attention to the answers. His love for kids seemed very clear, and Sera's heart sighed happily. He was hot, liked dogs, *and* he loved kids. She was going to have to date him after all. Only an idiot would lose a guy like that, and she wasn't an idiot.

Kenneth hadn't known what to expect from 'Brian's shop,' but he knew he would have never guessed right even if he had tried. The small building had large glass windows that displayed brilliant bolts of cloth and handcrafted clothing. Racks of more clothing as well as blankets, curtains, and anything else that could be made of cloth stood in the middle of a slightly overzealous garden.

The bell over the door chimed merrily as they walked in the front door. Inside the tiny room were rows and shelves upon shelves of more beautiful work. A counter wedged into a corner with an old-fashioned cash register on top. Beside it sat a jar that said 'tag trade.' "What's that?" Kenneth asked Sera as the girls ran for a door leading further into the building.

"Tag trade? It's what we do around here. Say I wanted a blanket but didn't have the money. I would take the tag from the blanket and write my name on the back. I'd then drop the tag into the jar. Brian could bring that tag to me and trade it for one of my art pieces of equal value."

"And who said that the barter system couldn't work in America."

"The same people who think the moon landing was a hoax."

They exchanged a grin as a man walked out of the backroom

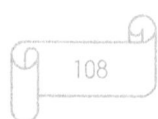

with a twin attached to each ankle. "Did you lose something, Sera?" he asked her dryly, his blue eyes twinkling merrily behind his glasses. He glanced at Kenneth and lifted a brow curiously. Sera had never brought a male over to the shop before. "Well. Hello. I'm Brian Matthews. I own this shop."

"You're one hell of a weaver," Kenneth said sincerely. "And my name is Kenneth."

"Nice to meet you." Brian put the two girls down gently. "I bet you might find some snacks in the fridge," he told them softly. He smiled as they darted into the back happily. "I get them buzzed on sugar and then give them back to their father," he explained to Kenneth. "My grandmother says that it's his just desserts for waiting so long to give her grandkids."

"What are you working on right now?" Sera rummaged through the racks as she spoke. "Anything fancy other than 'that' project?"

"No." He shook his head slightly. "No more special projects for me." She looked at him with fear, and he gently skimmed his hand down her hair. "I'm under contract," he told her. "All I can do is hope and pray."

Kenneth withheld his questions, sensing that there was something very serious being discussed that he didn't understand. Instead, he watched with amusement as Sera and Brian haggled price over a dress she liked. By the time they left the shop, she had the dress in a bag, and Brian had a tag to be used in exchange for a poster.

As they walked down the sidewalk, Kenneth asked softly, "Under contract?"

Her gaze lowered. "Around here that means that he's been signed into Enforcers' direct protection. It always finds a way to ensure that whatever is wrong is made right, but it's never easy." Her hands clenched together. "He's cursed, Ken. And that's all I'm going to say."

"He seems like a nice guy," he offered softly. "He'll get his happy ending."

"Yeah." She shook it off visibly. "Let's find something else to talk about."

"Like what?"

"I don't know." She smiled. "I'm just happy to be with you."

Abruptly, he couldn't keep up the farce anymore. He couldn't bear lying to her, and he was definitely lying by omission. "Can we talk?" he asked softly. He skimmed his fingers through her hair.

"Of course." She glanced around and saw a more secluded spot under some trees. She headed over and leaned against the trunk. Her stomach churned with nerves. He looked very serious, and a little grim. He couldn't technically break up with her if they weren't seeing each other, but if he had decided he didn't want to see her again, she didn't know what she would do. "This isn't going to be some sappy break up, is it?"

"No!" He framed her face with hands. "Get that out of your head right now. I'm not intending on leaving you. I just . . . have something to tell you. And I know you're going to be mad at me, so I'm not sure where to start."

"You're married."

"No."

"You joined the army?"

"No."

"Pity, you'd be hot in uniform." She let out a long breath. "Okay, what's this great secret, Ken?"

"I . . . hell." He lifted her chin slightly and kissed her with all the desperate longing in his heart. As she sensed it, her hands gently rested over his heart. Just that touch seemed to soothe him, and he gentled the kiss. When her lips parted on a soft sigh, he contentedly deepened the embrace. Desire surged at its chains when she teasingly curled her tongue around his, but he held tight to control.

He lifted his head slightly, and her eyes opened. The golden color looked dark and drowsy, and her lips were swollen and sensual. "If that's what you do to me with a kiss," she said huskily, her fingers trembling where they pressed to his chest, "I'm almost afraid to have

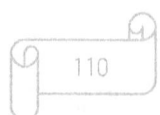

you for a lover." She took a ragged breath. "You're really scaring me, Ken."

He took a breath just as ragged. "Sera, I am . . ."

"Kenneth Dease!" a woman's voice exclaimed. "What a wonderful surprise!"

He hastily stepped back as the woman hurried over with a wide grin. Sera eyed the older woman intently, recognizing her as a TV news anchor from Manhattan. The cameraman following her looked just as amused as the reporter did. The name belatedly sank in, and she finally realized why Kenneth had been familiar. "Oh my god," she blurted. "You're Cameron's brother! You're Sarah's brother-in-law!"

He blinked. "The friend you said married an executive was Sarah?" He should have known!

"Yeah." Her eyes narrowed slightly. "And that means you're an executive too."

"Kenneth," the reporter quickly broke in, "can I have a minute of your time? I really want to ask you about your company's new campaign using Aenya Michaels. I came here to see her, and finding you was a lucky break."

He cursed softly under his breath. "Later, okay? I was *trying* to fit in."

"Oh." The reporter looked at Sera, saw the temper in her eyes, and winced. "Oh my."

"No worries." Sera took several steps to the side, carefully concealing the fact that her heart felt as if it was shattering inside her chest. She had never known a pain that sharp before. "We were done here, I think." She added softly, "I'm not mad at you, Ken. Okay? Trust me. Around here, we know what it's like to want to find a place where we don't stand out. And . . . Sarah was right about you. You're different than others I've known."

"Sera!" He reached for her arm but she evaded his grip. Before he could stop her, she ran off down the street. "Dammit!"

Miserable, the reporter said, "Kenneth, I'm so sorry. I didn't have any idea."

"No, how could you?" His eyes narrowed on her and the cameraman alike. "I trust I won't be seeing this on the six o'clock news."

"No, of course not! I'm not that kind of reporter." Genuinely unhappy, she added, "Did I mess everything up?"

"No . . . I think the fault lies with me." He took a long breath. "Call me for a comment later." He turned and walked away without waiting for consent. He would call a cab and get back to the office as soon as he could. He needed to talk to Sarah and find out everything he didn't know about his Sera. The woman of his dreams had entered his life, finally, and he would be damned if he let her get away now.

CHAPTER ELEVEN

Sarah was sitting on the side of Cameron's desk and watching him sign something when Kenneth walked in without knocking. "Help," he said without preamble.

His siblings looked at him and two sets of brows winged upward. He looked a little more frazzled than either was used to seeing, and Cameron was fairly sure that he recognized the frustration in the line of his brother's face and body. "Would you like to be more specific?" he asked politely.

Kenneth sighed and sank down in one of the visitor chairs. "Sarah, you have a friend named Sera?"

"Yeah, Sera Thomason." She smiled. "We always called it our personal joke that we had nearly identical names. But we're almost totally opposite in personality. I'm kind of like a peppermint and she's like a red hot."

"More like a cinnamon gumdrop," he muttered.

She pursed her lips as she tried not to laugh. There was only one way he would have known that. "Well, that explains where you've been the last two days. I take it she was wearing that cinnamon lip gloss she likes so much?"

He sighed deeply. "Yeah, she was."

"Okay, this I have to hear." Cameron grinned. "How did you find out what her lip gloss tastes like?"

"Yesterday, I went to the 3rd District to see what they might need in way of advertising. You know we were talking about taking on small businesses, and I figured that since Sarah was from there, we ought to start there. It's an amazing place. Well, I met Sera, with an E, when I almost got into trouble. Milly was doing an impersonation of a Rottweiler."

"You should see her German Sheppard impersonation," Sarah noted gravely.

"So I heard. Well, she, Sera I mean, agreed to show me around and answer my questions. Somewhere between Carroll Lane and Tolkien Avenue, I think I fell in love." He raked his hands through his hair. "And she hates executives. So there I was, stuck between a rock and a hard place. I was *going* to tell her, but I ended up kissing her instead."

"Actions speak louder than words?" Cameron struggled not to laugh.

"Boy do they! I couldn't tell her yet. I was so afraid she'd hate me. I had lunch with her and her mother. Then I went over there again this afternoon. I met more people, fell in love with her a little more. I wanted to make her fall for me before I told her. I think I was close to succeeding when disaster struck."

"Someone recognized you," Sarah guessed.

"Yeah. That stupid reporter from Channel 2 spotted me and gave me away before I could explain. Sera said she understood why I'd hid my identity, but she ran off before I could stop her! Damn it, Sarah, help me out here! What don't I know? Why does she hate executive types so much?"

Sarah tapped a finger against her cheek while she thought about it. "Okay, how much did she tell you about her dad?"

"Just that he died six years ago."

"Okay, so she didn't mention *how* he died?" When he shook his head, she sighed. "He was in a car accident with a drunken driver. The driver who hit him was an executive from one of the big hotel chains. He pretty much bought his way out of a manslaughter charge. Sera and her mother have been struggling hard since then. She won't even let *me* help her, Ken. All she has left is pride. You could go knocking on her door, but she wouldn't let you in anymore. If she

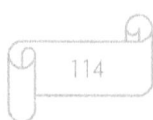

climbs out of being lower class, it'll be because she did it herself."

Cameron propped his chin on his hands. "How long would it take her?" he asked.

"I can't guess. It would probably help if she could get a job in her field and make a steady paycheck. She's working part-time."

"Not anymore. She said she was fired," Kenneth muttered.

"Well . . . hell."

"I need a distraction." He got to his feet. "I'm going to start going over applications." Thinking of Sera, he asked wistfully, "Did we really insist on a Bachelor's degree for our lead designer?"

Thinking the same thing, Sarah said, "Afraid so." She handed over the stack. As the door shut behind him, she sighed. "Well, now what do we do? We wanted him to find love, right?"

"Yeah." Cameron sat back in his chair. "We'll figure something out."

Lorcana was getting her nails done when her cell phone rang. She glanced down at the number and recognized it. She carefully pressed the answer button; she always wore an earpiece for her phone in case of just such a situation. "Hello, Patricia. What can I do for you?"

"It's more what I can do for you," her friend said. "You know that lamp thing you were interested in? I just heard about a kid in 3rd District who can *shapeshift*. My son had a college class with her and said she was pretty open about the skill. He even saw her shift once. She might be able to get that lamp for you."

"What's her name?"

"Sera Thomason. I have her address and everything. Actually, the name is familiar. I think my husband had dealings with her family once. I'm not sure. I don't really remember, frankly. She's so deep in the lower class that I'm surprised she even went to college."

"Email me the address," Lorcana said decisively. "If she can get me what I want, I'll be glad to pay her a nice sum. Money talks, even among those weirdoes in that District." She hung up the phone, her lips pursed. Really, she had nothing to lose at that point.

As soon as her nails were done, she called for her chauffeur and gave him the address Patricia had emailed her. She formulated her plan of attack on the way. She was well aware that lower class people clung stubbornly to their petty pride. She couldn't just throw money at the girl; she would probably refuse out of spite. No, she would have to figure out what she really wanted or needed and use that for leverage.

She hated the 3rd District. She always felt out of place there, and she was sure she hadn't mistaken the hostile looks fixed on her. She rang the doorbell on the ramshackle house and resisted an urge to wipe her finger on her skirt. This part of the District looked like it belonged in a slum; a historical slum, but one nonetheless.

When the door cautiously opened, she strove for a friendly smile. "Hello. Are you Sera Thomason?"

Warily, Sera asked, "Why? Who are you? You lost, or something? You're not from the District, that's obvious."

"No, of course not. My name is Lorcana Dease."

Sera knew immediately that she had to be looking at Kenneth and Cameron's mother. It only made her more wary. She knew what Sarah and Cameron had gone through, and the events had put Lorcana very far down in Sera's estimation. What the hell was the old broad doing at *her* house? Did she know about Kenneth? "What can I do for you, Mrs. Dease?"

"May I come in?"

"No, my mother is asleep." She stepped outside and firmly pushed Milly back into the house. The retriever was growling very low in her throat in a way that meant she liked Lorcana no more than Sera did. "Sorry, she's protective." She shut the door. "My mother is ill right now, and I don't want her to wake."

"Understandable. Now, I have a proposition for you, my dear. I

understand you're a shapeshifter. There's an item at the bottom of a well that I need you to get for me. I'd be willing to pay you for your time." Lorcana smiled casually. "I own a large company. I assure you, my money is good."

Sera bit her tongue before she asked if that was all that was good about her. "What well, what item, and how much are we talking?"

"The Frisk Well, it's an old lamp, and name your price."

"The Frisk Well? No wonder you need a shifter. Only frogs could get down there safely! Those bricks are slippery as hell." She crossed her arms. "Look, I appreciate the offer, but I'm not interested."

"Not even to buy medicine for your mother?" Lorcana made her voice sympathetic. "It must be very difficult, having a sick mother. Things are so expensive nowadays, after all. Do you have insurance? Does it cover everything?"

"Yes, we do, and no it doesn't." Her eyes narrowed slightly. She really wanted to kick Lorcana to the street. She was everything that Sera had always hated in bigwig, high power executives. She had also tried to make Sarah miserable. Sera was more of a 'two strikes' woman than a three strikes.

And yet . . . she couldn't deny that the money would be well used. It was a job, and god only knew that she had done some she hated for people she intensely disliked. "How much?" she asked again warily.

"Ten thousand?" Lorcana offered. "Would that work for you?"

Ten thousand would cover the medical bills, medicine, *and* groceries for at least a few months. She wouldn't have to rush into a new part-time job. Maybe she would even have a breather to find something she liked. "Okay," she decided. "Deal." She reluctantly shook Lorcana's hand. It seemed slightly stunning to think such a cold female had given life to two such amazing men. "You know where the well is?"

"Unfortunately, no. Do you?"

"Sure. It's not far from here. Follow me." She tucked her hands in her pockets and headed down the sidewalk, leaving Lorcana to follow at her own pace. Unable to resist, she asked innocently, "Didn't I read somewhere that your son got married?"

"Yes." The word was bitten out. "I just couldn't bear to be in the way of true love."

"You're such a good mother. You must love your sons a lot." She hid a grin as she heard Lorcana make a strangled agreement. Served her right!

The Frisk Well sat near the brooks that fed the Gentle Brook Inn less than a mile away. It was old gray stone covered in mossy vines, and the wooden roof had darkened with age. It was considered a wishing well around the District, and few ever asked for a wish that didn't come true. As such, when someone wished, they made sure it was something they really needed and wanted. Sera had never bothered to wish for her life to be better; it was way too much work for one poor wishing well.

As they stopped next to the well, she lightly put her hands on it. She stayed silent for several moments and Lorcana asked warily, "What are you doing?"

"Thanking the well for letting me jump down inside. Scoff if you like, but we take things seriously around here." A breeze tugged at the streaks in her hair teasingly and the sunlight glinted across her eyes.

Lorcana rubbed her hands over her arms. "Just hurry up."

"Sure thing."

Before her shocked gaze, Sera promptly turned into a small green frog. The older woman took a step back sharply, her heart pounding like mad. First the thing with the pea and the mattress, and now this. She had been pulled into some stupid faerie tale and she *loathed* it. "Get the lamp and get out. This is madness."

Sera hopped into the well and nimbly hopped down the slippery walls toward the water at the bottom. She turned into a fish just before landing and checked the depth of the water. It was only three feet or so, and she went back to normal to stand on her own feet. "Let's see if I can find that lamp."

It was dark as hell down that far since the sun couldn't reach all the way, but she finally found the small lamp wedged into a crevice in the wall. She pried it loose and studied it as best she could. It felt surprisingly heavy for its size. "Now how to get this out."

"Did you find it?" Lorcana called.

"Yeah," Sera called back, "but I'm not sure how to get it out. It's heavy. Seriously. The only bird I could turn into big enough to carry it wouldn't even fit in here! And I can't hop out like a frog."

On a little screech of frustration, Lorcana slammed the lid down on the well. "Rot for all I care! What a useless excursion this was!"

Sera could only stare up at where there had been, moments before, a circle of blue sky. "Hey!" she shouted. "No freaking way she just locked me in here!" She dropped the lamp and turned into a small bird to fly up to the roof. Try as she might, however, she couldn't push the heavy wood out of the way. Furious, frightened, she went back down to the water and changed back once more. "That bitch!"

Psst.

The faint feminine voice had her going very still. "Pardon?" she asked carefully.

The lamp! Rub the lamp, silly!

She scooped up the lamp, poured out the water that had gotten inside, and warily rubbed the side. She had seen stranger things in her life, including faeries who lived inside computers, so she wasn't going to be surprised to find a wishing well spirit living in a lamp.

She *was* surprised, however, when a tiny pink streak shot out the spout and bounced erratically off the sides of the well. On a shriek, she ducked and covered her head protectively before she got hit by flying sparks.

A warm light began to illuminate the area and she cautiously lowered her arms. Her eyes slowly widened as she straightened and stared at the small creature hovering in front of her. "No way," she breathed. "Are you . . . a dragon? Wait, I thought *genies* lived in lamps."

The small dragon snorted and ruffled the fins on her head. "And who said genies had to be human-like, huh? That smoky, wispy thing is *so* out of date." She landed on Sera's shoulder. "I'm Dazzle, and I'm a genie-in-training! You got my lamp, you summoned me, and so you get to use my power! As long as you wish for non-selfish things, I can grant you wishes forever. Selfish wishes deplete my power, and eventually I won't have any more."

"What happens then?"

"I lose the ability to grant wishes. Eventually, if I can't regain any power, I'll disappear."

Sera frowned. "Then would wishing myself out of here be selfish?"

"Nope! That would be a wish of self-preservation, so it's totally cool." Dazzle's face wrinkled up as she concentrated. She began to glow hot pink as she called on her power. "I'm new at teleporting, so hang on tight."

"Oh god." Sera squeezed her eyes closed as she felt the spell hit. When she carefully opened her eyes a moment later, she found herself at the top of a large tree. "Gah!" She grabbed the branch she was on and held tight. "Damn it, aim *lower* next time!"

"Er, sorry about that."

She just sighed and turned into a monkey to climb her way down. She turned back at the bottom and brushed at the muck on her jeans. "Yuck. Man, what a disaster that almost was! I knew she was a bitch, but I didn't know she was *that* nasty. She could have killed me!" She crossed her arms and tried to ignore the fact that Dazzle flew alongside her with the lamp. "No wonder she wanted your lamp. She must've heard it granted wishes."

"Yup yup. That's right. But now I belong to you. You're my master, okay?"

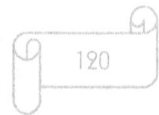

"Just call me Sera." She opened her front door and went inside as quietly as possible. Milly slept near the door but woke up to follow Sera to her bedroom. If she was at all unnerved by Dazzle, it certainly didn't show.

Once the bedroom door shut, Sera stripped off her wet clothes. "I cannot believe this. I don't even know *what* to wish for. And I don't want to wish for selfish things. Can you tell me if something is selfish so I can decide if I really want it?"

"Sure, there are no rules against it."

"Is there anything you can't do?"

"Interfere with free will," was the prompt response. "I can't do something to someone that they wouldn't do by themselves on their own. Like . . . I couldn't make Lorcana a decent person even if every person in the world wished for it. She's bad to the core, seriously. But I could give her horns." She brightened, the fin on the tip of her tail twitching happily. "Wish for that!"

"*No!*" Sera had to grin though. "Tempting as it is." She pulled on fresh clothes and sat down on her bed. "Okay. If I was going to wish for anything, I'd wish for my mom to be healthy again. Can you do that?"

"Absolutely! I can't do it all at once, but I can start making all the problems get better." Dazzle flew over to land on the footboard. "I'll turn her medicine into vitamins." She nodded firmly. "She'll be just fine within a week, just another of the District's miracles."

Sera let out a long breath. "That's fine with me. I just . . . can't lose her too."

"So . . . what do you want for yourself?" Dazzle climbed up the poster on the footboard and perched at the top. "You made a big unselfish wish, and now you can have a selfish one. What do you want?"

"Hmm." She looked at the battered computer sitting on her desk. It barely ran its operating system let alone the programs she needed. "How about a new computer and the non-bootleg versions of the programs I need to do my art?" She laughed. "Well, technically, they'd still be bootleg, huh?"

"I dare anyone to prove that they aren't legal." Dazzle flew over to the computer and around it so fast that her glow blinded Sera briefly. When the glow faded, the old desktop had been replaced with a shiny new model and a stack of discs sat beside it. "You'll have to install them," she apologized. "I'm still learning. Last time I tried to auto-install something, I made the whole machine start speaking in tongues."

"I'll enjoy every minute of it, no worries. How'd you know what kind of comp to give me?" She ran a hand over the top reverently. She also had not one but *two* huge monitors.

"Hey, I might be only just learning my powers, but I know my way around computers. My last master taught me a lot. She was really good with them."

"That's really cool."

"So . . . now what?" Dazzle landed on her shoulder. "There's got to be more. I mean, if you had everything you needed to be happy, then you wouldn't have even woken me up. So there's got to be more."

"I want a job I can love," she said softly. "But I don't think that's something you can give me, Dazzle."

"Hmm." Dazzle thought about that. "What would you need to get your job?"

"A degree, for one thing." A rolled up paper appeared and dropped into her hands. "No way. You did *not* do what I think you just did."

"Sure did." The fins on her head cocked at different angles as she grinned. "It's just a piece of paper. You've got the stuff you need in here." She patted Sera on the head. "And it's all official and stuff. Anyone who checks will see that you graduated this semester."

"Do I have a good GPA?" Sera asked dryly.

"I left it where it was. You can't knock a B+ average, y'know. Now what? I'm having fun! I like granting you wishes. They aren't selfish at all. There's too much good in your heart for that. You're like

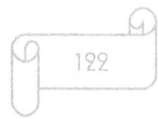

my last master. She was good too. So I'm gonna do my best, okay, Sera?"

"I feel . . . dazed." She sank down and sat on the floor against her bed. When Milly moved closer, she scratched her ears lightly. "I can't believe this is happening. I mean, sure, I believe in the impossible, but this is surreal even by District standards."

"Well . . . what else do you want?"

Unbidden, an image of Kenneth popped in her mind. "Something you can't give me," she murmured

Speculatively, Dazzle asked, "A man?"

"Bingo."

The dragon-genie tapped her claw on her jaw as she thought about it. "Kenneth Dease, right?"

"I'm not even asking how you knew that."

"Good idea. Well . . . I can't get you *him* per se, but I can get you close to him. Did you know his company is looking for a lead graphic designer?"

Her head jerked up sharply. "What?"

"Yeah, they're doing interviews tomorrow. I could get you an interview. You'd have to get the job yourself, but you'd be close to him." She wiggled her butt in a manner not dissimilar from a cat about to pounce, and a folder appeared on Sera's lap. "That's their qualifications and what you need to bring."

"Let's see." Sera flipped the folder open and ran a finger down the list of knowledge requirements. "I have all these. And I've got the portfolio to prove it." She groaned suddenly. "Wait, I can't do this. Lorcana's going to know who I am."

"She's not doing the hiring." Dazzle's voice sounded smug. "She's being transitioned. You'll be interviewing with Kenneth and Cameron. And they're businessmen enough to hire you only if you're good. They wouldn't hire you *just* because they like you. It'll help though. Ooh! You'll need a nice suit!" She glowed and a stylish black suit appeared on the bed.

"I didn't wish for that," Sera noted warily.

"Pre-emptive wish. You would've wished for it eventually."

"I . . . hmm." She studied her genie. "So just where did you come from again?"

"The lamp." The dragon smiled angelically.

Somehow she got the feeling that that wasn't the whole truth, but she didn't push the issue. She'd had enough to deal with for one day!

CHAPTER TWELVE

Kenneth didn't sleep that night. He couldn't. There were simply too many thoughts tumbling in his mind for him to shut everything down and rest. He wanted to go to Sera. He had to go to her. But what was he supposed to say? She was too conscious of the difference between their classes.

The sleepless night turned out to be more visible than he thought. When he arrived at work the following morning, Louise handed him her cup of coffee as he walked past her desk. "Do I look that bad?" he asked wryly.

"Worse."

"Great." He took the coffee with him as he headed for his office. He had gone over the applications before passing them to Cameron to review. They had five designers they were interested in, and all were available for interviews that day.

To his surprise, there was another application sitting on his desk. "Where'd this come from?" As he picked it up, he went very still. It couldn't be a coincidence. There were no coincidences.

The applicant was Sera.

"That was on my desk when I got here," Cameron offered from the doorway. "I had Sarah call her to come in. She's way more qualified than anyone else we're seeing today. If her portfolio is as good as I'm hoping, our decision will be easy."

Kenneth ran a finger over where she had written 'Bachelor's in Graphic Design, 2016.' "I thought she said that she didn't have her degree."

"I called the college and checked. They confirmed it. Something weird is definitely going on, Ken." He grinned. "But I'm not knocking our luck. If she's coming to you, all the better. You look a little . . . sleepless."

"Get out of my office, Cam."

With a snicker, his brother backed out. "Try not to hit on her during the interview."

"Smartass," he muttered. He tossed the application down on his desk and crossed his arms. Something was definitely up, and as soon as he had a chance, he would pin Sera down and find out what had happened.

He was forced to bide his time. Sera ended up as the last scheduled interview and that meant he had to sit through five other applicants. Not that they weren't talented or genuinely likeable. They just weren't the person he had waited his entire life to find.

Sarah was in the middle of checking out one applicant when she saw Sera walk in. "Sit," she ordered. Her friend smiled wryly and sat down, and she grinned at the young man she was currently helping. "I've known her for years. I can get away with things like that."

He grinned. "I have a friend like that." He winked at Sera. "Good luck."

"Thanks." She waited until he headed out and then walked over to her friend's desk. "Well. Nice digs. That your husband's office behind you?"

"Sure is. He used to have a closet but upgraded recently." Sarah studied her. "Degree, huh?"

"It's a really long story. I promise I'll explain everything later. Let's just say that yesterday hit a whole new level of unreal, even for the District." She blew out a hard breath. "How do I look? I've never worn a suit before."

"You look amazing." Her eyes twinkled. "Sort of sexy, so I do hope Ken can concentrate on your art portfolio and not your physical one." She got to her feet. "I'll show you to the conference room."

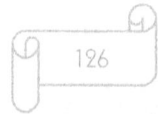

"Yeah, sure." Sera's hands tightened around her portfolio as she tried to ignore the way her stomach dipped and rolled like a particularly unhappy ocean. The lamp was tucked safely in her purse but it wouldn't be much use. She was on her own and she knew it.

Kenneth looked up when the door opened and his jaw dropped as he saw her. He was on his feet before he even being conscious of moving. A tailored black suit did amazing things to an already amazing body, but he missed her paint-streaked jeans. She was an artist, not an executive. "Sera."

She held her portfolio like a shield. "I'm interviewing," she warned him. "Keep your hands off!" When Cameron cleared his throat, she found a smile for him. "Hi again. You sure you two aren't twins?"

"Positive," he said dryly. "Nice to see you again, Sera. Now hand over that portfolio." He took it when she held it out and then dropped it on the table to spread out the pieces inside. "While we look at this, tell us what you can do."

She sat down and took a deep breath. She could do this. "Well, I've been self-taught for a long time, but I just completed my degree as well. I know the Adobe Creative Suite . . ."

The brothers listened intently, most of their attention on the work she had brought. Without bias, she had by far the best portfolio of anyone who had interviewed. Kenneth had been expecting it after seeing the piece she had done for the club, but the work in her portfolio was even better. "How are you at work on the fly?" he asked.

She blinked. "Good. Why?"

He slid a sketchpad across to her. "I'm going to describe a concept, and I want you to draw it." He slid across a box of pencils as well.

"Go for it." She held one pencil in her hand and stuck different ones over each ear so they were in easy reach. The gum eraser was brand new; she had to stretch and squish it around until she felt surer it would pick up pencil cleanly.

Unbeknownst to her, all of her actions got added like points to her already high score. "Okay, here's the idea. It's a poster. Flashy, modern, and edgy," he began. "It's an ad for sunglasses. The background is sharp angles so the round edges of the glasses pop. The glasses are red, so give a green background."

"Blue," she argued. "If you want it to pop, then clash your colors. Red against blue will be much more dramatic." She twirled her sketch around. "See? And anyway, people are conditioned to see red and green and think Christmas. You have to be careful with them."

The brothers exchanged a long look. "Okay," Cameron said finally. "You're hired."

The pencil hit the table with a clatter. "I'm *what*?"

Kenneth grinned at her. "Don't sound so shocked. You've got the best qualifications, you've got the best portfolio, and you were willing to argue with your future bosses when they were wrong about an art concept. You're absolutely hired."

"I think I'm going to pass out." She pushed back from the table, her head spinning. "Or I'm going to be sick. I got the job?" She shook her head hard when he came around the table. "Don't touch me. I'm freaking out here. Do you know how badly I wanted this?" she demanded. "It's my *dream*."

"And now you have it." He tugged her up to her feet and kept her possessively tucked under his arm. "And now that business is done, we have some personal things to talk about." He held tighter when she tried to get free. "You might be almost as tall as I am, but I'm certainly stronger. I'm kidnapping Sera," he added as he dragged her past Sarah's desk.

She grinned. "Good."

"Traitor!" her friend muttered. She glanced up and saw Lorcana and felt her stomach clench with fear. "Oh crap."

He spotted his mother and held her tighter. "Problems other than the obvious?"

"Part of the explanation I owe you," she whispered.

Lorcana walked closer and stared intently at Sera. She knew

she wasn't imagining things. Really, how could there be two tall females with pink streaks in their hair? The little twit must have found a way out of the well after all. "And you are?"

"Our new lead designer," Kenneth informed her coolly. "And if I play my cards right, she might even agree, finally, to go out with me. She might be your next daughter-in-law, so I wouldn't be burning your bridges yet, Mother."

She hissed something unpleasant under her breath. Suspicious, she eyed them as they walked away. Something smelled rotten around here. What was that little nobody up to?

"Precisely where are you taking me?" Sera demanded.

"My office." He ushered her inside and shut the door firmly. "I don't want interruptions."

"I guess you really want that explanation."

"That's not all I want." He framed her face with his hand and kissed her hungrily. His other hand dropped to her waist and dragged her tighter against his aching body. Desire? It had gone beyond that. This was obsession. Craving. "So you won't date me," he muttered against her lips. "Can we skip to the part where you'll put me out of my misery and let me be your lover?"

"Ken." It was little more than a moan as his hands opened her jacket and got to work on her blouse. She desperately grabbed for control and caught his hands before he could make her forget her name. Her entire body vibrated like a piano string with too much tension in it. "I will not have my first time on top of a desk."

His head lifted quickly. "Pardon?"

She scowled. "Weren't you listening when I said I wasn't casual?"

"You're twenty-one," he said with a matching scowl. "I'm entitled to have believed you'd had to have had at least one serious relationship."

"Not *that* serious. You're the first guy I've ever wanted to be serious about in that way, okay?" She let go of his hands and carefully refastened her blouse, her fingers trembling as she did. He wasn't the only one going out of his mind. How the hell did a body crave something it hadn't had before? No wonder it was called frustration!

He took a long breath. "I used to have self-control. Then I met you." He took a healthy step backward and put his hands in his pockets. It was either that or tumble her down onto the floor. She had worn that damned lip-gloss again and it only enhanced her natural flavor. She looked rumpled and flushed and *damn it* he wanted her so bad it hurt. "Talk. Quick."

She drew a shuddering breath and pressed her fingers to her lips. "So I had a surprise visitor yesterday morning . . ."

By the time she finished explaining, he was staring at her in disbelief. That his mother had tried to kill her was little surprise; he knew her ruthlessness knew no bounds. And that there was a genie-dragon hybrid in a lamp didn't seem so hard to swallow either. It was having all of it together that blew his mind. He slowly sat down in one of the chairs. "Well."

"Please don't be mad," she said softly. "I just . . ."

"Why on Earth would I be mad?" he asked wryly. "We didn't hire you because of your wishes, and I sure as hell wanted you well before you had them. It's just a lot to take it." He pressed his hands together and tapped them against his chin while he thought. As far as he was concerned, nothing had changed. Nothing except that a few more barriers had been knocked down between him and the woman he loved.

"Alright." He got to his feet. "I'm simply going to count my blessings now I have you close enough at hand that I can chip away at your stubbornness." When she warily backed up, he moved closer and trapped her against the desk. His lips skimmed tenderly over her cheek. "Let me be yours," he breathed softly. "I need you, Sera."

Her lashes fluttered closed as his lips claimed hers in a kiss so tender that it stole all the strength from her body. It felt, almost, like he loved her. Could he? Of their own will, her arms wound around his waist to hold on tight. She loved him so much.

They eased apart and his trembling fingers skimmed through

her hair. "Let me come over for dinner. You don't have to date me," he coaxed, "but let me be part of your family."

She was so doomed. "Alright," she finally conceded. "Come over for dinner tonight. Mom was feeling so well this morning that she's going to be bored real soon. She'd love company. She likes you a lot."

"Good. Now that we have that settled, let's talk business." He smiled. "You need to meet the people you're going to be working with, and over."

As she heard them approaching the door, Lorcana beat a hasty retreat. Her heart pounded hard with a combination of fury and desperation. Sera had used the lamp. She should have known that was what was going on! At least it was true that the lamp gave wishes. Now she just had to get her hands on it!

When Kenneth and Sera walked into the area where the other designers were located, Louise had to work to cover a smile. "Nice to meet you," she told Sera solemnly. "I'm Louise, but most call me Lou. Since you're not officially my supervisor yet, I feel free to tell you this: please put Kenneth out of our misery. He's been hell to live with these last few days."

"Hush!" Kenneth scolded her. "I'm working on her all by myself, thank you. She's letting me have dinner with her and her mother."

Torn between horror and amusement, Sera had nothing to say to that. She was greatly enjoying herself regardless. It seemed a little . . . daunting that she would not only be working in her field, but that she would be overseeing the work of this many other talented people. She was equally flabbergasted when he showed her into the office she would use. "It's huge!"

"Yeah, our last lead had been here forever. He picked the spot when the place was made. You get to reap the rewards." He leaned against the door and smiled. "Do you still think you're walking through a dream?"

"I should be waking up any minute now," she admitted. She held up her hands warily when he stepped closer. "Don't you dare touch me, Ken!" She darted out of his reach. "Don't you have any self-control?"

"Where you're concerned? No." He snagged her wrist and tugged her close. "Let's get some lunch. Not a date," he assured her. "Just lunch. You've got to be hungry. I know I am. There's a cute bistro not far from here."

"Oh just go out with him!" a male scolded as he went past the open door. "We saw your work; we know you didn't seduce your way into your position."

"Pity for me," Kenneth murmured.

Sera groaned and covered her face with her free hand. "Fine. Alright. Let's get lunch. I didn't eat breakfast, so I am kind of hungry." She freed her hands and stuck them in her pockets. "No more holding my hand, got it?"

"Fair enough." Instead, he lightly rested his hand on the small of her back. The gesture was very possessive and as subtle as neon. Not touch her at all? Over his dead body. This was practically a war that he fought, and he would be damned if he lost.

The bistro was small but lively, and he was a frequent enough visitor that the waiter happily found them a small table out of the way of the crowd. As they settled in with sandwiches and coffee, Sera felt some of the tension fading from her shoulders. She let out a long breath.

"Decompressing?"

She smiled wryly. "Finally. I think it finally sank in. The weights just lifted from my shoulders. I mean, I know my mom is going to get better, but now I can support us until she's on her feet again. I can't depend on Dazzle for everything. That would definitely be selfish."

"You know," he said softly, "my dad would have adored you. He was hell on wheels, but he loved Cam and I. When we were little, and old enough to realize our mother hated us, he told us that he stayed with her because of us. He knew the courts might side with a mother over a father, and he didn't want that chance. If he'd known he would die from lung cancer, he'd have quit smoking."

She gently covered his hand with hers. "I almost envy you," she said just as softly. "You had some warning it might happen. I had none. Dad went out to get ice cream, and a few hours later, a member of Enforcers was at our door to tell us what had happened. A drunk driver."

"Enforcers told you?"

"Yeah. If something affects a member of 3rd District, the Enforcers are notified first. They personally tell the people involved."

"I knew they had clout, but, damn." He turned his hand over and laced their fingers together. "I liked it there," he admitted softly. "When Cam told me it felt like being home, I didn't really understand until I was there myself."

"I can't envision living anywhere else."

He softly rubbed his thumb over her palm. "But could you? Would you be happy in a big place with plenty of room for artistic expression?"

Her heart began to beat harder. "If I knew I was somewhere I would be loved, yes. I can put down roots anywhere as long as I know I will be happy." Barely breathing, she searched his face. "Why do you ask?"

He brought her hand to his lips and kissed her wrist tenderly. "I'll tell you tomorrow morning," he said huskily. "I want to talk to your mother first." He reluctantly released her hand, his fingers caressing her skin as he did. "How do you feel about starting work this afternoon? We have a meeting with a company, and we definitely need your on-the-fly art skills."

"As long as my pay starts this afternoon," she smiled, "I don't mind at all."

He laughed. "A woman after my own heart."

He had no idea, she thought morosely, how bad she really wanted his heart. And his smile. And his body. And damned near everything about him. Men like him could easily make a woman completely lose her sanity.

"By the way," he added an hour later as they walked back into the office, "feel free to dress more casually when you're not going to be at a meeting. If you look around, you can get an idea for the style around here. But if we've got a meeting, then you'll need to break out this lovely suit." Wistfully, he said, "I never thought I'd look forward to meetings."

She glanced down at the suit, half-expecting to find it had suddenly become skintight and made of leather. "It's just a normal skirt."

"On your legs, it's an invitation to ogle." He brought her hand briefly to his lips. "See you at 3:00."

She blew out a breath as he walked away and then firmly walked into her new office. She sat down behind the desk and dropped her head on the top. "What have I gotten into?"

"Ahem."

She glanced up and found Louise in the doorway. "Sorry. Did you need something?"

"Your first official duty." She walked over and put down her timesheet. "Sign please." She eased a hip onto the side of the desk, a smile teasing her lips. "So. Do tell what's going on with you and Kenneth. Obviously you two knew each other before you interviewed."

"By three days. Or maybe two and half?" Sera signed the timesheet and slid it back across the desk, marveling at the concept. *She* approved time now? "It's complicated. I didn't even know he was a Dease until some reporter gave away his identity." She rubbed her forehead. "And there I was, falling real fast for some guy, and he turned out to be in charge of a huge company. I was, until today, seriously low class, Lou."

"A classy low class," Louise told her. "All that bull about position is just that. Around here, it doesn't matter where you're from so much as what you do with your life. Kenneth fell for *you*, hon. He didn't fall for what you might become. Did he even know you were interviewing here?"

"No. Heck, I didn't even know until last minute." She frowned

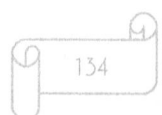

thoughtfully. "You think he might love me?"

Louise sighed affectionately. "You're so cute." She hopped to her feet. "I always wanted a little sister; now I have two between you and Sarah. I just find it ironic that you both supervise me now."

"You're not offended?"

"Heck no! I'd rather focus on my work than keeping this loony bin in line *any* day." She winked. "Just let me know if you need someone to talk to, okay?"

Sera found herself smiling. She would definitely like Louise. Having a big sister sounded pretty wonderful. "You got it. Now get to work." Her smile became a grin. "I always wanted to say that."

"Fun, huh?" With a grin, Louise headed back to her desk. She would have to talk to Michael and Becky and they could start planning a secret bridal shower for Sera. There was no question in her mind how this would end.

Cameron had entered the lobby of the building after running out for a sandwich when he was surprised to see a stranger studying the elevator listing. She was *tiny*. Not only short but overall delicate and slender. Her silvery hair seemed more like feathers than human hair. When she turned and smiled at him, her violet eyes sparkled merrily. "Hello," she said.

"Well, hi." He smiled as he stopped next to her. He had to smile. There was something that felt genuinely likeable about her. "Are you looking for someone?'

"I was looking for you." She held out a folder. "This is important, Cameron, okay? You need to make sure Kenneth and Sera sign this contract."

"Contract?" His eyes widened. "Wait, are you from Enforcers?"

She giggled and ran off through the lobby. "Bye!" she called over her shoulder. She narrowly missed bumping into both the security desk and a person entering, but everyone who watched her had a smile.

Wondering what she had given him, he flipped open the folder and started reading. A slow grin began to cross his face as he saw what was being set up. Not that he had doubted a happy ending, but this would just be insurance. Still, he could only shake his head in bemusement as he hit the call button for the elevator. Enforcers employed some really interesting people. He would have sworn he had just met a wingless faerie.

Sera had settled into her new office by the time the meeting drew close. She had found the supply closet, been cheerfully helped by a graphic geek named Michael, and now had most of what she needed. The other items, such as her preferred choice in sketchpad and drawing utensils, she would bring from home. Electronic drawing tools came courtesy of the job, and she was a very happy camper.

After a glance at the clock, she gathered up her things and headed for the conference room. As she left her office, a cheerful woman with pale blonde hair walked up. "Hi. I'm the tech geek around here."

Sera grinned. "I'm the new art geek. Normally I'm called Sera."

"Emily." She saluted with a CAT cable. "I'm here to hook up your email and stuff. It'll be done by the time you're back from your meeting."

"Great. Thanks." Still marveling at the day, Sera headed for the meeting. She was doing what she loved, and she got to work near the man she loved. Could it get any better?

Cameron waited for her outside the meeting room. "Hey, there you are," he said with a smile. He held out a document. "Your signature, ma'am. Some of the last paperwork for your position. We're informal on most things except procedure."

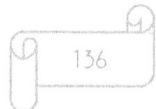

"Sure." She signed at the bottom without looking twice. "Any hidden language about servitude?"

"It's standard language. Ken didn't write it." He grinned when she stuck her tongue out at him. He had always wanted a big sister. Sure, she wasn't *that* much older, but it still counted. Whistling softly, he waited for Kenneth. When he spotted him, he said, "Last formality and Sera is officially ours. Yours. Well, something to that effect."

Kenneth grinned and scrawled his signature next to Sera's. "Anything about servitude in there?"

"You two think far too much alike." He folded the contract and tucked it safely into a pocket inside his jacket. He refused to let it out of his sight until he was positive it was no longer needed. Like after the honeymoon.

As he walked into the conference room, Lorcana edged around the corner she had been standing near. She checked twice, made sure no one was paying attention, and hurried to Sera's office. The tech was finishing up, and she hid where she wouldn't be seen. Internally, she bemoaned her current state. She had gone from being in charge to being forced to hide so she could steal a lamp from a stupid peon.

Emily left the office and Lorcana darted inside, heart pounding. She spotted Sera's purse and opened it quickly. The lamp sat inside. She snatched it up, zipped the purse closed, and scuttled out of the office. She didn't breathe until she entered the tiny office she had to use until she left for good.

Hands trembling, she rubbed the lamp quickly. A bright pink glow lit the area and she held her breath. When the glow cleared, a small dragon hovered in front of her. "A dragon?" she demanded. "Shouldn't there be a genie?"

"Uh-oh." Dazzle stared at Lorcana. "You're not Sera."

"No." She smiled tightly. "I'm your new master, and you need to grant my wishes. I want the company." She paused as she thought about it. "You know, I want more than that. I want revenge on that stupid shifter and my idiot son. Give me a contract that says Kenneth is willing to marry the woman of my choice and will turn over his shares upon marriage."

Dazzle reluctantly produced the document. "I can't forge his signature," she warned. "It would be interfering with free will; he'd have never signed this willingly, and I can't make it look like he did."

Lorcana scoffed. She picked up a pen and signed Kenneth's name at the bottom of the document; the signature looked nearly identical to his real one. "I've forged my boys' signatures for years. If no one gives me what I want, then I take it. I used to forge their father's signature as well." She studied the contract in satisfaction. "I'll call that nice woman who was willing to marry Cameron and see if she wants Kenneth instead. Everything is going to be just the way I want it." She frowned as Dazzle lost lift and plopped onto the side of the desk. The dragon didn't look . . . healthy. "What's wrong with you?"

"I'm tired. Can I rest, master?"

"Oh. Sure. I'll call you if I need you again." As Dazzle disappeared into the lamp, she picked up the phone and began to punch numbers. Finally. Finally she was going to get what she deserved. And once she had Kenneth's share, it wouldn't be long before she got rid of Cameron as well. Her wish granting dragon would see to it.

CHAPTER THIRTEEN

The meeting went smoothly, and better than expected. While ideas fired from all around the table, Sera kept up with the demand. She produced sketch after sketch, made dozens of changes, and was fast enough to ink anything that became set in stone so she could change around it safely. Though Cameron and Kenneth had come up with the original concept, the company receiving it was very particular about their promotions.

Still, when they left at the end, they looked very happy with the result. They had two print ad concepts that Sera would turn digital, and the ideas from those print ads would be given to the 3D animation unit to be made into a gimmicky television commercial.

The door shut behind them, and Sera held up her carbon covered fingers. "I look like a coal miner," she said ruefully. "I didn't start pushing my hair out of my face, did I?"

"No, you're clean," the lead animator, a woman named Becky, assured her. She grinned suddenly. "And now you know why I work with computer pencils and not physical ones. I never walked out of an art class looking like a zebra." She pondered that. "Okay, I did once, when they made me take fundamentals of art. I vowed off charcoals ever again."

Sera grinned back. "I could tell some horror stories too." She rolled her shoulders and gratefully accepted the napkin Kenneth offered. "Thanks, Ken." She wiped at her fingers. "I've never made so many changes so fast before. It was fun."

"Thank god," Cameron said sincerely. "I was afraid you'd run screaming. You artists are so temperamental."

"We grow artists tough in the District."

Kenneth glanced at the clock. "That's it for the day, guys. Let's break and meet tomorrow morning at eleven. Will that give you enough time to get a rough digital outline?" he asked Sera.

"Since I'm starting at eight, sure." She looked at Becky. "I can send you the digital frame to use to make the character models. You'll have it by ten-ish, okay?"

"That's perfect."

Kenneth smiled as he fell into step beside Sera as they left the office. "You're fitting in like you always belonged here." His hand lightly rested at the small of her back. "I definitely don't care how you got here. I'm just glad you did." He followed her into her office and shut the door behind him.

She eyed him warily. Since the office only had windows to the outside, no one in the main area would see them. Then again, she doubted it would stop him. She edged back as he stalked toward her slowly. There was something not quite civilized in his eyes as he approached. Something dangerous and predatory in the small smile on his lips. She bumped into her desk and leaned back when he leaned in. Her pulse began to beat harder as her entire body heated to flashpoint.

"It was torture," he said raggedly, his voice rough, "to sit there and watch you across the table. I'm shocked I didn't say something stupid. I'm more shocked I didn't simply pounce on you. Are we still strangers?" His hot hands closed around her arms and he gave her a little shake. "Are we strangers, Sera? I don't think we are."

"You terrify me. It's just all too much." She shuddered as he pressed a hot kiss to the side of her neck. Her entire body ached for his. She could actually feel her breasts throbbing with the need to feel his hands. Everywhere she had a pulse, it beat out a crazy rhythm that demanded his caress. Colors whirled at the edge of her vision, hot and bright.

"Sera."

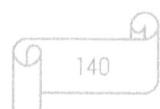

On a moan, she turned her head and found his mouth with hers. His tongue thrust hungrily into her mouth and her knees nearly gave out. Only his hands held her up. The kiss devoured her, dragging her into the erotic spell he could weave so easily over her. She surrendered on a shudder. It hurt too much to fight. She loved him. Needed him. She would never stop. "Your place or mine?" she asked huskily.

His head lifted sharply and his darkened green eyes searched hers. All he saw was a melted pool of hot and welcoming gold. Something mysterious, something feminine, lurked in the depth of her gaze, and a small, ancient smile touched her kiss-swollen lips. "Are you sure?" he demanded.

"I never say anything I don't mean." She wound her arms around his neck and rested her forehead against his. "So, which is it?"

"Mine." His lips slowly curved. "I still want to have dinner with you and Cecily. Then I'll kidnap you back to my place and sneak you into my room."

"Will you have your wicked way with me?"

"I'm going to have you any way I can." His teeth nipped at her lip in a sensual threat. "Consider yourself warned." He slowly released her and his hands slid slowly over her skin as he did. His fingers laced with hers. "Let's go."

She was nearly in a daze as she followed him. To those who observed their exit, there wasn't a single doubt that the couple was on the verge of self-combustion. In fact it seemed quite obvious that they wanted to be alone together, and as quickly as possible. Into the silence of their exit, finally someone said, "At least Ken will be easier to live with tomorrow."

"How did you get here?" Kenneth asked as he escorted Sera out of the building.

"Bus. I don't own a car, and I sure as hell can't ride a bicycle this far."

"That'll change," he said determinedly. "Until you can get a car you want, I'll carpool with you." His lips curved ever so slightly. "Then again, you'll be at my place most nights, so it won't be hard."

How permanent was he thinking? She couldn't guess and she was too afraid to try. He hadn't said he loved her. Did he? He liked her, she knew that. And he definitely wanted her. Was that enough for her to get her happy ending?

Her thoughts halted when she saw the vehicle they approached. Her lips twitched. Her tough, high-level executive boss drove a Volvo. And not just any Volvo, but one that looked like it had been popular before he was born. It was clean, well-taken care of, and certainly dent and scratch free, but it was no flashy sports car. "I was totally not expecting this."

"Hey, I never claimed to go for the high life in everything." He looked at her evenly. "I work in advertising, Sera. I know how to look beyond the surface and see if what's inside is quality. And I don't hesitate to choose the best . . . even when it might not be considered top of the line."

She had the feeling they weren't talking about cars anymore but said nothing about it. She just got in without a word. She felt . . . odd. Suspended in a bubble. It was as reality no longer existed. The world had gone away. There was only her and Kenneth.

She was half-afraid she wouldn't be able to carry on a conversation with her mother, but when she let them into the house, she was surprised to find it empty. "Mom?" She went into the kitchen and saw a note on the fridge. Bemused, she read it twice to be sure.

"Where is she?" Kenneth asked from the doorway.

"On a date."

"A date?" His brows shot up.

"With Doc Matthews." She laughed suddenly. "I *knew* he seemed to have a personal interest. I'm really glad, for them both. They need each other. Seriously, the way he watched Mom was totally not how a normal doctor looks at a patient." She turned with a smile that slowly faded as she saw the look on Kenneth's face. Her breath caught.

"Exactly how did he look at her?" he asked softly.

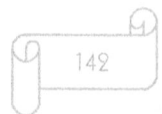

"Offhand," she managed to whisper, "I'd say it would be roughly like how you're looking at me right now."

The tension stretched as they watched each other. They were alone. They would be alone for hours. She found herself walking toward him slowly, drawn by a force she could not fight. He moved forward equally, and his hand lifted to brush his knuckles over her cheek.

The mood broke rather abruptly when Milly ran into the kitchen with a happy bark. She knocked into Sera, threw Kenneth off balance, and then proceeded to smother both with happy kisses when they landed in a heap on the floor.

"Damn it, Milly!" Sera started laughing as she tried to shove her dog away and get herself untangled from Kenneth at the same time. "What a way to spoil the moment!"

Kenneth propped himself up on his elbows with a grin. "But it's not a bad thing. I was two seconds away from tearing that suit off you and taking you on the kitchen counter." He rolled lithely to his feet before kneeling and lifting her into his arms.

"Gah!" She grabbed his shoulders desperately. "Okay, I know I'm not that heavy but I'm not *that* much smaller than you."

"I just happen to be that much stronger." He nuzzled his nose into her hair so that he could tease the hoop on the top of her ear with the tip of his tongue. Her breath broke and desire clawed at his body. "Direction?" he asked huskily.

"Hall. Left door." The ability to use words of more than one syllable had taken a hike along with her blood pressure.

Milly followed them but stopped when Kenneth shut the door in her face. Content, she curled up outside and her tail wagged happily. She liked her Sera to be happy. And she liked Kenneth. He was a keeper. She would have to teach him to play fetch.

Kenneth slowly let Sera's legs go so that she could stand on her own feet. He glanced around the room curiously and began to smile. It was obvious an artist lived there. It looked a whirl of color and pattern, somehow oddly chaotic and yet entirely harmonious. He couldn't wait to set her loose on his house.

He glanced at her to find her watching him, and the smile slowly left his face. He softly cupped her cheek and drew her in to could kiss her softly. The explosive force of the passion between them had suddenly tamed. Time. They had time. He deepened the kiss one breath at a time until her hands dropped to her sides in surrender.

He slowly eased back and began to unfasten her jacket. Her hands lifted and he brushed them aside. "Let me," he urged huskily. "I've wanted to do this all day." He slid the jacket down her arms and it fell onto the floor softly.

She couldn't find her breath or her will. There was so much more to this than she had ever imagined. She couldn't even tell whether it was her heart or her body that ached more. Couldn't be sure where she ended and he began. When his fingers slid inside her open blouse and skimmed across the top of her breasts, fire licked through her body. What was it in his touch that felt so good to her? "Only you," she said softly, her lashes lowering. "I was waiting."

His hands trembled for a moment. "Sera." Wonder filled his gaze as he let the blouse fall. She seemed impossibly perfect to his eyes with her curves barely held in check by the scrap of white silk hiding her from his gaze. "Look at you," he breathed.

Her lips slowly curved. "I'd rather look at you." She tugged on his tie until he leaned in closer for a kiss. Her nerves had evaporated. She didn't even remember them. Teasingly, she nibbled on his lower lip the way he always did to her. "I used to like my males to be much taller. But your height is so convenient, Kenneth." She eased up only slightly on her toes and blew lightly on his ear. "See?"

Any blood that had still been in his head seemed to gather much lower, fisting into a hard ache that demanded relief. Her fingers teasingly walked down his chest, and his stomach tightened in anticipation. "You're a tease." It was barely more than a rumble.

"Maybe." She nudged at his jacket and watched with hungry eyes as he shrugged out of it impatiently. The white-collar shirt he

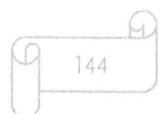

wore just emphasized the strength in his shoulders and made them seem wide and powerful, perfect for a weary shifter to rest her head on. She unfastened the buttons and laughed as she encountered his undershirt. "And men say women wear too many clothes."

"You do." He shrugged off the shirt and then tugged off his undershirt. Gloriously bare, he rested his hands lightly on her hips as his fingers played with the zipper of her skirt. "How's that?"

She traced a finger down the sculpted line of the muscles on his chest, loving how the pale hair covering them teased her touch. "I wouldn't have expected this from a guy who panders posters."

"He also lifts weights."

"Lucky me." Her lashes lowered slightly as she felt her skirt sliding down her legs. And slowly her lips curved as she heard his breath catch. "I'm not a pantyhose girl," she said solemnly, sensual laughter lurking in the tone.

"Now I'm the lucky one." He reverently skimmed his hand down her leg and tugged at the top of her thigh high stockings. He couldn't even say what was so sexy about them, but the way they emphasized her almost outrageously long legs was beyond belief. He caught her around the waist and lifted her onto the side of the bed. Slowly, like a man unwrapping a particularly anticipated present, he peeled the stockings down her legs and then off entirely.

She fell over onto her back and closed her eyes as she savored the feel of his hands on her body. The bed moved as he sat beside her and she looked up to see him leaning over her. Something beautiful filled his eyes. Something that might very well have been love. Emotion welled and stole her voice. All she could do was reach for him desperately.

He sank into her arms on a groan and kissed her deeply, his tongue dueling hotly with hers. One hand tangled in her wild black hair. The other swept up and down her body without course, almost as if he was memorizing her. Every touch fed the fire and spread the pleasure until her whole body quivered with desperate need.

He grasped the front of her bra and tugged hard. The back

broke open and he pulled the offending piece of clothing away and tossed it aside. He bent his head and greedily captured one tight nipple in his mouth. She was cinnamon everywhere; hot and spicy but sweet underneath.

Her back arched wildly and she grabbed his shoulders for balance. Every tug of his mouth tugged at something deeper and made a hot fist begin to gather inside. The ache seemed to center between her legs and spread outward. His name was little more than a cry of desire as he began to trail hot kisses down her stomach. "I'm going nuts," she managed to say.

"I've been nuts for days," he countered thickly. "Jesus, Sera. Where have you been all this time? I didn't even know I needed you." He stripped away her silk panties and eased back enough to sweep a possessive gaze over her naked body. His. Only his.

His fingers slid between her legs and softly slid through the silky black curls hiding her from his touch. Her mouth opened to say something but all that emerged was a soft moan when his fingers found where she ached most.

She was wet and hot, nearly burning him alive. He grasped wildly at control. He hurt with the need to be inside her. And she was ready for him. Dear god, she was ready. Her desire for him was as powerful as his for her. He watched her face raptly as he slowly slid a finger inside her body. His thumb teasingly brushed over the sensitive nerves at the apex of her legs.

Her hips arched wildly and her hands grabbed the covers for support. When he slid a second finger slowly, teasingly, into her, she suddenly jackknifed up and grabbed for him. He fell over onto his back with a rich masculine laugh. "Problem?"

"Two can play that game." She tossed her hair out of her eyes, and their golden color glowed with power and promise. "And you're not naked."

His grin turned dangerous. "That can be fixed."

They unfastened his belt and pants together, and she fiercely stripped them and his shorts down and off his body. When he was as

naked as she was, she sat back to look at him. That something deep inside heated and fluttered wildly as she saw how aroused he was. He wanted her. It seemed a glorious thing that he wouldn't care where she was from or that she might not be normal.

His breath hissed in as she lightly ran a fingertip down the length of his throbbing erection. His fingers dug into the blanket beneath him as he fought the urge to drag her over the top of him. The look in her eyes, the nearly wondrous discovery, was worth every agonizing second of torturous pleasure.

Her lips teasingly traced across his chest before nuzzling one flat nipple. Her tongue flicked lightly, as if to just taste, and his body jerked. Thrilling to having him at her mercy, she caressed and petted him softly, tasting anywhere she liked. His shoulder. His stomach. He was impossibly beautiful, impossibly perfect.

Her hot breath teased the tip of his arousal and he cursed under his breath. He caught her around the waist and rolled to pin her again. The soft skin of her legs caressed him as she naturally wrapped them around his hips as if they had been lovers forever. Her hands softly framed his face, her eyes darkening nearly to black as he slowly took her, and the sight was wildly erotic.

When he was as deep as he could go, he buried his face against her neck, his body trembling fiercely. "Sera." It was all he could say. She fit him so perfectly, her body made to align to his. The sensation was pleasure that bordered on pain.

She had no words for him. She could only kiss him, pouring everything she was into that simple thing. It was enough. He took her again and again, each time a little deeper, a little harder, until that something broke inside. It broke with the force of a hurricane, ecstasy rushing over her so hard and fast that there was no resisting it. No words to describe it. And when it took him as well, she could only hold onto him as tight as possible, never wanting to let go.

He caught most of his weight on his elbows as he collapsed against her, but that was the limit of his ability. After a few moments, when he felt surer his voice would work, he asked huskily, "Are you comfortable?"

"Don't mind me." Her eyes didn't open and her voice sounded drowsy with satisfaction. "I'll just stay here a while."

His lips curved. "I guess there's no need to ask if you enjoyed it."

"Never ask questions with obvious answers." She made a disgruntled sound as he gently disentangled their bodies. "I liked you where you were." She felt him leave the bed and opened her eyes curiously. "I thought post-coital glow was supposed to be one of the best parts."

"It is." He opened the door just enough for Milly to dart in. "But someone was being neglected."

Her heart happily melted. When he got back into bed and tugged the covers over them, she cuddled in as close as she could. A thrill filled her at how his arms went around her just right. She watched Milly curl up on the end of the bed with her favorite squeaky toy in her mouth, and she wondered why she didn't simply implode with joy. "I'm so glad my bed is big," she said with wry humor. "It can actually hold two people skirting dangerously close to the six foot mark and a Golden Retriever that doesn't realize she's almost as heavy as her owner."

He smiled and combed his fingers through her hair to tease out the pink streaks. "I always wanted a dog, but we couldn't have pets. They would make a mess. Or they might break something."

"Or they might make you happy," his lover muttered.

"Probably," he admitted. "Sure as hell the house has been happier since Mother went into the guesthouse. Cam's birthday is in barely a week. At that time, she's out for good from both the company and our lives. I can't even call it burning our bridges. There were never any bridges to burn."

"You going to stay all night?"

"I wish I could." He trailed a finger down her arm slowly. "Your mom might be miffed at me."

"Nah, she thinks you're hot. She wouldn't blame me at all."

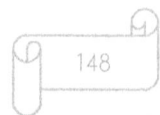

He snorted softly. "Be that as it may, I still want to talk to her. Then you and I are going to talk about us."

She sighed happily. "I can handle that."

Since there was no knowing when Cecily would be home, he reluctantly left around ten. Sera walked him to the door, wearing nothing but a robe covered in splotches of bright color. She was as vibrant as the art she made and glowed beautifully like a diamond in the rough. He loved her more than anything.

His good mood lasted only until he got home. When he walked into the house, he found Lorcana waiting for him. His smile faded as he hung up his jacket. "What?" he asked her curtly. "I'm tired and you're not welcome in *our* house."

Her smile more closely resembled a sneer. "We'll see about that, Kenneth. I have something you might want to look at. Be glad you got your lust for that little nobody taken care of. You won't be seeing her again."

A chill went slowly down his back. "Now what have you done?"

"Let's go into the office and talk about that, shall we?"

CHAPTER FOURTEEN

Sera woke the following morning feeling as if her entire world was finally right. She had her dream job. The man she loved might just love her as well. Nothing could possibly ever pull her down again.

She had no meetings that day. She opted for a pair of casual pants and a bright shirt that she knew Kenneth would love; he had the soul of an artist, too. She went to collect her purse, and she was startled to realize it wasn't anywhere in the house. In fact, she didn't remember grabbing it out of her office when she left. She wouldn't have normally worried, but Dazzle's lamp had been in there.

She waited for ten minutes, but Kenneth didn't arrive to pick her up. A feeling of trepidation began to fill her heart as she ran through the District to Brian's place. He was always awake early, and though puzzled, he was amiable to driving her to work. He didn't ask anything on the way; he could sense something going on.

She ran into the building, shoved through a surprising crowd of people in the lobby, and impatiently waited for the elevator. She couldn't shake the feeling that there was something terribly wrong. When the elevator dinged, she didn't get a chance to step inside because Louise stepped off. "Thank god," she said. She took Sera's arm and pulled her down the hall. "Sera, there's a big problem."

"What's going on?" She grabbed Louise's arm in turn. "Lou, what's going on? I can feel it. I can feel something wrong."

Louise took a deep breath. She hated what she had to say. "Ken arrived at work this morning looking as if his world had ended. I was so sure he'd be all smiles. We all knew he and you were going to take

the logical step in your relationship. He was supposed to be happy!" Her hands curled into fists. "But he wasn't. Apparently he's getting married."

"Wait. What?" Sera leaned against the wall before her legs could give out. Bile rose and she firmly pushed it down. "He's getting married? To who?"

"Janice Benton." Her blue eyes snapped with angry lights. "Let's just say that she and Lorcana get along *fabulously*. I tried to get Ken to tell me what the hell was going on, but he just shut down. All he would say was that sometimes you couldn't win."

Sera shoved past her and scrambled into the elevator. Her new friend stayed right behind her. "I can't accept this. I can't."

"There isn't much time, Sera. The wedding is in less than an hour."

The doors were barely open before Sera ran down the hall into the executive suite. No one in the office smiled. No one laughed. People watched her with sadness and with grief. She barely noticed. She went right into Kenneth's office without knocking. "Ken?" Her heart sank as she saw him sitting with his head in his hands.

He looked up slowly. The woman of his dreams. He had found her and he couldn't even keep her after all. One memory of one beautiful night was going to have to sustain him for a very long time. But her . . . she could have happiness. He just had to make her hate him first. He slowly got to his feet. "Hello."

Her hand curled tightly into the frame of the door. "So. I hear you're getting married in an hour."

"Yeah. Surprised me too. But I'd asked her a long time ago and she'd put me off." He jerked one shoulder up in a mockery of a casual shrug. "Guess our fun is over. Since we're going to have to work together, try not to make any scenes, okay?"

Not Kenneth. The voice seemed to whisper in her mind, but she didn't need to hear it. She knew she was not hearing the truth. For a man supposedly marrying the woman he wanted, he looked amazingly miserable. "Is that what you want, Ken?"

He averted his eyes. "Yeah."

She turned and walked away without another word. It almost seemed to him that he could literally feel her tearing out the biggest part of his heart and soul. On a violent oath, he doubled over and slammed a fist on the top of his desk.

"What the fuck is going on?" Cameron demanded sharply from the doorway. He walked in and violently kicked the door shut. "Ken, what's going on? You left before I could see you this morning, and Sarah and I hurried here expecting you to be walking on air. Instead we're hearing that you're marrying *Janice*. Damn it, bro, you want to explain?"

Kenneth slowly sat down. "You know all that paperwork that we had to sign to transition Mother out? Apparently she snuck something in when we weren't looking. A contract relating to that company we intend to absorb. Among the terms and conditions is a clause saying that, to cement the entire deal, I have to marry Janice because she's the niece of the owner. I can't back out, Cam. Do you realize how many people in that company will lose their job if we don't absorb it?"

"That's impossible." Cameron lightly touched his jacket pocket. Inside it was the contract he had made Sera and Kenneth sign. Suddenly it made all the sense in the world why he had been given it. "She had to have forged it. It has to be fake, Ken."

"And how are we supposed to prove it?" his brother demanded. "And it doesn't matter now anyway." He buried his face in his hands. "I sent Sera away. She must hate me now . . ."

Sera made it halfway through the office before sudden fury made her change her direction. She couldn't work there anymore. She couldn't bear to see Kenneth and know he would never be hers again. But if she was going out, she would go out with a big bang. Someone needed to tell Lorcana Dease off, and she was more than happy to do so.

Lorcana wasn't in her office. Disappointed, she started to leave when she spotted something sticking out of the desk. She moved closer to look and horror filled her. The lamp. It was the lamp. She pulled it out of the desk drawer and stared at the tarnish on the side. Lorcana had stolen the lamp. Had she done something to Kenneth?

No. No, she couldn't have. Dazzle couldn't impact free will. Whatever had happened, he had to be willing. She took a deep breath and rubbed the side of the lamp. Dazzle slowly appeared, but with none of her usual flare preceding her. The small dragon looked tired and sick, but when she saw Sera, she found a smile. "Sera. My real master."

"Oh Dazzle." Sera hugged her close. "I'm so sorry. If I hadn't left your lamp at work, this wouldn't have happened." She rubbed her cheek over her head. "Are you okay?"

"Lorcana's selfish wish used up nearly all my power." Her eyes closed for a moment but opened again. "I can grant you only one more wish, Sera. Then I won't have any more power. But I want to do this. I want you give you something." Her eyes closed again. "You made me so happy with all your unselfish wishes. I wanted to be with you forever . . ."

Sera bit back a sob as she hurried out of the office. She snuck back into her own and put the lamp back in her purse. She knew no one could see Dazzle. She wrote out a letter of resignation and left it on the top of the desk. Then, still keeping Dazzle close, she left the entire area and caught an elevator going down.

The lobby had packed with even more people. The wedding was being held in the auditorium, and even for such short notice, plenty of people had turned out. Other business owners were there, and people from the company Janice represented. Media had arrived, too, from several stations and at least one newspaper.

She made her way through the crowd and edged into the back of the auditorium. The wedding had only just started. Kenneth still didn't look like a happy groom, but Janice certainly glowed happily. Sera had to wonder if anyone had noticed her bouquet was already dying. The red roses had wilted almost entirely.

As the minister began to talk, Dazzle asked softly, "What's your final wish, Sera?"

There was no question in her mind what she wanted. If all Dazzle could grant was one wish, then there was only one thing to be done. She deserved to grant one last unselfish wish to make up for what Lorcana had done. "I want Ken to be happy." The weight of the lamp disappeared from her purse and Dazzle slowly dissolved from sight. Arms empty, heart breaking, she walked out of the auditorium. There was nothing else she could do.

Cameron was sitting in the front row, arms crossed and eyes narrowed, when Sarah suddenly grabbed his arm. He followed her gaze and his eyes widened as he saw the soft pink glow around the corner. He looked around quickly but saw no one looking at him. He promptly snuck from his seat and into the hall. To his surprise, the glow was a dragon. "Who are you?"

"I'm here to grant one last wish for my master." Dazzle glowed softly and a cassette tape appeared in Cameron's hand. "Lorcana Dease forged Kenneth Dease's signature. The evidence is on that tape from her phone. He is not bound by a false contract, but he *is* bound by a true Enforcers one."

He looked down at the tape and then up again but Dazzle had disappeared. A grim set to his chin, he snuck around to where the audio system was situated. He put the cassette in, thanking the gods that the system hadn't been upgraded, and then flipped the switch that transferred the speakers from the microphones to the internal audio.

Seconds later, Lorcana's voice came over the speakers. *Janice, you want to marry Kenneth?*

Janice's voice answered, *Like he wants to marry me. He's onto your games.*

Yeah, well, it doesn't matter. I've got his signature on a contract that says he'll marry you to cement that merger, and once married, he has to give his shares to you.

How'd you get that?

Ha. How do you think? I forged it. It's not the first time I've done

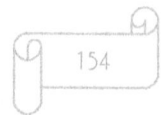

154

it. You think I ran all decisions past those two idiots I gave birth to? Please.

The entire auditorium began to buzz. Horror filled Lorcana's face as angry expressions slowly turned toward her. Reporters leapt forward and shoved microphones into her face. Janice began to look just as terrified as many eyes turned toward her as well.

Cameron darted around the system and jumped up onto the small podium beside his brother. "I've got more proof!" he announced firmly. He pulled out the contract. "This is a different contract entirely. Kenneth signed it willingly not even a few days ago. It states that he will marry the person he loves and no other. It was also signed by Sera Thomason. Sera is from the 3rd District, and this contract is overseen by Enforcers." He grinned at his brother. "And Kenneth remembers signing this one, doesn't he?"

"You sneaky . . ." Kenneth said softly as he understood. "Paperwork, my ass."

"Hey, it was true." He punched his big brother lightly in the shoulder. "Turnabout is fair play. You did it to me."

Before Kenneth could react, Dazzle suddenly appeared before both males. "Don't worry," she told them, "no one else sees me. Ken, you need to hurry! I'm the genie Sera told you about. She used her last wish—my last wish—to wish for you to be happy. So whatever it takes to make you happy, then that's what I am bound to do."

"Take me to Sera," he said instantly. "I need her to be happy. I only need her. Please, take me to her!"

"Okay!"

The bright flash momentarily blinded Cameron. When he could see again, Kenneth had disappeared. As people looked around in confusion, he covered his face with his hands. "Wonderful. How am I going to explain that one?"

Sera hated riding the bus, but there was no way she could walk home. She simply curled up in the back and stared sightlessly out the window as streetlights and signs rolled by. She felt dead inside as if everything had stopped all at once.

When her stop arrived, she barely acknowledged the driver's farewell as she disembarked. She just didn't care about anything. With a deep breath, she turned to go home . . . and felt her broken heart freeze inside her chest.

Kenneth stood behind her.

Her purse hit the ground with a thump. "Ken?" It was little more than a whisper. "I thought you were getting married."

"Someone wished for my happiness." He slowly walked toward her, his eyes dark and intense. "I'm here to take that happiness."

Her hands slowly curled into fists at her side. Tears welled in her eyes but she refused to let them fall. "And what do you need to be happy?"

His hands tenderly framed her face. "You." He rubbed his thumb over her cheek. "You're my happiness, Sera. I love you more than anything. I have from the day I met you. I want you to be my wife. I want you to turn my house into a place of color and laughter. I want you to boss me around at work even though I'm supposed to be in charge."

Her lips trembled into a smile. "I tried to quit."

"It's not official. You have to yell at me and storm out dramatically. It's a rule."

She gave a hiccupping laugh. "You know me. I love rules." His lips found hers and her hands curled around his wrists to keep him close. The tears welled up from somewhere inside that she hadn't known could cry.

"Stop. Sera, please. Stop." His lips rushed over her face to steal her tears.

"I was so scared," she whispered shakily. "I wanted to die, Ken. I knew you weren't happy, even when you were trying to lie to me." She hit his shoulder hard enough to make him wince and then curled her fingers into his shirt to hold on. "I was going to go yell at Lorcana when I found the lamp." Her voice broke on a sob. "Dazzle. She lost her power. Lorcana killed her!"

A bright pink glow startled them both and they looked up in

shock as the dragon-genie appeared with a shower of sparks. She looked vibrant and healthy as if she had never been so frighteningly weak. "I'm right here!" she said happily. She flew in loop-de-loops around the lovers. "I told you, didn't I, that good wishes negate selfish ones. So I'm okay now." She landed on Sera's head and peered down into her face. "I can't grant wishes anymore though."

"I don't need anything else." She wound her arms around Kenneth's neck and smiled. "I've got everything I want right here."

It took nearly an hour to get rid of everyone in the lobby. Cameron let Sarah take care of the media while he took care of the guests. Janice and Lorcana were 'taken care of' by two policemen who had just happened to conveniently show up. Louise categorically denied calling them, but no one believed her. One of them was her cousin.

As Cameron waited for the elevator, he felt a presence and turned to see the silvery-haired woman standing behind him. She smiled, her eyes twinkling. "Hi again."

"Hi." He pulled out the contract and handed it to her. "Here you go." Softer, he added, "And thanks."

"You're welcome!"

As she ran off, Sarah stepped up beside him and slipped her hand into his. She softly rested her head on his shoulder. "Bet we see her again."

"Oh?"

"Ever hear the saying about things coming in threes?" Her eyes slid to where Louise stood bickering with a security guard.

He followed her gaze and began to smile. "The best things do, right?"

CHAPTER FIFTEEN

Rhianna was in her office when Rayna walked in with the contract. It read as 'Complete' very clearly across the front. "Tada!" she said as she put it on Rhianna's desk. "Here you go, Rhi."

Rhianna read over the document, added some notes, and slipped it into a folder. It also reflected complete, and she swiveled in her chair to add the folder to a drawer clearly labeled 'Dease.' She closed the drawer, and it remained entirely blank.

"One more, right?" Rayna asked.

"Naturally. In fact, I've been waiting for this one for a long time. It's well overdue for an ending." Her lips curved. "A happy one, of course."

Violet eyes sparkled merrily at her. "Of course."

Status: File In Progress
Analysis: A diamond in the rough always shows its true colors when held by someone who can see the value inside.

Folder Three
LOUISE

CHAPTER SIXTEEN

(Six months ago . . .)

It was warm and sunny in the 3rd District, but it made no difference to those who worked and lived there. Warm or cold, bright or cloudy, those who ran businesses kept their doors open for anyone to walk in. When it was winter, customers might find themselves receiving hot tea or cocoa to combat the chill outside. When it was summer, iced tea or lemonade might be on hand.

Ever since the Faerie Club and the Gentle Brook Inn had taken off in society, the District had had a renewed interest from people on the outside. Rather than rebuff those who came wandering in curiously, the District had opened their doors and their wares and offered a rare glimpse into the magic of their homes.

Among the favorite small shops to visit was the tiny building where Brian Matthews sold his beautiful clothworks. The gentle shopkeeper had a way of making a loom sing, and if it was sewn, it was sewn by hand. He owned only a single old-fashioned sewing machine, but it got little use. The more tedious the detail, the more pride he took.

The irony was, of course, that at least half of New York had seen or owned his work and simply didn't realize. The pieces he sold through big name stores were sold under the pseudonym B. R. Matthews. Brian liked his quiet. He liked his life to be peaceful. And as his twenty-eighth birthday crept dangerously close, his only solace came from his work.

When he turned twenty-eight, he would die.

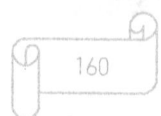

Marked across his upper chest for all of his life had been twenty-eight small birthmarks shaped like needles. Every year, one more disappeared. His uncle, the doctor in the family, had finally made the connection as to what was occurring when he had seen Brian suffer a minor heart attack on his sixteenth birthday at the very moment one mark faded. The weaver was cursed, and no one knew why.

Brian went on with what was left of his life to the best of his ability. Really, what else could he do? He opened his shop, made his art, and enjoyed the company of his nieces and nephews.

The bell chimed merrily over the door, and he left the back room to see who had entered. To his surprise, he found a familiar red-haired woman waiting for him. "Well." He tucked his hands into his pockets. "Hello, Ms. Taber. I wasn't expecting to see you." He had never met her, but everyone knew the Enforcers' head honcho on sight.

Rhianna smiled at him. "Most aren't. How are you, Brian?"

"Well enough." He held a stunning green dress in front of her. The nearly Grecian style suited her in some elemental fashion. "This was made for you." He offered it with a smile. "My work chooses who it belongs to."

She draped the dress over her arm, and her fingers moved over the soft material gently. "I'll wear it quite proudly." She searched his cerulean blue eyes intently and suddenly smiled. "You would never tell me, would you? You're not the type to burden others."

"Why tell what everyone knows?" he said simply. "Talking of it will not change it." He went behind the small counter. "Tea?"

"Yes, thank you." She put the dress down and accepted the cup he offered. "Brian . . . yours is a gift that we do not want to lose. You are an important part of this District. Everyone who lives here is. The way you can heal with your craft is too needed to be lost."

"But what can you do? We don't even know why I am this way." He rubbed his hand over where the last mark rested on his chest.

She studied him for long moments before murmuring, "Even

without Truth here, I can see you are lying, Brian. You know why this is happening."

He looked away. "And it cannot be changed."

"Why can't it?" She reached into her jacket pocket and pulled out a sheaf of papers. "This is a contract, Brian. Enforcers wants to do whatever it can to aid you." She put the contract down in front of him. "We will provide you with ancient thread that will serve as a lure to the right person. With this thread, you must weave a scarf that will have a strand of your hair. Sell it under your pseudonym. It will find its way to the person who can break the curse. At that point . . . you will have to do the rest."

He stared blindly at the contract. "I couldn't survive seeing her again," he said softly, achingly.

Even softer, she said, "And you won't survive if you don't. Time changes people. Souls learn more with every rebirth. You can end things right this time."

"I don't even know how it ended before . . ."

"Then that, too, you must find."

He closed his eyes for a moment before straightening his back. He grabbed a pen and signed the bottom of the contract before he could change his mind. Beside him, a roll of softly glowing multicolored thread appeared on the counter. When he touched it, he could feel the age and the power. The ancient spool had Latin carved into the side, and though he was rusty at the language, he could still read it. "'From the loom of Hestia.'" He glanced at Rhianna. "Where did you find this?"

A little smile touched her lips. "I found it lying around." She tapped a finger lightly on the contract. "It's up to you, Brian."

He smiled wryly. "Wasn't it always?"

(Present day)

Louise was the black sheep in her family, but one that was well loved. She had two older sisters, two older brothers and two younger ones, six aunts, six uncles, fifteen cousins, one or two second cousins,

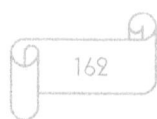

and five nieces and nephews. Of that massive family, of those old enough to have a job, she was the only one who was an artist.

She could lay claim to lawyers, police, businesspeople, a fireman, two ranchers, and assorted other desk job type people that she was related to, and not a single one of them knew a paintbrush could be used for more than painting a wall. She preferred her paint to be electronic these days, but she knew her way well enough around a canvas.

She lived alone in a small apartment in Manhattan. It was the most centralized location to all her family in the city (some were scattered across the country), and it was also close enough to work that her commute didn't become a nightmare. She felt happy enough where she was, but she was also discontent with her life. At twenty-six, she knew her whole life lay ahead of her, but she simply didn't feel truly happy yet.

As she brushed her thick auburn hair and desperately tried to convince her curls to behave, her phone began to ring. She hit the speaker button. "Hi, Mom."

Evelyn Pram sighed deeply. "Lou, you know I love you."

"Oh lord."

"Could you *please* make a flyer for your cousin's wedding?"

She just smiled wryly. Her family accepted her artistic side mostly because they loved to take advantage of it. "Which cousin this time?"

"Elly. She's marrying that nice attorney I told you about."

"Great, more lawyers in the family." She gave up on her hair and tied a bright blue ribbon around it to keep it back from her face. "Shoot me an email with all the details. And, no, I will not be a bridesmaid. That last time I was a bridesmaid for one of my relatives, I ended up looking like the Great Pumpkin in heels."

Her mother snorted softly. "Get married yourself and you can have revenge."

"Ha. I actually have aesthetics, remember?" She hung up the phone over her mother's sputter, but she was smiling as she did. Her parents were very careful not to pressure her into getting married or 'settling down' even though she knew they both worried over how alone she felt.

With a shake of her head, she pulled on her favorite sundress. Summer had hit NYC with a vengeance, and the sun was bright and hot in double doses. The air, smoggy as it could be, seemed fresher and cleaner. Going to work was now a great feeling, and she looked forward to every minute. Her job hadn't changed. The entire company had changed. It had been months since Cameron had claimed his shares, and he and his brother had done a clean sweep to remove all traces of their mother (their not-so-happily-jailed for fraud mother) from the place.

Louise was a happy camper. Her bosses, both of which were more like her brothers, were happy. The women they had married, both of which were like little sisters to her, were happy. She loved working for Sera. She was able to be both supervisor and friend, and she didn't take crap. Especially not from Kenneth, and Louise had snickered more than once to hear them shouting at each other. It was a match made in heaven as far as she was concerned.

The message light on her answering machine blinked as she entered the living room, and she pushed the play button. One message was political junk; some assemblyman wanted to be re-elected. She couldn't have cared less for him or his policies. Another message was to tell her that the DVD she had ordered was at the store for pick-up.

The last message was from her favorite older brother. *Lou, go on a damn vacation and stop stressing everyone out. You're like a paint can that's been shaken too hard. You're going to spew everywhere.*

"Love you too," she muttered. Still, she had to think about it. Maybe she *should* take a day off and play hooky. She could con Sera and Sarah into going with her; they had a dual wedding ceremony coming up and were still hunting for dresses. They had promised Louise that she could pick her own bridesmaid dress, so she had

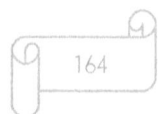

reluctantly agreed to be a shared maid-of-honor.

Her phone began to ring again, and she sighed as she answered. "Hi, Dad."

"My favorite daughter!" Craig Pram had a big booming voice that could keep rowdy teenagers in line as effectively as it did unruly defendants in court. "Would you do your loving father a *big* favor?"

"Now what do you want?" It was more affectionate than exasperated.

"Well, Harry is retiring soon . . ."

"More flyers? Seriously, Dad, you could just open any Office program and fake it yourself."

"But then they wouldn't be professional."

"Professionals get paid. I get emotionally blackmailed!"

"Love you."

She sighed. "No wonder you indulged my desire for art school! Alright, alright. Send me the info and his photos and whatever else you need."

"That's my girl!" He paused and then added, "You know, Lou, we were thinking you really ought to take a vacation. Those Dease boys can spare you a few days."

"Oh don't you start too!" She hung up the phone and glowered at it for long moments. And only the pigeons outside the open window heard her mutter, "I don't need a vacation from work. I need one from my family!"

CHAPTER SEVENTEEN

The first thing Louise did when she got to work was get a cup of coffee. On one sip, she knew Sarah had gotten there first; she made the best brew in the company. Louise had watched her once, and she still had no idea why hers always tasted better. Coffee in hand, she sat down at her desk and booted up her computer.

She had only just started to troll through the half dozen emails when Sera suddenly walked up and leaned on the side of the cubicle. "You," Sera said.

"Me. What's up?"

"Wanna play hooky?"

Louise slowly looked at her. "You're doing that creepy thing again. Stop reading my mind! I was just thinking how nice it might be to take a day off."

Sera grinned. "And even better, it's not being AWOL because your supervisor is making you go. Sarah and I found this sweet shop that we want to look for dresses at. And you've got to come along because you need a dress too."

Sarah suddenly popped up on the other side of the cubicle. "And, seriously, we still need to fill our closets at home. I mean, what's the point of making our husbands complain about losing their closets when we don't even take up a quarter of the space?"

Louise laughed. "Hey, far be it from me to argue!" She closed her mail and began to shut down the computer again. "I still think it's going to be *amazing* to have the double ceremony. I'm not even stressing over being maid-of-honor."

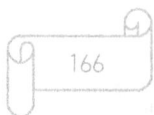

"Why would you be?" Sera asked curiously.

"Haven't you heard about that old superstition that a woman who is too many times a bridesmaid will never be a bride?" She held up her hand. "This will mark my sixth walk down the aisle without being the one in a veil."

Sarah pursed her lips slightly. "I admit that I've never seen you date in the months I've known you. So what gives? You don't want to be married? It's perfectly fine if you don't, you know."

"Hmm." Louise slung her purse over her shoulder as she stood. "I do," she decided at last. "I just haven't met a guy lately that I wanted to date, let alone think about marrying. And I *was* engaged once," she offered, "but it didn't last long. He became convinced that I was seeing someone else, and I wasn't. Kind of put a damper on things."

The two sisters-in-law fell into step beside her and they headed for the exit. Kenneth and Cameron already knew they were sneaking out, so neither worried that they might be missed.

"What exactly are you doing about your dress?" Louise asked Sarah. "I mean . . . you have to have everything specially made for you, so . . ."

"That's the curious thing, Lou." A light summer breeze teased her rusty hair as they walked outside. "Ever since I married Cam . . . my sensitivity has gone down to a much more manageable level. I still bruise like a grape. I still feel *much* more acutely than a normal person. But some of the harder issues are gone. I can feel the threads in cloth, but only if I'm thinking about it."

"It served its purpose," Louise murmured.

Sarah grinned at her. "You're starting to sound like one of us, Lou. You sure you're normal?"

"Normal as I can be considering my family. Hey!" The last was a yelp as a particularly strong wind snagged the ribbon in her hair and whisked it away. It sailed out of sight before any of the women could think about grabbing it. Now freed, Louise's curls danced wildly around her face. She blew a lock out of her eyes. "I need a perm."

"But your hair is curly already," Sera said in confusion.

"Believe it or not, it helps tame the beast. Ah well. At least the wind feels nice." She pulled out her keys and twirled them around a finger. "I'll drive."

The shop that Sera and Sarah had found was located in a nearby mall. The crowds didn't look too bad at that time of morning, and they found a parking spot miraculously close to the entrance they wanted. The shop itself was actually a boutique, and Louise recognized it as they walked in the door. "I've been here," she said decisively. "With all five of the prior brides I've been in a ceremony with. Good choice, gals. They have some sweet dresses here." She winked. "And though pricey, you can afford it now."

A handsome gentleman in a suit and turban came up with a wide grin on his face. "Louise, are you here again? Tell me you're getting married this time."

"Nope. That would be these two." She put a hand on each of her friends' shoulder. "Sera, with an E, is the tall one. Sarah, with an A and an H, is the redhead. They're having a double ceremony since they're marrying brothers."

His brows winged up as the names and the scenario clicked for him. "Ah, the two women who married the Dease brothers, correct? Welcome to Bridal Dreams." He smiled. "I'm Rashid, and I'll be helping you out today. Louise knows I know my dresses."

"He can't get rid of me," she agreed cheerfully. "He keeps hoping I'm going to get married so he can prove his skill by finding me, the pickiest female in the world, the perfect dress."

Sera snickered. "Well, we're picky but not that picky. I'm all about being streamlined and simple. Sarah is totally a romantic and needs a princess' dress. And we need a hot and sexy bridesmaid dress for Lou. She can choose whatever she wants as long as it is blue or green since those are our colors. Any shade of either, too."

Rashid stepped back for a moment and studied all three females intently. Sera looked tall and shapely, as striking as a model. Sarah looked cute and spunky, but somehow innately regal. Louise

S.J. GARRETT

looked, as always, vibrant and wild-spirited. "I might just know what you need. Let's find a fitting room to get your sizes."

Sera and Sarah got rooms right across from each other. Louise opted to wait to look for her dress until they had what they wanted. That they would find it, she had no doubt. She had seen Rashid in action. He had an amazing ability to read people perfectly.

He returned shortly with two dresses. He gave one to each female and sat down beside Louise on the padded bench in the hall. "So." He looked at her pointedly. "Elly is getting married. She's younger than you are, kid. When Evelyn called to tell me and Jess, she was bemoaning the fact that all her children except you are paired off. Even Deke just got married, and he's your baby brother."

"Twenty-two," she murmured. "Not so much a baby, 'shid."

"We're family, Lou." He bumped her shoulder. "I think I know you well enough. What's going on, hon? It can't be just that you're picky. You're not still hung up on that idiot from three years ago, right?"

"Yes and no." She frowned. "He accused me of cheating. The thing is . . . I *felt* like I was cheating. But not on him. I felt like I was cheating on someone else *with* him."

He sat back. "Huh."

"The few dates I've gone on since have made me feel the same way." She sighed. "I figure if I ever find a guy that I don't get that feeling from, he was probably the person I was cosmically cheating on." She dropped her face into her hands. "I used to think oogie-boogie stuff was crap. Then I met the two dingdongs trying on dresses. Let's just say . . . they changed my mind."

"Who're you calling a dingdong?" Sera demanded.

Louise looked up with a smile but her words got stuck. "Wow," she finally said. "Wow, Sera. You look amazing!"

The gown was pure white silk. No lace or frills adorned it. It clung to Sera's entire body until mid-thigh where it began to flare into a train. The very faintest of shimmery patterns wove into the material and reflected light as she moved. The bodice dipped enough to tease without being overly sexy.

A little giddy, Sera turned in front of the mirrors lining the hall. "I can't believe how beautiful it is! Kenneth's eyes are going to pop out of his head if he sees this." She swung around, eyes sparkling. "I want it. It's perfect!"

"Rashid, one. Picky brides, zero." Louise crossed her arms on a grin.

"Make that Rashid, two." Sarah stepped out of her dressing room with her skirt held in her hands so she could walk. "It's so perfect."

The dress had a full ball gown skirt made of layers of silk, satin, and lace. The top had a corset that laced down the front with fat white ribbons to her waist where the streamers fell into the folds of the skirt. It had no straps or sleeves which suited her smaller frame perfectly. The skirt dragged on the floor behind her for at least two feet. Everything was shimmering white but very faint cream touches brought vivid emphasis to her bright hair.

"I think we might have to hold the men up at the altar," Sera told her sister. "Ken's definitely going to pass out, and Cam's probably going to stutter through everything."

Rashid rubbed his hands together. "Now let's find some accessories. We can then get you in with our seamstress for any alterations needed, though I think there may be few. You are lucky enough to wear off-the-shelf sizes!" He turned his gaze on Louise. "And as for you, I have a few things that ought to be perfect."

Sarah lifted a brow as he headed down the hall. "I get the feeling he knows you other than when he helped your other brides."

"He married my cousin," Louise admitted dryly. "So I'm sort of related to him."

Veils were decided on, along with hairpieces. As soon as Sera and Sarah got back in their street clothes after seeing the lady who would make the alterations, Louise found herself shoved into a dressing room. "No orange!" she said over the door fiercely. "I still haven't forgiven you for that!"

Rashid just laughed and headed for the racks. When he returned, he had a dress draped over his arm in a blue identical to her eyes. He passed it into the dressing room and then winked at the other two women. In a soft voice so his cousin didn't hear, he told them, "If she ever gets to an altar, I already have her dress picked out."

"Nice." Sarah sighed happily as she saw Louise walk out of the dressing room. "Done. Sold. Pack it up, it's going home."

It was a simple dress in silk and satin, but it both clung and swirled around Louise's body in a way that made her look as if she walked through water. Beads scattered across the dress glimmered and rippled in the light. The skirt went to just past her knees and the top stayed up by thin beaded straps. The faintest of green color could be seen if the light hit the dress just right.

"Rashid, three?" he asked hopefully.

Louise could only sigh as she ran a hand down the dress. "Okay, I forgive you for the Great Pumpkin incident."

The gown was added to the other two, and they headed up front to be rung up. As Louise reached for her wallet, Sera caught her wrist. "Add hers to our total," she told Rashid. "We're the ones making her be in the wedding, and that means we pay for it." She arched a brow at Louise when her friend stared at her. "No arguing. I'm your boss and I said so."

Sarah giggled softly. Rashid grinned. "Just for that, I'll give you the employee discount I was going to give Lou." As he handed over the receipt, he added innocently, "There's a lingerie store just down the way that most of our brides go to as well. Tell them to give you the Dream Honeymoon discount."

"Thanks!"

After a giggling tour of the lingerie store, they emerged with several bags among them. Even Louise hadn't been able to resist some of the fancier pieces. Just because she had no one to show them off to didn't mean she wouldn't enjoy wearing them anyway.

That stop set the course for the whole day. They went in and out of nearly every store, and they always came out with more than what they had gone in with. Realizing that it wouldn't all fit in Louise's car, Sarah called for the chauffeur to pick her and Sera up in a few hours.

It was nearing late afternoon by the time they found the last accessory shop on their list. It was a specialty place that sold unique and one-of-a-kind items. The windows had been filled with everything from shoes to purses to hats to scarves. Books and trinkets lined the walls, and revolving stands with jewelry dotted the aisles.

The three women split up to peruse the wares, and Louise found herself wandering a little aimlessly. Many things intrigued her, but nothing really jumped out at her . . . until she reached the back of the shop. Amid the rows of assorted neck and head accessories, there was a satin cushion sitting by itself on a small table. Folded on the middle of the cushion sat a scarf of such brilliance and color that she took a sharp breath.

"Ah." The owner had come up beside her without her knowledge. As old and wrinkled as he was, he looked as if he would be quite at home on a porch yelling at kids to keep off his damn lawn. His faded brown eyes still held wizened intelligence as he studied her and the scarf in turn. "You like this, yes?"

"It's beautiful." She reverently touched the scarf and was sure she felt it tingling all the way from her fingers to her shoulder. "Can I pick it up?"

"I don't know. Can you?"

She scooped it up and unfolded it so that its beauty was unconfined. It felt as soft as silk, as thin as air, but as warm as fleece. She could nearly see through it, and as light passed through, it cast multicolored rainbows on the carpet. It reached roughly four feet in length and six inches wide. The way it slid over her fingers felt nearly sensual. "It's so beautiful." She brushed it against her cheek and marveled at the craftsmanship. She knew it had to be handmade. "Where's it from?"

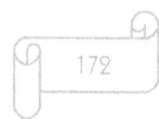

"It was made by B. R. Matthews."

"Really?" She looked at him in surprise. "I've admired his work for years but could never afford it." Very reluctantly, she forced herself to put the scarf down. "It's probably too expensive for me." She rubbed her fingers over the scarf softly. She just couldn't stand to let go.

The owner picked up the scarf and wrapped it around her neck before she could stop him. "Sometimes the art picks the owner," he told her softly. "This is yours, my dear. I am sure Mr. Matthews would be very pleased."

"Really?" She looked in a mirror and was enchanted with how the scarf seemed to fit perfectly. It wrapped just once around her neck, and the ends fell to her waist in the front and back. It was also light enough it didn't get in the way. In fact, she almost couldn't tell she wore it at all. "Are you sure? It must be worth a fortune."

"I am sure."

Sera came around the corner of a rack and her brows shot skyward as she saw Louise. "There you are. Whoa!" She moved closer and leaned in to see the scarf better. She recognized the work instantly. "B. R. Matthews. Niiice. He makes amazing stuff." She straightened and found a smile though her stomach had begun to quiver with a dangerous combination of nerves and hope. Why hadn't she suspected this sooner? It made sense of *everything*. "It suits you."

"Thanks." Louise knew she shouldn't accept such an expensive gift, but she simply had no willpower to say no. "Thank you, sir," she told the owner softly.

"You are most welcome."

It was evening by the time she helped unload at the Dease manor the bags that had been stuffed in her car. With only her own indulgences left, she headed for home. She felt curiously lighter and more content. Taking a day off had definitely helped.

Her answering machine was blinking faster than a nearsighted blonde with new contacts. She hit the play button and listened with half an ear as she unpacked her purchases. It seemed as if every family member she could lay claim to had called to tell her something or another. Her family intimidated people like Sera and Sarah who had had exceptionally small families while growing up. She couldn't imagine *not* having a big family.

As the apartment fell into blessed silence, she found herself looking into a mirror. She had changed into a nightgown and robe for the evening, but she had left the scarf on. Bemused at herself, she removed it and placed it gently on her dresser. She started to walk away, and it snagged on her sleeve. She freed it and used it to tie her hair back instead, and she let the ends flutter behind her sassily. Someday she wanted to meet B. R. Matthews and tell him how much she loved his work. It seemed to speak to her very soul.

"B. R. Matthews" had a vastly different day. Brian awoke in the morning to the sound of banging on the roof, and he recognized it as the sound of the neighbor's cat hunting birds. Since it was as good an alarm as any, he went ahead and got out of bed.

As always, his day started by putting on a pot of coffee before unlocking the shop. He set out what would be displayed outside and then cleaned up the inside. While he drank his first cup of coffee, he went through the tags in his jar. There weren't many. He would swing by their places later and make the trade final.

Tags sorted, he got his computer running to check his email. There were several new messages. One from his uncle; he had just come back from his honeymoon and wanted a belated wedding gift for his bride. Brian just shook his head. It still amused him that the woman who had always been like his sister was now his step-cousin. He also just glad that Lewis and Cecily had found each other; sometimes true love just took a little longer to go from simmer to boil.

Another message had the weekly newsletter from the Faerie Club. Aenya was expecting her second child and she wanted to hold a party. A second personal message for Brian alone accompanied it. She wanted a baby blanket; she felt sure she would be having a boy this time, but she didn't want to go with the traditional blues that regular stores hyped on, just in case she might be wrong.

By the time he finished the emails, people were already starting to wander in and look around. Friday mornings were always the busiest in the District, followed closely by Sunday afternoons. It was a fascinating phenomenon that he had always found amusing. He sold two blankets and six banners and then helped a very pregnant mother find a dress for her niece's graduation party.

When a lull arrived, he closed for lunch and went into his workroom. An immense loom took up most of the space, but it was all that he needed in there. This was where he worked on his most special projects. He was working on his biggest project at that very moment, and he knew very well that it might be his last. He had been under contract for six months. His birthday stood only days away.

A gust of wind blew the front door open around mid-afternoon, and two identical little girls came running into the shop shrieking, "Cousin Brian!" at the top of their lungs.

He ducked behind the counter. He had played the game with them since they had been old enough to walk. He smiled as he heard their footsteps pattering around the hardwood floors. Then, suddenly, two matching faces popped around the side of the counter. "Found you!" Tawny shouted.

"I just can't hide from you well enough!" He scooped up both and hugged them tight. "How are my favorite girls?"

"We get summer break." Tammy looped her arms around his neck and eyed him owlishly. "How come adults don't get summer break? It's not fair. We want Sera to play with us."

"Sera has a busy job. Unfortunately, adults don't get to play like little kids." He carried them into the kitchen and put each down on a different chair. He got two cups of milk and two cookies and handed one of each to each girl. He sat down at the table with them, an ear cocked toward the front in case anyone came in. "Are you happy with your new sister and mommy?"

Both nodded enthusiastically. "Mama is really nice, and she only scolds if we're really bad," Tawny said. "And she and Daddy are always cuddling, but they let us cuddle too. We get to go spend the weekend with Sera and Ken! They got a puppy to play with Milly, and we get to play with him too!"

"How come there are two Seras?" Tammy demanded.

"They spell their names differently." Brian poured himself some tea. "And it's just one of those little things that life likes to throw at us to make us giggle. Like brothers marrying women with mostly the same name. That sort of thing."

"Oh." The twins nodded, eyes wide, as if they understood entirely.

He covered a smile and let them be while he headed up front to help another customer. When he returned, both girls had started drawing with the paper and crayons he always kept on the table for them. Tammy had no real aesthetics. You had to guess to be sure what she had drawn. Tawny was very much Sera's sister; the girl had a talent beyond her years.

"Brian?" Tammy had stopped drawing.

"What is it, Tam?" He knelt next to her chair.

"Daddy says you're going away soon." Her lower lip quivered. "I don't want you to go away."

"I'm sorry, honey." He gently smoothed back her hair. "I wouldn't go if I had a choice. But this is something beyond my control."

"Where are you going?" Tawny asked. She climbed off her chair and walked over to hug him tightly. "Can we visit you there?"

"No. Someday, when you're a little older, your daddy and mommy will tell you everything. You're not old enough to understand yet. I'm sorry." It broke his heart as both girls clung onto him tightly with tears in their eyes.

"Adults are silly." Tawny wiped her eyes on his shirt. "How come you have to have secrets?"

"Well, when you grow up, you can have your own." It disheartened him to think he wouldn't be there to see them turn into young women. He knew they would be troublemakers, and with Sera for a role model, they would be ass kickers as well. A lethal combination, to be sure. "I tell you what," he said softly. "You want early birthday gifts?"

"Yeah!" Both brightened. Their birthday was in a month, and they had been sad that he wouldn't go to their party. He had always been the most fun to play games with, and he had never once been mad if cake got thrown.

They followed him to the main room of the shop where they found a younger couple exploring things. As Brian rummaged in the racks, the twins went over to the woman and smiled up at her. "Hi."

"Well, hi." She knelt to their height and smiled. "Do you live here?"

"Nuh-uh. Brian's our cousin! We know where everything is." Tammy nodded firmly. "You want help?"

"We were just exploring." The man smiled as well. The twins were too cute to not be smiled at. "But I guess I could use a new tie."

"Okay!" Tawny scampered off and returned momentarily with an armful of ties. "Here! You can find one. Brian makes lots of nice ones." While the man went through them, she asked, "How come boys wear ties?"

"To make up for women wearing pantyhose," the woman explained dryly.

Brian covered a smile. "Tawny. Tammy. Come over here."

"Kay!" The girls skidded around the racks and stopped quickly as they saw him holding up two small dresses. One in blue, Tammy's favorite color, and the other in green, Tawny's favorite. Both looked like something a princess would wear.

"Oh my," the woman murmured as she looked over the top of a rack to watch. "How lovely!"

"Are . . . are these ours?" Tammy gingerly touched one of the dresses.

"I think they might be." He handed the blue one to her and the green one to her sister. "Happy birthday. I figured you might want to wear them to your party, so you get them early."

Tawny hugged her dress tight. She liked the clothes he made. She always felt as if he was hugging her, and he was the best hugger ever. Her lower lip wobbled. "I'd rather you stayed here."

He knelt and hugged them both tightly. "I know," he said softly. "I know."

The twins went home with their father an hour later. Brian helped some more customers and made a brief detour to take care of the tag trades he had pending. He lucked out too; the traded items would make good last gifts for his family. Then, with all that done, he began to work on something else. He had put it off long enough.

As the sun began to set, he finally brought in everything from outside and shut the front door. He turned over the Closed sign, turned the radio on low, and went to get some dinner. He had to admit he loved working from home. The convenience couldn't be beat. He would have said he would miss it, but he had no idea precisely how the afterlife worked. It would be interesting to find out.

His phone began to ring while he was washing the dishes. Since it was the line that connected to his fake name, he answered, "Matthews."

"Hello, Brian."

The familiar old voice made him smile. "Hello, Mr. E. Don't tell me you're out of stock already."

The old man laughed. "Nearly, my boy. Anything of yours seems to simply fly out of here at lightning pace. After all, I carry the elite B. R. Matthews at discount prices. You can't get these sales anywhere else."

Brian laughed and leaned against the counter. "It still amuses me that people don't even realize I'm just a lowly weaver from the District. I don't hide who I am. No one chooses to see." He took a long

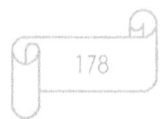

breath. "Just so you know, I finished my will today. I'm leaving whatever is left in stock to you. I know you'll take care of selling it and getting the money to my family."

"Don't be so quick to have that witnessed, Brian. Something interesting happened today."

The weaver nearly stopped breathing. He slowly sank down onto the chair beside him. "The scarf?" he managed to ask.

"Her eyes were blue."

"Blue eyes." His own cerulean ones closed. "Naturally."

"When she walked in, I knew she would be the one. She had no purpose. No reason to be there. And without asking, without being guided, she found her way to the scarf. She could not put it down. I sent it home with her, Brian. I think if I hadn't, she might have died herself. There is hope, my boy."

He slowly hung up the phone and got to his feet to go look at the tapestry he had been working on. It was more than three-quarters done with only the end left to be completed. Starting from the top, it told a story in memories and vignettes. In the center, surrounded by the story, rested a man and woman.

She had blue eyes.

Very softly, tenderly, he traced a finger over her nearly imperceptible features. "Come back to me," he murmured huskily. "I never stopped waiting for you, just as I promised so long ago."

CHAPTER EIGHTEEN

It took less than two days for everyone to realize Louise was attached to her scarf. Almost literally in some aspects for she never took it off. If it wasn't around her neck, it was tied around her hair. Sometimes she looped it around her waist. It didn't matter where she wore it; no one saw her without it.

Kenneth didn't think too much of it until he saw his wife watching her nearly constantly. He caught Sera's arm and pulled her into the office. He shut the door and asked quietly, "You want to tell me what's wrong? And don't tell me it's nothing. I know you better than that."

Her hands curled together. He pulled her into his arms and she pressed her face to his shoulder. "I'll tell you later when . . . when things end. However they end. I'm just scared and hopeful and feeling useless."

He softly ran his hand down her back. "Okay," he said softly. "When you're ready, tell me. But tell me sooner if I can help."

"No, I need to take the next step. Maybe I'm not supposed to, but I'm damned well not sitting around." She tugged free of his grip and left the office. "Hey, Lou," she said as she crossed to her friend's desk.

"I've almost got the ad for the billboard done," Louise said without glancing up. "Ten minutes or so. I'm currently wrestling with layout. I'm just not happy."

"That's great, but that wasn't what I wanted to ask about." Sera flicked a finger at the ends of the scarf. It was currently tied as a

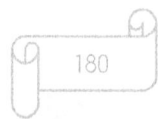

headband around Louise's hair, and it somehow seemed to miraculously be able to keep the riotous curls in line. "You don't take this thing off, Lou. If you told me you slept in it, I wouldn't be surprised." Louise's cheeks warmed, and she gripped her hands together tightly. "I know him," she finally said.

"What?" Louise's head swung around. "B. R. Matthews? You know him?"

"It's a fake name. He's actually my step-cousin. His uncle is my stepfather. The B stands for Brian. The R for Robert. He lives in 3rd District and runs a small shop there. He sells his normal work in big stores and keeps the specialty stuff at home." Somehow she found a smile. "We always laugh at how people buy some poor weaver's wares and never realize they have what is technically a designer label."

"Can I meet him?" Louise snatched up a pen and paper. "Address, please. I've always wanted to meet him and tell him how much admire his work. It's a silly dream, I know. I'll go this weekend."

Sera wrote down the address and wondered how her fingers could be steady. "Actually," she said casually, "he won't be open this weekend. If you want to go, you better go today. It's only mid-morning. If you wanted to take off, I wouldn't stop you. Hey, trust me, I know all about silly dreams and reaching for them, so it would be perfectly fine with me."

"You're the best! I'll finish this then take off." Louise went back to her work, a giddy feeling in her heart and stomach. She would finally get to meet someone she had admired for years. No one knew what he was like, but she felt prepared to like him since Sera so clearly did.

Once she finished the layout and sent it to Sera for review, she shut down her computer and gathered her bags. She knew how to get to the District, and she didn't worry about losing her way. And since it wasn't *that* big, she knew she could find parking and just walk however far she needed.

It was a good plan, except for the fact that she had no real sense of direction to begin with. She was sure she followed Sera's directions precisely, but it didn't take very long before she was rather hopelessly lost. She couldn't even be sure which way went back to her car. She could see the Enforcers immense building in the distance to her left, but it had almost always seemed to be there, no matter how many turns she made.

With a deep sigh, she sat down on one of the benches along the street. A crack of thunder had her morosely looking up at the sky. It had been cloudy all morning, but the weathermen had sworn it wouldn't rain.

A few fat drops of rain landed on her hand and head. It was her only warning. In less than a minute, the clouds opened and it began to pour. She didn't bother to dive for cover. Really, the damage had already been done. She knocked a soggy lock out of her eyes. At least her hair would stay in place for a while.

An umbrella suddenly moved over her head and the rain was kept at bay. Startled, she looked up and found herself staring into a pair of cerulean blue eyes so beautiful that they took her breath. They were set into a face just as shockingly handsome. A trim goatee hugged the line of a strong jaw that she really wouldn't have minded running her fingers down. His black hair had been tied into a small ponytail at the back of his neck.

"Thanks," she managed to say as she felt her entire body flush with heat. Something needy gathered deep inside. Holy hell, what did they put in the water in this District? People, almost as a whole, were utterly gorgeous!

Brian offered her a hand. "Come on. My shop isn't far. You can take shelter there. I had just brought everything inside when I saw you." As her fingers slipped into his, he fought the urge to draw her into his arms. The violent and ferocious desire was the least of his problems, though it did not help. Finally. Finally she had come back to him.

She let him draw her to her feet, and her heart raced wildly as he tucked her under his arm protectively to keep her out of the rain

as they hurried down the sidewalk. She hadn't felt a desire like that before, and she didn't even know the guy! She knew he was shorter than average since he didn't tower over her, but boy had Mother Nature used those lesser inches well.

He ushered her into his shop and shut the door as another thunderclap echoed loudly across the sky. He shook the umbrella out and set it aside before pulling off his glasses and wiping them dry. "You must be freezing in those wet clothes."

"Only a little." She wrapped her arms around herself and looked around the shop curiously. It didn't take her long to realize that the wares for sale appeared to be very, very familiar. Her fingers curled into the ends of her curiously dry scarf. "Wait. Don't tell me you're Brian Matthews."

He smiled and handed her a cup of hot tea. "The one and the same."

"What a lucky coincidence." She smiled at him. "I was coming to see your shop. I was given this scarf the other day, and I've always admired your work. I just wanted to tell you how amazing I think it is." She offered her free hand. "I'm Louise Pram. Everyone calls me Lou. I work for Sera."

He should have known. "It's nice to meet you, Lou, and thank you very much for the compliment." He eyed her critically. "You can't go out in this weather, and you certainly can't stand around like that. Why don't you borrow something to wear and wait out the storm?"

"You wouldn't mind?"

"Not at all. I'd rather talk to you than to myself." He went through the racks, studied items, and finally picked a colorful skirt and matching top. "Here." He offered them to her. "These were made for you. You can go through that door," he pointed, "and change. Toss your wet clothes in the dryer."

She ran her fingers over the silky material of the clothes. "I really shouldn't."

His eyes twinkled. "But you will anyway."

She laughed. "I can't help it. I'd never turn down a chance to wear something this beautiful." She hurried into the back and shut the door. She didn't bother to lock it. There was no rational reason why, but she absolutely trusted him. She felt safe with him. She couldn't shake the feeling that it wasn't their first meeting. Everything about him . . . his eyes, his smile, his voice . . . even her attraction to him felt familiar.

The skirt hung to her ankles and felt so light and airy that she decided it had been made of clouds. The top was her favorite kind since it had built-in breast support. That meant she could toss her bra in the dryer too. Thankfully, her underwear had stayed dry. She added her socks to the dryer and set her shoes aside to air dry.

Her sopping wet hair couldn't be helped, but when she walked back into the front, Brian offered her a towel. "Thanks." She rubbed at her hair briskly and studied him curiously. "You've been on the market for ten years, but I'd swear you couldn't be much older than me."

"I turn twenty-eight in a few days." He leaned on the counter to watch her. She glowed brilliantly inside his small space as if it simply couldn't contain the wildness of her soul. "What about you?"

"Twenty-seven in five months." She saluted lightly as she pulled the towel off her head, and she knew, without looking, that her hair had to be a mess. A little smile played at her host's ridiculously kissable mouth. "That bad?" She tugged at a curl.

"Come here."

She didn't think to question why. She simply walked over to where he stood. She didn't find a single protest to voice as his fingers combed through her hair and easily coaxed the curls into taming. He truly wasn't much taller, though she herself stood on the shorter side, and he seemed strong and warm. Secure. The scent of his skin made her feel as if she had come home.

His fingers were still tangled in her hair as if he couldn't quite let go. She couldn't catch her breath as she looked up at him. She had never thought of glasses as sexy, but on him they looked outrageously hot.

Another clap of thunder broke the tension. She stepped back and he picked up his coffee. By tacit agreement, neither said a word about what had almost happened. Instead, she sat down on one of the seats at the counter. "Thanks again for the rescue. I have no sense of direction."

"None at all?"

"Afraid not." She winced wryly. "I'm the only artist in the family. I think that anything related to practicality was used up before my parents got to me. Then again, I have younger siblings that turned out okay, so maybe there was a temporary shortage on genes." She propped her chin on her hand with a smile.

"How many siblings?" He sat down across from her and picked up a bundle of material to begin stitching a hem.

"Six total. I'm fifth in the line-up." She watched his hands in fascination. She had always considered sewing to be slightly feminine, but his nimble hands bespoke pure masculinity. The delicate way they handled the cloth made her wonder what it would be like to feel his touch on her body. "What about you?"

"Only child," he admitted. He glanced up to find her watching him and his fingers tightened on the needle and thread as his body throbbed with hunger. His scarf had curled around her neck and the end lightly danced over her breasts. He wanted to be the cloth covering her, to tie her up in him so she could not escape again. He just did not dare. "I have a couple aunts and uncles," he said, his voice huskier, "one of which is Sera's stepfather."

She very carefully sat up straight, her pulse beating quickly. She knew she had not mistaken the desire in his eyes. It called to the passion inside her so swiftly, so fiercely, that it took her breath. She waited, looked, but that strange feeling of cosmic cheating did not come. Was he the one she had been looking for?

She cast quickly for a neutral subject. She had just met the man! She couldn't jump over the counter and pin him to the floor, no matter how tempting it sounded. Never mind that she didn't feel like she talked to a stranger. "Do you make your own cloth? I'd swear I've never seen anything like it before."

"I do. If I don't weave it by hand, there's a place I can send my designs to and have them make it. I use them only for large projects. Most of the time, it's all by hand." He saw her fingers lightly moving over the scarf and his body tightened with need. He wanted to be the one she touched in that way. "Your scarf was woven by me."

"I never take it off," she admitted. "I just can't bear to let it go." She took a deep breath. "What are you working on there?"

"A shirt." He held it up so that she could see it. "I'm not sure who it will belong to. My work always picks its owner."

"Is that your gift?" When he lifted a brow at her, she smiled. "C'mon. You were born here. Was I not supposed to know? Have you *heard* what's been going on at my office over the last few months? I work for Aladdin!"

"It is my gift. I can deliberately imbue certain items with the ability to heal or give someone protection or help. When I make an item for someone in particular, it becomes attuned to them. No one else will see it in the same way the owner does."

Her heart skipped a beat. Had he . . . made the scarf for her? That was impossible. He had never met her until now! "I think it's amazing," she said honestly. "When Cameron and Kenneth said that the District was like homecoming, I didn't fully understand until I was here. Even when I was lost and wandering the streets, I didn't feel out of place. I could have been happy to wander for hours."

"We often say that those drawn to the District have inside them something that they need that only can be found here. What do you want, Lou? More than anything."

"To be loved." Her color rose as she heard her words. "I know it sounds cheesy," she stammered quickly, "and don't think I don't have a great family, because I do, but I just don't have anywhere to fit in, and my family sometimes looks at me weird and . . ."

He gently pressed his fingers to her lips. A soft smile curved his lips and made his eyes warm. In the lamp lit room, he looked mysterious and welcoming at the same time. A gentleness inside him simply effused the air. It called to her like a lodestone.

"Don't explain yourself," he told her softly. "When you said 'you don't fit in anywhere' it made perfect sense why you were drawn here. We don't belong anywhere else except here." He rubbed his thumb over her cheek and softly brushed at the curls tumbling in her eyes. Was there hope this time? She was very different from the woman he had known before.

Her lips began to tingle with the desperation to feel his on them. "Brian."

His hand lifted as he got to his feet. "Let me show you something."

She took a moment to press her hands to her heart and take a breath. She was quivering, literally trembling, from head to toe with desire. Every tiny brush of his skin against hers brought dizzying pleasure. And it wasn't a *new* feeling. It seemed as if her body already knew his touch, already knew what he could do to her. "Jesus," she muttered.

"Lou?"

She got to her feet and hurried to where he stood near another door. As she walked, the skirt fluttered around her legs. The silky material caressed her suddenly sensitive skin. She would have *sworn* it felt like his hands touching her instead. "Sorry. I was wool gathering."

She watched rather helplessly as a slow smile curved his lips. "I don't work with wool," he told her, "but I could make an exception if you supply some." He put his hand on the small of her back and nudged her into the room. "In here."

The practical part of her brain told her it was stupid to be alone with a man she barely knew because he might have dastardly intentions. The rest of her prayed that he did. She ignored both and stepped into the room. He turned on a lamp and she blinked in the glare. When she saw the loom in the center of the room, her breath caught. "Oh. Oh wow."

She slowly touched the tapestry and felt it pulsing with power.

"It's beautiful, Brian," she said softly. She ran her eyes over it, sensing it might be more than just decoration. "What is it? Does it tell a story?"

"It does." He didn't need to see the images to know how it went. It had been engraved inside his soul. "Have you ever heard the tale of the Weaver's Wife?"

"No."

"Do you want to?"

She lightly ran her fingers over the faces within colored thread. "Yes." It came out as little more than a whisper. Somehow . . . she could feel the importance.

"The story starts a long time ago."

She found a smile. "Doesn't it always?"

His knuckles brushed down her arm softly. "There was a poor weaver who lived by himself along the sea. He had no fortune, no claim to fame. His was a simple life. One day, as he was walking to town for thread, he came upon a young woman on the road. She was a wild spirit in a conservative family life, and she did not look upon him poorly. They walked together. They talked together. And they were in love before they reached the town.

"Her family was reluctant to allow her to wed the weaver, but he offered woven silks, the finest ever seen, and her family relented. The two were married and she wore a gown made by her groom's hand, tailored perfectly to fit only her. They were happy together for many years, living by the sea while the waves came in."

He took a step away, seeing only the past. "The weaver could feel a restlessness in his wife. Her spirit could not be tamed. And so he said to her 'go into the world. I cannot go with you.' She went into the world, traveled to a foreign place, and then came home. Her restlessness grew worse, and he told her again 'go into the world. I cannot go with you.' Again, she went to see a far off land. She came home, and she was so restless that the weaver knew she could not be kept. He told her 'go into the world. I cannot go with you." Very softly he said, "And she went."

She found herself gripping the edge of her scarf like a lifeline. Her throat had tightened with pain for the weaver in the tale. How he must have loved his wife to let her go! "And what happened?" she whispered.

"I don't know." He let out a long breath. "I've never known. I don't think anyone knows what happened. I keep hoping I will figure it out so I can finish my tapestry." He finally turned to look at her, and his heart broke at the sight of tears on her cheeks. He rubbed his thumb under her eyes to steal them away. "I did not tell you to make you sad."

"It's not that." She turned her face into his hand almost helplessly. "It's just . . . I could swear I had been there. I felt it so deeply." She drew a ragged breath. "Well, I hope you find that ending, Brian. I'd like to know too."

He led her back into the front shop, and they could both see that it had stopped raining at last. "I suppose I should keep my things indoors tomorrow, just in case," he said wryly. "Whenever they say something on the news, I always assume the opposite."

"That's because you're smart." She sighed. "Guess I better put my clothes back on and get out of your hair."

"You can keep what you're wearing," he told her softly.

"Really?" She looked down in surprise at the clothes. "But . . ."

"Tell you what." He smiled as he leaned against the counter. "You visit me again, and we'll call it a fair trade." He snagged a bag from a hook and held it out. "Put your things in here and I'll walk you to your car." His eyes twinkled. "And I'll be sure to point out the right way to get here."

She had to grin at that. "I don't get embarrassed by the truth." She hurried to the dryer and pulled out her warm clothes. She tucked them into the bag and slung it over her shoulder. "I really am grateful to you."

"Then come back very soon."

She tilted her head slightly and her curls danced around her face. He kept his hands in his pockets before he got his fingers in the auburn locks once more. "Why?" she asked. "You sound like you're in a hurry."

"I won't be here much longer," he said simply.

"Oh." Sadness wrenched her heart. Not that she blamed him if he had decided to move; he really needed more space with the way he was busting at the seams, so to speak. His tone just seemed to indicate that he would be going very far. The thought of not seeing him again terrified her. "I'll come back tomorrow then." She glanced away shyly. "I like spending time with you."

He held out a hand and she took it hesitantly. He laced their fingers together and tugged her closer. She held her breath, praying for a kiss, but all he did was give her a gentle hug with his free arm. Fed up with both of them, she freed her hand and wrapped her arms around his neck firmly. "Hold me. Just once, I want to be held."

The hitch in her voice shattered his control. His arms banded fiercely around her waist as he lifted her off her feet. He buried his face in her hair, savoring the fragrant scent and silken texture. She still smelled like summer and sunshine. He had never forgotten. "Lou."

"It's stupid," she said shakily against his shoulder. "It's ridiculous. But I can't let go of you. I'm scared, Brian. I don't even know why. I feel like something terrible will happen to you if I do. I want to say I just met you, but I didn't. I know I didn't. What's wrong with me?"

"I don't know. But you're not alone. I knew you when I saw you. I think I knew you subconsciously all along." He eased her back and caught a handful of the scarf. "I made this for you." He spoke so softly, so intensely, that she believed him. "It could belong to no other." He brushed a tender kiss across her forehead. "I'll take you to your car."

If it hadn't been for him holding her hand, she knew she would never have had the strength to leave. They stepped outside and she shivered in the still chilled air. Summer storm it may be, the air still felt cool on her skin after being indoors. He released her hand to go back inside, and when he came out again, he wrapped a soft shawl around her shoulders. "I shouldn't accept this," she scolded him.

He smiled. "But you will." He combed his fingers through her hair just for the enjoyment of seeing the curls cling to his fingers. "After all, no smart woman turns down free designer clothes. You seem pretty savvy to me."

She laughed. "I can't argue with any of that." She leaned against his shoulder as they walked down the sidewalk. She saw people smiling at them and couldn't help but smile back. When someone waved, she blew them a kiss. "I bet they think I'm your secret girlfriend."

"They've been bored lately. The giggling will do them good." He tucked her under his arm securely.

"I have to ask. How tall are you? I mean . . . I'm five-three and I'm not very shorter than you."

"Five-six."

She sighed happily. "I could grow fond of shorter men." They had reached her car and she reluctantly stepped free of his arm. She unlocked the door and turned to say goodbye when she realized how close he stood. The urge rose so fast that she couldn't resist. She tossed her bags into the car and then went on her toes to kiss him. She let him go almost as quickly as she had grabbed him and ducked into the car. The taste of him was as wildly tempting and achingly familiar as the rest of him.

He bent to look in the car at her, and his blue eyes burned with passion barely kept in check. "I'll let you go with that," he warned huskily, "but now I owe you one." He shut the door and walked away before she could say a word.

On a shaky breath, she dropped her forehead onto the steering wheel. She had the panicky feeling of going under for the third time and couldn't even remember deciding to get into deep water. She knew she should stay away, let him go, and move on. But she couldn't.

She just couldn't.

CHAPTER NINETEEN

After a sleepless night being haunted by too familiar cerulean eyes, Louise woke very early. She ignored her answering machine, didn't bother to check her mail, and got dressed in clothes to combat the still threatening storms. Another had come overnight, and most assumed another would hit that day.

She hoped to play hooky again, so when she got to work, she didn't bother to start her computer. She instead lurked outside Sera's office. She had a lot of questions for her friend. And as soon as she saw her, she demanded, "I want to know about Brian."

"Yikes!" Sera pressed a hand to her heart. "You came out of nowhere, Lou! I'm too young for a heart attack." She unlocked the door and nudged her older friend inside. She shut the door where no one could overhear and put her bags down behind her desk. "Okay, what do you want to know?"

"Where is he going?"

"Can't tell. That's his choice."

Louise sat down in one of the chairs and gripped her hands together tightly. The scarf tied around her hair seemed oddly less colorful as if responding to her emotions. "What *can* you tell me?" she asked softly. "Please, Sera. I'm begging. I'm in over my head. You've been there."

"Yeah." Sera propped her chin on her hand as she leaned on the desk. "It's damned scary, that's for sure. Why don't you tell me what happened yesterday, and I'll decide what I can tell you. Brian is . . . secretive. There are things only he should tell you."

"I went to see him yesterday and got lost in the storm. He took me to his place and gave me dry clothes. We talked. He told me a story of a tapestry he's making." She took a deep breath. "And we struggled with one ridiculously powerful attraction. We both . . . we both recognized each other somehow. He said he made this scarf for me."

Sera took a long breath. "There's not much else I can tell you other than the fact that he's one of the most amazing people I've known. He loves so much. Gives so much. He would sooner be the one unhappy than see anyone else suffer. I've never heard him raise his voice. Never heard him use anything stronger than 'hell' and that was only when the loom nearly fell over on one of my little stepsisters."

"What am I supposed to do?"

"I don't know," her friend said simply. "I wish I did. But you're of no use to us like this, so take another day off, okay? Go see him. I think any answers that the two of you need can only be found with each other."

"Thanks, Sera." She got to her feet and hurried out of the office.

As Sera buried her face in her hands, Kenneth walked into the office. He went to her side without a word and pulled her into his arms. He had a strong feeling he knew now what was happening. It was scary for everyone involved. There was a lot more at stake here than he had ever imagined.

The neighbor's cats awoke him again, but Brian didn't immediately get out of bed. Truth be told, he hadn't really been sleeping. He hadn't slept much the entire night. He had been tormented by dreams of the past and memories of the present. How was it possible to crave another person so badly? He couldn't remember if it had been like this in the past, but he wouldn't have been surprised.

When he finally dragged himself out of bed, he put on coffee and got to work boxing up items he knew wouldn't sell in the next two days. There was no fear in him. No real sadness. He'd had a long time to get used to his fate. He didn't even want to think that he might be freed of his curse; it was too painful to think of trying and losing.

His regular phone rang and he picked it up. "Hello?"

"Brian, I hear you were seen with a lovely lady yesterday."

He smiled wryly. "You heard right, Uncle Lewis. Her name is Louise Pram. She's a friend of Sera's, and also one of her employees. She got lost out here and I gave her shelter from the storm."

Lewis was silent for long moments. Then, "And?"

"And I don't know," he said simply. "I'm not going to trap her, Uncle. I could not bear it. Am I supposed to sacrifice her happiness just so I can live? I don't think so. I'm sorry. Enforcers tried their best, but I don't think it's going to work." He hung up the phone and considered the merits of locking the front door. He just didn't feel like seeing anyone. She wouldn't come back to him.

"Brian?"

His head jerked up in shock at the sound of her voice. She hovered just inside the front door, something hesitant in her eyes as if she wasn't sure he would welcome her. "Lou." He breathed her name softly, unable to believe she really stood there. "You came back."

"I promised, didn't I? Am . . . am I interrupting anything? I can leave."

"No!" He crossed the room and caught her in his arms. "Don't you dare walk out that door." He buried his face in her hair and savored how it felt to hold her. Even if it was only one more time, at least he could see her. Could touch her. "I didn't really expect you to come back again."

"I had to." She curled her arms around his shoulders and held

on tightly. Everything was alright again. Now that she was in his arms, everything was alright. "I needed to see you again."

He let her go with visible reluctance. "Well, you can help me then. I'm working on packing. I know you'll enjoy seeing all the different things I've made." He smiled suddenly. "Say, you want to help me out? I have several things I need to finish and my dressmaker dummy fell apart on me. They should fit you well enough for me to make sure I'm putting them together right."

She cocked her head and smiled. "Sure. That sounds like fun." She laughed. "Gee, I always wanted to be a model but they said I was too short."

"Pity." Something hot filled his eyes as he looked her over slowly. "You certainly have the body for it." He let his fingers linger on her cheek and then dropped his hand and went to the front door. He turned over the Closed sign to give them privacy before leading the way into the back room where he kept works-in-progress.

"How many rooms are there?" she asked curiously. She was ignoring, to the best of her ability, the way he seemed to be looking at her. It wasn't good for her pulse or her control. "I've seen two others than the front now."

"Four, not including the bathroom. The other two rooms are a small kitchen and my bedroom." He hung a sheet from the ceiling to make an impromptu changing area for her. "Here you go. Now you won't worry about modesty." He turned around and lost nearly every thought in his head as he realized she had stripped off her jacket and shirt. The plain black bra gently hugging her beautiful breasts was all about practicality, and he wanted very badly to remove it so that she wore nothing except the light.

Her stomach quivered with nerves but she managed to keep her tone light. "I've never been very modest. And . . ." Much softer she continued, "And I just don't feel uncomfortable with you. I know you somehow. I trust you."

"Don't trust me too much, love." He focused on pulling clothing out of drawers. "I want you very badly."

She had known it, but hearing it sent a thrill through her body. What would it be like to make him lose his control? To have her gentle weaver go wild? She somehow knew that he was the still waters whose depths became dark and volatile. Perhaps that was the very water she had been pulled under. "I trust you," she said again with absolute conviction. "You would not hurt me."

"No," he agreed quietly. "I wouldn't." He handed her a handful of cloth and added casually, "And if you are wondering, I'm comfortable enough with half or completely naked women as well."

"At almost twenty-eight," she murmured drolly, "I would certainly assume so." She shook out the material she had been handed and discovered it was a dress of some kind. Curious, she shed her jeans as well and pulled the dress on over her head.

He closed his eyes as he watched her shimmy into the outfit. This hadn't been such a good idea after all. It would be one serious test of his self-control. She was perfectly formed, her body designed to be held by his. When he opened his eyes again, he found himself grinning despite his desire. "Hmm."

Her lips twitched. "I think this belongs to someone taller than me." The collar of the dress tried to dip toward her waist, and the waist tried to go to her knees. "I think Sera needs this more than I do."

He grabbed a tape measure but briefly paused before lifting it. "Do you mind?"

"Not at all." She held up her arms to allow him to get her measurements. As he checked her bust size, she added in amusement, "The only man in the world who could probably guess my measurements without being offensive is also the only man who would think of double checking."

"I'd have been wrong." He wrote down the numbers on a pad of paper. "You're a bit more curvaceous than I was admiring."

"As opposed to assuming, you were admiring?"

He glanced up from measuring her hips. "I'm not blind." He straightened and smiled. "Strip."

"Yet another thing you can say without being offensive." She tugged off the dress.

"It's a gift." He put the dress in a box with a note for it to be given to Sera and then grabbed another article. "This ought to be much closer."

Much to her relief, it was. Rather than being distinctly too big, it was only a little bit off. She could even see where he hadn't finished piecing it together; among other things, it only had one sleeve. The material felt so soft and silky that she knew he had woven it.

Truthfully, she suspected she would always know the difference. It just seemed that anything he had woven by hand caressed her skin intimately. She was only glad he didn't make lingerie. There was no telling what it would do to her.

She stood patiently while he pinned the missing sleeve in place and held the tape measure so that he could check the length. "I think it's a funny length." She looked down. "The edge hits that no man's land between calf length and ankle length."

"I agree. Let's see if I have something to fix that." He went through three drawers before he found a roll of lace. "Here we are." He knelt at her feet and pinned some in place. "I think that's much better."

"Definitely." She turned in a circle to help him pin all the lace, then gingerly removed the dress with his help so that she didn't get stuck by anything. Even with his care, one of the needles scraped over her shoulder. "Ouch!"

"I'm sorry, Lou." He lightly touched the scratch where it looked angry and red against her fair skin. "It's not bleeding, thankfully." He skimmed his thumb down her shoulder where he could see only a faint tan line. "Sunbathing or tanning salon?"

"Hey, if I'm going to tan, I do it in real sun, not artificial." She couldn't fight a shiver of delight as he trailed his fingers over her skin. His fingers were as soft as the silk they handled, and just as delicate in their touch. "Brian."

His hands curled around her waist hotly as he pressed a tender kiss to the scratch. "I just needed to touch you."

The quivering started from inside and moved outward as his lips softly trailed across her shoulder. Barely breathing, she leaned her head back against his shoulder helplessly. Heat rose with shocking swiftness, her body eagerly craving more of the wicked pleasure. *He wasn't even really touching her.* Just those tiny kisses over her shoulder and his hands around her waist. She was so sharply attuned to him that it began to alarm her. "Brian," she said again.

This time he let her go. "I'm sorry." He averted his gaze. "Get dressed."

She slowly pulled on her clothes again and found them oddly distasteful after having worn his work. Striving for a neutral subject, she asked, "When Sarah had so much trouble with her skin, did you make her clothes? Sarah Davidson, I mean."

"I knew who you meant." He made himself busy by sealing boxes. It was either that or tumbling her down onto the hand woven rug and getting reacquainted with everything new and everything familiar. He wanted her so badly that even his teeth hurt. His jeans felt far too tight on his aching arousal, and he knew full well that there was no hiding it. "And yes, I did. I had always hoped to make her wedding dress someday, but, well, things have happened to both of us."

"That's one way of putting it." Fully dressed again, she bent to help him pick up some pieces of clothing when there came a very loud clap of thunder right over the shop. It was followed closely by the sound of heavy rain. "Seriously," she said dryly, "why have meteorologists when they can't even predict the weather correctly?"

"I have a second cousin in Sacramento, Cali." He shook his head. "She says that if you wait five minutes, the weather changes. More mood swings than the local government."

"Which local government?"

"Any."

They shared a grin. She handed him the items she held and turned to get more. Her toes promptly caught on the rug and it slid

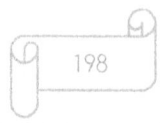

across the hardwood floor. It threw her entirely off balance and would have sent her onto the floor if he hadn't moved swiftly and caught her in his arms.

Sadly, he slid on the rug too. They went down hard but landed on a pile of material that cushioned them. She shook her head to clear it and looked up to see him smiling wryly. "Sorry about that," she said sheepishly. "Did I mention that the directional genes weren't the only ones that went on strike when I was born?"

"I've seen the world's greatest dancer slide on this thing. It's not you, trust me."

His smile slowly faded as he looked down at her. She had ended up beneath him in the fall. Her body pressed along every inch of his. Her wild hair reflected more red than brown as it caught the warm hues of the material she laid on. Her perfect mouth curved into a smile, and her blue eyes shimmered in the light.

Her smile disappeared as she stared up at him and saw the look in his eyes. Instead, her lips began to tingle and throb, as if knowing precisely how his mouth would feel and craving the sensation. With trembling fingers, she ran her thumb over his lips and then over his face before burying her hands in his hair.

He bent his head and took the kiss they both needed so badly. His lips were soft and firm all at once; hot and hungry but gentle and tender. The conflicting emotions tugged at everything inside her until the trembling had spread through her whole body. Her lips parted under the pressure of his and a soft whimper caught in her throat as his tongue immediately thrust into her mouth aggressively.

Something broke inside her. She could hear it, let alone feel it. With a low cry, she arched up to deepen the kiss, her fingers curling into his hair to keep him close to her hungry mouth. She couldn't get enough of his taste. She was starved for it.

His hands fisted into her curls and held her head still as he took the kiss even deeper. The taste of her was engraved inside him, so familiar and so welcome that his throat tightened with a swell of emotion he could not fight. He broke free of the kiss and raced wild kisses over her face. Her soft breaths seared him. "Lou. I love you."

She went very still. "What?"

He lifted his head and met her eyes evenly. "I love you. Stay with me."

Terrified, she broke out of his grip and scrambled to her feet. "This is too much. Too fast. I'm not like this. I can't get involved with you." She backed toward the door, breathing too hard and too fast. "I don't know what's wrong with me."

She fled the room and he closed his eyes as he heard the front door open and slam closed. Pain welled up endlessly. He had reached for her again only to encounter the one thing he could not fight: her desperate longing to be free. He fell onto his back and covered his face with his hands. It was over.

She had run two blocks before the tears caught up and forced her to stop. With a low sob, she sank down to the ground against a wall. Just what was she running from? Was she running from his feelings or her own? Why had she panicked? "I'm a coward," she whispered, her face buried in her knees.

She had finally found the person she was cosmically tied to, and she had run away when he told her he loved her. It was fast, outrageous, and it shouldn't be happening. Yet it *was* happening . . . and she could not find the will to change it.

She was in love with him. She had been all along.

A soft throbbing warmth had her lifting her head. Her scarf was pulsing. The gentle touch of the material over her skin had the same sensation as Brian's touch. She gently rubbed the cloth between her fingers. From the day she had picked it up, this moment had been inevitable.

So what if he was leaving? Providing he wasn't going to the moon, she could go with him. If it wasn't far, they could commute. If it was far, she could find another job near him. The only thing she could not give up was Brian himself.

She scrambled to her feet and called herself every name she could think of as she ran back through the pouring rain. Though she

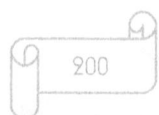

had always before gotten easily lost, she found her way to the shop as if something pulled her there. And something did. The man she had loved since before her birth.

The door was still unlocked. She threw it open. "Brian!"

He looked up sharply and felt a wild sense of déjà vu as he saw her in the doorway. She was soaked and shivering, her hair longer than usual because the curls had pulled out. Her eyes weren't quite tamed, were certainly a little wild, and a lot terrified. "Louise." He stayed where he was in the middle of the shop. He could not go to her again.

"It's not you," she said fiercely. "It's me. I'm a coward. I ran from my feelings, not yours." She took two trembling steps toward him. "I love you. I have all along."

Heart pounding, he held his arms out. She cleared the floor in nearly a single leap, her arms going fiercely around his neck even as her legs hooked around his hips. She clung onto him as if he were life itself. "Lou. Dear god, Lou." He held her as tightly as he could, shaking from the inside out.

"Don't let me go," she whispered as she trailed desperate kisses over his neck and face. "Not even for my sake."

He would have to. He knew he would have to. But this was a reprieve from hell, a chance at heaven. He buried his fingers in her hair and dragged her head up for a wild kiss. Unable to release her, he whirled and carried her down the hall to his room without once releasing her lips. She was wild in his arms, her body twisting and pressing against his, her tongue not only accepting the mating thrust of his but returning the gesture readily.

When he swung her around, she broke free of the kiss with a breathless laugh. "Wait! Don't get the bed wet! I'm soaked to the skin!"

He dropped her onto her feet and nearly tore the shirt she wore off over her head. It landed with a wet plop somewhere in the room. "I wanted to do this all day," he admitted roughly. His hands ran up and down her sides just a little harder than usual. "You shouldn't wear anything." His mouth ran hotly down her neck and his teeth tugged at the strap of her bra. "And if you wear anything," he added more fiercely, "it should mine. I'm the only one who can touch you."

"I knew it." Her head fell back as his teeth scraped deliciously. It was only his arms holding her on her shaking legs. "I knew it felt as if . . . as if anything you had woven was touching me like a lover." She laughed huskily. "Don't make me lingerie. I'll lose all ability to think."

"How you tempt a man." He unfastened her jeans and slowly peeled the wet denim down her long legs. She still wore her sandals and he tossed them across the room without care.

Her head was still spinning when he stood and dragged her up for another kiss. The feeling of his clothes against her sensitized skin was erotic, but not nearly close enough to what she wanted. With more desperation than finesse, she rushed to open the buttons on his shirt. One popped off. "Sorry."

His laugh sounded low and seductive. "You know a good tailor."

"Boy, do I." Her sigh came long and happy as he shrugged out of his shirt. He wasn't necessarily built like some men she had known, but his body was defined with just enough muscle to entice. Everything looked gentle about him, and she craved that tenderness even in the middle of the storm surging through her body. "You're beautiful."

"Am I?"

She looked up in surprise. "You sound surprised."

His fingers curled into her thick hair. "Everything is different when you're in love." He tugged her up again and kissed her with a slowly famished heat. The shudder that ripped through her body clawed at him with desire.

He released her and swiftly divested her of her bra. Her underwear went next. As he straightened and stared at her hotly, she realized what he meant. It was one thing to know you were attractive. It was another thing entirely to see yourself in the eyes of the one who loved you.

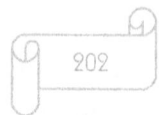

She reached out a finger and lightly touched the needle shaped mark on his shoulder. "Tattoo?"

"Birthmark."

"How appropriate." She eased in and lightly tasted the mark, and her tongue teased it gently. His strong body jerked and the rush of power filled her. "Just how much can you take?" She nuzzled her way across the dark curls on his chest. "You've been seducing me for days. It's my turn now."

"I've barely touched you." His voice broke as her lips closed over a nipple and tugged. "Lou."

"With your hands, you've barely touched me." She scooped up the fallen scarf and slowly trailed the ends across her skin. "This has touched me all along. You touched me all along."

He looped the scarf around her neck and jerked her against his aching body. "I never stopped touching you." He lifted her and tumbled her down onto the bed. When he saw her lying there, the scarf dancing over her beautiful body, his control broke. He stripped off the rest of his clothes and slid onto the bed beside her. "I need you," he said roughly as he buried his face between her breasts. "Please, Lou."

His mouth captured her nipple and sucked so strongly that her back arched. The ache that had never gone away erupted into a wildfire. She could feel the throbbing need between her legs and she curled a leg over his hip enticingly. "Hurry."

The breathless plea was more than he could bear. They could tease each other later. They had been teasing each other for centuries. On a tortured groan, he caught her mouth with his as he fumbled blindly for the nightstand. "Damn it," he said against her lips when he couldn't open the drawer.

A wild thrill went through her entire body. She nipped sharply at his ear and savored the way he quivered in her grip. "I wonder if I could make you get really creative." Her tongue teased the line of his jaw.

A bit desperately, he got the drawer open and grabbed

protection. When she saw the foil packet in his hand, her heart fluttered with emotion. That he would remember something like that even as hungry as they both were . . . it was simply the way he was. Everything about him was so perfect for her. She grabbed his wrist before he could tear it open. "No," she said softly. "Not this time."

It was risky and irresponsible. He had never been either of those things, but he didn't want anything between them either. She was his in a way she would never be anyone else's just as he was hers. He threw the packet to the side and dragged her closer. Slowly, his eyes burning into hers, he began to take her, savoring the sensation of her tight flesh welcoming his possession.

When he was as deep as he could go, he simply stayed there for a long moment. Homecoming. It wasn't a new feeling. He still remembered how it felt to make love to her. How every moment felt perfect. He framed her face with his hands and kissed her ravenously. "I love you."

Her hips arched helplessly, trying to urge him into moving. No cosmic cheating here. *This* was what she had been seeking. She dug her nails into his shoulders demandingly. "I love you. Please!"

He shuddered and gave them both what they needed, thrusting into her again and again until her breaths were sobs and she clung onto him wildly. The tension gathered and coiled, the ceaseless pleasure driving him to take her as hard and deep as he could. He fought it, needing her to be there with him.

It wasn't a long wait. Ecstasy could not be resisted by either. It grabbed them sharply and wouldn't let go, waves of pure delight tearing through their bodies. It went to a level beyond their flesh, into their hearts and souls, even into their minds as the joy of reunion, not discovery, claimed them both.

In the silence after, she lay curled against his chest, listening to him breathe, and realized that she wanted to be nowhere else. She needed nothing else. Finally she had found where she belonged.

CHAPTER TWENTY

The sound of the storm finally clearing woke Louise later that evening. She had lost track of the passage of time entirely. There had been nothing but her and Brian inside her world. Her body ached and tingled after the last few hours, and she savored every sensation. She would have called her lover insatiable, but, really, she was just as bad. She couldn't shake the feeling that they had been making up for lost time.

She turned to cuddle against him and discovered his side of the bed was empty. Startled, she sat up. "Brian?"

"Down here," came his voice from somewhere in the house.

She slipped out of bed and spotted a gorgeous silk robe lying on the end of the mattress. It was a blushing rose pink with a paler cream pattern across it. Enchanted, she lifted it and rubbed her cheek over the soft material. It teased and caressed her like the touch of its maker's fingers, and she knew he had made it for her.

When she slipped it on, it fit perfectly. She used her scarf as a belt and headed down the hall toward Brian's voice. She found him standing at the loom, studying the story of the Weaver's Wife. She slid her arms around his waist and pressed against his back. "What's wrong?" she asked softly.

"I can't see the end." He kept his voice even with effort. He couldn't see the end and the mark had not faded. She loved him, but he could not keep her. Nothing had changed except that he would die knowing what it was like to truly live.

"Is it important?"

"Yes."

She rubbed her cheek against his back. "Why?"

"I can't explain it." He turned and pulled her into his arms. "I knew this robe would be perfect on you." His fingers danced down the sleeve of the robe, caressing the skin beneath as if the silk wasn't even there. "I suspect that if I go through the shop, I'm going to find a lot that I made with you in mind."

"I wouldn't mind wearing a wardrobe entirely created by you." Her lips curved. "Of course, considering my sensitivity to your work, there's no telling what it'll do to me. I might have to take long lunches just to find you and seduce you."

Sadness filled his heart. There would be no long lunches together. He buried his face in her hair for a moment and held on with all his strength.

She paused as she sensed his desperation and then held him in return. She wanted to tell him that whatever was wrong would be made right, but she could not find the words. "What's wrong?" She framed his face with her hands as he lifted his head. "Tell me," she urged softly. "I can't stand to see you so sad, Brian."

"I was just thinking of a cousin of mine. He was diagnosed with cancer and told he only had months to live. He asked me what I would do if I only had a day left to live, and I had no answer for him." He searched her eyes. "What would you do?"

She didn't have to think about it. "I would do everything I had never gotten to do. Then, when I felt that my last moment had arrived, I would choose how I left this world." She softly kissed him, hurting for him. "I'm so sorry, Brian. It must hurt to lose someone you love. And your family is small to begin with."

"I've accepted it." He released her and looked at the tapestry. "I need to ask you a favor," he said softly. "If a time comes that something happens to me before I finish this, I want you to burn it."

"Burn it?!" She took a step back in horror. "You want me to burn something so beautiful?"

"Please, Lou."

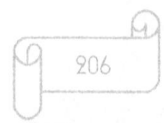

Very reluctantly, she finally said, "Alright. But you'll finish it. I know you will." As he turned toward her, she slid her arms up around his neck. "I didn't like waking without you," she told him softly. "I don't even want to be away from you for a minute."

His lips curved. "I think my cousin's leniency with your time off might go only so far, my love." He softly trailed kisses over her face and savored her taste. It had been burned inside him for all time. It would remain there always.

"Oh, I dunno. I bet she wouldn't mind. I have plenty of vacation time owed to me. I hadn't taken a day off in a year or two." She slid her hands slowly over his chest, and her fingers danced across the little needle mark that intrigued her. "And I think she and Sarah and the boys think this is my just desserts. They wanted me to find someone."

He lifted her into his arms and headed back down the hall toward the bedroom. "I'm not wasting a minute," he muttered fiercely. "I've waited too long for you as it is." He lowered her down onto the bed and untied the robe. "I love you, Louise."

The desperation was in his touch again. She didn't question it. She simply gave herself to his embrace with all the love she had. She tried to give him everything, somehow sensing he needed to hold onto her. The wordless fear had come back again, but she absolutely refused to lose him.

The next time she awoke, it was morning. She also awoke to her lover's hands softly moving over her body. The sunlight poured in the window but it did not feel nearly as hot as his skin. She opened her eyes and found herself looking into his cerulean gaze as he watched her tenderly. With a sigh, she tugged him down for a lingering kiss. Now *this* was her idea of starting the day right.

Clanging and banging on the roof broke the mood. "What is that?" she asked warily.

"Neighbor's cat chasing pigeons." He skimmed his hands over her before reluctantly getting out of bed. "Shower?"

She admired the line of his back and decidedly delicious ass and then hopped out of bed as well. "My hair must be a mess." She looked in a mirror and winced. Her curls had officially gone out of control. "I tried to grow my hair out once, hoping it would stretch the curls. It didn't work. I just looked like I had hair that went out of style in the 80s."

"They're not that bad." He caught a handful and tugged lightly. "I love your hair." He turned on the shower full blast and waited for the water to heat. "In you go. There's room enough for two."

Only barely, she found out a moment later, but she wasn't complaining with any excuse to be in close quarters with his amazing beauty. She even let him wash her hair for her, though she had never imagined she would ever want to share that kind of an intimacy.

After the shower, she dried her hair while he shaved. The domesticity of the scene staggered her. Her few lovers had never felt that . . . right to her. Even disregarding the 'cosmic cheating' issue, she had just never felt like having anyone that deeply in her life. Things had been casual. The curious thing now was that this *was* casual. Casual intimacy. Brian fit so perfectly in her life it was as if he had always been there.

She commandeered the small kitchen to cook breakfast while he made coffee. He disappeared to put on clothes and shortly returned to catch her in his arms. He rested his chin on her shoulder contentedly. "I threw your dirty clothes in the washer."

"I can't go naked all day," she noted dryly.

"More's the pity. Actually, I picked something out for you."

"Now you really *are* spoiling me, B. R. Matthews."

His lips curved into an innocent smile that still looked slightly wicked. "Can I help it if I made that many pieces of clothing with you in my mind? I never know something was made for someone until they come and claim it. There's much here for you to claim."

"Well, if you want to put it that way . . ." She dished up the scrambled eggs she had made and grabbed the toast. "Simple and yet protein filled. We need our energy after last night. And yesterday. I can't believe either of us is walking."

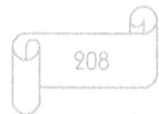

He just smiled and picked up his fork.

While he did the dishes, she went and found the clothes he had laid out. To her amusement, in addition to a lovely pale blue skirt and pink camisole, she also had a matching pair of panties and bra, both in the same pale pink. She was further amused to find they fit perfectly. The only downside was that the material had a way of gliding over her skin that most assuredly would be distracting all day. "When'd you start dabbling in women's unmentionables?" she called down the hall.

"I always did," he called back. "It's just not the biggest part of my trade. I literally make just about anything."

Bemused, she picked up the phone and called her office. Sera cheerfully let her take another day of vacation, but this time Louise was sure she heard a note of strain in her friend's voice. As she slowly hung up the phone, she looked to where Brian stood in the doorway. "She's worried about something. She tried to hide it, but I could hear it. I better take only today and go in tomorrow. Something must be falling apart and she's trying to be nice."

"That might be best." He tugged her to her feet and admired how she looked in the clothes he had made. While she had been on the phone, he had boxed up items he wanted to be given to her some time after he was gone. There had been many, just as he had thought all along. "You know what I want to do today?"

"What?"

"Go out."

"I could be persuaded." She tied the scarf around her hair to keep it out of her face and teasingly fluttered the end under his chin. "Where do you want to go?"

"There's a carnival a few blocks away. I've never been to one."

"Really? In that case, we absolutely have to go." She laced her fingers with his as they headed through the house. The front area had been nearly entirely packed. She wanted to ask where he was going, but something kept her from speaking about it. She really wanted him to ask her to go with him, but she wasn't sure if he would.

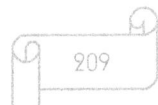

Maybe he needed to move away for a little while and miss her a lot. Then she could call and nag him into letting her go wherever he was. She didn't doubt he loved her, but she suspected he intended to let her go for what he thought was her own good. Over her dead body, he would!

The carnival was lively and fun. He proved to be adept at several of the midway games, and she found herself the reluctant carrier of several strange toys. She didn't mind. She had fun just watching him explore everything. He resembled a big kid who had been let loose on the grounds, and the sudden mental image of a little boy with cerulean eyes and her curly hair nearly took her breath. She really wanted a future with Brian. One that included marriage and kids. Rashid could finally pick her out a dress.

They tried out some of the rides, and all the coaxing in the world wouldn't let Brian convince Louise to get on the most hair-raising one. "No thank you," she said firmly. "My feet stay on terra firma, mmkay?"

"What're you afraid of?" he teased. "It's perfectly safe."

"Not a chance in hell." She crossed her arms and set her chin. "You go ahead. I'm staying right here."

"Spoilsport." He brushed a kiss over her lips and hurried to get into line.

She just smiled and sat on a bench to wait for him. She *hated* large roller coasters. She would sooner find a nice, plain one that didn't do loops and turn her upside down or drop her fifty feet in two seconds.

The ride was only a few minutes, and he returned shortly. When he reached her side, he scooped her up into his arms, bags and all, and swung her around in a happy circle. "I saw you from the top," he told her. "And you were so beautiful that it took my breath."

She kissed him with a happy sigh. "Just for that, I might someday go on a larger coaster with you." She felt as much as saw him flinch slightly and her smile faded. "What aren't you telling me?"

"Nothing important." He put her down but kept her close in a

way that acted more protective than possessive. It was almost as if he feared she would be torn away. "You want to go for a drive with me? It's only early afternoon. I've always wanted to go into the mountains. Ever since I found you, I've felt like I can do everything I always wanted to."

"I'd go anywhere with you." She smiled. "You drive. You know me and my sense of direction."

The drive was two hours long, but they enjoyed every minute. They took turns switching radio stations and made fun of cars that were either an ugly color or simply looked weird. His car had a convertible top, and they left it down. It ruffled his hair and made her curls dance wildly.

"Just what was it like growing up with six siblings?" he asked her curiously.

"Interesting. By the time I was born, Mom and Dad had things down to a science. Unfortunately, I threw them for a loop. Here they were with four kids who liked science and law and numbers and suddenly their newest one wanted paint and pencils. That sustained me until I discovered the joys of computers and digital art."

"Seduced by the dark side."

"They had good cookies." She shot him a grin as he laughed. "One time, when I was about ten, I really, really wanted to paint a mural. I don't know why. But I really wanted to. No one would let me. So I painted the side of the house."

He tried not to smile. "I'm sure your parents greatly appreciated your talent."

"The fact that mural is still there did not stop them from grounding me at that time." She contentedly leaned back. "What about you? Did you get into trouble as a kid?"

"Who didn't? Let's see . . . my most memorable moment had to be when I got mad at a cousin and sewed him into his blankets. Since I used special thread, he couldn't break out. I was about thirteen at the time. He got revenge by filling my room with frogs. I still hate those things to this day. They give me the creeps."

"I guess I shouldn't wear my cute froggie earrings, huh?"

"Not unless you want to see a grown man cry." He turned off the freeway down a beaten road that wound around some rather sharp bends. From the corner of his eye, he saw she had her eyes tightly closed. "You don't like mountain roads?"

"Not in a car going fifty."

"We're going twenty."

"It feels like fifty!" She opened her eyes only when the car stopped and delight filled her at seeing that they had arrived at a scenic outlook. "Oh how beautiful!"

"I hear it's even better up the bike path." He came around the car and took her hand with his to lace their fingers together. "Come with me."

"Always," she promised softly.

By the time the sun set, they were sitting together on a bench that looked out over the rest of the mountain. From that perch, they could see the skyline of their city beginning to glow in the twilight. His hand softly covered hers, and she knew she had never been happier. She had never spent so much time with someone and loved every second.

"I guess you have to work tomorrow," he murmured softly. He rubbed his thumb over her knuckles tenderly.

"Unfortunately. I need to see what Sera is so worried over. Will you miss me?" she teased.

"Every second."

That something was in his voice again and she straightened up. "What's wrong?" She grabbed his shoulders when he would have turned away. "Damn it, Brian. I know there's something wrong. I can feel it. If you're ready to get rid of me, just say so!"

"No, never that! I'm just thinking of my journey." He rubbed his thumb softly across her cheek. "I thought I was ready, but maybe I'm not."

"I'll come visit you," she promised fiercely. "You can't get rid of me."

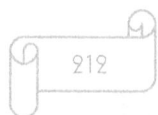

ARRETT

Somehow, he managed a genuine smile. "I would never want to get rid of you." He got to his feet and tugged her up as well. "Let's go home. It's getting late, and you need sleep if you're going to fix whatever your coworkers broke."

"I'm just glad I'm not in charge anymore. I mean, I was good at it, but it's just not my thing. I like the peacefulness of letting someone else lead."

He drove her back to where her car was parked in the District and stood patiently beside her as she unlocked it. When she looked up at him, he couldn't bear it any longer. He pulled her into his arms and kissed her as if it would be the last time. "I love you," he said against her lips.

"Brian?" She frowned when he released her. "You're scaring me."

"It's okay. I'm just not sure how to handle my emotions." He stepped back. "Better leave before I don't let you go at all."

"That's more tempting than you want it to be, I'm sure." She slid into the car and looked up at him. "Good night, Brian."

"Goodbye, love."

It wasn't until she got into bed later that she realized what he had said. He had said goodbye, and it hadn't been in a casual 'see you tomorrow' sort of way. Terror stabbed into her heart. *What was wrong*?

She didn't sleep all night. Bright and early the next morning, she made her way to work. She had tucked her fear away to the best of her ability. As soon as she was done with work for the day, she would go by Brian's place and hopefully catch him before he left entirely. He couldn't get all of it done in just eight hours.

She was at her desk when Sera walked in. The taller female went utterly white as she saw her. "Why are you here?" Sera demanded as she rushed to Louise's side. "Why aren't you with Brian?"

Louise leapt to her feet and slammed her hands on the edge of the cubicle wall, drawing startled eyes from everyone there. "What

13

the hell is going on?" she nearly shouted. "What aren't you two telling me? Damn it, Sera! If you know, tell me! Brian wouldn't tell me what was going on, and I *know* he was afraid of something!"

Sera grabbed her arms sharply. "Go to him! Hurry, Lou! You have to go to him before it's too late! He should be at his shop. Make him tell you what's going on! I *can't*. Don't you think I would have if I could? The terms of his contract—" She shut up quickly.

"Contract. He's under contract with Enforcers. There *is* something wrong." Without waiting for consent, she snatched up her purse and rushed out of the office. Tears burned her eyes and closed her throat, and terror clawed at her heart. Even the soft material sliding over her skin could not soothe her. He would not be under contract unless there was a danger of something terrible happening. She needed to save him from whatever was wrong!

It wasn't long before she parked and rushed toward the shop, but it felt like a century. A For Sale sign sat in the front yard, and the blinds were drawn in all the windows. The door was miraculously unlocked and she rushed inside only to stop sharply. Everything was boxed and labeled clearly. The labels didn't have a forwarding address. They had names and instructions. She grabbed some at random.

'Give to Brie.'

'For Aenya; tell her that I made sure it would aid with restless nights teething'

'Sera; she can have it altered by anyone if needed.'

"What is this?" she whispered. She dropped the tags and went into the kitchen. Empty. The bathroom was empty. The bedroom was empty. There was no sign of Brian. Everything was neatly packed and labeled, ready to be distributed to different people. Nothing indicated it would be sent to his new location.

She went into the room with the loom and stopped still. The tapestry was still there, and it was as yet still unfinished. Boxes with her name stood against the walls, and there was a letter pinned to the bottom of the weaving. With trembling hands, she picked it up

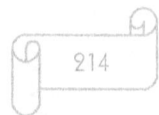

and recognized her lover's handwriting.

My Louise,

If you're reading this, then you obviously came looking for me. I'm so sorry I couldn't tell you this in person. I just didn't want to ruin what little time we had together. It was precious to me, and much more than I had ever dreamed of.

I'm cursed. The mark on my chest will disappear at the hour of my birth on my birthday. That day is today. When that mark fades, I will die. I've lived with this knowledge most of my life. I was resigned to my fate . . . until you walked in the door.

Three hundred years ago, I was a poor weaver. You were the daughter of an affluent family. You wanted to be free. I let you go. To this very minute, I don't know what happened after that. The tale of the Weaver's Wife is the tale of my life. Of my wife. Of you.

I'm taking your advice to heart. I did things I had never done before. Now I will choose how I go. My last gift to you is in those boxes. The greatest thing I can do for you is to set you free. You would never be happy caged.

I'll love you forever.

Brian

Tears running down her cheeks, she tore open the first box. It was clothing. Every box held more. She could feel the love he had poured into his weaving and knew that he had given her a piece of his soul.

She turned and looked at the tapestry. He had wanted her to burn it if he was unable to finish it. Yet as she stood there and stared at it, she slowly began to realize something. It flowed into her mind as flashes and snippets and images.

She knew how the story ended.

She rushed from the shop and back to her car. The entire time she drove on the freeway, she prayed she wouldn't be too late. She never once worried that she would be lost. She could feel the threads tying her to Brian, and they led her true. Her scarf pulsed hotly around her neck and seemed to be urging her on. Those turns on the mountain that normally terrified her were barely even noticed.

Dirt flew as she parked quickly at the scenic overlook. Desperately, she made her way up the path. "Brian!" she shouted. "Brian, answer me!" No answer returned, but as she rounded a bend, she saw him standing at the edge of the cliff where they had watched the sunset together. His open black shirt rippled in the wind, and the mark on his chest was stark and terrifying.

He sensed her presence for it was engraved inside him. His head lifted sharply and he turned toward her. His eyes flared wide with shock. "Lou. What are you doing here?"

"You idiot!" she shouted at him. Her hands curled into fists at her sides. "You're an idiot! What do you think you're doing?!"

"I'm giving you what you need most," he said simply.

"That was always your problem!" she countered furiously. She swiped at the tears in her eyes. "You were so convinced that I wanted freedom that I believed it too! *I want you*. That's all I've ever wanted! You know how that story ends? I do. I know how it ends!"

He very nearly stepped toward her but forced himself to stay put. "And how does it end?"

"She went to the last foreign land and realized that she wanted her husband to be at her side. She had no care for travel without him. That was why she'd been so restless. She thought he didn't want her!"

His mouth opened and closed. There were no words he could find to that. "What are you saying?"

"I'm saying you cursed yourself, you idiot!" She hurled her shoe at him but he ducked. "So stupidly blind, thinking you knew what I wanted! *I* would have cursed you too!" She kicked the other shoe off and moved closer a step. "You want me to be free? You want to let me go? I'll never be free of you, Brian Matthews. If you think you've got the guts, take away the scarf you gave me. It's a piece of you, isn't it?"

"It is." He carefully walked toward her, every step weighted in lead.

When he reached only a foot in front of her, she grabbed the scarf and flipped it around his neck. She dragged him down and kissed him wildly, pouring everything she was into it. Her heart, her soul, and her tears. She eased back a breath and whispered, "When she got home, she railed at her foolish husband for thinking he knew what she wanted. And what did the weaver say?"

His trembling hands framed her face. "Stay with me. Never leave again."

The mark on his chest glowed brightly for an endless instant and then softly dissolved away until there was nothing left. Her hands, spread on his chest, could feel the steady and powerful beat of his heart.

"I'm alive," he murmured.

"For now!" Her hand curled into a fist and beat against his shoulder. "I'm going to kill you for putting me through this! Damn you, Brian. I would have died without you here."

He tugged the scarf off and curled it tenderly around her neck once more. His hands moved over her without stopping, as he couldn't help himself. He could barely believe that she was there, that he was there, and that they were together as they had always wanted to be. He tugged her up for another kiss that lingered achingly. "Marry me," he whispered against her lips.

She laughed and wrapped her arms around his neck. "I think I did that once. But I'd be willing to do it again. My cousin Rashid will be ecstatic. I think he's had my wedding dress picked out for years."

"Rashid." A smile began to curve his lips. "Does he work at Bridal Dreams?"

"He does." Her brows shot up. "Don't tell me . . ."

"I told you I made a little of everything. If he's been holding the dress that I think he has, then he was right. It was assuredly made for you." He lifted her and began carrying her back toward the car. "We're going to need to go on a long honeymoon somewhere. Where do you want to go?"

"Anywhere," she answered simply, "as long as I have you.

That's all I ever wanted. Just you by my side. Never let me go again."

      Sitting on a shelf in the quiet shop, the contract from Enforcers had been overlooked for months. As it registered that the conditions in the agreement had been fulfilled, it began to glow softly. The word 'Complete' appeared across the front, and the document folded itself up tightly. Its work was done.

EPILOGUE

Rhianna was in her office reading her email when the front desk paged her to let her know she had a package. With a smile, she went downstairs to the lobby. "What have you got for me, D.J.?"

The receptionist smiled and held out a bubble wrapped package. Across the top, it read *Fragile!* Rhianna opened it very carefully and found two items. One was a contract that glowed brightly. The other was a folded tapestry. When she unfolded it, everyone who watched caught their breath. It was, without question, the most beautiful thing anyone had seen.

She turned and handed it gingerly to D.J. "Have it hung down here so everyone sees it," she told him. "Put it next to Taylor's paintings of the other . . . jobs we've done."

"Yes'm." He gingerly took the tapestry and carried it over to the wall that she had indicated. There was enough room in the center to hang the tapestry, and he waited patiently for a ladder to do so.

Spreading outward from the center where the newest story would hang were brilliant depictions of other tales. One showed a tattered pair of dance shoes sitting on the edge of a banister. Another was of a swan and a nightingale curled together. A third showed a glass slipper and golden pocket watch. The next showed two wolves running under a full moon.

On the other side of the tapestry were more paintings. One showed a princess sleeping in a field of morning glories with a prince kneeling beside her. Beside it hung a picture of a faerie holding a red apple and a soldier keeping a wand out of her reach. The third in the set showed an image of a golden locket with seven sets of stars surrounding it.

As the tapestry was being hung, another worker brought over two new paintings to go with the weaving. One was of a princess lying on a stack of mattresses, smiling down at the man watching her. In his hand rested a pea. The other painting was of a golden genie lamp whose smoke seemed to form the image of a couple embracing.

On the wall across the room could be found two additional paintings. One showed a raven carrying a pink ribbon. The other was of a fat golden bird carrying a set of wooden rings in its beak.

It was quite a collection. Rhianna loved every single one. Still smiling, she went back upstairs to her office. She added notes to the newest contract and slipped it into a folder. As it also glowed in completion, she tucked it securely into the drawer labeled 'Dease.' She shut the drawer and locked it, and the word 'Finished' appeared in red.

Content, she sat back in her chair and stretched her hands high over her head. She had known all along how the story would end.

It had been worth the wait.

Status: File Complete
Analysis: Where there is love, there is always freedom. Sometimes it just takes a while to recognize it for what it is.

Come back with me to the world on the other side of the River Styx. Their stories might just be as critical to safety of the 3rd District as the work Rhianna does is . . .

Bonus Folder
TERRA

CHAPTER ONE

It was hot. It was hot and humid. It seemed as if the very sky was sweating, the oppressive heat clogging the air so that when someone breathed, it felt as if they were breathing molasses.

It was days like those on Mirage that often offered glimpses of the Earth. It hovered there in the distance, just beyond the sight of most. Was it real, or was it a myth? Most knew it was real. Others laughed it off. Yet more wondered what it must be like.

Terra Evermore didn't have the time to wonder, though she had seen the blue planet from the corner of her eye as she drew water from the well. Her day had started early and it would end late. Even in the middle of the day, even under the hottest part of the sun, she had work to do. Her muscles ached and threatened to cramp, and sweat slid down her back under her threadbare tunic and leggings. Her bare feet, callused though they were, still wanted to blister as they crossed over stone and dirt that was hard baked and so hot that water evaporated when it dripped.

When the bucket of water was full, she lugged it precariously toward the manor that she lived in. She could not call it home. It had never been home. Truthfully, she did not really live in the manor at all. She slept out back under a leaky tool shed roof. She was only allowed to sleep inside if snow came; after all, she was no use if she was dead.

Her mistress stood on the steps leading into the kitchen. "What took so long?" she demanded.

"I didn't want to waste water." Terra knew better than to ask for a drink though her throat felt dryer than the dirt under her feet. She simply lugged the bucket up the steps and handed it over. "What do you need me to do next, Mrs. Arcwood?"

Mrs. Arcwood put the bucket of water on the counter in the kitchen with a little grunt. She still couldn't fathom how such a small female could carry the water bucket with little effort. Terra was of slightly shorter than usual height for Mirage since she stood only around five-six or so, and she looked as slender and lithe as a willow. Yet, she was still somehow as strong as a tree that bent in the wind rather than break.

Mrs. Arcwood reluctantly cared for the girl. She had ever since the child had been bought from a servant merchant. Even at ten, Terra had been lovely and smart, and in the eight years since, she had blossomed into a young woman that more than one passing male farmer had admired wistfully.

However, Terra was neither for sale nor was she free. She was an indebted servant sold to pay off her family's debts. She would serve the Arcwoods until she died. Mrs. Arcwood kept her affection for the girl a secret. She knew her husband cared little to nothing about her, and she knew her son did not act the kindest toward females of equal station let alone lesser.

As she poured water into the pot on the stove, she said casually to Terra, "Has Vin been bothering you, Terra? His father and I have told him that he is not to give you orders, and he took it with great resentment."

Terra's stomach rolled. She did not like Vin. She never had. He was five years older than she was, and ever since she had come to the Arcwood household, he had delighted in terrorizing her. He looked at her in a way that made her absolutely terrified to be alone near him. She couldn't be sure what he would do to her, but she knew it would be bad. "I do not be alone near him," she admitted softly. "He . . . alarms me."

Mrs. Arcwood looked at her sharply. "Has he touched you?"

"No!" She shook her head vehemently. "That is why I am always

so careful. I get sick when I see him."

"Make sure it stays that way." Mrs. Arcwood handed her a basket. "Chickens."

"Yes ma'am." She headed back out into the heat and over to the chicken coop. Among her chores, this was her favorite. It meant she could get, even briefly, out of the sun.

She was halfway through with the task when a shadow filled the doorway. She looked up quickly and saw Vin standing there. She edged back, her free hand closing around the pitchfork behind her.

A sneer curled his lips. He was handsome, fair and beautiful enough to be a prince, but something cruel always clung to the corner of his eye. "Look what I found," he said slyly. "All alone, little Terra?"

Her pale green eyes narrowed sharply. The color appeared nearly iridescent in the light, and it shimmered in the dark. It was offset by long, and thick, silvery-brown hair. She wore it braided nearly constantly, but it still offered an enticing sight to most men, as much as her slim and lovely body did. "I'm working, Vin. Please leave me be."

He clucked his tongue. "That's *Master* Vin to you."

Her chin lifted slightly. "Mrs. Arcwood has told me that she and Mr. Arcwood have refused you the right to order me around. Therefore you are no master to me. You never will be."

The smile faded from his face as his eyes went cold. "My parents won't be around forever. You won't always avoid being alone near me." He began to stalk closer. "You can be willing or not. I don't care. You're just a slave."

As he moved closer, she swung the pitchfork around and jabbed it lightly into his stomach. He barked out a laugh. "You wouldn't dare!"

"Try me." Her hands tightened. "I'll die before I let you touch me." She pushed harder when he tried to step forward.

He saw something in her eyes, some steady determination, and backed up. "You'll be whipped for this," he snapped. "When I tell my parents that you assaulted me!" He turned and stalked out, and it seemed as if the very air cleared with his exit.

The pitchfork fell on the ground with a clatter as she lost her grip. Shaking, she sat down against the wall. She probably would be whipped, but it would be a better fate than finding herself in his hands.

"Terra!" The roar came from the house, and it was recognizably Mr. Arcwood's voice.

She finished gathering the eggs and left the coop on shaking legs. Her hands tightened around the basket handle as she saw Mr. Arcwood standing at the kitchen door. The same cruelty in Vin's face existed in his father's face. In one hand, Mr. Arcwood carried a familiar cart whip normally used on horses. "What's this I hear about you attacking Vin?" he asked in a viciously soft voice.

Protests were useless, but she tried anyway. "I didn't! He tried to grab me in the coop and I fought him off! All I did was aim the pitchfork at him; he walked into it himself, and not even very hard!"

He grabbed her arm and swung her around to shove her toward the shed where she slept. "If Vin is grabbing you, then let him," he snapped. "What, you think it matters to anyone if you're 'pure'? You'll never be any man's wife, Terra. Don't you dare raise a weapon against anyone in this family again!"

She said nothing. She had never lied before, and she would never lie in the future. If Vin grabbed her, she would fight to her last breath. When they got to the shed and she was released, she turned her back and bowed her head.

He raised the whip . . . then slowly lowered it again. There was something inside her in that moment, some goodness, that stayed his hand and his heart. He dropped the whip to his side. "Next time," he snarled, "I won't be so gracious!"

She turned sharply, shocked, and watched as he stalked into the house. Trembling, she slowly sat down in what little shade the broken roof provided. Her only consolation was that they would all go on a long journey starting the next day; Vin would not have any

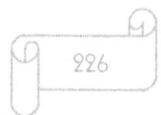

chance to get her alone.

Even before dawn the next day, she helped to load the wagon. They were going to the kingdom several days' journey away to celebrate the upcoming festival. The king had been gone on a long sabbatical, and he was expected to return in a week. The festival promised parties and celebrations and exotic wares from across the land. Though she would not get to buy anything, Terra looked forward to at least seeing the city.

When the wagon had been fully loaded with supplies and provisions, they set out. Mr. and Mrs. Arcwood rode at the front of the wagon to drive the horses, and an umbrella mounted over their heads shaded them. Vin rode inside the covered wagon where it was cool. Terra rode on the very back, precariously perched on the step. There was no shade, and it was certainly bouncy, but at least she did not have to walk.

"Don't we have to go through those nasty woods?" Vin suddenly asked his parents. "I hear it's cursed."

"So people say," Mr. Arcwood agreed. "But I've never heard of anyone getting eaten in there. Mostly, they say that the Oak Woods is full of trees that are living."

"Aren't all trees living?" Terra asked and then hastily covered her mouth.

Thankfully, Mr. Arcwood didn't take offense at the question. "Perhaps I should have said sentient. It is said that the trees in the Oak Woods are full of will and thought. There's a story about it. Something about an oak tree that lost a love, or whatever. You know how Mirage is." He stopped the wagon so that a crowd of Brownies could scuttle across the street. "Everything is never what it seems."

It was mid-afternoon by the time they entered the woods. Terra loved them instantly. The trees stood immense and towering, stretching thick branches up toward the sky which could barely be seen between the leaves. Roots crisscrossed the land, brown where the sun hit and mossy where they rested in shade. The horrible heat dissipated there, and it was even on the cooler side. The air smelled crisp and clean.

"This place gives me the creeps," Mrs. Arcwood muttered suddenly.

Startled, Terra looked over her shoulder toward the front of the wagon. "It certainly is depressing," Mr. Arcwood agreed.

Terra had no idea what they were thinking; the woods were beautiful! Peaceful and serene. She would have happily stayed there forever. The only downside was that the sudden shift from the hot sun to the cool shade had her shivering after several moments.

Vin leaned out of the wagon and put a blanket around her shoulders. Into her ear, he purred, "Wouldn't want you to get frozen. I like my women to be soft."

She jerked away from him and nearly jerked off the step. "Don't touch me!"

"Vin!" Mrs. Arcwood snapped sharply.

He started to answer when the wagon came to an abrupt halt and sent him tumbling to the ground inside. A pot banged against his head sharply. "Ow! What's going on?" He stuck his head out the front and got his answer. Bandits. Half a dozen bandits had surrounded the wagon.

"Get the goods," one said to the others. His voice cut the air like a whiplash. "Take everything we can carry."

As the bandits walked closer, Terra scrambled down off the wagon and darted around the side. She ran right into Mrs. Arcwood who tugged her closer protectively. Vin and Mr. Arcwood joined them, all of them too terrified to say a word. They could only stand there and watch as the wagon was torn apart and anything of value got stuffed into bags and sacks. When the wagon was only a shell, one of the other bandits lit it on fire.

"What do we do with them?" yet another asked. He ambled closer to Terra and caught her braid in his hand before she could jerk free. "She's a beauty, isn't she? Is she your daughter?" he asked the older couple.

"Yes," Mrs. Arcwood blurted.

"No!" Mr. Arcwood countered. "She's just a servant! You can take her if you let us go."

"Why don't we make this easy?" the lead bandit said casually. "Someone grab the girl. Kill the rest. Then it won't matter, will it?"

Swords and daggers were drawn. Sneers filled faces that crossed everything from boring to handsome. As one grabbed Mrs. Arcwood's arm, she gave Terra a powerful shove and sent her stumbling. "Run!" she shouted. "Run, Terra!"

One of the bandits lunged for Terra, and she whirled and dashed into the trees. Behind her, she could hear Vin starting to scream. It raised the hair on her arms and she clamped her hands over her ears. Equally chilling was when the screams cut off sharply. Desperately trying to shut out the raucous, nearly maniacal laughter, she ran ever deeper into the woods. She didn't know if they were chasing her. She didn't want to stop to find out.

It was only when she realized that she couldn't hear them anymore that she stopped running. She had no idea where she was. She could see nothing but trees and roots everywhere. There was no sign of an exit. The woods were supposed to be days wide and days long. She wouldn't be leaving anytime soon.

Tears rose and choked her as she sank down under an unusually small oak tree. She buried her face in her knees as she sobbed, her whole body shaking violently. Even if she managed to find her way to an exit, what was she supposed to do? She had no money. No food, no water. She had no skills or abilities that she could use to make money. If she didn't die before she found people, she would no doubt find herself as another servant.

By the time the tears spent themselves, it was turning into evening. The woods were growing darker. She had seen no sign of animal life, but it didn't worry her. She had always gotten along with animals of all kinds. Even known predators did not offer her harm. She had even heard Mr. Arcwood once tell a neighbor that their fields were never tormented by wolves or coyotes because she was there. He had seen them sleeping near her shed peacefully, and they had never attacked another animal again. Terra didn't doubt him, though she had never seen the beasts that supposedly liked her.

As twilight began to turn into night, exhaustion caught up. She leaned back against the tree, intending to simply close her eyes and rest. She was cold, tired, and hungry. It would be impossible to sleep. And yet, it was only moments before she was out, her body simply unable to keep up with her emotions.

The calm of night descended and the oak tree stirred. Slowly, tenderly, two branches folded down to curl around her protectively.

Finally. Finally she had come home.

CHAPTER TWO

It was hunger that woke Terra a few hours later. Something smelled so delicious that it had crept into her sleep and called to her. It made her stomach clench hard; she hadn't eaten all day, let alone eaten well for longer. She didn't want to open her eyes to see what was being cooked. She felt warm and secure for once, and the feelings were just as foreign as the thought of being full.

When her brain actually clicked awake a few moments later, she went very still with fear. Memory had rushed back in. That warmth and security actually came from a pair of arms wrapped around her. She was on someone's lap, held against someone's chest. A man's chest; that much she knew for sure without looking.

Her eyes flew wide and she found herself staring up into a shockingly handsome man's face. He looked rough and powerful, his dark brown hair shaggy and uncontrolled. And he was *huge*. Even on his lap, she was shorter and smaller.

Terrified, she began to struggle wildly. "Let me go!" she shouted. She beat at his shoulders and tried to pull out of his arms, but he was vastly stronger than even she was. He continued to hold her firmly and oddly gently. "Let go! Let go!"

In her panic, it took a long time to realize he was saying something. His words slowly permeated the haze in her mind, their soft cadence finally catching her attention. "Calm down, you're safe," he said over and over again. "I'm not going to hurt you. Please, calm down."

Out of breath from the fight, she slumped against him. Tears slid down her cheeks. "Don't hurt me."

The plea in her voice broke his heart. He released her carefully, slowly, wanting to be sure she knew what he was doing. The instant she was free, she shot off his lap and backed away across the entire room. She ducked into a corner and all but curled into herself, her skin white and her green eyes too large in her face.

As slowly as he could, he got to his feet and walked toward her. He kept his hands held out so that she could see he was unarmed. "My name is Nikolas Rivers," he said softly. "What's your name?" There came no response and he knelt down. He knew that his size alone had to be intimidating her; he was much taller than average and very powerful in his build. She looked as if a strong wind might whisk her away. "Please," he coaxed. "Tell me your name."

"Terra," she whispered, her eyes locked on his hands. "Terra Evermore." Her eyes slammed shut as he lifted a hand toward her. When his fingers simply brushed away a smudge of dirt on her face, she looked at him swiftly. Her eyes searched his dark green ones. There appeared to be no sign of malice or cruelty in him. Only gentleness. "You're . . . you're not going to hurt me?" Her voice broke on the words and then came out with a rush. "Please, let me go. If I was trespassing, I didn't mean to!"

"Terra." He took her icy hands in his and softly blew on them to warm them. "I will not harm you. You are safe with me. I saw what happened with the bandits. I am only trying to help you. I would not hurt you."

"Why would you care?" she asked quietly. Her hands laid passively in his grip as if she thought fighting to be futile. "I'm just a servant."

"You looked like a frightened willow tree," he countered. "When I saw you running in the woods, you were so lovely. I treasure trees, and I will treasure you." He tugged lightly on her hands and pulled her to her feet. "You were very brave."

"I was terrified!" she disagreed shakily. She swayed on her feet suddenly, the dizziness sweeping through every inch of her body. She

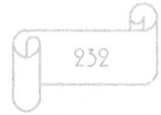

found herself instantly lifted into his arms once more. The fear did not return this time. She hadn't been held in a long time, if ever, but there was something in his touch that felt so kind, so nearly reverent, that she trusted she was safe.

He put her down on a chair next to a table. "You must be starving. When did you last eat?"

"Yesterday." Honesty made her admit, "But it wasn't very much. I didn't often get a lot of food. Just enough to make sure I wouldn't get sick." She took a wistful sniff of the air. Whatever was cooking on the small stove certainly smelled heavenly.

He waited, but when she did not ask for anything, he tucked his anger away carefully and walked over to the stove. "Do you like stew?" he asked her.

"I've never had any."

"Here's your chance."

"I can't repay you," she said miserably.

"Did I ask you to?" He brought a bowl over and put it in front of her. He added a chunk of bread and a glass of water so clean that it looked more blue than clear. "Eat," he urged as he sat down across from her. "There's plenty. I eat a lot, therefore I make a lot." When she still hesitated, he reached over to lift her chin so that she met his eyes. "If you want to repay me for saving you," he said pointedly, "you'll eat. Seeing you fade away would be a complete waste of my time and effort, wouldn't it?"

A sudden smile lit her face and turned her lovely face into an unbearably beautiful one. "I suppose it would." She picked up her spoon and began to eat. The stew tasted as delicious as it smelled, and she forced herself to eat it slowly. She didn't want to get sick, and she didn't want to rush through what might be her only good meal for a long time. "Where are you from?" she asked him. A hesitant smile touched her lips. "I mean, if you don't mind telling me."

"I'm from here," he said simply. "I live in these woods."

"Oh, a woodsman." Well, that certainly explained his build. She looked around the room curiously. There were no windows, and the walls looked more like dirt than wood, though it was rather hard to tell in the light from the single lamp. The room claimed a large bed, a stove, and the table and chairs she sat at. "Where are we?"

"Underground." He smiled when she looked at him in surprise. "There are many mysteries in these woods, Terra."

Something fluttered low in her body at the way he said her name, and it had nothing to do with being hungry. Breathless, she could only stare at him. He was truly the most handsome man she had ever seen, though she wouldn't have called him necessarily beautiful. A sudden heat rushed through her body, shocking and unexpected. She averted her gaze quickly as her cheeks flushed pink.

He curled his hands into fists under the table. He had wanted her from the moment he had laid eyes on her. Her shimmering hair begged for his hands to be lost in it, and her iridescent eyes reflected her every emotion. Though malnourished for too long, her body didn't seem to be thin. She was willowy and slim instead, her figure lithe and seductive without effort.

Holding her as he had for those hours had been self-inflicted torture, but he had done it to combat the terrible chill she had gained from being in the woods too long. More than once he had wanted to kiss her awake. He had never dared hope she would want him, especially not after her initial reaction to him. But now . . . for a moment, there had been something in her eyes. A startled desire followed quickly by shame.

He reached out and covered her hand with his. Her blush deepened. Tenderly, he said, "Terra, look at me." Her eyes reluctantly lifted, and he brought her hand slowly to his lips. Without hurry, keeping his gaze on hers, he softly kissed each slender finger before kissing her palm. His lips pressed to her wrist and he could feel the rapid race of her pulse. "Don't be afraid," he said huskily. "I could not hurt you."

"I'm a servant," she said miserably.

"Your masters are dead." She flinched, and he pressed her hand to his cheek. "You are free, Terra. There is nothing to be

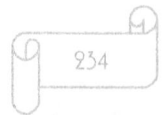

ashamed of if you desire me." He slowly smiled. "I'm glad that you do. I wanted you when I saw you in my woods."

Her breath hitched as that something inside stirred. The lethal smile touching her rescuer's lips seemed to simply beg to be kissed. Certainly, she had never kissed anyone before, but he made it very tempting. But he was a woodsman, and she was a former servant. A more unlikely pairing didn't exist.

She dropped her hands into her lap when he released her. "What am I supposed to do, Nikolas?" she asked softly. "I have nowhere to go. I have no skills at anything. I don't even know how to get out of these woods."

"You can stay here tonight," he countered softly. "I must leave soon, but you are welcome to stay. The sleep will do you good."

She looked at the bed longingly. It seemed far too fine for her to touch. "Just give me a blanket and I'll curl up in a corner. I can sleep anywhere."

He didn't push the issue though he had no intention of letting her sleep on the floor. "Since I have a little time left, tell me about yourself," he offered softly. "I'd like to know about the willow I saved."

"I'm a servant, as I said. I was bought eight years ago by the Arcwoods, when I was ten. My parents got into debt very badly." Her gaze lowered. "My mother was ill. My father sold everything to pay for medicine, but it did no good. When she died, he simply . . . gave up. He was gone soon after. The debt fell on my shoulders. The holder of the debt said if I would be a servant, he would call it even. I didn't have a choice."

"So you've been a slave for eight years to a couple who, obviously, cared little about your health." He fought to keep his voice even. "Do you live in the kingdom?"

"No. We're part of the land owned by the king and under his jurisdiction, but we were not in the actual kingdom. When we were attacked, we were heading for the festival."

"It disgusts me that the kingdom would have no idea that

children are being sold to pay a debt they had no control over." He ran his hand down her hair softly, the calluses on his fingers snagging on silken strands. The tendrils seemed to lift and follow his touch. "What was it like on the farm where you lived?"

"It was okay, I suppose." His fingers skimmed down her cheek and she rubbed against them unconsciously. His touch was so loving, so tender. It was an alien sensation, but one that she couldn't help but soak up eagerly. That anyone might care about her . . . "I slept outside most of the time, but when it snowed I slept in the kitchen. I always slept with a knife in case Vin found me."

"Vin?"

"The Arcwoods' son." She shuddered. "He always tried to touch me."

"Touch you how?" His voice sounded as grim as he felt.

"He wanted . . ." She made a helpless gesture, embarrassed. "You know what he wanted. You said you did too."

"Wrong." She looked at him in surprise and he drew her hands up to rest over his heart. "He wanted to hurt you in a way no man ever should hurt a woman. I want to love you. I will not, *could never*, hurt you."

She searched his face intently, and slowly, a little flower of happiness began to unfurl inside her heart. It seemed miraculous, but she could see in his eyes, and hear in his voice, his sincerity. Whatever he wanted of her, it was nothing like what Vin wanted. "I trust you, Nikolas," she said with conviction.

Relief nearly made him lightheaded. "Hey, at least call me 'Nik.' You don't need to be formal with me." He hesitated for only a moment before lifting her off her seat and settling her on his lap. She went very stiff for a long moment and then her body slowly relaxed against him. Her head fit perfectly on his shoulder. "There," he said softly into her hair. "Someone around here is long overdue for some cuddling."

Suddenly drowsy, she found herself smiling. "You're a bit big to cuddle but I can try." He laughed out loud and it sounded wonderful

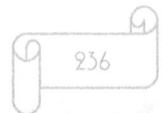

on her ears. She rubbed her cheek over his chest softly. He smelled like the woods did. Pure and clean and free. "How tall are you?"

"Six-seven."

He reached an entire foot taller than she did, but it no longer seemed so scary. Somewhere between the way he had treated her after she had attacked him to the way he now held her so safely, her fear had evaporated entirely. She felt . . . happy. Safe. Maybe she was in love with him. She didn't know. She had never loved anyone before. Maybe it was just gratitude. Maybe it was just desire, though 'just' seemed a misnomer the way her pulse clamored at his every touch and every smile. "Nik?" she asked softly.

"Sleep," he countered just as softly. Her soft breath feathered across his skin as she relaxed, and he continued to hold her until he knew for sure that she truly slept. Her skin was nearly translucent even though it carried a soft gold tint from the sun. Dark circles showed starkly under her eyes.

He got to his feet and carried her as if she was the most precious thing in the world. He placed her very softly on the bed and tugged a blanket over her. She snuggled deeper into the pillows with a wordless murmur, and he brushed at the hair falling in her face. He had waited a long time to find her. He had nearly begun to give up hope.

"I won't let you go again, my willow," he promised softly.

He stayed by her side until he sensed the dawn approaching. As he felt the first rays calling him, he softly brushed a kiss across her lips. She stirred, her hand moving as if to reach for him, and he straightened swiftly. With a last longing look, he walked away. It would be a long time until sundown arrived and he could hold her again. He did not worry for her safety. There was nothing in the woods that could harm her. Neither plant nor animal would ever be a danger.

The willow had returned to where she belonged.

CHAPTER THREE

Terra awoke to the sound of birds chirping and a morning breeze caressing her skin. Startled, she sat upright and found she had been sleeping in a soft bed of grass beneath the branches of a tree. She looked around but there was no sign of any shelter nearby, even one that might be underground.

A soft cooing sound caught her attention, and she looked up to see a small dove sitting on a branch over her head. She smiled as she got to her feet. "Hello," she said softly. "Am I hogging your tree?"

The dove cocked his head slightly. "I would not say so," he said after a moment. "I own nothing in these woods. I simply fly where I am needed."

She blinked once, then twice. "You talk?"

"Certainly. Do you?"

She suddenly smiled. "Sometimes my talking got me into trouble. I suppose I do not mind that a dove can converse with me. Do you have a name?"

"I do not. It does not matter though," he added gently. "I would always know when you spoke to me though you spoke not my name." He flew down and landed delicately on her shoulder. "What will you do today, Terra?"

"I do not know." She crossed her arms around herself as she began to walk aimlessly. "I feel a little . . . surreal right now. Did I dream everything? Am I still dreaming? Was Nik even real, little dove?"

"He was as real as you are," he promised. "And you shall as yet

see him again. Today is yours. Tonight is his. The time in between is waiting time. So I ask again, what will you do today?"

"I suppose I can only start walking and see where I end up." She tilted her face up toward the sunshine coming through the leaves. "It is so peaceful here. I don't know why people call these woods cursed. Are the trees really sentient?"

"Everything that lives has a spirit. It just so happens that these woods are slightly more willful than most other places." He hopped around to sit on her other shoulder. With his beak, he tugged on a lock of her hair where it had escaped her braid. "Why do you plait your hair?"

The colloquial term sounded fascinating from a dove, but she accepted it at face value. She knew her companion was not normal. Perhaps he was a good spirit in disguise. "I braid my hair to keep it out of my face when I am working. And it is so hot on the farm!" More reluctantly, she added, "And it hides how dirty it is. I only bathe when I can be sure I will not be found. I haven't had a hot bath in years."

"I suspect you have not had clean clothes in years either."

She looked down at her tunic and leggings. Both were caked with dirt, worn all the way through in places, and practically falling to pieces in others. The only thing she wore that remained in any decent condition were her underwear and bra; those were necessities in her book, and she treated them far more carefully than her outerwear. If she could only wash one thing, it was that.

"Well," she said, "I haven't worn these all my life, you know. I only finished growing a short while ago. But they are all I own now." She frowned deeply. "I do not know how I will make money to buy anything should I get out of these woods."

A secretive smile crossed the dove's face. "By the time you get out, you will not have any worry for it any longer."

"If I get out." She sighed and sat down under a tree. "I am so tired. My feet hurt so badly. Yet I know I shouldn't complain; I'm alive." She leaned against the tree trunk and closed her eyes. "I almost wish Nik had not saved me."

The dove flew down to land on her lap. "Would you wish away meeting him?"

"No." She softly stroked the small bird's head and was rewarded by a trilling coo. "That is why I said 'almost.' Last night . . . for the first time, I felt like someone cared about me. I want to see him again," she admitted even softer. "I don't know what I feel. But I want to be with him. He may never love me, but that's okay. I just want to be with someone who cares about me."

The dove watched her for long moments and then flew off into the sky. She let him go and closed her eyes to rest. It was a curious situation to find herself in, to be sure. This sort of thing was supposed to happen to other people, not to people like her.

Sadness suddenly filled her heart. Mrs. Arcwood had tried to save her. She had always found the older woman to be more gentle than her husband or son. She had liked her. Now she was no doubt dead along with Vin and Mr. Arcwood. Try as she might, she couldn't regret that the two males were gone. They had been horrid people. She would carry the scars from Mr. Arcwood's whip forever.

After a brief rest, she got back on her feet and started walking again. She couldn't even tell where the sun sat in the sky, and she had no idea if she was going forward or backward. Nothing looked familiar, but she could not be sure if she would remember what she had already seen. There was no way of knowing how far from the incident that Nikolas had taken her.

Her feet began to hurt. She tried to balance herself on a tree to see if she had cut herself but she was tired enough that she missed the trunk. She instead stumbled past it, and her shirt snagged on a bush that tore out a chunk of material.

The sudden urge to cry welled and she fought it. Crying changed nothing. She simply squared her shoulders and freed her shirt from the bush. If she had to walk naked in the woods, then that's what she would do. There wasn't anyone to see her anyway. Maybe she could make clothes out of leaves.

She rested under a different tree hours later when twilight

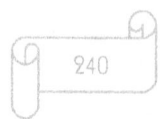

crept in. As she looked around for a place to sleep, the dove suddenly returned. He flew down to land on her shoulder and dropped a small gold key into her hand. "What is this?" she asked.

"A key."

Exasperated, she said, "I see that!"

He smiled. He had known there lurked a spirited heart under her quiet exterior. There had to be. She would not have endured that long without it. "It is a key to another home under a tree. Follow me; I will take you there. You may take shelter there tonight."

She curiously followed the dove as he flew through the trees. It wasn't very long before he stopped before a mighty pine tree with a trunk wider than Terra. She ran her hands lightly over the bark, and her fingers brushed across a small hole. When she looked closer, she discovered it was a keyhole. She put the key in and turned it, and the entire trunk opened like a door to reveal a staircase.

More fascinated than alarmed, she went down the dark stairs carefully. At the bottom, she found a small room just like the one she had woken in before. A fire burned welcomingly in the stove, and when she went closer, she discovered that technically nothing burned at all. It simply gave light and heat. "Magic," she whispered, enchanted. She had always wanted to see magic.

The dove flew down and landed on a trunk sitting against the wall. "Terra. Come here."

She walked over and opened the trunk. Inside, she saw clothes of silk and satin, the colors rich and the fabrics luxurious. "Oh," she breathed. "They're lovely."

"Wear something," he urged.

"They are too fine for me." She shut the lid regretfully. "And I am filthy in any case." She spotted a basin of water and a washcloth and went over to at least scrub her face and hands clean. Just that simple thing felt delightful. She glanced at the bed wistfully but instead went to sit in front of the stove. It was quiet and calm, and she was tired. Maybe she could take a nap before the owner came home.

When Nikolas came down the stairs less than an hour later, he came to a sharp stop as he saw her curled up in front of the stove. Why wasn't she in the bed, or wearing the clothes he had provided? He walked over to her and knelt down. The dark circles had begun to fade from under her eyes, and her skin seemed healthier. The woods as much as the rest were beginning to take their effect.

He softly smoothed his fingers down her cheek, savoring how it felt to have her close once more. He eased her into his arms and stood, his heart tightening fiercely as she instinctively cuddled against him. One delicate hand curled over his chest as if to grab onto the heart inside.

He placed her softly on the bed and brushed her hair out of her face. Unable to resist, he gently kissed her, needing nothing as much as he needed her taste again. She stirred, a soft sigh captured by his lips, and her lashes lifted slightly. A warm welcome filled her eyes, and she curled her arms around his neck. Her lips parted to invite a deeper embrace.

He groaned softly and took the gift she had given so freely. It was near impossible to keep his touch tender, but he would be damned before he frightened her. Even as he deepened the kiss, his tongue teasing hers and enticing her to return the gesture, his hands ever so lightly skimmed down the side of her body.

A shiver rippled down her nerves of pure delight. Shy but unafraid, she hesitantly began to return the kiss, following his lead without question. He tasted as wonderful as he smelled, his flavor as instantly addicting as the pleasure beginning to steal through her body. She couldn't breathe anymore, but she really didn't care. Breathing wasn't important anyway.

He slowly broke the kiss and searched her eyes. They glowed more iridescent than ever, and looked very sultry with an unconscious sensuality. Not a single trace of fear could be found in her gaze. As her fingers softly traced his lips, he asked huskily, "Did I frighten you?"

"No. It was beautiful. I'd never been kissed before."

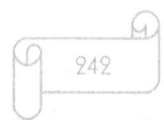

Warily, he asked, "Kissed the way I kissed you, or at all?"

She smiled. "At all. I never met anyone I wanted to kiss, and certainly no one wanted a servant girl enough to kiss her without consent."

"I really should apologize."

Her eyes deepened with warm laughter. "But you won't."

His lips curved. "No, I won't." Fascinated, enchanted, he framed her face in his hands. She was warm and vibrant, giving and brave. And smart. He was sure she would disagree, but she seemed to accept and absorb so much so swiftly. A servant? She should be a princess or queen. "You're not going to hit me?" he asked solemnly.

"That would be silly when I kissed you too." When he released her, she sat up gingerly and tried not to touch the bed too much. She didn't even remember getting into the bed, and she felt rather embarrassed at getting the covers dirty. She could see the smudges from her clothes. "I thought I was in front of the stove."

"I moved you." He frowned. "Why didn't you change clothes, Terra? Or get in bed if you were tired?" He fingered the great tear in her tunic. "This is falling apart."

She shook her head. "I couldn't take those things. They were too fine for me."

Temper lit his eyes and he shot to his feet to pace away. "Too fine, she says!"

Wary but not entirely afraid, she watched him carefully. "They were silk, Nik. At best I might someday be a farm girl, but I will never be in a position that deserves to wear something that lovely." She got out of the bed before she made it dirtier.

He swung around and stepped closer so that he towered over her. "I may not be very old," he told her fiercely, "but I have seen my share of ladies, noblewomen, and princesses. Only half of them deserved to wear the silks you claim are too fine for you. It has nothing to do with your birth, willow, and everything to do with what is inside." He blew out a hard breath. "And stop looking at me like that. I'm not mad at you. I'm mad at the idiots who made you think you were without worth."

"I'm sorry." She made a helpless gesture. "I've always had to be very careful of Mr. Arcwood's temper and I couldn't help but be wary of yours. I know you won't hurt me."

There was a significant silence before he asked very softly, "Why were you careful of his temper?" No answer. "Did he hit you?" Again, silence. Nausea churned in his stomach. "Whip you?" Her lashes flinched, and he cursed softly.

Before she quite knew what he would do, he crossed to her and spun her around. Red color flooded her cheeks as he knelt and lifted her tunic away from her back. "Don't look! It's horrible!"

His fingers, though shaking, remained tender as they traced the thin scars on her back. Most were faded and would no doubt disappear entirely someday. Others were much newer, much starker, and would be there for much longer. One particularly vicious mark reached nearly an inch wide. He softly traced the length of it. "He must have been particularly furious."

"I was so tired coming back from the coop that I dropped the basket of eggs and broke everything." A little tremor ran through her body. "Please. Stop looking, Nik."

He smoothed her tunic down and curled his arms around her waist as he pressed his face to her back. "I would never hurt you, let alone like this," he vowed softly, "no matter how angry I might be." He reluctantly released her and got to his feet.

She took a deep breath as she turned to look at him. She could believe him. The horror in his voice, and the pain in his eyes, at seeing how she was marked felt true. This was a man who had no cruelty inside him. "Okay." She started to say something else when her stomach rumbled loudly. Her cheeks went bright pink as he smiled at her. "Uhm."

"I suppose I had better feed you again." He caught her hand and brought her wrist to his lips for a moment. "Come sit down. I'll make something. Or do you want to?"

"I don't cook very well," she admitted shamefully. "Mrs.

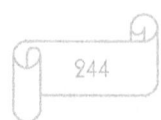

Arcwood tried very hard to teach me, but I lack some sort of skill at it. At least, when it comes to a stove. I can bake with a stone oven well enough, but those are such luxury items."

"And it seems like only yesterday that running water was a luxury." He competently began to assemble the ingredients for his stew. "Ah, well. I like to cook. Until I was on my own out here, I never really had a chance."

"How old are you?" she asked curiously. "You said 'you may not be very old' and yet you seem much older than me . . ."

He smiled over his shoulder. "How old do you think I am?"

"Thirty-five?"

"Ouch. Twenty-five."

She winced good-naturedly. "Sorry." She propped her chin on her hands and watched him. How such a strong and masculine male could be that gentle amazed her. "Where are you really from, Nik? You talk like a city boy, and yet you are very much a woodsman."

"I am from the city," he admitted after a moment. Letting the stew simmer, he sat at the table and handed her a small loaf of bread to nibble on. "Coming out here wasn't an intent, exactly. I simply found myself unable to leave."

"It is beautiful," she agreed softly. "A dove was telling me that the trees are living creatures. Are they? Can they talk and think? Do they feel?"

"Of course." His voice sounded simple. "They feel and love. They are no different from you and I other than the form they reside within. Those of pure hearts, such as you, find the woods to be beautiful and peaceful. Those who carry malice find the woods to be frightening and uncertain. It is how the trees protect themselves from those who would chop them down carelessly without a single thought for how they feel."

Something painful lodged in her chest. "I don't know why," she said softly, "but it hurts to hear you say that."

She was more sensitive to what happened around them than he had thought. Carefully, he said, "You are a very giving person. I

would imagine it would hurt you to think of someone being cruel."
He went over to the stove and dished up two servings. As he placed
a bowl in front of her, he said teasingly, "My lady."

She smiled shyly. "I am no lady."

"Of birth." He shrugged one shoulder carelessly. "At heart,
certainly you are. I'm older and I say so, so you'll just have to trust
me."

Her smile spread. "Well, I guess I cannot argue with that." She
contentedly began to eat her stew. It was still a marvelous feeling to
think that not only was she having a real meal, but that there was
someone who wanted her around. If it meant being with Nikolas, she
would have been happy to never leave the woods again.

"Terra?"

She looked up quickly. "Yes?"

His breath caught at the glow in her eyes. "Don't look at me like
that, willow," he said faintly. "I am having enough trouble keeping my
hands off you." He reached out with trembling fingers to caress her
cheek. "From the moment you fell into my arms," he murmured
softly, "I have never wanted anything more than to have you for my
own. I love you very much, willow."

Her mouth opened and then closed. Wonder slowly filled her
face and her eyes. She reached out to touch him, her fingers tracing
over his beloved face. The warmth unfurled inside her, and finally she
understood what it was. It wasn't gratitude. It wasn't just desire.

It was love.

"Nik," she breathed softly.

He reached out and pulled her onto his lap so swiftly that the
empty bowls bounced off the table onto the floor. She didn't care.
She threw her arms around his neck and met his kiss with all the pent
up emotion inside. But this time . . . she realized something distantly.
His touch was not unfamiliar. The hunger that stirred inside her blood
was not unfamiliar. Even before his arms went around her to hold her
close, she knew exactly how it would feel.

Aching, fit to burst, he broke free of the kiss and buried his face

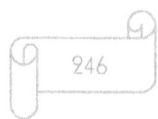

against her neck. She quivered in his arms, her breaths coming as quickly as his. Her fingers seemed to be convulsively moving against his scalp as if she couldn't stop herself from caressing him.

"Ask me to stay with you," he pleaded roughly. The faintest of trembles of fear went through her body, and he lifted his head instantly. Confusion had filled her eyes. "It's alright, Terra," he promised gently. "There's time yet."

"I don't understand," she said softly. "Why am I suddenly afraid?"

"You've been through a lot the last few days. Your life has changed completely beyond your control. Now I threaten to change it again." He brought her hand to his lips and tenderly kissed her palm. "You will make this choice, willow. It is entirely your choice if we become lovers. I will wait as patiently as I am able to."

"I'm so sorry, Nik." She pressed her face against his shoulder. Her body felt achy and restless, desperately craving the feeling of his hands, but it couldn't entirely override her nerves. She *wanted* to be his. Why couldn't she ask him to stay?

When she suddenly yawned, he found a real smile. "I suppose it is just as well. I wouldn't want you to fall asleep while I was making love to you. After, perhaps, because then I could have you in my arms."

Only the lightest of blushes on her cheek, she countered, "I'm already in your arms."

"But frustratingly clothed."

She sat upright, eyes wide. "You would want me to sleep *naked* in your arms?"

He arched a brow. "You expected to be wearing boots?"

"Or a nightgown at the least!"

He leaned in and teasingly nibbled at the line of her jaw. "You won't need one. And when you eventually are there, you won't even think of it." The little stinging kisses made their way down her neck to her shoulder. "You shouldn't wear anything except your beauty. Or me."

Flushed with an entirely different heat, she had no words to say to that. She felt silly and naïve, but she had always assumed that couples wore pajamas to bed. But then, really, what did she have to base her assumptions on? The Arcwoods hadn't been an affectionate couple, and Nikolas was proving to be *very* affectionate. She soaked up his attention like a tree would soak up the sun.

Another yawn caught her by surprise. He softly tugged her closer. "Go to sleep," he urged softly, his voice nothing but a rumble in his chest. "I will hold you until I have to leave."

"I wish you did not have to leave," she said sleepily. She curled her hand over his heart. "You seem so tired when I see you, Nik. I can feel it." She sighed softly and closed her eyes. "I want to take care of you too. If I could be with you, I would never want to leave this place."

He closed his eyes as he struggled for control. Even after she slept, he continued to hold her. Every time he left her, it took another piece of his soul. Through the whole long day, even when he could not feel anything else, he felt hunger for her smile and her laugh. For her kiss and her touch. How much longer would he have to wait?

CHAPTER FOUR

Terra woke the following morning to once more find herself outside. This time she did not feel quite so startled by it. The magic in the woods was something to simply be accepted. And she did accept it. She could accept anything.

The sound of a brook caught her attention, and she made her way toward it carefully. Her feet still ached, but not nearly as bad as they had the day before. She was more than happy to sit on the bank of the brook and let her feet dangle inside. The cool water felt wonderful. If she could have found some soap, she would have even bathed. The next time she saw Nikolas, she really wanted to look as good as she could.

"A woman who loves is a vain woman." The dove flew down to land beside her.

She smiled. "I never imagined I would be in love, so I had no real care for my appearance. I suppose that since Nik has seen me at my worst, I ought to be unconcerned, but I don't want him to regret picking me."

"It is natural instinct," he countered gently. "Love is a survival mechanic. It triggers the desire to mate and produce offspring. It, therefore, produces the urge to look your best for your mate. Feeding the beast, if you will."

"You sound like quite the expert."

He ruffled his feathers. "I suppose you could say that."

"Well, perhaps you'll then explain why love is said to be blind."

For a moment, something old and sad crossed the avian face

beside her. "When you love," he said softly, "you are supposed to be blind to flaws. You will find your love to be perfect to you. Though others may see them as plain, beastly, or perhaps even a little cold, you will see beyond it to the inside. Blind to the outside, perhaps is the best way to say it. Blind to the outside, accepting of the inside. Loving regardless of both."

She watched him for long moments and then asked softly, "So who was blind to your inner flaws?"

His wry laugh sounded a little sad. "I was blind to my own." He shook it off visibly. "Ah well, we were discussing you, were we not? You love Nikolas as he is. You would love him no matter how he appeared, yes?"

"Yes." There was no question in her mind or heart.

"Good." He hopped closer to the water to look in. He nearly slipped down the bank, but she caught him. "Thank you," he told her. "I am not quite used to this form just yet." His head tilted when she smiled. He smiled as well. "You do not seem surprised."

"Little surprises me anymore." She opened her hands and let him fly up into the air. Feeling refreshed once more, she got to her feet and stretched largely. "I don't know where I will go today," she decided softly, "but I'm not in any hurry or desire to find the exit anymore. If I looked for Nikolas, would I find him?"

"Possibly, but you may not recognize him as he is right now. You are not ready to."

She considered that as she began to walk. Why wouldn't she recognize Nikolas? He was distinctive in many ways. She felt sure she could never pass over him in a crowd, and she felt even surer that there was no way he could disguise himself that she could not see through. She felt attuned to him, as if something at the core of him called to something at the core of her.

She took her time walking through the woods. To her delight, the woodland creatures finally came out of hiding. Birds of all kinds nested in the trees, trilling to one another and to her alike. A long-eared jackrabbit hopped along at her side for a ways before

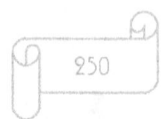

scampering off to play.

Two wolves, a mated pair, welcomed her when she approached where they rested in the shade of some boulders. Tiny cubs curled against the female's side, and Terra cuddled each in turn, giggling when they licked her face. The male wolf rubbed against her softly, and she combed her fingers through his fur to pick out twigs and briars. "There you go." She kissed his forehead softly, marveling at how a beast that wild, that free, could be so welcoming to her.

Deeper in the woods she found a small herd of deer. A large stag with a mighty rack oversaw the many doe that walked at his side. Two tiny fawns teetered on legs that were too long for their bodies. With tiny bleats, they wobbled over to Terra and contentedly bumped against her.

The stag was a little intimidating when he got close for he was much bigger than Terra, and certainly carrying more muscle, but he acted as gentle as the fawns as he bumped his nose against her. She scratched his head around his antlers and smiled at the soft and fuzzy fur that covered them. She wouldn't have guessed his antlers would feel like that.

As twilight drew close, she was sitting under a thick fruit tree with a wildcat purring on her lap. Well, with its head on her lap. The beast was much bigger than an average housecat. The dove flew down from out of nowhere and landed without fear on the beast's back. The cat opened one eye, sighed, and closed it again. Terra just smiled. "Hello."

The dove dropped into her hand the golden key he carried. "There is a place waiting for you."

She gently nudged the wildcat and it reluctantly wandered off. With a large yawn, she got to her feet to follow the dove. "These are called the Oak Woods, but more than oak grows here."

"It used to be all oak trees," the dove explained, "but seeds were carried in by birds and a few other species have sprouted. In the beginning, when the woods were first formed, there were only two trees, and only one was an oak."

"Hmm." Interested but sensing he wouldn't tell more, she instead asked, "I don't suppose I can keep one of these little homes? I love the woods, but a place to actually live would be wonderful."

"They have a purpose, and when they serve it, they will be gone."

"Oh." A little disappointed, but not entirely surprised, she used the key on a lock in a large fir tree. She went down the stairs revealed and found another small room. This one, much to her delight, had one feature that the other two hadn't: it had a bathtub behind an elaborate screen. And not just any bathtub, but one full of steaming hot water. On a chair beside it sat a dish with a bar of soap, a couple fluffy-looking towels, a brush, and a bucket to rinse her hair with. "Is . . . can I use that?" she asked in a hushed voice.

"It is there solely for you."

She didn't need to be told twice. She stripped off all of her clothes and draped them over a chair. She unbraided her hair so that it fell to her hips in a curtain of silvery-brown color. It didn't quite sway with her steps for it was quite dirty, but she had every intention of fixing that as well.

She gingerly got into the tub and found it to be the perfect temperature and depth. She sank in to her chin with a sigh of near bliss. The hot water felt wonderful on her sore muscles and aching feet.

She only lingered a little while. She didn't want the water to go cold, and she didn't know when Nikolas would arrive. She grabbed up the soap and fiercely scrubbed herself clean. It felt as if she removed several layers of dirt. She treated her hair to the same thing, scrubbing it with soap twice before it actually felt clean again. She used the bucket to rinse off the soap and then wrapped herself in the towels to get out.

To her immense chagrin, when she went to grab her clothes to wash them, she discovered they had disappeared. The dove was also nowhere in sight. "You *sneak*," she muttered under her breath.

She reluctantly eyed the trunk sitting to one side. Unless she

wanted to go naked for the rest of time, she had no choice but to dig into the fine materials. She hastily dried her hair enough that it didn't drip and then opened the trunk.

She really had no idea if she had any taste since everything looked beautiful to her. She finally settled on a shimmering pale green dress that was so soft and delicate that she felt clumsy just handling it. There was a matching bra and panties to go with it, for which she was grateful since that fink dove had taken *all* of her clothes, but everything was *silk*.

She felt beyond decadent as she pulled the clothes on, but the dress fit so perfectly that she just couldn't bring herself to take it back off and look for something plainer. It fit snug to her chest and waist, and flared out to a fuller skirt as it went to brush the floor. It laced up the front, thankfully, and she got into it easily enough. The sleeves went to her wrists where they flared into a bell shape. Around the edge of the sleeves and the skirt went dark green embroidery of leaves.

There were slippers to match, but she left them off. Her feet felt too happy to confine right then. Instead, she sat down in front of the fire in the stove and began to brush her hair. The concept seemed completely foreign to her, and she had to struggle with several tangles before they let go. She had almost never brushed her hair before; the few times she had been able to wash it, she had braided it immediately after. Perhaps that was why her hair had so many waves; she couldn't recall having wavy hair as a child.

She heard a step on the stairs and looked up with a smile as Nikolas walked in. He stopped sharply as he saw her, and his eyes widened. Nervously, she twisted a lock of hair around her finger. "Do I . . . Do I look okay? I wasn't going to . . . but the dove . . . I mean, he said I could . . ."

"Stop." He took a deep breath for control and came the rest of the way down the stairs. "I just didn't believe my eyes at first." He knelt beside her and caught a handful of her hair. It was as soft as the silk of her dress, resilient, and thick. "You're beautiful, Terra," he said huskily. "You look like a princess."

"Really?" She looked down shyly. "I was hoping you'd like it. I don't know anything about clothes, but I thought that you might like green because you love the woods." And his eyes were green as an oak's leaves, but she kept that to herself, not sure if the observation would embarrass him. Truly, green was becoming her favorite color too. She loved his eyes.

"I like green," he said agreeably, "but I like it when it is the same color as your eyes. Eyes as green as a willow's leaves." He used his grip on her hair to tug her up for a tender kiss. "I missed you," he murmured against her lips.

"I missed you." She buried her face against his shoulder as he held her.

"Would you . . ." He took a deep breath. "Would you be happy here, Terra? Would you be happy with me even if I was a simple woodsman who could not be with you during the day?"

"I could be happy anywhere if I was with you. I just wish I could keep one of these houses! I want so much to have a home to live in. I've never had one. And I could try to learn to cook, so I can take care of you the way you took care of me." She searched his eyes, her breath held. "Why?"

"Will you . . . Can you . . ." He blew out a breath. "Damn it. I've used some of the smoothest lines in the world and I can't even ask the woman I love if she would be my wife."

Her smile lit not just her face but also the entire room. "Yes."

His lips slowly curved. "I didn't actually ask."

"The answer is still yes." She laughed as he shot to his feet with her in his arms, but the laughter died shortly as he kissed her wildly, as if the dam on his emotions had broken free. He didn't kiss her; he consumed her. A kiss such as that would have frightened her even the day before. All it did now was bring her desire for him wildly to life. When he finally released her, all she could say breathlessly was, "Nik."

"If I make love to you," he warned huskily, "then it is our

wedding night. Ceremony or no, you will be mine and I will be yours. Do you want that, Terra?"

Her lips trembled. "I've never belonged to anyone. No one belonged to me." She wrapped her arms around his neck. "I love you, Nik. I want nothing more than to be with you. Don't let me go."

With a shuddering breath, he carried her over to the bed and gently put her down on the side. He knelt in front of her and searched her eyes for any sign of nerves. All he saw was a shimmering, welcoming glow. Her hands softly framed his face before skimming back into his hair.

He eased onto the bed beside her and began to slowly unlace the dress. His hands looked large and powerful against her delicate build, but there was such a lack of fear inside her that his own nerves faded. He was so afraid of hurting her! But she was strong. Much stronger than even he had guessed. She bent. She did not break. And she came back more resilient than before.

As he tugged the dress slowly up her body, she began to unlace the ties at the collar of his tunic. She released him so that the dress could be tugged off and promptly went back to working on his tunic when it was gone. With his help, the tunic got removed as well.

In wonder, she spread her hands slowly across his chest. He was beautiful. As powerful as an oak, but as gentle as a spring breeze. The muscles of his body looked starkly defined, a reminder of his strength, but the sight of them only made heat gather low in her body. Such a magnificent creature wanted her. She would not question her luck.

"Look at you," he breathed softly. His hands brushed down the outside of her breasts and she caught a breath. "So lovely." He tugged the straps of the bra down until her breasts came free of the cups. The nipples were tight and flushed, begging for his touch. Unable to resist, he bent his head and took one in his mouth gently. Her body jerked in shock and a soft moan rippled from her lips as he sucked softly. She tasted like nothing he had ever known. He couldn't get enough.

Every tug of his mouth tugged deeper. She caught his hair and held him closer, her body arching instinctively in a plea for more. The depth of the pleasure his touch wrought was faintly astonishing. Yet, at the same time, each caress made her want more. She teetered back and forth between hunger and delight until she couldn't breathe or think. "Nik." It was almost a sob.

Her bra disappeared over the side of the bed. He lifted her onto his lap for a ravenous kiss, his hands buried in her hair to keep her possessively close. Her fingers dug into shoulders desperately as she countered his kiss, just as hungry, just as needy. When he didn't deepen the kiss fast enough to suit her, she nipped at his lip warningly. A low masculine laugh rumbled in his chest as he gave her what she wanted, his mouth plundering every secret from hers.

When he released her, she gulped in air that was hot and humid in a way that in no way resembled the farm. It burned her deep inside, and his scent seemed seared into her lungs. She found herself flat on her back with him looming over her, and there was still no fear. Her fingers trembled with need as she ran them over every inch of his body that she could reach. She couldn't feel enough fast enough.

He stripped away her panties and raked his gaze over her swiftly. She was long and graceful with all her height carried in her legs. Her waist was trim, her breasts delicate rather than lush. The silvery-brown curls between her legs served as a delicious lure that sent his fingers trailing slowly down her body.

As his fingers scraped across her stomach, her muscles quivered and tightened. He began to make his way across her skin with his lips and dropped hot little kisses over every inch. The deceptively fragile line of her ribcage, the intriguing little dip near her bellybutton. There was nothing he didn't savor.

Her legs shifted restlessly as he nuzzled the curls that had intrigued him. Then, before he could ask, her legs parted to let him closer. A shudder ripped through his body as every muscle tightened to the point of pain. He skimmed a finger across her most sensitive flesh and listened to her breath break. He kissed her, tasted her, and savored her cries. She was hot and wet, more than ready for him, but she was small enough that he couldn't stop his fear that he would hurt her.

"Nik." The desperate plea in her voice cracked his control. "Please." She didn't know what she asked for, but knew only he could give it to her. Her entire body was aching and tight, straining wildly for an end to the ceaseless pleasure. It was so sharp that it nearly became pain. "Nik!" It was a cry as he kissed her again.

He slowly made his way back up her body until he could take her mouth again. The kiss went wild and carnal, her taste branding them both. She fiercely wrapped her arms around his neck when he started to release her. "No!"

"I'm not leaving you." He stripped off the rest of his clothes as fast as he could. Her green eyes looked dazed with desire, her lips red and swollen. A fine tremor ran through her entire body, and her lovely breasts lifted with her every breath. He sank into her arms again with a tortured sound of need. "I love you." He caught her arms and drew them up around his neck. "Hold me, Terra."

Her arms tightened fiercely. Without asking, as if somehow knowing, she curled her legs around his hips. She held onto him tightly with all her strength. She would never let him go!

Her lips parted on a swift breath as she felt his hard flesh slowly pushing into her body. There was only a brief moment of panic. Just as her body started to tense, she looked into his eyes and saw the wellspring of his emotions. It stole all her fears as surely as it had stolen her heart. She turned her face up for his kiss, telling him without words that she wanted him.

He surged into her completely, and her startled cry was muffled by his lips. He stayed fiercely still, his body shaking. "Are you alright?" Her hips twisted against him and it was enough. He began to thrust in and out slowly at first, giving her time to adjust, but as she began to arch into every motion, his control collapsed entirely. He took her again and again, each time a little deeper, a little harder.

She buried her face against his neck to stifle her cries as the tension broke free and wild ecstasy went cascading through her body. It felt as if she had somehow imploded into a million pieces, never to be whole again without him. He buried his face in her hair as he drove into her one last time and his release claimed him as surely as he had claimed her. It was nothing he had ever experienced before. Nothing he had imagined might exist.

He let himself fall to the bed beside her, and he found a smile when she automatically tightened her leg over his hip to keep them joined. He didn't want to leave her either. He sighed long and deep as he tugged her even closer. "Still want that nightgown?"

The rough quality to his voice seemed to stroke over her body. "S'okay. I think I'll just stay here a while." She smoothed her hand softly across his chest. Neither his heartbeat nor hers had steadied yet, but she loved it. The lingering aches in her body were of a kind that she had no desire to soak out in a tub. "Are you going to touch me again?"

His lips curved. "Let me catch my breath first. You wore me out." He trailed his fingers down her arm slowly. He caught her hand and brought her fingers to his lips. The calluses on her fingers marked of her hard life, and they created pure magic on his body. When she eventually discovered her own power as a lover and tried to have him at her mercy, he would be in trouble. He couldn't wait.

Softly, she asked, "What do you do during the day, Nik?"

He hesitated. "Watch over the woods."

She tilted her head back and looked up at him. "The dove told me that there were once only two trees in these woods. Do you know the story?"

"Mm. Do you want to hear it?" When she nodded, he tugged her closer. "Many centuries ago, most of Mirage was flat and without trees. Seeds fell from the Earth, or so they say, and found themselves to be in exceptionally fertile land. Soon trees grew everywhere. In this area, only two seeds fell. One was a willow seed, the other an oak.

"In this rich land, the two seeds grew with minds and wills. The willow was delicate, tossed about in every wind. The oak grew closer and closer, wishing to protect his beautiful companion. Under the protective shade of the oak's branches, the willow stayed safe from the wind and grew tall and beautiful. As the two trees continued to age, they grew closer and closer until they entwined. When you looked into the branches, you could not tell which was which save for the shape and leaf.

"Other oak trees began to grow around the two, drawn to protect their lord and lady. Soon everyone knew of the mysterious entwined trees, and people came from all over to look and wonder. One who came was a huntsman. He looked upon the trees with disgust. Grown as they were, they overtook the land where he wished to build a home. And so he took an axe and cut them down."

She made a sound of pain, and his arms tightened protectively. "The spirits of the two trees were released, and the sound of the willow's weeping melted the huntsman's cold heart. He could only look with horror at what he had done. But it was too late. The deed had been done. Some say he still lives somewhere in these woods, lamenting what he had so carelessly destroyed."

Her breath hitched on a little sob. Somehow she couldn't believe it was nothing but a story. It cut her far too deep inside. *It was as if she had been there.* "What happened to the willow and oak?"

"No one knows. They say their spirits wander the world, always seeking one another, never able to share the sun again as long as the curse lives." He framed her face with his hands and began to tenderly kiss away her tears. "Shh. I did not tell you to make you cry." When it seemed the tears would not fade, he turned and tucked her underneath him once more. "I'll make you forget," he said huskily.

But even in his loving embrace, she could not entirely forget the tale. It felt important somehow. She was no fool. Her lover called her a willow. She could not see him during the day. She often associated him with oaks. If there was a curse on them, then she was

going to break it. He had saved her, and now she needed to save him.
It was that simple.

CHAPTER FIVE

Terra awoke sharply the next morning as she realized she was alone and outside. She sat up quickly and clutched tighter the blanket that had been wrapped around her. Folded on a fallen log close by sat her discarded clothing of the night before, and the slippers had been placed lightly on top.

It belatedly dawned on her that the tree she slept under had its branches curved quite deliberately to form a shelter around her. She looked up swiftly and recognized it as the smaller oak tree she had seen that very first day when she had been running for her life. It stood only a foot or so taller than she did, but its presence just bespoke regality.

Tears welled in her eyes and slid soundlessly down her cheeks as she got to her feet. She wrapped her arms around as much of the trunk as she could and pressed her face to the surprisingly soft bark. "I still love you," she whispered fiercely. "I will never stop loving you, my oaken lover."

The dove suddenly flew down and landed delicately on a branch. "Terra?"

With a yelp, she clutched her blanket tighter. "I'm naked!"

Politely, yet chuckling, he turned his back to let her scramble into her clothing. "Are you decent?" he asked after a few moments.

"Yes, thank you."

He turned around and flew down to land beside where she sat on the log. She was looking at the slippers a bit helplessly, but as much as he wanted to help, he couldn't. He didn't have hands. He pointed a wing at one shoe and then at the proper foot. "Left."

She blushed. "Thank you." She pulled them on gingerly but found them to be surprisingly comfortable. It would be much nicer walking in them than barefooted. She straightened up and ran a hand through her tangled hair. Unbound, it showed the effects of her husband's hands having been in it. "What do I do?" she asked achingly. "He is the oak, and I am the willow. Am I right?"

"You are right," he agreed simply. "The huntsman did not just curse himself; he cursed the entire woods. The minute Nikolas entered the woods, he was forced to retake the oak form during the day. If he leaves the woods before the curse is lifted, the following dawn will find him becoming an oak forever. But you . . . you could break the curse. Only you could for only you have the gentleness inside to forgive even the worst of beasts. That is why all creatures are drawn to you. Near you, there is always peace."

Her eyes lingering on the form of her oak lover longingly. Even like this, he seemed beautiful to her. "What must I do?"

"Sign this." The dove glowed, and a scroll and quill appeared. "We good spirits do things formally around here," he apologized. "And this will give me the authority to tell you *exactly* what needs to be done. You have to do precisely what I tell you!"

A little smile touched her lips as she signed the bottom of the scroll. "I spent my life doing what people told me. I doubt three days has made me forget. If I ever found myself in a position of telling someone *else* what to do, I wouldn't know how to handle it."

He picked up the scroll with his beak and it disappeared. "You would be better at it than most for you are kind. Now then." He hopped onto her lap and ruffled his feathers. "I will lead you to where the huntsman still lives. You must go into his home and walk past him without a word. Do not listen to him! In the room beyond him, you must light only a single candle. With that candle, search for two rings. One will be made of oak wood, the other of willow."

Her brows shot up. "He . . . he made rings from the trees he cut down?"

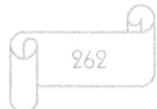

"He made *wedding* rings," the dove confirmed softly, "for he had seen too late the beauty of the union he had destroyed. The oak ring will fit you; put it on. The willow ring needs to be tied to a ribbon on your bodice. Once you have done those things, go back to the huntsman. You must forgive him, Terra, even though he has cursed the one you love. Even though he may seem to be a cold and cruel creature."

She took a deep breath. "I will do it. I have to. I can't let Nik down. I have to save him as he saved me."

"Good girl." He flew up into the air. "Follow me."

She got to her feet and followed quickly. With her new slippers, she found it much easier to cross the land of the woods. The only downside was that the skirt made it a little more difficult to navigate over and under assorted obstacles. Yet, she was not alone in her journey. When she reached a tall boulder she needed to climb over, a great bear came forward and let her climb onto his back to reach high enough to pull herself up.

When she hit a river that looked too deep to cross safely, beavers swam down the waters pushing a raft made of twigs and logs. They ferried her to the other side without mishap. When she found her sleeve caught by a sticky briar, an eagle flew down and used its sharp beak to free her without tearing away her gown.

It seemed to be hours that she followed the dove. She didn't argue once. He clearly knew where he led her. And soon enough she found her answer as to their destination. He stopped flying and landed on a tree. "There," he said softly.

She stepped around the tree and found herself looking into a small clearing. Trees had been cut away, their stumps left to rot and blacken in the sun. In the place where the willow and oak had stood, there was nothing but broken ground that had never grown back. A hut stood only feet away, beaten and weathered and grayed from age. Some of the panels of wood had rotted and sagged. A pallor hung over the entire place. No smoke curled from the chimney. No light shined from within the filthy windows.

Her hands curled into fists. She braced her shoulders and walked determinedly toward the hut, her heart beating madly inside her chest. She could barely breathe. Her mouth was dry and her throat was tight.

Only the lightest of pushes caused the door to fall open. She stepped into the opening and barely kept back a flinch. The interior looked just as bad as the exterior. Holes in the floor caused the wood to sag. Cobwebs hung in every corner. Dust coated all surfaces. Molded food sat abandoned on a table.

And there, sitting in a rickety chair before a dead hearth, was an old man. He looked shriveled and worn, as battered as his home. His eyes had sunk far into his head, and wrinkles within his wrinkles pulled down his entire face. He was gaunt and pale, his hands gnarled where they gripped the arms of his chair. His clothes resembled something a huntsman might have worn, but they were dirty and torn. The dust on the floor around the chair seemed to say he had not moved from that spot in years.

As she stepped into the home, the floor creaked. Eyes that were a little mad, a lot miserable, and greatly furious fell upon her. "Get out." The voice rasped like dry leaves.

She didn't say a word as she edged across the floor and tried to avoid the rotted places. The thump of his foot on the ground made her flinch but she did not falter.

"Worthless!" the voice spat. "Useless! Unwanted little cow! Who would care to have you around? *Slave*. You are nothing but a servant without a master! No one would want you!"

The words grew ever viler the closer she got to the broken door at the back of the room. She flinched at every syllable, but she did not stop. She did not say a word. Years of cruelty at the hands of Mr. Arcwood and Vin had taught her that silence was the only weapon that worked. She had no need to defend herself.

Her hands shook but she managed to open the door and slip into the room. It was pitch black as she fumbled for a table. Something fell over and broke but she ignored it. At long last, her

fingers closed around a candle and a match. She lit the candle and a small area became illuminated. She put the candle in a holder on the table and looked around. The room appeared to be barely more than a closet, and the shelves held boxes upon boxes of junk. Objects of all kinds sat on the floor and crowded a tiny table.

After a few moments of blind fumbling where the candle's light did not reach, she finally found a handcrafted box. She slowly opened the lid. There, resting on a bed of dried leaves, were two wooden rings. One ring was made of wood the same dark brown as Nikolas' hair. The other was a wood of silvery-brown, just like hers.

She picked up the oak ring and slid it over her finger. It fit perfectly. The lighter ring was also bigger, and she knew it would fit Nikolas. She tied it to the ribbon on her dress and then blew out the candle. Shoulders squared, she walked out of the room.

The old man had fallen silent. He neither looked at nor spoke to her as she walked softly toward him. She knelt beside him and looked up into his face. She could not hate him. Sadness welled inside her as she gently covered his hand with hers. "It's okay," she said softly. "I forgive you. How could you know? You've paid, huntsman. You've paid a thousand times over. Only you cannot forgive yourself."

Tears slowly gathered in the old man's faded eyes. They rolled down his wrinkled face as it slowly crumpled. "Willow." His voice broke as he began to sob softly. "How can you forgive me?"

"I never hated you, huntsman. *We* never hated you. You hated yourself. I forgive you. Please. Let go. You do not have to stay here any longer."

A long sigh unraveled from the huntsman's lips. "Thank you, willow." He began to dissolve into shimmers of light. "At last I can rest . . ."

Even as he disappeared, the hut disappeared as well. In moments, she found herself alone, kneeling in the middle of the clearing. Grass already began to grow in where only an hour before it couldn't. Softly, she asked, "Did I . . .?"

"You did," the dove confirmed just as softly as he flew down near her. "The curse is broken."

She immediately turned and ran back the way she had come. She wanted to find Nikolas. She had to find him! If the curse was broken, then surely he would be a man again. She would be able to see him in the sun, to wake in his arms in the morning.

Search as she might, she could not find him. She could not even find the oak tree he had become. Disheartened, she took shelter under another tree entirely. The dove had not arrived. She knew there would be no more little houses under trees. They had, as the dove had said, served their purpose.

Somehow she managed to fall asleep. It was not an entirely restful sleep. Her dreams were tormented by haunting images of oak trees dancing just beyond her reach. She wanted Nikolas. She wanted to be with him so terribly. Had they come that far only to still never be together?

The sunlight on her face woke her in the morning. Sore and stiff from sleeping on the ground, she carefully sat up. Her beautiful clothes were very dirty now, and so was she. Thankfully, when she looked around, she discovered the unexpected yet familiar shape of the trunk that had held her clothes. She instinctively checked for the willow ring and found it had disappeared from her ribbons. "What?"

The dove flew down and landed on the top of the trunk. "Good morning, Terra."

"Good morning," she said softly. Her gaze lowered. "I did not find him, dove. I looked for him, but could not find him."

"Naturally not. He is waiting for you elsewhere. I can lead you to him." He smiled when she looked up swiftly in surprise. "But first, you cannot go back to him looking like this! Come with me. There is a place to bathe not far from here."

She followed him eagerly, caring not so much for the bath as for the hope that soon she would be with her husband. Her *husband*. It was a marvelous thought that someone would belong to her in such a way, and she would belong to him.

The place she was led to turned out to be a small hot spring

that looked barely bigger than a tub itself. Soap and towels waited. The dove flew off to give her privacy, and she wasted no time in taking off her dirty clothes and getting into the water. She scrubbed herself clean, thoroughly washed her hair, and dried off as much as she could. Her hair was so thick that it would take an hour, at least, to fully dry without help from a fireplace.

By the time she finished, her dirty clothes had disappeared. In their place came a new gown of pale silver with the same leaf pattern around the sleeves and skirt. It much resembled her last dress, but it had a much fuller skirt, nearly a full bell, like a ball gown. As she tightened all the laces, she startled herself to see her own reflection. She looked like a princess!

Slippers also waited, and she pulled them on her feet. She got them backwards and quickly had to switch them. Maybe wherever she and Nikolas made their home would be the kind of place she could mostly go barefoot. She had a feeling she and shoes might never fully get along.

"Decent?" the dove called.

"Yes, thank you."

He flew down and dropped the cloak he carried. As it landed in her arms, he offered, "Put it on. It will keep you warm and clean."

She almost didn't want to accept the gift. The cloak was real velvet! But, since the dove didn't seem inclined to leave until she did as told, she pulled the cloak on and fastened it securely. It felt very warm, and very comfortable. "Lead the way."

He did so unwaveringly. As the first few hours passed, she began to realize the trees were growing thinner. The sounds of a city had started to grow louder. "Are we leaving the woods?" she asked.

"We are. Nikolas waits in the city."

"Oh." Well, that made some sense. He had said that he had not intended to live in the woods. Perhaps only the curse had kept him there. If he wasn't an actual woodsman, then what was he?

The woods stopped where a road began. The city started not even a hundred yards away. Trumpets blared and the people cheered and laughed loudly. Flowers and banners hung from every rooftop and decorated every corner that she could see. Belatedly, it dawned on her. "That's right, the king was returning after a hiatus." She frowned at the dove. "Are you sure we should go into the city? It must be packed!"

"You will find him." He landed on a fencepost.

"You're leaving me?"

"You do not need me any longer. Goodbye, Terra."

"Goodbye," she said softly as he flew off. With nothing else she could do, she pulled the hood of her cloak over her hair and made her way down the road toward the city. It was amazingly bright and cheerful, a whirl of light and color to a girl who had lived her entire life on farms. She was enchanted with the shops and fascinated by the people who milled the streets. She missed the quiet of the woods, but the city seemed amazingly beautiful in its own way. It was, in fact, liberally covered in trees itself.

"The procession is coming!" someone shouted from a rooftop.

She shortly got crushed in the crowd as people gathered on the sidewalks to wave and cheer. She was both warmed and bemused by the people's obvious love for their king. She had been listening to conversations, and apparently he was a fairly new king. He had inherited the throne only a few years before when his father had died. His sabbatical had been one to mature himself into a better leader.

As the procession began to approach, she couldn't see anything. The crowds had gotten really thick, and most people were taller than she was. She pushed her way through to the front, but someone unintentionally shoved her rather hard and sent her stumbling into the street. The entire procession came to a halt before they ran her over.

Terrified, she covered her face with her hands as she heard someone dismount their horse and approach. She would get into so much trouble! She squeezed her eyes shut as her hood got tugged off her hair. "I'm so sorry!" she blurted.

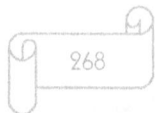

A tender hand tangled into her hair with an achingly familiar touch. Her head jerked up and around, and she stopped breathing entirely as she beheld the man that knelt beside her in the clothing of a king.

It was Nikolas. *He* was the king.

The morning sun shone down on his hair and made his eyes glow softly with joy as he looked at her. She forgot entirely that there was a crowd watching. She carefully reached up to frame his face with her hands. He turned his head to press a kiss to her palm and then tugged her left hand to his lips. He softly kissed the ring she wore. "My willow."

Lips trembling, she whispered, "The willow ring."

He held up his hand, and the silvery ring resided where it belonged on his finger. It fit perfectly. "When I left to find myself," he murmured huskily, framing her face in his hands, "I never expected to find you as well." He slowly stood and pulled her to her feet as well. Belatedly remembering the crowd, he looked at all the faces of his people. The expressions ranged from surprise to confusion. "The woman before you," he said clearly, "is my wife. She is your new queen. Without her love, without her bravery, I would never have returned home."

The crowd began to cheer loudly, and Terra blushed brightly. "I can't be a queen!" she whispered strongly to him.

His lips curved slowly. "Of course you can. You married a king." He snatched her off her feet into his arms and kissed her with all the love in his heart. To see her in the sunlight, to feel her touch even in the middle of the day . . . He could ask for nothing else. "I love you!" he said fiercely against her lips.

Joy rose and blinded her. "Nik! I love you so much!" She gave a hiccupping little sob, threw her arms around his neck, and kissed him just as wildly as he had kissed her. She would never let him go again!

The cheers became whoops and catcalls as the people realized their king and new queen did not seem intent on ending the embrace anytime soon. "Get a room!" someone shouted over the laughter of the crowd.

Nikolas laughed as well and scooped Terra up off her feet. "If you insist!" He put her on the back of his horse and swung up behind her. He held the reigns with one hand and kept his other arm firmly around her waist. He didn't think he would ever be able to let go of her without fear for at least a few more years. Perhaps centuries. "Are you happy at last, my willow?"

"Very happy." She looked up at him. "But who was that dove, Nik? He was always there for me. He told me everything I needed to do. He claimed to be a good spirit but I don't . . . I don't think he was."

"That was the messenger of love," he told her softly. "The one who helps ensure that we all have a happy ending."

She sighed contentedly and snuggled closer. "Then I guess that's what we had better do."

EPILOGUE

Rhianna Taber was in her office studying a list of names when she felt as much as saw a soft glow coming from her desk. She slowly lowered the document in time to see a scroll tied with a golden ribbon appearing before her. The scent of peaches seemed to dance along her nose and dig velvet claws into her heart and soul.

She carefully unwound the scroll to read it. In classic Enforcers' fashion, the word 'Complete' was boldly marked across the front in red. Yet it was not a contract that had been issued from Enforcers. There was only one other being that could do something like that.

Her trembling fingers were well controlled as she wrote some notes at the bottom of the scroll. She slipped it into a folder and slowly closed it. It was too painful to think about. It was too painful to hope.

Eric Mason had been watching her the entire time, and he quietly shut the connecting office door before turning to look at the other three people behind him. Taylor Vincent stood staring at his hands in a way that did not bode well. "Burning?" Eric asked quietly.

Taylor took a long breath. "I haven't felt this in a long time. There's something dangerous out there, Riku. And it's coming directly for Rhi."

A little shiver roughened Gwyn Vincent's skin, and she turned into his arms. "It's somehow familiar," she said softly, "the dark cloud hovering around her. The scales are *balanced*. I can't understand it."

Even Eric had never known everything about his oldest friend and partner. He tugged his wife, Rayna, into his arms and drew what little comfort he could from her. Whatever was coming for Rhianna would have to go through the four of them first. She was not alone.

The Enforcers protected their own.

Status: File Complete
Analysis: Even the hardest of hearts will soften when faced with an oak's dedication and willow's tears.

S.J.GARRETT

Author Notes

We are now three books deep into the 3rd District series, and the stakes are going up! Did you enjoy The Weaver's Wife faerie tale that encompassed Brian and Louise? I sure hope so, since it was my first attempt to create a completely original story in the same vein as the classics.

The next book in the series will be THE LUCINO FILE. Hot-tempered and passionate Italians who have their own brush with the magical District, but whose happy endings might just come at a much higher price! Look for it in May 2017.

If you loved this story, or any of my stories, please leave me a review on Amazon! Reviews are the bread and butter of an author's life, and even a simple "More, please!" will keep us going.

You can keep up with me on www.facebook.com/stacyjgarrett or www.stacyjgarrett.com or follow my blog at stacyjgarrett.wordpress.com. I sometimes lurk on Twitter (@stacyjgarrett), and Tumblr as well (stacyjgarrett.tumblr.com).

I can't wait to see you again within my magical District! Until then, keep looking for those happy ever afters!

Stacy J Garrett

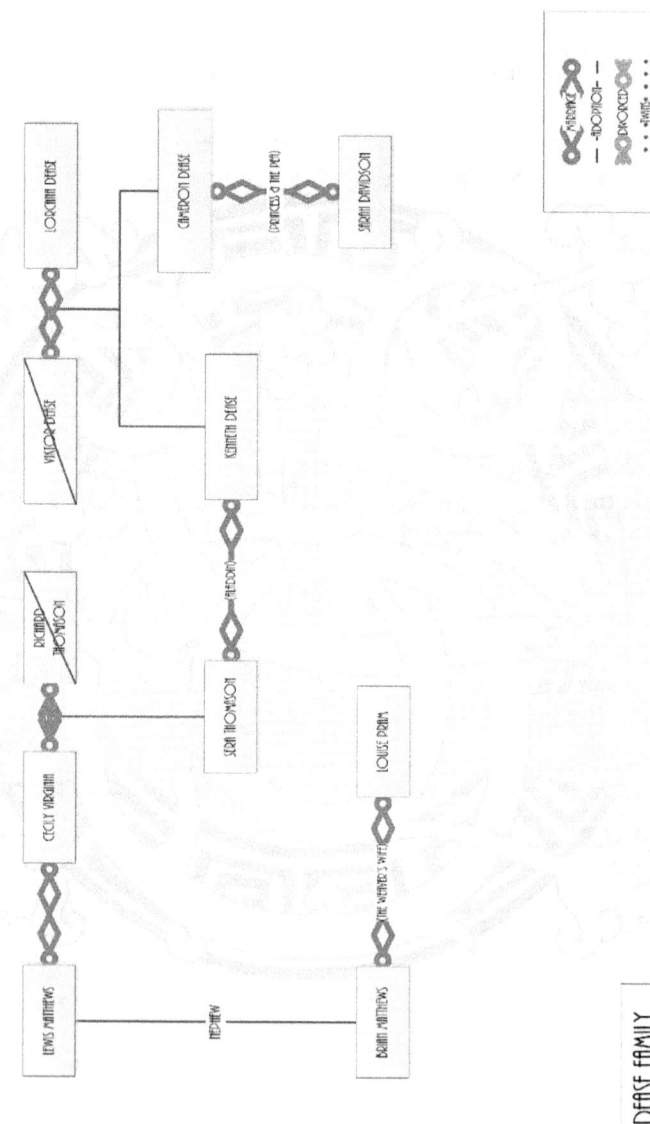

DEASE FAMILY

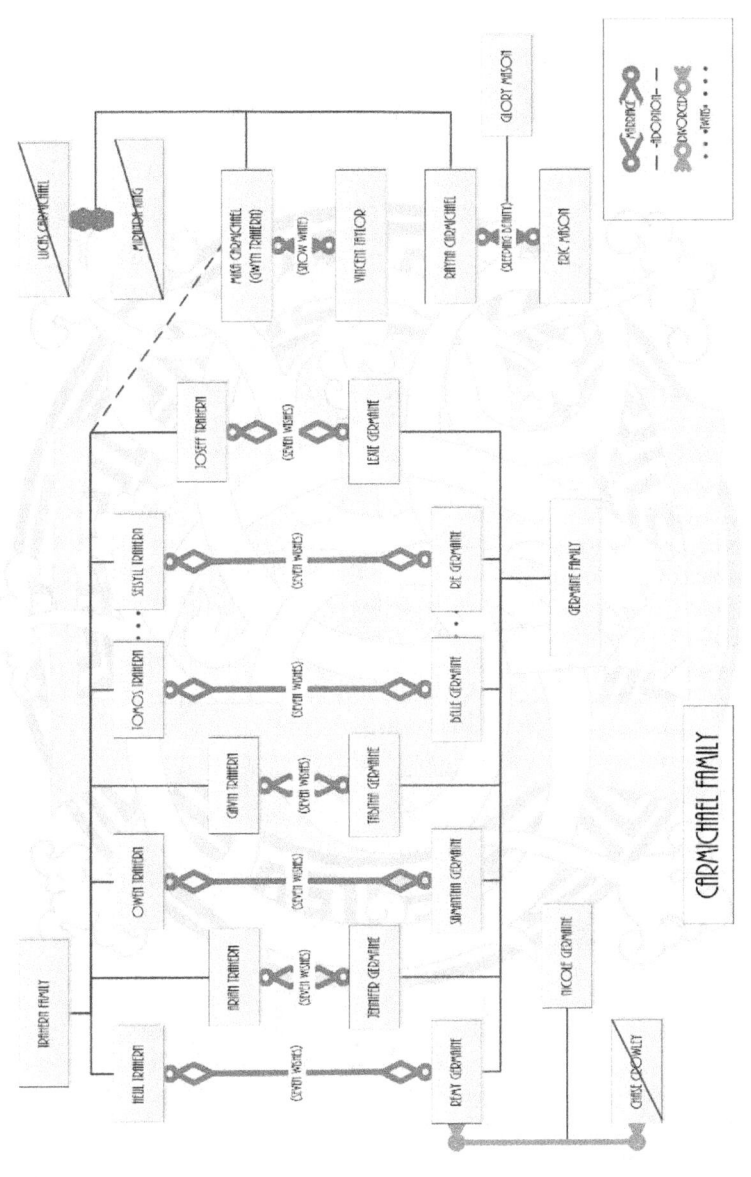

CARMICHAEL FAMILY

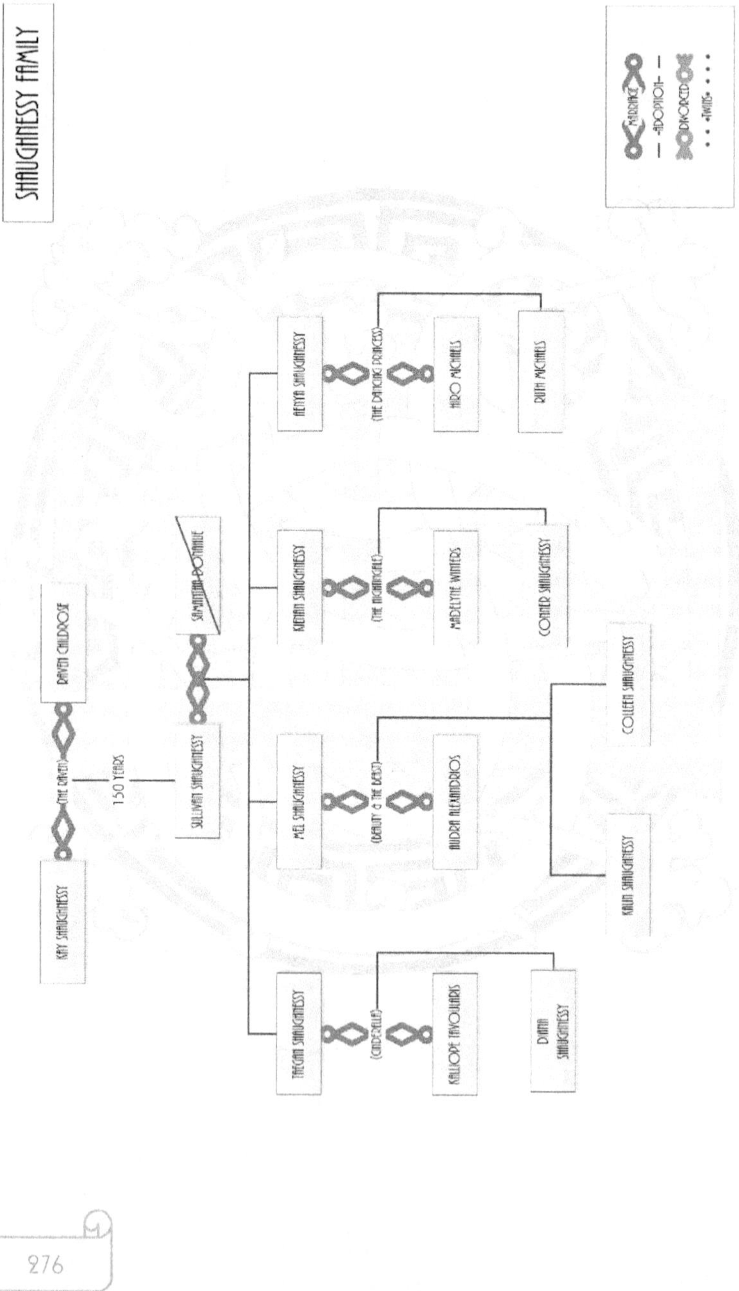

THE DEASE FILE

SHAUGHNESSY FAMILY

Legend:
- MARRIAGE
- —ADOPTION—
- DIVORCED
- · · · TWINS · · · ·

KAY SHAUGHNESSY — (THE DEACON) — DAWEN CHILDCOKE
150 YEARS
SEPARATION—CONTINUE

SULLIVAN SHAUGHNESSY

TEAGAN SHAUGHNESSY — (CINDERELLA) — KALLIOPE TAYLOUVERIS
  - NEILLOPE TAYLOUVERIS
  - DARIN SHAUGHNESSY

MEL SHAUGHNESSY — (QUENTIN & THE BEAST) — MADORI ALEXANDROS
  - COLLEEN SHAUGHNESSY
  - KAILIN SHAUGHNESSY

KIERAN SHAUGHNESSY — (THE BACHELORS) — MACKAYLYN WINTERS
  - CONNER SHAUGHNESSY

ALENNA SHAUGHNESSY — (THE CAROLINE PRINCESS) — HIRO MICHAELS
  - DIANA MICHAELS

Stacy J. Garrett was made in England but born in Sacramento, California, and like the redwoods of the state, her roots have dug deep. Her destiny as a bard was somewhat inevitable. Little else can explain how she constantly told her mother tall tales so outlandish that she couldn't even get grounded for them. Her mother and grandmother had her reading by age three, and that love of a good story propelled her through so many books that Scholastic Books gave her a medal. A love of worlds created by others eventually brought out the desire to create her own, and she has never looked back.

Stacy has seen both good and evil in her life, and her stories, like life, have no half measures. Even in a fantasy world of dragons and faeries, even in a modern city where magic abounds, she knows that the constants of real emotion never change. Dreams come true, love can be found at first sight, princesses can rescue their princes, and maybe there really can be happily ever after. Her happy endings never come without cost, though, for she truly believes we can't appreciate the good and the joy without the bad and the pain along the way.

Her current haunt is a comfy house in her beloved Sacramento where she wrangles four feline fur-kids and consumes peppermints like mana in order to balance a calendar filled with more creative venues than a sane person should realistically undertake. If she's not chained to her desk, she's stomping through the scenery in search of equally fantastical photographs.